EMMA

A MODERN RETELLING

Alexander McCall Smith

PANTHEON BOOKS   NEW YORK

All rights reserved. Published in the United States by Pantheon Books, a division of Random House LLC, New York, a Penguin Random House company. Originally published in Great Britain by The Borough Press, an imprint of HarperCollins Publishers, London, in 2014.

Pantheon Books and colophon are registered trademarks of Random House LLC.

Library of Congress Cataloging-in-Publication Data
McCall Smith, Alexander, [date]
Emma : a modern retelling / Alexander McCall Smith.
pages   cm
ISBN 978-0-8041-9795-3 (hardcover).
ISBN 978-0-8041-9796-0 (eBook).
1. Young women—England—Fiction.   I. Austen, Jane, 1775–1817. Emma.   II. Title.
PR6063.C326E46 2015   823'.914—dc23   2014025558

www.pantheonbooks.com

Jacket illustration by Iain McIntosh
Jacket design by Kelly Blair

Printed in the United States of America
First United States Edition

2 4 6 8 9 7 5 3 1

For my daughters, Lucy and Emily

1

Emma Woodhouse's father was brought into this world, blinking and confused, on one of those final nail-biting days of the Cuban Missile Crisis. It was a time of sustained anxiety for anybody who read a newspaper or listened to the news on the radio, and that included his mother, Mrs. Florence Woodhouse, who was anxious at the best of times and even more so at the worst. What was the point of continuing the human race when nuclear self-immolation seemed to be such a real and imminent possibility? That was the question that occurred to Florence as she was admitted to the delivery ward of a small country hospital in Norfolk. American air bases lay not far away, making that part of England a prime target; their bombers, she had heard, were on the runway, ready to take off on missions that would bring about an end that would be as swift as it was awful, a matter of sudden blinding light, of dust and of darkness. Quite understandably, though, she had other, more pressing concerns at the time, and did not come up with an answer to her own question. Or perhaps her response was the act of giving birth itself, and the embracing, through tears of joy, of the small bundle of humanity presented to her by the midwife.

There are plenty of theories—not all of them supported by evidence—that the mother's state of mind during pregnancy may affect the personality of the infant. There are also those who believe that playing Mozart to unborn children will lead to greater musicality, or reciting poetry through the mother's stomach will increase the chances of having linguistically gifted children. That anxiety may be transmitted from mother to un-born baby is an altogether more believable claim, and indeed Henry Woodhouse appeared to be proof of this. From an early age he showed himself to be a fretful child, unwilling to take the risks that other boys delighted in and always interested in the results when his mother took his temperature with the clinical thermometer given to her by the district nurse.

"Is it normal?" was one of the first sentences he uttered after he had begun to speak.

"Absolutely normal," his mother would reply. "Ninety-eight point four. See."

This disappointed him, and he always showed satisfaction when a doubtful reading required the insertion of the mercury bulb under his tongue a second time.

In due course this anxiety took the form of dietary fads, one after another, involving the rejection of various common food-stuffs (wheat, dairy products, and so on) and the enthusiastic embracing of rather more esoteric fare (royal jelly and malt bis-cuits being early favourites). These fads tended not to last long; by the time he was eighteen and ready to go to university, he was prepared to eat a normal vegetarian diet, provided it was supplemented by a pharmacopoeia of vitamin pills, omega oils, and assorted enzymes.

"My son," said his mother with a certain pride, "is a vale-tudinarian."

That sent her friends to the dictionary, which gave her additional satisfaction. To dispatch one's friends to a dictionary from time to time is one of the more sophisticated pleasures of life, but it is one that must be indulged in sparingly: to do it too often may result in accusations of having swallowed one's own dictionary, which is not a compliment, whichever way one looks at it.

Henry Woodhouse—known to most as Mr. Woodhouse—did not follow the career that had been expected of generations of young Woodhouses. While his father had assumed that his son would farm—in an entirely gentlemanly way—the six hundred acres that surrounded their house, Hartfield, the young man had other plans for himself.

"I know what you expect," he said. "I know we've been here for the last four hundred years . . ."

"Four hundred and eighteen," interjected his father.

"Four hundred and eighteen, then. I know that. And I'm not saying that I want to go away altogether; it's just that I want to do something else first. Then I can farm later on."

His father sighed. "You would be a gentleman farmer," he said. "You do know that, don't you?"

The young Woodhouse smiled. "I've never quite understood that concept. What exactly is the difference between a gentleman farmer and a farmer pure and simple?"

This question was a cause of some embarrassment to the

older Woodhouse. "These matters shouldn't need to be spelled out," he said. "Indeed, it's not a question that one really likes to answer. And I'm surprised that you feel you need to ask it. A gentleman farmer . . ." There was a pause, and then, "A gentleman farmer doesn't actually farm, if you see what I mean. He doesn't do the work himself. He usually has somebody else to do it for him, unless . . ."

"Yes? Unless?"

"Unless he doesn't have the money. Then he has to do it himself."

"Like us? We don't have the money, do we?"

"No, we don't. We did once, but not any more. And there's nothing dishonourable about that. Having no money is perfectly honourable. In fact, having no money can often be a sign of good breeding."

"And a sign of poverty too?"

There was another sigh. "I feel we're drawing this out somewhat. The point is that it would be a very fine thing if you chose to farm rather than to be . . . What was it you wanted to be?"

"A design engineer."

This was greeted with silence. "I see."

"It's an important field. And we need to do more engineering design in this country or we'll be even more thoroughly overtaken by the Germans." This, the young Woodhouse knew, was a fruitful line of argument to adopt with his father, who worried about the Germans and their twentieth-century lapses.

"The Germans do a lot of that sort of thing?"

"They do," he assured his father. "That's why they've been

so successful industrially. Their cars, you know, go on virtually forever, unlike so many of our own cars that I'm afraid won't even start."

"Engineering design," muttered his father—and left it at that. But the argument had been won by the younger generation, and less than a year later Mr. Woodhouse was enrolled as a student of his chosen subject, happy to be independent and away from home, doing what he had always wanted to do.

It proved to be a wise choice. After graduating, Mr. Woodhouse joined a small firm in Norwich that specialised in the design of medical appliances. He enjoyed his work and was appreciated by his colleagues, even if they found him unduly anxious—some even said obsessive—when it came to risk assessment in the development of products. The work was interesting, but perhaps not challenging enough for the young engineer, and in his spare time he puzzled over various drawings and prototypes of his own invention, including a new and improved valve for the liquid-nitrogen cylinders used by dermatologists. This device was to prove suitable for other applications, and once he had patented it under his own name—rather to the annoyance of the firm, who mounted an unsuccessful legal challenge—he sold a production licence to a Dutch manufacturer. This provided him with financial security—with a fortune, in fact, with which he was able to renovate Hartfield, revitalise the farm, and set up his increasingly infirm parents in the gatehouse. Their ill health unfortunately robbed them of a long retirement, and within a very short time Mr. Woodhouse found himself the sole owner of Hartfield.

He had married by then, and in a way that surprised people.

Everyone had assumed that the only person willing to take on this rather anxious and obsessed engineer would be either a woman of great charity—and there are plenty of women who seem prepared to marry a *project husband*—or a woman whose sole interest was financial. His wife was neither of these, being a warm and personable society beauty with a considerable private income of her own. Happily married, Mr. Woodhouse enjoyed the existence of a country gentleman even if he continued with his engineering job for some years. A daughter was born in the year following their wedding—that was Isabella—and then another. This second daughter was Emma.

When Emma was five, Mrs. Woodhouse died. Emma did not remember her mother. She remembered love, though, and a feeling of warmth. It was like remembering light, or the glow that sometimes persists after a light has gone out.

Had he not had the immediate responsibility of looking after two young daughters unaided, Mr. Woodhouse could well have lapsed into a state of depression. With the irrationality of grief, he blamed himself for the loss of his wife. She may have died of exposure to a virulent meningeal infection as random and undetectable as any virus may be, but he still reproached him- self for failing to ensure that her immune system was not in better order. If only he had insisted—and he would have had to insist most firmly—that she had followed the same regime of vitamin supplements as he did, then he believed she might have shrugged off the virus in its first exploratory forays. After all, the two of them breathed much the same air and ate the same things, so surely when she encountered the virus there was every chance that he must have done the same. In his case, however, vitamins C and D had done their job, and if only he had persuaded her that taking fourteen pills a day was no great hardship, if one washed them down, as he always did, with breakfast orange juice . . . If only he had shown her the article from the *Sunday Times* which referred to work done in the United States on the efficacy of that particular combination of vitamins in ensuring a good immunological response. She scoffed at some of his theories—he knew that, and took her gentle scepticism in good spirit—but one did not scoff at the *Sunday Times*. If only he had taken the whole matter more seriously then their poor little Isabella and Emma would still have their mother and he would not be a widower.

Such guilty thoughts commonly accompany grief and equally commonly disappear once the rawness of loss is assuaged. This happened with Mr. Woodhouse at roughly the right stage of the grieving process; now he found himself thinking not so much of the past but of how he might cope with the future. In the immediate aftermath of his wife's death he had been inundated with offers of help from friends. He was well liked in the county because he was always supportive of local events, even if he rarely attended them. He had given generously to the appeal to raise money for a new scout hall, uncomplainingly paid his share of the cost of restoring the church roof after a gang of metal thieves had stripped it of its lead, and had cheerfully increased the value of the prize money that went with the Woodhouse Cup, a trophy instituted by his grandfather for the best ram at the local agricultural show. He never went to the local pub, but this was not taken as a sign of the standoffishness that infected some of the grander families in the neighbourhood, but as a concomitant of the eccentricity that people thought quite appropriate for a man who had, after all, invented something.

"He invented something," one local explained to newcomers to the village. "You don't see him about all that much—but he invented something all right. Made a ton of money from it, but good luck to him. If you can invent something and make sure nobody pinches the idea, then you're in the money, big time."

He was surprised—and touched—by the generosity of neighbours during those first few months after his wife's death. There was a woman from the village, Mrs. Firhill, who had helped them in the house since they had returned to Hartfield, and she now took it upon herself to do the shopping for the groceries as well as to cook all the meals. But even if day-to-day requirements were met in this way, there was still a constant stream of women who called in with covered plates and casserole dishes. Every Aga within a twenty-mile radius, it seemed, was now doing its part to keep the Woodhouse family fed, and at times this led to an overcrowding of the household's two large freezers.

"It's not food they need," remarked Mrs. Firhill to a friend, "it's somebody to tuck little Emma in at night. It's somebody to take a look in his wardrobe and chuck out some of the old clothes. It's a wife and mother, if you ask me."

"That will come," said the friend. "He's only in his thirties. And he's not bad-looking in the right light."

But Mrs. Firhill, and most others who knew him, disagreed. There was a premature sense of defeat in Mr. Woodhouse's demeanour—the attitude of one who had done what he wanted to do in the first fifteen years of adult life and was now destined to live out the rest of his days in quiet contemplation and worry. Besides, it would try the patience of anybody, people felt, to live with that constant talk of vitamins and preventative measures for this and that: high-cocoa-content chocolate for strokes, New Zealand green-lipped mussel oil for rheumatism, and so on. It would not be easy to live with that no matter what the attractions of Hartfield (eleven bedrooms) and the financial ease that went with marrying its owner.

And in this assessment people were right: Mr. Woodhouse had no intention of remarrying and firmly but politely rejected the dinner-party invitations that started to arrive nine months after his wife's death. Nine months was just the right interval, people felt: remarriage, it was generally agreed, should never occur within a year of losing one's spouse, which meant that the nine-month anniversary was just the right time to start positioning one's candidate for the vacancy. But what could anybody do if the man in question simply declined every invitation on the grounds that he had a prior engagement?

"There's no need to lie," one rebuffed hostess remarked. "There are plenty of diplomatic excuses that can be used without telling downright lies. Besides, everybody knows he has no other engagements—he never leaves that place."

The fact that no new Mrs. Woodhouse was in contemplation meant that something had to be done about arranging care for Isabella and Emma. With this in mind, he consulted a woman friend from Holt, who had a reputation for knowing where one could find whatever it was one needed, whether it was a plumber, a girl to work in the stables, a carpet layer, or even a priest.

"There's a magazine," she said. "It's called *The Lady*, and it's—how shall we put it?—a bit old-fashioned, in a very nice sort of way. It's the place where housekeepers and nannies advertise for jobs. There are always plenty of them. You'll find somebody."

He took her advice, and ordered a copy of *The Lady*. And just as he had been told, at the back of the magazine there were several pages of advertisements placed by domestic staff seeking vacancies. Discreet butlers disclosed that they were available, together with full references and criminal-record checks; trained nannies offered to care for children of all ages; and understanding companions promised to keep loneliness at bay in return for self-contained accommodation and all the usual perks.

He wondered who would still possibly require, or afford, a butler, but the fact that butlers appeared to exist suggested that there was still a need for them somewhere. It was easier to imagine the role played by "an energetic, middle-aged couple, with clean driving licences and an interest in cooking"; they would have no difficulty in finding something, he thought, as would the "young man prepared to do a bit of gardening and house maintenance in return for accommodation while at agricultural college." And then, at the foot of the second page of these advertisements, there was a "well-educated young woman (26) wishing to find a suitable situation looking after children. Prepared to travel. Non-smoker. Vegetarian."

It was the last of these qualifications that attracted his attention. He thought it hardly necessary these days to mention that one was a non-smoker; it would be assumed that any smoking would be done discreetly and away from others, it now being such a furtive pastime. Far more significant was the vegetarianism, which indicated, in Mr. Woodhouse's view, a sensible interest in nutrition. And as his eye returned to the text of the advertisement he saw that even if it was included in a column in which it was the sole entry, that column was headed "Governesses."

Governesses, he thought, were perhaps on the same list of endangered species as butlers. He did not know anybody who had had a governess, although he had recently read that in Korea and Japan, where ambitious families took the education of their children in such deadly earnest, the practice of hiring resident tutors to give young children a competitive edge in examinations was widespread. These people, if female, could be called governesses, and were probably no different from the governesses that British families used to inflict on their children in the past. Of course the word had a distinctly archaic ring to it, being redolent of strictness and severity, but that need not necessarily be the case. He recalled that Maria von Trapp, after all, was a governess—as well as being a former nun—and she had been anything but severe. Would this well-educated young woman (26) possibly have a guitar—just as Maria von Trapp had? He smiled at the thought. He did not think he would make a very convincing Captain von Trapp.

The advertisement referred to a box number at the offices of *The Lady*, and he wrote that afternoon asking the advertiser to contact him by telephone. Two days later, she called and introduced herself. He noticed, with pleasure, her slight Scottish accent: a Scottish governess, like a Scottish doctor, inspired confidence.

"My name is Anne Taylor," she said. "You asked me to phone about the position of governess."

They arranged an interview. Miss Taylor was available to

travel to Norfolk at any time that was convenient to him. "I am not currently in a situation," she said. "I am therefore very flexible. There are plenty of trains from Edinburgh."

He thought for a moment before replying, reflecting on the rather formal expression *not currently in a situation*. There were plenty of people not currently in a situation, and he himself was one of them. Some were in this position because they had tried, but failed, to get a situation, and others because they had a situation but had lost it because . . . There were any number of reasons, he imagined, for losing one's situation, ranging from blameless misfortune to gross misconduct. There were even those who lost their situation because the police had caught up with them and unmasked them as fugitives on the run, as confidence tricksters, even as murderers. *Murderers.* He imagined that there were non-smoking, vegetarian murderers, just as there were nicotine-addicted carnivorous murders, although he assumed that as a general rule murderers were not regular readers of *The Lady* magazine. Murderers probably read one of the lower tabloids—if they read a newspaper at all. The lower tabloids liked to report murders and murder trials, and that, for murderers, would have been light entertainment, rather like the social columns for the rest of us.

Miss Taylor noticed the slight hesitation. She was not to know, of course, of his tendency to anxiety and the way in which this operated to set him off on a trail of worries about remote and unlikely possibilities, worrying about murderers advertising in *The Lady* being a typical example.

"Mr. Woodhouse?"

"Yes, I'm still here. Sorry, I was thinking."

"I could come at any time. Just tell me when would suit you, and I shall be there."

"Tomorrow," he said. "Tomorrow afternoon."

"I shall be there," she said, "once you have told me where *there* is."

There was a delightful exactitude about the way in which she spoke, and he suspected, at that moment, that he and his daughters had found their governess.

2

It did not take Mr. Woodhouse long to confirm his earlier suspicion that Anne Taylor would be exactly the right person for the job.

"You seem to be entirely suitable," he said, a bare hour after her arrival for the interview. "All we need to do, I suppose, is to sort out when exactly you can start and, of course, the terms. I doubt if any of that will be problematic."

Miss Taylor stared at him. She seemed surprised by what he had said, and for a moment Mr. Woodhouse wondered whether he had unwittingly committed some solecism. He had been careful to call her Miss Taylor rather than Anne, even if that sounded rather formal—so it could not be that. Had he said anything else, then, to which she might have taken exception?

"I have yet to indicate whether I shall accept," Miss Taylor said quietly. "One does not assume, surely, that the person whom one is interviewing wants the position until one's asked her."

"But my dear Miss Taylor," exclaimed Mr. Woodhouse, "how crassly insensitive of me. I was about to raise that very issue with you and—"

"There is no need to resort to *spin*, Mr. Woodhouse," interrupted Miss Taylor. "When one has said the wrong thing, I find that the best policy—beyond all doubt—is not to make things worse by claiming to be doing something one was not going to do." She paused. "Don't you think?"

He was momentarily speechless. He had not imagined that the person he had invited for interview would end up lecturing *him* on how to behave, and for a moment he toyed with the idea of ending their meeting then and there. He might say: "Well, if that's the sort of household you think you're coming to . . ." or "My idea was that I should be employing somebody to teach the girls, not me." Or, simply, "If that's the way you feel, then shall I run you back to the railway station?"

But he said none of this. The reality of the situation was that he had two young daughters to look after and he needed help. He could easily get some young woman from the village to take the job, but she would almost certainly feed them pizza out of a box and allow them to watch Australian soap operas on afternoon television. He *knew* that would happen, because that was what girls from the village did; he had seen it, or if he had not exactly seen it, Mrs. Firhill had told him all about it. And even she was not above eating an occasional piece of pizza from a box; he had found an empty box a few weeks previously and it could only have come from her. This young woman, by contrast, was a graduate of the University of St. Andrews, spoke French— as any self-respecting governess surely should do—and had a calm, self-assured manner that inspired utter confidence. He had to get her; he simply had to. So, after a minute or so of silence during which she continued to look at him unflinchingly, he mumbled an apology. "You're right. Of course you're right . . ."

To which she had replied, "Yes, I know."

He opened his mouth to protest, but she cut him short. "As it happens, I think this job would suit me very well. What I suggest is a three-month trial period during which you can decide whether you can bear me." And here she smiled; and he did too, nervously. "And whether *I* can bear *you*. Once that hurdle has been surmounted, we could take it from there." She paused. "I do like the girls, by the way."

He showed his relief with a broad smile. "I'm sure that's reciprocated," he said.

Mrs. Firhill had been on hand to help with the encounter and had shepherded the girls into the playroom while this discussion with Miss Taylor took place. Mr. Woodhouse could tell from his housekeeper's demeanour that she approved of Miss Taylor, and in his mind that provided the final, clinching endorsement of the arrangement. Accepting Miss Taylor's suggestion, he called the girls back into the room and explained to them, in Miss Taylor's presence, that she would be coming to stay with them and that he was sure that they would all be very happy.

"But we're happy already," said Isabella, giving Miss Taylor a sideways glance.

"Then you'll be even happier," said Mr. Woodhouse quickly. "But now, Miss Taylor, we must all have a cup of tea. I prefer camomile myself, but we can offer you ordinary tea if you prefer."

"Camomile has some very beneficial properties," said Miss Taylor.

Mr. Woodhouse beamed with pleasure.

.   .   .

The briskness with which Miss Taylor moved into Hartfield surprised Mr. Woodhouse—she arrived, with several suit-cases of possessions, within a week of her interview—but it was as nothing to the speed with which she reorganised the lives of the two girls. In spite of her earlier enthusiasm for the appointment, Mrs. Firhill took the view that she was moving too quickly: "Children don't like change. They want things to remain the same—everybody knows that, except this woman, or so it seems." These were dark notes of caution, uttered with a toss of the head in the direction of the attic bedroom that Miss Taylor now occupied, but the housekeeper, too, was in for a sur-prise; neither Isabella nor Emma resisted Miss Taylor, and from the very beginning embraced the ways of their governess with enthusiasm. The new regime involved new and exotic academic subjects—French and handwriting were Miss Taylor's intel-lectual priorities—as well as a programme of physical exercise and, most importantly, riotous, vaguely anarchic fun. A bolster bar was erected in the nursery, under which soft cushions were arranged. The girls were then invited to sit astride each end of this bar, armed with down-stuffed pillows. The game was to hit each other with these pillows until one of them was dislodged and fell on to a cushion or occasionally the bare floor below. In order to level the playing field that age tilted in Isabella's favour, Emma was allowed to use two hands, while her sis-ter was required to keep one behind her back. White feathers flew everywhere like snowflakes in a storm, and the shrieks of laughter penetrated even Mr. Woodhouse's study, where he sat engrossed in the latest crop of scientific papers in the dietary and nutritional journals to which he subscribed.

He was bemused by the changes that he saw about him, by

the constant activity, by the new enthusiasms. He watched as scrapbooks filled with cuttings from magazines and papers; as cut-out dolls found their way on to every table; as rescued animals and birds took up residence in shoe-boxes lined up at the base of the warmth-dispensing Aga; as the current of life, which had grown so sluggish after the death of his wife, now began to course once more through the house. He welcomed all of this, even if it failed to relieve his own anxiety. It was all very well to be cheerful and optimistic when one was the girls' age, but what if you were getting to the age—as he was—when life for the immune system became much more challenging? There were dangers all about, not least those identified by the medical statisticians, whose grim work it was to reveal just how likely it was that something could go wrong. And every time he contemplated the results of new research, there was the task of adjusting his regime to increase his level of exercise—or reduce it, depending on the balance of benefit between coronary health and wear and tear on the joints; to increase the number of supplements—or decrease it, depending on whether a novel product, attractive in itself, was likely to react badly with something that he was already taking. Such balancing was an almost full-time job, and left little time for other pursuits, such as the assessment of engineering risk—a task that he was well qualified to carry out but that could be inordinately demanding if one took it seriously, as Mr. Woodhouse certainly did.

The purchase of a new lawnmower was an example of just how complicated this could be. Hartfield was surrounded by extensive lawns that gave way, to the east, to a large shrubbery, much loved by the girls for games of hide-and-seek. Those games themselves had been the cause of some anxiety, as it was always possible that hiding under a rhododendron bush might bring one into contact with spiders, for whom the shade and dryness of the sub-rhododendron environment might be irresistible. Spiders had to live somewhere, and under rhododendron bushes could be just the place for them.

Mr. Woodhouse had heard people saying that there were no poisonous spiders in England. He knew this to be untrue, and had once or twice corrected those who made this false assertion. On one occasion he had gone to the length of ringing up during a local radio phone-in programme when a gardening expert had reassured a caller that there were no spiders to worry about in English gardens.

"That's unfortunately untrue," said Mr. Woodhouse to the show's host. "There are several species of spider in England that have a very painful bite. The raft spider, for instance, or the yard spider can both administer a toxic bite that will leave you in no doubt about having encountered something nasty."

The host had listened with interest and then asked whether Mr. Woodhouse had ever been bitten himself.

"Not personally," came the answer.

"Or known anybody who's been bitten?"

"Not exactly."

"Well then," said the host, "I don't think we need worry the listeners too much about what they might bump into in their gardens, do you?"

"Oh, I do," said Mr. Woodhouse. "A false sense of security is a very dangerous thing, let me assure you."

His concern over spiders was fuelled by the information that the Sydney funnel-web spider, known to be one of the most dangerous spiders in the world, had taken up residence in the

London Docks and was apparently thriving in its new habitat. That did not surprise Mr. Woodhouse at all, who had long thought that the ease with which goods and people could now be transported about the world was an invitation to every dangerous species to take up residence in places where they had previously been unknown. It was inevitable, he thought, that at least some travellers from Australia would bring in their luggage spiders that had taken refuge there while their suitcases were being packed. If bedbugs could do it—and they did—then why should spiders resist the temptation? He shook his head sadly; the green and pleasant land of Blake's imagining would not be green and pleasant for long at that rate. And if spiders could do it, what about sharks, who had to swim no more than a few extra nautical miles to arrive at British beaches? Or snakes, who had only to slither into a bunch of bananas in Central America to arrive within days on the tables of people thousands of miles away? And what if they met, en route, an attractive snake of the opposite sex? Before you knew it you would have a deadly fer-de-lance population comfortably established in Norfolk. That would give those complacent gardening experts on the radio something to think about.

"Nonsense," snapped Miss Taylor when he raised the issue of spiders under rhododendron bushes and queried whether the girls might not be banned from going into the shrubbery to play their games. "We cannot wrap ourselves in cotton wool; just imagine what we would look like. Moreover, girls and spiders have co-existed for thousands of years, as is established, I would have thought, by the continued survival of the two species: the British girl and the British spider. *Cadit quaestio.*"

The expression, *cadit quaestio*—the question falls away—

was one that Miss Taylor often used when she wished to put an end to a discussion. It was virtually unanswerable, as it is difficult to persist with a question that has been declared no longer to exist—anybody doing so seems so unreasonable—and it was now being used by the girls themselves, even by Emma. She had difficulty getting her tongue round the Latin but had nonetheless recently answered *"cadit quaestio"* when he had asked her whether she had taken her daily fish-oil supplement.

The size of the lawns around Hartfield meant that a mechanical lawnmower was required. For years Sid, who helped with the farm and with some of the tasks associated with the garden, had used an ancient petrol-driven lawnmower that he pushed before him on creaky and increasingly dangerous handles. Mr. Woodhouse had decided to replace this, and had looked into the possibility of a small tractor under which was fitted a powerful rotary blade. This would enable Sid to sit on a well-sprung seat as he drove the lawnmower up and down the lawn, leaving behind him neat stripes of barbered grass.

The tractor brochure portrayed this scene as a rural idyll. A contented middle-aged man sat on his small tractor, a vast swathe of well-cut grass behind him. The sky above was blue and cloudless; in the distance, on the veranda of a summer house, an attractive wife—at least ten years younger than the man on the lawnmower—waited to dispense glasses of lemonade to her hard-working husband. But Mr. Woodhouse was not so easily fooled. What if you put your foot just a few inches under the cover of the blade? What if you fell off the tractor because the ground was uneven—not everyone had even lawns—and your fingers, or even your whole hand, were to get in the way of the tractor and its vicious blade? Or what if a dog bounded up to greet its owner on the tractor and had its tail cut off? The woman dispensing lemonade so reassuringly would shriek and run out, only to slip under the lawnmower and be sliced like a salami in a delicatessen. It was all very well, he told himself, trying to avoid these possibilities and pretending that nothing like that would happen, but *somebody* had to think about them.

The enthusiasm that Isabella and Emma felt for Miss Taylor proved to be infectious. Although Mrs. Firhill had misgivings about the governess and the pace with which she introduced her changes, she found it hard to disapprove of a woman who, in spite of a tendency to state her views as if they were beyond argument, was warm and generous in her dealings with others. The conviction that she was right—the firm disapproval of those she deemed to be slovenly in their intellectual or physical habits—was something that Mrs. Firhill believed to be associated with her having come from Edinburgh.

"They're all like that," a friend said to her. "I've been up there—I know. They think the rest of us very sloppy. They are very judgemental people."

"I hope that it doesn't rub off on the girls," said Mrs. Firhill. "But I suppose it will. There's Emma already saying *cadit quaestio*—and she's only six."

"Oh, well," said the friend. "Perhaps it's the best of both worlds—to be brought up Scottish but to live somewhere ever so slightly warmer."

Mrs. Firhill nodded—and thought. There was already something about Emma that worried her even if she was unable to put her finger on what it was. Was it headstrongness—a trait that you found in certain children who simply would not be told and who insisted on doing things their way? Her cousin Else's son had been like that, and was always getting into trouble at school—unnecessarily so, she thought. Or was it something rather different—something to do with the desire to control? There were some children who were, to put it simply, bossy, and little girls tended to be rather more prone to this than little boys—or so Mrs. Firhill believed. Yes, she thought, that was it. Emma was a *controller*, and it was perfectly possible that Miss Taylor's influence would make it worse: if you were brought up to believe that there was a very clear right way and wrong way of doing things, then you might well try to make other people do things your way rather than theirs.

Once Mrs. Firhill had identified the issue, the signs of Emma's desire to control others seemed to become more and more obvious. On one occasion Mrs. Firhill came across her playing by herself in the playroom, Isabella being in bed that day with a heavy cold. In a corner of the room was the girls' doll's house—an ancient construction that had been discovered, dusty and discoloured, in the attic. Now with its walls repainted and repapered, the house was once again in use, filled with tiny furniture and a family of dolls that the girls shared between them. Long hours were spent attending to this house and in moving the dolls from one room to another in accordance with the tides of doll private life that no adult could fathom.

Unseen by Emma, Mrs. Firhill watched for a few minutes while Emma addressed her dolls and tidied their rooms.

"You are going to have to stay in your room until further notice," she scolded one, a small boy doll clad in a Breton sailor's blue-and-white jersey. "And you," she said to another one, a thin doll with arms out of which the stuffing had begun to leak, "*you* are never going to find a husband unless you do as I say."

Mrs. Firhill drew in her breath. It would have been very easy to laugh at this tiny display of directing behaviour, but she felt somehow that it was not a laughing matter. What she was witnessing was a perfect revelation of a character trait: Emma *must* want to control people if this was the way she treated her dolls. *Bossy little madam*, thought Mrs. Firhill. But then she added—to herself, of course—*without a mother*. And that, she realised, changed things.

3

oarding school?" said Miss Taylor. "I don't think that'll be necessary, do you? Not for your girls."

Mr. Woodhouse shifted uncomfortably in his seat. The conversation he was having with the governess was taking place in his study—his territory—and he would have imagined that he would have had the psychological advantage in such surroundings. It was a large room, furnished with a substantial desk, and to speak to somebody from behind such a desk surely must confer some degree of authority on one's pronouncements. He had read somewhere that Mussolini had a very large desk indeed, placed at the end of an exceptionally long room. This meant that visitors had to walk for some distance before they even reached the dictator, by which time if they had not already been intimidated when they entered the room they certainly would be by the time they reached his desk. And it was not just dictators who were keen on such tactics: there were several democratically elected presidents who were known to use elevator shoes, to stand on strategically placed boxes to gain height, or to insist when group photographs were being taken on being placed next to those shorter than themselves. He generally needed none of this, being secure enough in his estimation of himself, but Miss Taylor had a knack of making him feel perhaps slightly less than authoritative, as she was doing now, even in his own study.

"I think that their mother would have expected it," he said. It was sheltering behind his late wife—he knew that—but it would be hard for her to argue with a pious concern for the feelings of the girls' mother.

"But she may well have changed her views," retorted Miss Taylor. "Had she lived, that is; I was not suggesting that views can change after one has crossed over, so to speak. Things have changed since . . . since her day. And both of them are perfectly happy where they are. Why send them off to some wretched boarding school, some Dotheboys Hall? What's the point of having children if you then just send them away?"

Mr. Woodhouse looked out of the window. It was all very well for Miss Taylor to barge in and give her opinions on this tricky issue, but she was Scottish and did not understand the nuances of English life. Highbury, their village, was the embodiment of England; and there was a social order, complete with nuanced expectations, that she could not be presumed to understand. The local primary school was perfectly adequate for young children—and Miss Taylor was right to say that the girls were happy there—but now that they were getting older, there arose the highly charged question of boys. If they went to the local high school, then they would simply become pregnant; Mr. Woodhouse was sure of that. That was what happened at the local high school. They would meet the wrong sort of boy whose sole ambition would be to make any girl whom he met pregnant.

He wondered if he could explain his fear to the governess, who was staring at him intently, as if trying to fathom the nature of his unsettling suggestion that the girls might be sent away.

Miss Taylor now spoke. "How long have I been here now? Almost three years, have I not?"

He nodded. She had become a fixture in their lives, and it seemed as if she had been there for much longer than that. And he hoped, quite fervently, that she would be there for much longer—indefinitely, really, as it was hard to imagine Hartfield without her now.

"Well," continued Miss Taylor, "it would be a pity if I were to drop out of their lives after all that time, simply because they've been sent off to boarding school."

Mr. Woodhouse gasped. "But there would be no need for that," he said. "You wouldn't need to leave."

"I don't see what the point of my remaining would be," said Miss Taylor coolly. "My role here is as governess. As *governess*, I must emphasise. I would have nothing to do were the place to be devoid of children."

"But there'd be the holidays," objected Mr. Woodhouse. "They would need supervision during the holidays."

"Mr. Woodhouse," said Miss Taylor reprovingly, "surely you wouldn't expect me to sit about for months on end with nothing to do."

He was about to say, "But that's exactly what I do myself . . ." but he stopped. He could not contemplate her leaving, and it had now occurred to him that there was a way in which this could be avoided.

"May I suggest a compromise?"

"I don't see what compromise there can possibly be," said

Miss Taylor. "Either they go to boarding school, or they do not. You weren't going to suggest that I accompany them? I'm not sure that that would be viewed with favour by the school concerned."

Mr. Woodhouse laughed. "You going off with them and sleeping in the dorm with the rest of the girls? Eating your meals in the school refectory? Playing hockey? Hah!"

She looked at him with disdain. "Very droll," she said. "Perhaps you could tell me what this compromise is."

"There's a school in Holt," said Mr. Woodhouse. "That's not far, as you know. You will have seen it. Gresham's."

"I could hardly miss it," said Miss Taylor. "I do not go about with my eyes closed, Mr. Woodhouse."

"They take day pupils," he continued. "I could drive them there in the morning, and then you could pick them up late afternoon."

Miss Taylor looked thoughtful. "It has a very good academic reputation, I believe."

"Exceptional. And some very distinguished people went there. Benjamin Britten, the composer, for example."

"My tastes are a bit more robust," said Miss Taylor. "That's a personal view, of course. There are those who like Britten, but what he has to say about Venice would hardly encourage one to visit the place . . ."

"And then there was Donald Maclean," mused Mr. Woodhouse. "He was at Gresham's too, and became a very well-known spy."

"I see. Neither of those would have made very good husbands, I think . . ." She gave him a wry glance. "One would not want one's husband to defect to the other side, would one?"

Mr. Woodhouse looked puzzled. He thought that there might be something subtly humorous about her remark, but he was not quite sure what it was. *The other side?* Moscow? That was a bit obvious. "Well, it's all different now," he said. "We would not be sending them there to find a husband. There'll be plenty of time for that, later on."

"Yes," said Miss Taylor. "There are those who believe that is what universities are for."

She rose to leave. She was not one to prolong a conversation once a decision had been made. "I'm not at all sure that Emma will be the sort to want a husband," she said quietly. "Isabella, yes. She definitely will. And sooner rather than later, I think. She's probably thinking of boyfriends more or less now. I know I'm talking about a twelve-year-old girl here, but character, Mr. Woodhouse, is formed at a very early stage in our lives, and there are some girls who, even though only just twelve, give very clear indications of what lies ahead in the amorous department. I have seen it, Mr. Woodhouse. I have seen it all before."

Mr. Woodhouse seemed lost in thought and did not pursue with her what she had said. This suited Miss Taylor, as she was not very sure herself what she would say if he were to press her on her judgement of his daughters' characters. She was sure enough of her assessment of Isabella, but when it came to Emma she was a good deal less confident. There was something very unusual about Emma, who was, she felt, considerably more complex and therefore more interesting than Isabella. That was not to be dismissive of the older sister; Isabella was a pleasant enough girl, and Miss Taylor was sure that she would be a social success, particularly with boys. It was much more difficult to make such a prediction in Emma's case. She was a pretty child and that would guarantee the attention of friends—the beautiful, Miss Taylor had noticed, are seldom lonely, unless they choose to be. But it seemed to her that Emma had depths that might well be lacking in Isabella and girls like Isabella. There was something about her . . .

An aesthetic awareness? Was that it? Shortly after she had first arrived at Hartfield, Miss Taylor had become aware of Emma's interest in how things looked. There had been a curious incident in which Emma had ventured into her governess's room and started to rearrange the toiletry items set out on the dressing table. These included two silver-backed brushes—one a clothes brush and the other a hairbrush—that had been given to Miss Taylor by her aunt in Aberdeen. "Scottish silver," the aunt had said. "The very best silver there is." Miss Taylor had wondered about that: How could Scottish silver possibly differ from all other sorts of silver? Silver, surely, was silver, wherever it came from. But that was not the point: the real point was the large ornate letter *T* engraved on the backs of the brushes.

Now these brushes sat alongside an eau-de-cologne dispenser in the form of a squat bottle of thick-cut glass, a tortoise-shell comb, a bottle of nail-varnish remover, and a small Wemyss Ware bowl containing cotton-wool buds. For the average young child, such a collection would have been a positive invitation to fiddle, to take tops off, to press and spray things. The eau-de-cologne dispenser would have been the greatest temptation, closely followed by the cotton-wool buds. But this was not what happened with Emma, who spent ten concentrated minutes moving the items about the dressing table until they were placed in a position that appeared to satisfy her.

"You're very busy," said Miss Taylor as she observed what was happening.

"They must be beautiful," said Emma.

"What must be beautiful, Emma?"

"Things."

Miss Taylor smiled. "But they are beautiful, these things of mine. Those lovely silver brushes, for instance—they're very pretty, aren't they?"

The young Emma nodded. "Like this," she said, moving the brushes to the side. "They go there. These go . . ." She shifted the eau-de-cologne dispenser to the centre of the table. "There. Right shape."

That was not the only incident of that nature. Miss Taylor soon realised that the furniture in Emma's room, along with the pictures on her wall, rarely stayed in the same position for more than a few weeks on end. There were three chairs in the room and they were shifted about with regularity: under the window, beside the wardrobe, at the end of the bed, and then back to the window. Similar things happened in the rest of the house, although that was less noticeable. However, Mr. Woodhouse once commented that somebody seemed to have moved two of the pictures in his study, swapping their position.

"I can't see why Mrs. Firhill feels it necessary to dictate what I look at," he said over breakfast.

"There are others who may have a tendency to rearrange things," said Miss Taylor. "I don't think that Mrs. Firhill has views on what pictures go where."

Emma, busy with her bowl of cereal, said nothing.

"Well, I wish they wouldn't," said Mr. Woodhouse. "Why can't people leave well alone?"

Miss Taylor thought about a reply to that. He was right, of course, but only to an extent: there were too many people who imagined that there was some sort of duty incumbent on them to change things. These people were often unwilling to leave things as they were, which could be irritating. Yet if nothing were ever changed, she mused, then wouldn't life be rather dull? She was distracted from this rather interesting question by the thought that some people not only liked to interfere with the way that inanimate things—possessions and paintings and the like—were disposed, but also liked to change the way in which people themselves were arranged. She glanced at Emma, who now looked up from her cornflakes and smiled at her.

Later that day, Miss Taylor said to Emma, halfway through their French lesson, "Tell me, Emma, why do you like to move things about? I'm not scolding you, darling, I'm just curious to know."

Emma stared at the book they were reading. It was the adventures of Babar the elephant, in the original French. The three young elephants, Pom, Flora, and Alexander, were in peril, and she wanted to continue with the story.

"To make them happier," she said. "Now can we carry on reading?"

The girls settled in well at Gresham's, and both Miss Taylor and Mr. Woodhouse became accustomed to their daily school run. In the mornings Isabella and Emma were driven to Holt in a mud-bespattered Land Rover that was normally used for farm work; in the afternoon, Miss Taylor, who insisted on wearing motoring gloves, cut a fairly dashing figure as she drove to collect them in a silver-coloured Mercedes-Benz that had belonged to Mr. Woodhouse's father.

With the girls at school for more of the day, Miss Taylor initially found that time hung heavily on her hands. But after she enrolled for a number of Open University courses, she discovered that the study and essay-writing that these entailed filled the gaps in her day. Mr. Woodhouse encouraged her in this, and insisted on making available a fund for the purchase of textbooks and other materials needed for her studies. In her first year she completed two courses on Medieval Spanish History along with a course on the Trade Routes of the Ancient Middle East. In her second, she achieved a particularly high mark in both Classical Culture and Civilisation and the Dance and Drama of Restoration England, and then embarked on a more advanced course on the Art of the Baroque.

For the girls she was by this time very much a stepmother in all but name, her relationship with Emma being particularly close. But while most stepmothers encounter resentment on the part of their stepchildren, she did not. This resentment is based on the feeling that the stepmother is harsh and unkind: a pattern so common as to attract a name—the Cinderella Syndrome, Cinderella having been the victim of an egregiously unpleasant stepmother and stepsisters. Just as Cinderella did, the stepchild pines for the mother who would have treated her better, and resents the usurpation by the stepmother of her place in her father's affections. At Hartfield, important elements in this psychological equation were missing: Miss Taylor was anything but unfeeling—in fact, she regularly and unapologetically indulged the girls. But then she was not married to their father—who had no interest in any relationship with her other than as an appreciative employer and, in a sense, friend. Without those complications, a fully blown psychopathology could hardly get started, and there was nothing to mar the reasonable, loving relationship that the two girls enjoyed with their governess. It was to Miss Taylor that they turned for advice; it was she who comforted them when they encountered the torments that beset any adolescence; it was she who looked after them and gave them the love that their own mother would have given them had she survived.

Shortly after her seventeenth birthday, it was decided that Isabella should not remain at school any longer. Most of her contemporaries were to spend a further year at Gresham's, but in Isabella's case it was felt that there was no point in persuading her to study for examinations that she had no desire to sit and that she would evidently not pass. She wanted to go to live in London and find work there. She had met somebody on a train who said that she could find her a job with a firm of fine-art auctioneers that specialised in providing employment for the daughters of county families. She would not be paid very much, she was warned, but that was not the point; she had a regular income from her mother's estate that would be more than enough to pay the rent and ordinary living expenses, and her father, she felt, would provide for any luxuries. London, with its plays and its parties, beckoned; it was as if its lights, bright and seductive, penetrated into the country even as far as Hartfield itself, lighting the winding way to the distant city.

Mr. Woodhouse, of course, felt that London was highly dangerous.

"I cannot understand," he said to his daughters when Isabella first mentioned her desire to go there. "I just cannot understand how anybody would wish to live in London. I can see why people might wish to go in for the day—to see what's on at the Royal Academy or the Science Museum or whatever. Perhaps even to do a bit of shopping. But to live there?" He shook his head in disbelief at the inexplicable nature of such a choice.

"But . . ." began Isabella.

She did not get far. "The very air is sixth-hand," continued Mr. Woodhouse. "Just think of it: when you breathe in places like London, you're taking in air that has already been in and out of goodness knows how many lungs."

"Twelve," said Emma. "Strictly speaking—if each person has two lungs and the air is sixth-hand."

"Well, there you are," said Mr. Woodhouse. "Twelve lungs. Imagine the microbial load, and the viruses . . ."

"But viruses are everywhere, Father," said Isabella. "We learned that in biology at school. Miss Parkinson—you should have seen her."

Emma giggled. "Old bag."

"A very good teacher, I believe," said Mr. Woodhouse. "And obviously aware of viruses—which is a good thing."

Isabella smiled. "She said that we need to be exposed to a few viruses in order to build up our immune system. She said that the rise in the number of people with allergies is partly to do with the fact that everybody is eating over-purified food."

"Should we eat dirty things?" asked Emma. "Should we wash the crockery maybe only once or twice a week?"

Mr. Woodhouse tried to smile at this suggestion, but he found the whole discussion acutely painful: one should not talk about microbes lightly, he felt; it was an invitation to disaster. Of course microbes could not hear what they were saying, but it seemed somehow foolish to talk about them as if they were not there.

"There may be a smidgeon of truth in what Miss Parkinson says," he conceded. "You do need to be exposed to a certain level of microbial activity, but London goes way, way beyond that." He paused. "No, I cannot see living in London as anything but foolhardy. Theatres and museums are all very well . . ."

"And parties," added Isabella.

Mr. Woodhouse glanced at her, but ignored the provocation. "These things may be all very well, but what if you're in such a wretched condition that you can't enjoy them? What then?"

"They look fine to me," said Isabella. "There are loads of people at Gresham's whose parents live in London—or work there—and they seem fine to me."

Mr. Woodhouse shook his head. "The air is far healthier out here," he said. "And if you lived in London, young lady, you'd know all about it. You'd have a streaming cold 24/7, as you people like to say. And you'd be running the risk of much worse, believe me. If the water's been through however many sets of kidneys . . . No, don't make that face, this is *science* I'm talking about. If London water has been through all those systems . . ."

"Through boys' systems too," contributed Emma.

Isabella smiled. She did not object to *that*.

"If London water has had that experience," continued Mr. Woodhouse, "then what's the chance of at least some viruses escaping the attention of the chlorine, and, I believe, ammonia they dose the stuff with? What about hepatitis? That's water-borne, as I think I've told you in the past."

"Hepatitis turns you yellow," said Emma.

"Yes," said Mr. Woodhouse, glancing at Isabella. She did not take these things seriously enough, he felt, and shock tactics were sometimes necessary to emphasise a point. "A fact worth remembering."

There were several such conversations about the dangers of London, but it seemed that none of them had much impact on Isabella's desire to move there as soon as possible. Mr. Woodhouse agonised over this in private, but also raised the subject with Miss Taylor.

"She seems dead set on going off to London," he said as they walked together one evening in the shrubbery. "I've talked to her about it, but it seems to go in one ear and out the other with that girl. In fact, I'm not sure that it even goes in one ear at all. I think that a lot of what I say is completely ignored. Emma's quite different, of course—she listens to what I have to say, but her sister . . ."

"Her sister is a very different girl," said Miss Taylor. "We all know that."

"I can't understand it," said Mr. Woodhouse, shaking his head with exasperation. "They have the same DNA."

"Not quite the same," corrected Miss Taylor. "They share some DNA but they have their own genes. They're not identical twins."

"Yes, you're right," said Mr. Woodhouse. "But they come from the same background and at least they have the same broad genetic inheritance, and yet . . ."

Miss Taylor reached out and placed a calming hand on his arm. "Isabella is more physical," she said. "It's as simple as that. In fact, I'm sorry to have to say this, but there's only one thought in her head at the moment: the opposite sex."

The words *the opposite sex* were carefully enunciated—as if she were speaking with gloves on—and uttered in a slightly disapproving Scottish accent. The effect was electric.

"Boys?"

Miss Taylor nodded. "Isabella is interested in boys. They are all she thinks about. They, I'm afraid to say, are her destiny."

He fell silent. He did not like to think about the implications of what the governess had said. Was this the reason why one had daughters—to hand them over to be seduced by lascivious boys? He shuddered. He did not want the world to claim his girls. He wanted them to stay with him forever, in the security— or at least the relative security—of Hartfield. Let the outside world do its worst, but let it do it outside, and not within the curtilage of this agreeable old house and these gentle acres.

"We need to marry her off," he muttered.

Miss Taylor frowned. "I didn't think people spoke in those terms any more."

"I don't care," said Mr. Woodhouse. "The fact of the matter is that I have a daughter who is going to get herself involved in all sorts of affairs if we don't." He hesitated, looking at Miss Taylor as if for advance confirmation of what he was about to say. "That will happen unless we find a husband for her as soon as possible."

"But Isabella's only seventeen," protested Miss Taylor. "She hasn't really lived yet."

"Many people get married at eighteen or nineteen," said Mr. Woodhouse. "The average might be higher, but remember that you only have to be sixteen."

"Child brides," said Miss Taylor dismissively.

"My mother was eighteen when she married my father,"

said Mr. Woodhouse. "And it was a very successful marriage, as I think you know. My own wife was twenty-two when we married."

Miss Taylor was silent.

He felt more confident now. "So you see, it's not so outrageous an idea to want to fix your daughter up with a husband in order to protect her from what might be a string of unhappy affairs with all sorts of unsuitable young men. In fact, the more I think about it, the more attractive it seems."

Miss Taylor now spoke. "But you can't *fix people up*, as you put it. She's a young woman now. She's going to have her own ideas of what she wants, and I'm sorry to have to spell it out, but those ideas won't necessarily be the same as yours." She frowned. "This is the twenty-first century, you know."

"That," he said, "is a fact of which I am only too acutely aware. And I'm also aware of the fact that you cannot choose your daughter's husband for her." He paused. "But what you can do is to let suitable people know that your daughter is about the place. That's all. Then nature will take its course—or at least you hope it will, and some suitable young man—somebody from round about here—will step forward and win her over. That's all."

Miss Taylor stared at him. She had wondered whether he was being entirely serious; now she understood that he was.

"And how do you let people know?" she asked.

Mr. Woodhouse smiled. "Do you read those copies of *Country Life* I get?"

Miss Taylor knew immediately what he had in mind. "You mean we should get Isabella's photograph into *Country Life?* On that page near the front where they have a picture each week of an attractive young woman, with details below of her parents and what she's doing?"

Mr. Woodhouse nodded. "It's a great tradition," he said. "They've been doing it for years, you know." He lowered his voice. "In fact, my mother had her photograph there. I've got the copy of the magazine in my study. I'm rather proud of it. To have a mother who had her photograph at the front of *Country Life* is quite something, don't you think?"

"I shall never completely understand the English," muttered Miss Taylor.

"Don't try," said Mr. Woodhouse. "There are some things that pass all understanding, as they say."

4

It was a matter, they said, of submitting a good photograph to the editor of *Country Life* and asking him to consider featuring one's daughter in a future issue. Success was by no means guaranteed, even for the highly photogenic: there were many girls in many counties, all most eager to appear, or at least all having parents who were eager on their behalf. And parental support in this was crucial; self-nomination was unheard of, as the very act of putting oneself forward would be incontrovertible proof that one was not suitable.

The photograph had to be reasonably interesting. *Country Life* girls did not simply sit for the camera against some featureless backdrop but were pictured striking a pose in surroundings that gave an indication of their normal social milieu or talents. The daughters of major gentry—those with stately homes—might be photographed leaning against a stone pillar, the clear inference being that this was just one of the many stone pillars owned by her father; those who had no stone pillars but who had, say, a small ornamental lake, would be photographed standing in front of this. Those who worked with horses—and this was a large group—might have a hunter in the

background, or at least a saddle. Dogs were a popular accoutre-
ment, usually Labradors, who would be at the young woman's
side, ready to retrieve or flush birds, enthusiasts all, and given
the same appraising scrutiny by the readers, in many cases, as
the young woman herself.

Not everybody, of course, lived in the country, although most
of those who were urbanites had at least some country connection. Parents might be described as being of Cheyne Walk,
Chelsea, *and* East Woods Manor, Chipping Norton, or whatever
it was that provided the country bolthole for those who lived in
town. And of course in any such juxtaposition it was Chipping
Norton rather than London that counted: anybody could live in
London, but not everybody could live in Chipping Norton.

The accompanying text also revealed the subject's plans.
Many young women were studying something at university—
particularly at Durham, Edinburgh, or Bristol. Many were
planning to work in public relations or in a gallery; one or
two—the lucky ones—had already opened their own interior-
decoration business. Some were planning to get married in
the near future, and the month of the wedding was given so
that the readers might know whether they had been invited or
passed over. If the wedding was to be the following month and
no invitation had yet been received, then the conclusion was
inescapable that one was not going. If, however, the marriage
was to take place next September or October, and it was only
May, then an invitation was still a possibility.

Mr. Woodhouse had never paid much attention to any of
this, which he regarded as the sort of thing that appealed to
women but not to men. The wording of any caption to Isabella's
photograph could be worked out later—his immediate task was

to find a photographer. This sent him off to the Yellow Pages, but he had not even begun to page through these when he remembered that he knew of a photographer who was right on their doorstep, or whose brother was.

George Knightley was the owner of one of the largest houses in the area, Donwell Abbey (twenty-four bedrooms). At the time at which Mr. Woodhouse was thinking of publishing his daughter's photograph, George was just twenty-five and had owned Donwell for four years. He had inherited not only a house, but looks too, his father having been described in a magazine article as one of the ten most handsome men in England. Knightley *père* had also been one of the most modest, as he never made any reference to this, or any other accolade that came his way. He had that endangered and most attractive quality: an old-fashioned Englishness, in appearance, garb, and manner, and a generosity of spirit that made him extremely popular in the neighbourhood. This ensured a sympathetic reception for his son when he took over the property. "Thank heavens," said people. "Think of what we might have had, with all these . . ." Typically there then followed a listing of those who might have bought Donwell Abbey had it been put on the open market: hedge-fund people, dot-com people, Russian oligarchs, celebrities of various stripes—the list was a long one and generally concluded with a sigh of relief that the Knightleys remained exactly where they had been for centuries.

His parents were divorced when he was barely seven. It was not an acrimonious parting: both parties had gradually grown away from each other and recognised that they were, quite simply, bored with the other's company and that this boredom was beginning to turn to irritation. They understood that when another's mannerisms begin to grate, it is probably too late to retrieve the situation, even if a relationship might be patched up with a lot of effort and forbearance. He went off to live in Vancouver; she stayed at Donwell, which had now been given to her as part of a generous divorce settlement. The boys stayed with her and, for reasons of geography, saw their father only intermittently. He lost touch with England and, to an extent, with his sons, although he had never intended to desert them. For her part, she developed a close friendship with a man she met at a bridge club, and ended up travelling with him to competitions all over the world. It was on one of these trips, a visit to an international bridge tournament in Kerala, that she was hit by a car—an old Hindustan Ambassador with minimal brakes—and died. Her last memories were of the sun above her—so brilliant, so unrelenting—and concerned faces looking down on her: a boy wearing a blue shirt, a man in a khaki uniform who was shouting at the others; and then the sun again, and darkness.

Under the terms of her will, George inherited Donwell and the estate surrounding it, while his brother, John, was given such investments as his mother had. It was a roughly equitable division and it suited both of them. George had a sense of duty that his brother lacked; he also rather liked the challenge of restoring the Donwell farm to profitability. For John, his inheritance of easily realisable assets would enable him to indulge his taste for expensive cameras, forget the house that he had always found hopelessly uncomfortable and dull, and buy a flat in a fashionable part of London.

The young George Knightley's commitment to Donwell was no passing fancy. Aided by his astute farm manager, he made sure that fields were used in such a way as to ensure maximum

European Union grants. Old farm machinery was replaced with brand-new equipment, and diversification—the saviour of many a farmer who had found it impossible to make a living growing crops—was pursued with single-minded enthusiasm. This meant that several farm cottages that had been lying empty were made suitable for holiday lets; that beehives were introduced and a centrifuge bought for the extraction of honey from the comb; that a large flock of rare-breed sheep was established, as well as a farm shop selling home-cured bacon, and jerseys and mittens made from the wool of the rare-breed sheep; in short, that every way of making a farm pay was examined, tried, and, if successful, implemented.

The proximity of Donwell Abbey to Hartfield meant that the Woodhouses and Knightleys saw a fair amount of each other. George Knightley had always been aware of the Woodhouse girls, of course, but they were, in his eyes, no more than two rather attractive teenage girls who had always been about the place and with whom he occasionally chatted. Isabella, of course, had always appreciated his looks, but the age gap between them made any thought of romance impossible. When she was sixteen, and beginning to take a strong interest in boys, he was twenty-four, and therefore impossibly old by teenage standards.

"Life after twenty?" Isabella said to a friend. "I don't think so!"

"Well, you're hardly *dead* when you're twenty-something," said the friend. "Maybe a bit past it, but not actually *finished*."

"That comes later."

"Yes, forty."

They had laughed, but they actually meant it.

George thought nothing of age gaps. He might be older than Isabella, but he was nonetheless amused by her. He compared her with some of the girls he had met at university: in a few years she would be exactly like them, he thought—a county girl itching to find the right husband from the ranks of those young men who would make up her social circle. It was a harmless enough fate, even if a rather predictable one.

He was not so sure about Emma. She was a good dozen years younger than he was, and so when he returned to Donwell at the age of twenty-one she was only nine—a mere child. Over the years that followed, though, he saw the uncoordinated adolescent grow into a self-assured and rather beautiful young woman. He often saw her when he went to visit Mr. Woodhouse, but it seemed to him that he was largely invisible to her. That, of course, was because he was a friend of her father and therefore of no interest to her other than as a vaguely avuncular figure. In spite of her indifference to him, he found himself appreciating her rather intriguing manner, her frequently unexpected, not to say mischievous observations, and her independent, insouciant manner. Emma, he thought, was growing up interesting.

Now Mr. Woodhouse remembered what it was that George Knightley had said to him. He had told him that his brother had become something of a success as a photographer and had actually won a national competition a year or two earlier. "John has a bit of an eye," he said. "He always has had one. Odd, really, given that I can't take a snap myself."

Mr. Woodhouse had not paid much attention at the time, but now it came back to him, and he thought that the simple solution to his quest would be to invite John Knightley to take the picture.

He asked George for his brother's number in London. Then, when he made the call, the telephone was answered after only one or two rings—always a good sign, thought Mr. Woodhouse—and John Knightley came on the line.

"We haven't seen one another for some time," said Mr. Woodhouse, trying to remember when it was that he had last seen John and wondering whether he still had an unhealthy complexion and rather lank hair.

"Ages," said John. "Yonks."

"Yes," said Mr. Woodhouse. "I see your brother quite a bit, of course. He often comes round here."

"He hasn't got much to do," said John.

Mr. Woodhouse sounded peeved. "He keeps busy enough, I'd say. He runs the farm rather well."

"With a manager, yes," said John, and then added, "Good old George."

Mr. Woodhouse ignored this remark. "You still taking photographs, John?"

"Yes, Mr. Woodhouse. That's my job. I'm a fashion photographer in London. *Vogue. Vanity Fair. Tatler.* That's me." He paused. "You won't have seen my work, of course."

Mr. Woodhouse cleared his throat. This was a very irritating young man—very different from his equable and well-mannered brother. "I need a photograph of my daughter."

"Which one? The tall sexy one?"

Again Mr. Woodhouse bit his tongue. "Isabella. She's seventeen."

"Great age," said John. "You want me to do it?"

"Yes. Can you?"

"Do dogs bark?" replied John. "Is the Pope a Catholic?"

Mr. Woodhouse frowned. "What?"

"The answer's yes. Happy to oblige, old son."

The tone now became formal. Mr. Woodhouse would expect John the following Saturday for the taking of a couple of portrait shots in the house and gardens. This was agreed and the conversation came to an end.

Mr. Woodhouse sat and reflected. It was all most unsettling: John came from a good county family, and had he not gone off to London might well have ended up helping his brother run their small estate. He had had a perfectly good education, too; like his brother, George, he had gone to Marlborough, yet here he was using the language of a cockney barrow boy—if barrow boys still existed—and if cockneys still existed too. *Old son! Is the Pope a Catholic?* What had the Pope got to do with it? Mr. Woodhouse asked himself. And of course dogs barked; did they not understand that in London?

Isabella required no persuasion to have her photograph taken. "In a mag?" she shrieked. "He'll put me in one of his actual mags? Are you serious?"

Mr. Woodhouse realised that they were probably thinking of different magazines. He knew that Isabella liked to read glossy magazines full of ephemeral news about celebrities and their doings; he had come across these magazines left lying about the house and occasionally sneaked a look at their contents. They were absurd, of course, and the people they featured were without any interest at all—highly made-up, unhealthy-looking specimens who appeared to have no other purpose in life than to evade the paparazzi who pursued them. But occasionally the very same hounded celebrities opened their doors to admit the photographers to their homes, and the resultant features, plastered with high-definition pictures of white sofas and opulent swimming pools, gave an indication of just how little taste these people had. And yet there was a certain fascination in seeing them in their natural habitat, and he had occasionally had to drop a magazine hurriedly and guiltily as a daughter came into the room. "Tidying," he would say quickly. "Why do you girls insist on leaving all these ridiculous magazines about the place?"

Isabella was rarely fooled. "What do you think of that photo of *her*?" she might ask. "Can you believe that he actually *bit* her? Did you see the love-bite—it's on her left shoulder—you can just make it out?"

"Most unhygienic," he muttered. "A human bite can be a very toxic thing. There are numerous germs on people's teeth."

"Not celebs," retorted Isabella. "A bite from a celeb is different."

Now he was faced with something of a moral dilemma. Should he tell Isabella that the destination for her photograph was not to be some glossy gossip magazine, but *Country Life*, where photographs of humans are often outnumbered by photographs of horses and dogs, or sometimes of old houses?

He decided to be honest—or at least a bit honest. "It won't be one of your glossy mags," he said. "It's another magazine altogether. A bit more sedate, but still."

He need not have worried. "I don't care where it goes," she said. "It's enough to have your photo in anything. Think what they'll say when they see it at school. They're all still sitting in the classroom and I'm posing! That's seriously cool."

"I'm glad that you're pleased," said Mr. Woodhouse. "The photographer will be coming tomorrow. He's George Knightley's brother. You'll remember him. He went off to London for some reason best known to himself."

Isabella looked thoughtful. She did remember John Knightley. She remembered thinking that he was rather good-looking and had long hair when everybody else around him seemed to have his hair cut short. And he had gone to London, she thought. *A London photographer is coming to do a shoot with me. With me.*

While most people drove sedately up the drive that led through the parkland to Hartfield, enjoying the trees and the view of the shrubbery in the distance, John Knightley arrived at speed on a 1982 Ducati motorcycle, a throaty roar announcing him well before anybody saw the handsome Italian bike and its equally handsome rider. Mr. Woodhouse went out to meet him and shook hands with the leather-clad brother of his neighbour.

"Sorry I'm a bit late," said John. "There was a pile-up on the motorway and I had to stop and get a few shots of it. Not my usual stuff, of course, but in my business you're always looking for things you can sell to the red tops. They love a bit of gore, those editors."

Mr. Woodhouse struggled to keep his composure. "An accident? You took photos of an accident?"

John took off his helmet. "Yup. I don't go in for anything too gory—not like some. There's a chap I know in London who does the really bad scenes—you know, hands and stuff lying about. Not for me."

"I should hope not," said Mr. Woodhouse.

"You're looking at respectability," said John, smiling. "You're looking at the upper echelons of the profession."

Mr. Woodhouse availed himself of the invitation to examine John Knightley. He was a very striking-looking young man— tall, as he had remembered him, but with a bit more weight than he recalled him having. The face, though, was by no means chubby, but had a sparse, sculpted look to it, and the head was topped by a mane of flowing dark hair. John Knightley, he decided, looked rather like a lion; an absurd idea, he told himself, and then went on to think: *Long hair requires frequent washing if it is not to become a sanctuary for microbial life.* His gaze descended to the leather jacket and tight-fitting trousers and then to the boots with metal attachments on the heel—spurs? he wondered; surely not. How quickly, he thought, could one effect a transition from one world to another; from the world of George Knightley, with his faultless taste, his life of understatement and simple English decency, to this world of leather jackets and . . . He had noticed the tattoo; he had missed it at first because it was so discreet, but now, as the sleeve of the leather jacket inched up following a movement of John's arm, he saw the small picture of an angel, or what looked like an angel, on his visitor's wrist and underneath it a few tiny words, illegible at that distance. He caught his breath; the social descent seemed to him to be complete, and terrible. Tattoos were unacceptable; they just were. People could argue as much as they liked that conventions had changed and a tattoo now meant nothing; that they said nothing about you; but tattoos, in Mr. Woodhouse's mind, constituted a line in the sand that one simply did not cross. John Knightley had stepped across that line.

"I think Isabella's in the morning room," Mr. Woodhouse said. "Would you care to come with me? We'll see her there."

John nodded. "I remember this place. We came here to a party once—my brother and I—when we were kids. He was sick in the conservatory, as I remember, and I tried to clear it up before anybody noticed."

"You're a loyal brother," said Mr. Woodhouse.

"Poor George."

"It sounds as if you feel sorry for him," said Mr. Woodhouse.

"Yes, I do. Being stuck out here in that great barn of a house and the tedium . . . My God, how does he manage it, having to put up with the same old people year in, year out?"

Such as me, thought Mr. Woodhouse.

"Mind you," said John. "I can't picture him in London, can you?"

Mr. Woodhouse felt that he must defend his friend. "I can't see myself in London either," he said.

John threw him a sideways glance. "No, possibly not."

They reached the morning room, a large rectangular room with French doors giving out on to a terrace beyond. It was a favourite room of the girls, and Isabella was waiting, nonchalantly pretending to read a magazine.

For all his preoccupations Mr. Woodhouse was not an unobservant man, and he noticed immediately the spark of response in Isabella's expression. As he did so, his spirits sank;

it had been a mistake to invite John Knightley to take Isabella's photograph, and even as he made this admission to himself he came to the further realisation that the consequences of this introduction could be serious, and long-lasting.

"I'll start in here," said John. "I've got my gear in my back-pack." He turned to Mr. Woodhouse. "OK. Thanks a lot. I'll see you before I go."

It was clear to Mr. Woodhouse that he was being dismissed, and it was equally clear to him that Isabella was anxious that he should not linger.

"Can't I help you in some way?" he asked. "Hold a light, or something?"

John shook his head. "It's easier if just two people are present at the shoot," he said, and then added, "Chemistry, you know. Energy flows. More intimate."

Isabella smiled. "See you later, Pops."

Mr. Woodhouse resisted the temptation to lurk in a corridor or peer out of a window when the shoot moved outside. Burying himself in his library, he spent the next half hour paging through an issue of *Scientific American* but retaining very little of what he was reading. He was convinced that John Knightley would take completely unsuitable photographs of Isabella, and that all that he would receive from *Country Life* would be a polite note about their inability to feature many young women who clearly would merit inclusion if only there were more room. The photographs would be gimmicky, he feared, with Isabella being draped seductively over the bonnet of a car or sprawled out wantonly on a pile of leaves; they would completely fail to embody the qualities of demure Englishness—mixed with an appealing and modest confidence—that could attract the right sort of husband.

He sighed, and laid *Scientific American* aside. It was important to have an understanding of particle physics—he had been reading about the Higgs boson—but the intellectual challenge of *Scientific American* was definitely secondary to a father's duty to protect his daughter. Rising to his feet, he retraced his steps into the morning room. This was deserted; Isabella and John had presumably left for the formal garden and the outside shoot. But when he looked out of the window he saw that they were not there, and nor was there any sign of them in the shrubbery, of which the morning room had an equally commanding view.

The unease he had felt up to this point was now replaced by real concern. Leaving the morning room by a French window, he made his way quickly round the outside of the house, scanning neighbouring fields for any sign of the young people. There was none; the ripening barley, swaying in the breeze, showed no signs of intrusion; sheep grazed in a neighbouring paddock undisturbed by human presence; it was a landscape quite without figures. It was only when he turned the corner of the house and reached the broad turning circle at the head of the drive that he spotted them.

They were standing by the shining red Ducati. John Knightley, having packed away his photographic equipment, was now busy extracting a helmet from a large metal pannier behind the motorcycle's seat. Mr. Woodhouse breathed a sigh of relief at the realisation that the photographer would be leaving, but then he noticed that there were two helmets: the one being taken from the pannier and the one that John was already wearing, the unfastened strap dangling casually under his chin. He watched as the photographer handed the spare helmet to Isabella, who took it, and laughed as he showed her how to secure the strap.

He called out, and she looked up sharply.

"Daddy," she shouted, as he approached. "Look at me. John's going to take me for a ride on his Duc . . . Duc . . ."

"Ducati," prompted John. "Just as far as Cambridge. We'll be back by eight tonight."

"But . . ." protested Mr. Woodhouse. He felt a sudden tightening of his chest, a symptom, he knew, of extreme panic. It was now, he thought, that he should have a stroke; at such a time as this, when fear sent the blood through his veins under such pressure that somewhere, in some obscure corner of the brain's plumbing, a tiny vessel might rupture and fell him just as surely as would a great blade. It was every bit as bad—worse indeed—as he had feared. "But you can't, Isabella. These things . . ." He gestured helplessly at the motorcycle; in his distress, words seemed to fail him. "These things . . . these things are Italian."

She burst out laughing. "What? Italian?"

He corrected himself, ashamed because John was smirking. "Lethal. I meant to say: these things are lethal."

He wanted to weep. He was convinced that as he watched her go down the drive it would be his last glimpse of his beloved daughter. He should do something to stop her: throw himself in front of the machine; or seize the key—if these things had keys—from John and run off with it, back to the house, ignoring his shouts. The most outrageous act on his part—even fetching his shotgun, his father's old engraved Purdey—and pointing it at John would be justified in order to save Isabella from this dreadful folly.

"It's perfectly safe," said John. "I'm a pretty careful rider, Mr. Woodhouse. Your daughter will be quite safe with me."

"See?" said Isabella. "There's nothing to worry about, Daddy."

"You mustn't, my darling. Please, please, I beg of you: you mustn't."

He did not think she heard him, as the flaps at the side of the helmet had now been fixed in position. She mouthed the word *Goodbye*. If only she hadn't done that, he thought. If only she hadn't tempted Nemesis to oblige and make it a real and final goodbye.

In slow motion—or so it seemed to the agonised Mr. Woodhouse—he watched Isabella mount the pillion seat. It was so prolonged, so deliberate—just as some article on human perception in *Scientific American* had explained it would be, because our minds register an event like that with heightened clarity, and that makes it seem to happen slowly.

"Isabella!" he called out. But his voice was drowned by the roar of the Ducati and the crunching sound of its wheels on the gravel, and she did not hear him. She waved, though, and waved again when they rode past him in a spray of tiny stones.

5

"Dearly beloved," began the vicar. "We are gathered together here in the sight of God and in the face of this congregation . . ." The echoing opening of the Wedding Service, couched in the Cranmerian prose of the Book of Common Prayer, could not but move every one of the one hundred guests attending the wedding of Isabella Woodhouse to John Knightley. Emma listened to each word, and was impressed by the sheer solemnity of what she heard: ". . . which is an honourable estate . . . and first miracle he wrought, in Cana of Galilee . . . and therefore is not by any to be enterprised, nor taken in hand, unadvisedly, lightly, or wantonly . . ." The resonant language brought home to her the significance of the occasion. This was *her* Isabella, her sister, taking such an irrevocable and adult step, leaving the security of her childhood home and venturing out as a married woman, as Mrs. Knightley. It was hard for her to accept that this was actually happening; it was all so sudden, and so dramatic—almost an elopement, but not quite.

She looked about her at the congregation almost filling the small Norman church in Highbury. The Knightley family

was led by George, and was well represented by an assortment
of cousins, even if somewhat distant ones; there were fewer
Woodhouses—not because various relatives had been passed
over, but because they were a smaller family. Then there were
people from the village: Miss Bates, an unmarried woman in
her fifties who occupied, on a fixed rent, a cottage in the village,
and who lived a narrow life in severely reduced circumstances;
James Weston, a widower whose Georgian house of eight bedrooms was barely a mile from Hartfield, and who had always
been a good friend to Mr. Woodhouse; Mr. Perry, an exponent
of alternative medicine, regarded as a charlatan by some (but
not by Mr. Woodhouse), and his wife, an illustrator of educa-
tional textbooks; and a number of friends whom Isabella had
known at Gresham's: Rosie Slazenger, Timmy Cottesloe, Kitty
Fairweather. Emma knew them too, although she was a few
years younger; Mr. Woodhouse had heard their names before
and had met some of them from time to time, but could never
tell which one was which.

Mr. Woodhouse had reconciled himself to Isabella's choice.
His attempt to marry her off had succeeded, of course, but not
in the way he had imagined. He had wanted her to find a husband in order to protect her, and she had done just that, with
alacrity and determination, although not alighting upon quite
the sort of husband he had envisaged for her. Still, it could
have been worse; and the most important consideration, he
knew, was her happiness. John Knightley made her happy. She
adored him, and as far as Mr. Woodhouse could make out, this
adoration was fully reciprocated. And he accepted that the fact
that he had a tattoo was far less important than the fact that they
were both happy. His tattoo, moreover, was a relatively discreet

one, and not something that people would necessarily notice, although it was a pity, Mr. Woodhouse felt, that the best man should choose to mention it in his speech.

Immediately after the wedding she informed him that she was three months pregnant, and that she was expecting twins. Emma, who was sixteen at the time, greeted this news with delight, but proclaimed, quite spontaneously, "Not for me! I'm never going to get myself pregnant! Yuck!"

She addressed this to Miss Taylor, who was surprised by the vehemence of her reaction. "But it's a wonderful thing to have children," she said. "You love children—I've seen you with those little girls in the village shop."

"Children, yes," said Emma. "But pregnancy, no. All that . . ." She assumed an expression of disgust. "All that fumbling."

Miss Taylor smiled. "You shouldn't worry about that," she said. "That'll take care of itself. The important thing is to meet a young man whom you love. Once that happens, and I hope it does, then everything else—fumbling, and so on—will seem quite natural."

Emma shook her head vigorously. No, Miss Taylor did not understand; how could she—at her age? "I don't ever want to get married," she announced. "Never. Never. Not in a thousand years."

Miss Taylor was tolerant. "Millennia come round so quickly, Emma." She smiled again. "I've already experienced one in my lifetime. And you may think that of marriage now, you know, but one's views do change."

"Mine won't," said Emma, with conviction. She was certain; she knew what lay ahead of her: she would continue to be pretty, clever, and rich. That did not include getting married:

pretty, clever, and rich people did not have to bother with such things.

"Oh well," said Miss Taylor. "There are other lifestyles. There is a great deal to be said for being single." And she thought: *Exactly what?* Not having to worry about another person; not having to accommodate a partner's wishes; not having to tolerate the slow, gravitational decline of the flesh into middle age and beyond, into that territory of sleepless nights and infirmity; not having to listen to familiar views on the same things, time after time? Not having to *have to*, in short. *And yet*, she thought, *if I had to choose between being a governess and having a man . . .*

Emma, having pronounced, now looked thoughtful. "Of course, I quite see how lots of other people want to get married. I can see how it's fine for them. In fact . . ."

Miss Taylor waited. "Yes?"

"It's probably rather fun to help other people find the right person. Yes, I think it must be." An idea had entered her mind. It was unbidden, but it excited her, and had to be expressed. "You, for example, Miss Taylor . . . What about you and James Weston?"

This was not an area into which Miss Taylor felt they should stray. She was, after all, Emma's governess, and there were boundaries to be observed, no matter how easy and familiar their relationship had been. "Leave me out of it," she said sharply. "*Cadit quaestio.*"

"*Cadit quaestio,*" muttered Emma, under her breath. "*Sed quaestio manet.*" She had asked her Latin teacher at school for a suitable rebuttal to *cadit quaestio*, and she had said that one might retort: *But the question still remains*, and that could be rendered *sed quaestio manet.* That was to put it simply, she explained. *Simpliciter.* Emma loved Latin because it gave her a sort of power. At school she had tossed a Latin phrase at a boy who had been staring at her in a disconcerting way, and he had been crushed—there was only one word for it: *crushed.*

Over the next couple of years, Isabella was more or less constantly pregnant; so much so that Mr. Woodhouse found it embarrassing to have to answer enquiries as to how his elder daughter was. The usual answer to this now was simply "pregnant" or "pregnant again," but this began to sound almost faintly disapproving—as if he were somehow censorious of her single-handed efforts to redress the demographic imbalance. He disapproved of excessive fecundity on the grounds that over-population inevitably created conditions in which microbes flourished. "The more there are of us," he said, "the more we invite the spread of infection. Superfluous human population leads to environmental degradation, and that leads to unhealthy water sources. That, in turn, encourages the proliferation of water-borne disease."

He wrote about this in a letter to the local paper, and the editor obliged by printing his letter prominently under the heading: "A Warning." He had hoped that this would lead to a lively debate in the columns of the newspaper, but it did not. There had been one or two letters on the subject, including one from a reader who said: "But this is nature's way, surely, of putting us in our place. And roll on the day when the next flu epidemic leads to a major culling of our species." That had drawn more responses than Mr. Woodhouse's original contribution. "It's all very well for you," wrote one correspondent in the newspaper. "You have access to antibiotics. What about all those poor people who don't have any antibiotics? What about them?"

Mr. Woodhouse had shaken his head over this letter. When would people learn that antibiotics were useless against viruses, and that penicillin would not have made all that much difference to the ravages of Spanish influenza—other than helping with incidental pulmonary infections? He had tried to explain the matter to Mrs. Firhill on numerous occasions, but the message had never got through, and she continued to say that the best treatment for a cold was a course of antibiotics.

But that issue, serious though it was, was only incidental to the main question of over-population, to which his very own daughter was contributing so enthusiastically. The first pregnancy brought twins: two boys, and they were followed at the shortest possible biological interval thereafter by a further set of twins, this time girls. While this enthusiastic breeding programme was being pursued in London, back in Norfolk Emma continued to attend Gresham's. At last the time came for her to leave, and she was driven away from the school one afternoon, zeugmatically, in floods of tears and the silver Mercedes.

"I feel so silly, crying like this," said Emma.

"It's not silly at all," said Miss Taylor. "I cried when I left school in Edinburgh. I cried when I left St. Andrews. It would be unnatural not to cry in such circumstances. It would demonstrate, I think, a certain indifference to separation—from place, from friends."

This set Emma off with renewed weeping. "All my friends," she sobbed. "Betty Slazenger," the name being uttered as if it were redolent of painful disaster, as are the names *Titanic*, Gallipoli, or the Somme.

"Rosie's sister?" asked Miss Taylor.

Emma nodded miserably. "And Pippa. Harry. Ellie."

"You'll see them again," said Miss Taylor. "You needn't lose touch. Isabella still sees Rosie Slazenger and Kitty, too, I believe."

Emma wept not just because she was leaving her friends; she wept because it was the end of a world—the brief, temporary world of school that we never feel is brief or temporary until it is suddenly over. But her regret did not last for long, as Miss Taylor had planned a busy summer for her: they enrolled, as fellow students, on a three-week course sponsored by the Victoria and Albert Museum, The English House Through Three Centuries. They went together on a fortnight's trip to Florence and Siena—a trip which Mr. Woodhouse was eventually persuaded to accept and finance, after a great deal of anxious hand-wringing and warning about the dangers of travelling in Italy, where the men, he said, were predatory to a degree that "we in England simply cannot comprehend"; where the drivers were "quite without concern for other road users"; and where "even the politicians were either certifiably insane or unashamedly criminal."

They returned to England unscathed by any of these dangers—although Emma did have her bag snatched in Florence by a dwarf on a motor scooter ("I warned you, my dear; I warned you," said Mr. Woodhouse). It was not this incident, though, that stuck in Miss Taylor's memory, but something altogether different—something that showed a side to Emma's character that people often did not see, but that, in Miss Taylor's view at least, was the real Emma. *Within us all,* thought the governess, *there is often more than one person, more than one self.* She had even discussed the subject with Emma—there was no point talking to Isabella about such matters, as she was given to yawning ostentatiously, though genuinely, when matters of the mind were raised. Emma, though, had listened as Miss Taylor told her about Plato's famous chariot.

"The chariot is the soul," she said, shaking her finger gently into the ether as if to pinpoint the insubstantial. "The chariot, you see, is driven by a charioteer but is pulled by two horses—one dark and one light. The dark horse represents all the brute appetites—concupiscence and so on . . ." She paused. "Concupiscence is to do with lust."

Emma closed her eyes. Was concupiscence really what they called lust in Edinburgh?

"Anyway," continued Miss Taylor, "the two horses that pull the chariot are of opposite inclination. The light horse is to do with the finer things: awareness of others, generosity, civilisation—the finer side of our natures, in other words. The job of the charioteer is to harness the energy of the dark horse and to make sure that the light horse is not pulled downwards by its companion."

Emma looked at her governess, imagining her, like Boadicea, in command of a chariot. And then something had occurred that distracted them: a telephone rang, and Miss Taylor for a moment or two seemed to be thinking about whether to ignore it or answer it, her chariot for an instant poised between the choice of ascending or descending. It ascended and she went to answer it, but it was the end of the chariot conversation.

And then, in Siena, on their Italian trip, while Miss Taylor sat at a table in the shell-shaped Piazza del Campo, looking down on to the bowl of the shell, Emma detached herself from her governess for a few minutes while they were waiting for their order of coffee to be fulfilled; and found herself in a small side street lined with shops selling Sienese ceramics. One shop window had caught her eye for the sheer beauty of a bowl that it was displaying. This bowl was white and lemon-yellow in its colouring. Around its sides were glazed figures of young men in Renaissance costume picking fruit, while a troubadour plucked at a stringed instrument. A hunting dog, its back arched, as the backs of such dogs so often are, pranced ready for the pursuit of some creature not shown. Emma stopped and stared, and then entered the shop hesitantly.

Fifteen minutes later she was back with Miss Taylor, who remonstrated with her, as the coffee was getting cold.

"I began mine. I couldn't wait."

Emma ignored her cup. "You have to come with me," she said. "I have to show you something."

Miss Taylor shook her head. "I'm not leaving until I have finished my coffee. You can't just leave such a beautiful place and dash off somewhere on a whim."

She waited impatiently until Miss Taylor was able to accompany her back to the shop. The window now had a large space where the bowl had been.

"These places . . ." began Miss Taylor, but was silenced by the effusive greeting of the proprietor.

"It is here," he said. "Then I will pack it and send it over for you. We guarantee its safe arrival."

"Safe arrival of what?" asked Miss Taylor.

The bowl was produced and placed on the glass surface of the counter. *"Eccolo!"* said the proprietor.

Miss Taylor reached out and touched the rim. "You understand," she muttered.

"It's for you," said Emma. "It's for you, from me."

It transpired that she had spent her entire spending allowance on the gift and during the remainder of their trip to Italy she would be able to buy nothing except essentials.

"I don't care," she said. *"Cadit quaestio."*

There was no arguing with the finality of *cadit quaestio*, and Miss Taylor, who had introduced the phrase, of course knew that. She knew, too, that there was a time to accept gifts, even the most extravagant ones, and to cherish them. She reached out and took Emma's hand and knew, at that moment, what the true nature of her young charge was. But then she thought of the chariot and the two horses, and she lowered her eyes and hoped.

Once back, there was university to think about, and the challenges of the decorative arts course at the University of Bath on which she had been offered a place. The choice of Bath had surprised Mr. Woodhouse, who said that he had not even known there was a university there. Miss Taylor had been more encouraging, even if she had her reservations; she would have preferred St. Andrews, which was, she pointed out, a mere six hundred years older. "Not that these things matter all that much," she said, in such a way as to indicate that they mattered a great deal.

For others, though—and this included her teachers at Gresham's—Bath somehow seemed a natural place for Emma to choose, although it would be difficult to say exactly why this was so. "She's that sort of girl," said the English teacher enigmatically. "She'll fit." And then, as an afterthought, expressed as if only to herself, "Perhaps she has *Bathos*." This reference eluded the chemistry teacher, who simply remarked, regretfully, "She never grasped chemistry. I tried, you know, but she never grasped it."

The course was certainly ideal: Emma had long been interested in patterns, whether in wallpaper, carpets, or in clothing. For her fourteenth birthday she had been given a book on the work of Edward Bawden, and had responded immediately and instinctively to his pictures of the English countryside—all plough horses and wayside pubs with suspended board signs; all fields of wheat and old-fashioned tractors; all open skies and wispy clouds. She tried to imitate his style, and that of Ravilious and the Nashes, succeeding sufficiently to be encouraged by her art teacher to persist; but what she really liked were Bawdenesque fabrics and wallpapers. She could gaze at these for hours, luxuriating in triangles and *trompe l'oeil*.

She had not given much thought to the need to work— Mr. Woodhouse had never mentioned the subject to his daughters—but Emma was far from lazy, and she felt that if she had a destiny it was in working with designs like these. She could start off as an interior decorator and progress to designing her own curtains and wallpaper; she would create fabrics for sofas and bedspreads. It was ambitious, but clear enough, at least, for her to find a course that would equip her to do just this. Her friends agreed. "Emma Woodhouse Designs," said one. "Brilliant. The name works, Emma—it really does."

Now that Emma was away at university, the question of Miss Taylor's continuing employment at Hartfield could hardly be avoided. Miss Taylor herself had tried to raise the subject several times even before Emma left, but had been fobbed off by Mr. Woodhouse, who either quickly changed the subject or, when more deliberately cornered by the governess, put it off until later that day. Then, of course, he failed to return to it or managed to ensure that he was not around at a time when it could be discussed. It was obvious that he was reluctant for her to leave, and that he simply wanted the normal routine of the house to continue as it always had, even if there was nothing for her to do. There was no reason why he should not continue to pay her—he hardly noticed her salary going out of his account each month, and, anyway, there was not very much for him to spend his money on, given that he rarely, if ever, left the house.

Disinclination to discuss a subject that needs to be discussed is never a solution: the topic merely assumes increasing prominence the longer it remains untouched. Every conversation that is then embarked upon, even if on a totally unrelated subject, will be conducted in the fear that it might suddenly be interrupted by the forbidden issue; every pause might be read as a sign that what has been unsaid so far might now suddenly be said. Eventually, of course, the strain tells, and the matter can be put off no more.

"My position," blurted out Miss Taylor one morning as she sat at the breakfast table with Mr. Woodhouse.

"On what?" he replied. "Your position on what?" It was a desperate, last-ditch attempt to evade the issue.

"No," she said firmly. "You know what I'm talking about: my position here at Hartfield. You may have observed that Emma is no longer here."

There were untapped wells of denial. "But she is!" he

exclaimed. "She's away at university during the term, and then she comes back. How can she be said to be away when she always comes back? If I go to London for a day or two and then return, I can hardly be said to be no longer here."

It was an improbable example. Mr. Woodhouse had not been to London for eight years, and showed no signs of changing his views on the undesirability of ever doing so.

"She is effectively now in Bath for more weeks of the year than she is here," said Miss Taylor. "In my view that means that she now lives in Bath. And anyway, she's eighteen, and an eighteen-year-old does not need a governess."

He looked at her with dismay. "But eighteen is so young," he said. "Remember what we were like at eighteen? We knew so little."

Miss Taylor shook her head. "That's not the way eighteen-year-olds look at it. When you're eighteen, you imagine you know everything. An eighteen-year-old will not accept guidance, I can assure you."

"But Emma doesn't have a mother," said Mr. Woodhouse. "You're the closest thing she's had to a mother since my wife died. If you were to leave . . ." He left the sentence unfinished; even this hypothetical talk of departure made him feel bereft.

"But I can't sit here and pretend to be a governess when both my charges have grown up," she said. "It just doesn't make sense."

"It's your Presbyterian background," muttered Mr. Woodhouse.

She stared at him. "What has the Church of Scotland got to do with it? I frankly do not see the connection."

"If you were a Catholic," said Mr. Woodhouse, "you would

have no difficulty with the idea of sitting around and doing nothing. That has never been a problem for Catholicism; it is only the Protestant outlook that makes us feel guilty about not being busy."

"Oh, really," she began, "this is nothing to do with John Knox, or Calvin for that matter."

"I beg you to stay," he continued, "I beg you, Miss Taylor. If you were to leave, then Emma would feel that a vital part of her home life was lost to her. I know that sounds extreme, but it really is true. You represent stability to her. You represent home."

She stared down at the floor, avoiding his anguished gaze. It would be easier to stay than to leave; she would not have all the bother of looking for a new job—who wanted govern-esses these days?—and she had to concede that Hartfield was extremely comfortable. The salary was generous, too, and since she did not have to pay for her board—or for anything else for that matter—it would enable her to continue to build up her savings, now standing at a total of eighty-seven thousand pounds. Reading that figure, recorded on her quarterly state-ments of account, filled her with pleasure: a governess had to look after herself and to ensure that she did not find herself, at sixty, penniless and homeless. And that meant saving, and not indulging oneself in non-essentials, unless, of course, a hus-band should materialise and bring with him financial security. But husbands, she reflected, did not appear that easily; there were plenty of women who lived in hope that a husband might suddenly descend; that they might draw back the curtains one morning and see, standing outside their window, a husband; or that they might take a seat on the train to work and find themselves sitting next to . . . a husband. That happened, of course, for some, but for others it did not, no matter how hard they wished, and no matter how much they deserved a husband.

Mr. Woodhouse suddenly brightened. "I've had an idea," he said. "I've always thought I needed a secretary." He looked at Miss Taylor with the air of one about to make an important announcement. "You could be my secretary—the pay and conditions would be exactly the same, but the job description would be different. You would not have to worry about being governess to a young woman who was away much of the time." He made a gesture of supplication. "Please say yes, Anne."

She had been about to concede, with a suitable show of reluctance, that she should continue as governess, but this new secretarial post—which she knew was almost certainly a sinecure—would do as well.

"All right," she said. "I accept." She paused. "What will the duties be?"

For a few moments he looked blank, but then he smiled and said, "Secretarial."

She nodded. There was no need to discuss the matter further, as everything, she imagined, would be exactly the same as it always had been. And that, of course, was what Mr. Woodhouse wished for above all else, and what Miss Taylor, for want of anything better, was prepared to accept.

6

It made no difference to Emma, of course: when she came back during university breaks Miss Taylor was there, as she always had been. And this continued throughout the four years of her degree course, which passed, she thought, as if the whole experience were some sort of pleasant dream. Norfolk, Bath; Bath, Norfolk; Bath again, and then Norfolk. There were saliences, of course: Paris for two months one summer, attending a course on the history of French décor during *la belle époque*, but then back to Norfolk, and then Bath; Edinburgh, another summer for a month, accompanied by Miss Taylor, for an internship with an interior-decoration firm, and then a blissful three weeks working with two university friends as a chalet girl in Morzine; then Bath once more and, before she was ready for them, her final examinations, and Norfolk again.

She did not stop to consider the curious role Miss Taylor occupied. Of course she was no longer her governess, being her father's secretary, but she realised that he still expected Miss Taylor to accompany her when she went off anywhere. In fact, he had even suggested once that Miss Taylor should go with her to Bath and take up residence there during university terms,

"Just in case you need her, Emma; it could be useful, don't you think?"

She had scotched that quickly. "Don't be ridiculous, Daddy! I'm an adult now and just imagine going to university with a keeper! I'd be the laughing stock. I'm not six any more."

She knew, though, that the suggestion came not from any distrust he had for her, but from his constant anxiety over her welfare. She knew that he worried about her and that Miss Taylor was meant to keep her safe from whatever it was that he dreaded. She allowed him this; he was her father, and she loved him; it was not his fault that he worried so much. Some people were just worriers, and there were worse things for a parent to be. The father of one of her university friends was a psychopath, she believed; he was a successful politician, but a psychopath nonetheless. If one had to choose between a worrier and a psychopath, she was in no doubt as to which she would choose. And indeed if one had to choose between a worrier and a politician, the same choice might be made. *At least my father, for all his peculiar ways, is harmless*, she thought. *That is all one can hope for in life: that one's parents are harmless.* She was rather proud of that aphorism, and dropped it into a conversation with friends. They looked at her admiringly. "You are *très* clever," said one.

After her finals, she returned to Hartfield.

"The end of Bath," said Miss Taylor. "And now?"

"I was thinking of finding another internship with a decorator," she said. "I've got some names. But there's nothing doing, apparently, until the autumn. I have the whole summer. I'll spend it here, I think. I've got tons of reading I want to do."

"And then you'll start your own practice?"

"That's the general idea."

Miss Taylor looked thoughtful. "Where? London?"

Emma shrugged. "You don't have to go to London. There's bags of work outside town."

"Your father would be pleased if you didn't go to London."

"I know. But it's not because of him—it's because I think that I can do just as well working in the country. Where do all the people with houses up here go for advice? They don't want to have to go to London."

Miss Taylor said nothing more, and they lapsed into silence. Their relationship was as easy as it always had been, and there were times when they could be together quite comfortably for hours on end without either saying anything to the other.

"What was that you said?" Emma once asked after they had been sitting together for almost an entire afternoon.

"I don't think I said anything," answered Miss Taylor, looking up from her book. "Or at least since about three o'clock, which is . . ." She consulted her watch. "Which is about two hours ago."

"That's what I meant," said Emma. "What did you say? I don't think I replied."

"I can't recall," said Miss Taylor. "Was it something about . . . No, I can't remember, I'm afraid."

"I thought I had views on whatever it was," said Emma. "But since you can't remember, then I can't really give my views."

"Perhaps not," said Miss Taylor; and then added, "Pity."

Over dinner, the conversation would naturally include Mr. Woodhouse, who never seemed happier than when he had the company of both Emma and Miss Taylor at the same time. These exchanges over the dining-room table often dwelled on

obscure and sometimes very technical issues arising from whatever it was that Mr. Woodhouse had been reading that day. On
days when *Scientific American* was delivered to Hartfield, this
might result in debates about immunology or astronomy; *The
Economist* could lead to discussions of the rights and wrongs
of liberal capitalism (Mr. Woodhouse was an opponent of the
greed that free markets encouraged) or to discussions of energy
policy. Emma was not greatly interested in such topics, but was
prepared to listen to her father, sometimes chiding him for
some factual error or misjudged conclusion, while Miss Taylor,
who knew about a surprising range of subjects, was more willing to engage.

Occasionally their dinner conversation was prompted by
something that Miss Taylor had read or heard on the radio.
At the beginning of that summer, shortly after Emma had
returned from Bath, an article in *The Scots Magazine* about
the remote St. Kilda Islands had triggered one such discussion. Mr. Woodhouse was interested in the evacuation of the
few remaining islanders in the late 1930s, and said that he had
always believed that this had been inevitable given the number
and variety of germs that would have thrived on islands that
were so heavily populated by flocks of seabirds. "I gather that
infant mortality was a problem for them," he said. "And frankly
I'm not surprised."

It was not this issue, though, that occasioned the intense
debate that evening, rather it was one of the photographs that
accompanied the article in *The Scots Magazine*. Miss Taylor
had been so struck by this photograph that she had shown it to
both Emma and her father. The picture was of one of the high
stone columns that rose out of the sea around the main island.

Here and there along the side of the column were patches of grass clinging to the rock at an angle of forty-five degrees—as hostile and impossible an environment as could be imagined, but home, it seemed, to a hardy breed of sheep that had lived there untended by any shepherd since the islanders left.

"Poor creatures," said Emma. "Imagine living at that angle, hundreds of feet above the sea. It's cruel."

"Very uncomfortable," said Mr. Woodhouse. "Of course they'll eventually have legs of different lengths, to cope with the angle, but that would take thousands of years, I imagine. Evolution doesn't happen overnight. Poor things."

"Poor things?" echoed Miss Taylor. "Those sheep, I imagine, are perfectly happy."

"They can't be," protested Emma. "Would you be happy living at that angle on a tiny patches of grass? With gales? With everything tasting of salt?"

"They may not be ideal surroundings," Miss Taylor conceded. "But they don't know any better, do they? They have no idea of gentle meadows in which sheep may safely graze, as Bach would have us believe."

"Bach?" asked Mr. Woodhouse. "What's Bach got to do with it?"

Miss Taylor looked at him. This was the reason, she thought, why I could never marry him, even if he were to ask me. It would be like marrying somebody who spoke an entirely different language. "Nothing," she said. "The point I was making is this: if you know no better, then you are happy with what you have. Those sheep have no idea that life may be any different from what they experience. Therefore they are happy or unhappy to the same degree as any sheep are, whatever their circumstances. I cannot imagine that the Duke of Northumberland's sheep are any happier than those St. Kilda sheep."

Mr. Woodhouse looked puzzled. "The Duke of Northumberland?" It was a most irritating habit of hers, he thought: bringing into a discussion people who had no business in it—Bach and the Duke of Northumberland: What light could they possibly throw on the issue of these unfortunate sheep?

Miss Taylor smiled. "I mention the Duke of Northumberland as an example of somebody whom one might imagine has contented and well-looked-after sheep. I do not know if that is the case; I simply assume it." She paused. "I believe that those St. Kilda sheep are not unhappy for the same reason that I am not unhappy with my lot."

Emma frowned. "But in your case you know that you could be happier than you are."

Miss Taylor turned to her. "Do I? Do you really think so?"

Emma did not reply for a moment. But then she realised that she knew the answer to this; she *felt* it. "Everybody can be happier than they are," she said. "They may not know it— yes, I accept that—but that doesn't mean to say that they can't be made happier. Other people can make them happier; other people can arrange happiness for them."

She was sure that she was right. She had not given the question much thought before this, but this discussion—this rather ridiculous discussion about sheep—had brought the matter into sharp focus for her. And just as she worked out what she thought about this, she realised, too, that this was something she could do with her life. She could make people happier by helping them to find happiness. It was very simple, really; all that was required was a willingness to take the initiative and show people where they should look. And as for those poor sheep on their cruel Hebridean columns, if only she had a boat she would take them away to some flat part of Scotland, some level lowland where they might live without fear of falling into the sea; where there was lush green grass and sunlight on their backs. She would take them in her small boat; she would be their shepherdess, their saviour.

She changed the subject. "Dinner," she said abruptly. "I think that I would like to have a dinner party."

Mr. Woodhouse put down his knife and fork. "Why?"

"Because I've been away for so long and don't want to get out of touch with people around here. You know how it is. You need to see people to keep in touch with them."

This pleased Mr. Woodhouse a great deal. He never dared confess his vision of Emma's future, which involved her staying at Hartfield forever, and not just for this final summer. She could have her design consultancy there—or whatever it was that she wanted to do—but she would stay in the house with him and Miss Taylor. Why go elsewhere? Why go and live in London in a house with two bedrooms—if you were lucky— when you already had a house with eleven? He could not see why anybody would want to do that; he simply could not understand the cast of mind that led people to live in what he saw as urban chicken coops.

"Of course you must have a dinner party," he said. "Whom will we invite?"

"The locals," said Emma. "George Knightley, of course."

She spoke almost without thinking, but now she wondered why she had mentioned George and why she had said "of course." Was it because she knew her father liked him, and she

wanted to make sure that he would feel involved in the dinner party? Possibly. Or was it something else? Recently she had
found herself thinking quite frequently of George Knightley.
He had crossed her mind when she drove her Mini Cooper
over to the garage to arrange for a service. She had imagined
what it would be like to be George and to be getting up in the
morning and deciding what to do with your day. Would he
shave before he took a shower, or did he shave after his shower
but before breakfast? Or perhaps he took a bath; there were
some people who looked as if they took showers and some
who looked as if they took baths. He was a shower person, she
thought, because he always looked so well groomed and energetic; bath people were more . . . more *dishevelled* perhaps,
less ready to go for a long run or do twenty press-ups on the
ground. It was a pointless, ridiculous thing to think about, but
it occupied her mind for a full ten minutes. And afterwards
she had felt quite uncomfortable—as if somehow she had been
there with him, watching him.

Then she had thought of him again when she lay in bed the
other night, waiting for sleep to overtake her. She suddenly saw
his face; she saw him looking at her and smiling, and she smiled
back in the dark, a smile seen by nobody else, of course, not
even by herself in a mirror, a passing smile, but a smile nonetheless. It was as if they were greeting each other; as if they
were complicit in some unspoken exchange. The real George
Knightley was available enough—she saw him reasonably frequently, and they chatted amicably, but this particular understanding did not pass between them in those real encounters—it
was something more private, and the more pleasurable for that.
Miss Taylor had said something about those sorts of thoughts;

she had spoken once of the memories that people bring out and savour, unwrapping them with all the care with which one uncovers some tangible souvenir, some cherished object. And now, quite suddenly, she thought of George with that sort of pleasure.

"Emma?"

Her father brought her back to the present.

"Sorry. Yes, the dinner party. George Knightley, and then Miss Bates. And Philip Elton too, in spite of Byzantine history and the Holy Ghost and all that sort of thing." She made a face. "He's a bit of a pain, but let's not be judgemental."

Philip Elton was the new young vicar who had recently been appointed to the parish of Highbury on a part-time and non-stipendiary basis, the diocese being too poor and the congregation too small to support a full-time clergyman. He was what was called a young fogey: a young person with the old-fashioned tastes and attitudes of one much older. Some young fogeys, of course, could not afford the well-made clothes and expensive shoes that successful young fogeydom demands, but Philip Elton could. A childless uncle had left him an office block in Ipswich along with a portfolio of flats in Norwich, and this provided him with a more than adequate income. A degree from Durham was followed by a brief period in theological college and an unsuccessful year teaching in a boys' boarding school. He had then enrolled for a part-time postgraduate degree in Byzantine history at the University of East Anglia, at the same time looking for a vicar's position in an undemanding parish. He was now twenty-seven, and would soon have his Ph.D. He had no intention, though, of competing for an academic post, as his financial circumstances made that unimportant.

An independent Byzantine historian could be perfectly happy living in a vicarage with seven bedrooms and a comfortable study. His duties as a non-stipendiary priest were hardly onerous: belief had waned, even in the country areas, and his congregation never numbered more than twenty. There were weddings to conduct, of course, because there were many who preferred the attractive parish church to the utilitarian shabbiness of the register office; and there were funerals, too, attended by many who were unaccustomed to ritual and who sang the Twenty-third Psalm out of tune, with puzzlement in their voices at the unfamiliar, lost language.

Mr. Woodhouse smiled. "Vicars are allowed to go on about the Holy Ghost," he said, and then added, "He's actually called the Holy Spirit these days. Holy Ghost is very old hat."

Emma shrugged. "Same difference," she said. "And then we should invite James Weston. Obviously he has to come."

"An excellent list," said Mr. Woodhouse. "*Le tout* Highbury."

Emma looked past her father, out through the window behind him. The names were so familiar to her and yet now, for the first time, she thought of them in an adult way; not just as parental friends and acquaintances, but as people open to her speculation and scrutiny. It was interesting.

Her father had said something, but she had not taken it in because she was thinking again.

"What?"

"I said that there was a young woman Miss Bates was speaking about, a Harriet Smith, I believe. We might invite her in order to balance numbers a bit."

Emma smiled. "How quaint. Nobody balances numbers any more."

"Don't condescend to me, Emma."

"Sorry, Daddy. Yes, by all means invite *la Smith*."

Miss Taylor pursed her lips. "To call somebody *la Smith* is similarly condescending. You don't even know her, Emma."

Emma made an insouciant gesture. "I'm crushed," she said, adding extravagantly, "like a clove of garlic in a garlic press."

"There's interesting new evidence about garlic," said Mr. Woodhouse. "Apparently the active ingredient in garlic significantly reduces the risk of heart disease and dementia. We've always known that, of course, but there's powerful new evidence pointing that way. Most encouraging."

"And vampires," said Emma. "It's very effective against vampires, I believe."

Mr. Woodhouse smiled. "If they existed, of course, I would have no doubt as to its efficacy in that regard. Their non-existence, perhaps, may be evidence of your proposition. Garlic has eradicated them." He laughed. "How about that, Emma? Would they appreciate that over in Bath?"

"Extremely amusing," she said. "*Très drôle*, Daddy."

"Your dinner party," said Miss Taylor the following day. "Don't forget to invite the guests. The most frequent cause of non-attendance at parties, I understand, is non-invitation."

"I can well imagine that," said Emma. "But yes, I'll invite them today. I'll start with Philip Elton, perhaps. He must sit in that vicarage of his and positively wait for invitations, but I can't imagine anybody invites him to much."

"He's a good-looking young man," said Miss Taylor. "I would have thought that his social life would be satisfactory enough."

"He's pompous," retorted Emma. "He's impressed with

himself and he's an intellectual show-off. As for that voice of his—people keep going on about it, but I think it's fake. Nobody talks like that, other than people who've been to drama school and have cultivated low, dark tones—you know, that deliberately *smooth* way of speaking some people have."

"Don't be too harsh, Emma. He does his best, no doubt."

Emma laughed. "But you could say that of anybody. We all do our best in one way or another."

"Do you think so?" asked Miss Taylor.

She waited for an answer, but Emma moved on to Miss Bates. "And then there's Miss Bates," she said. "I'll pop a note through her door. If I phone her, I'll never get off the phone. You know how she goes on, and on, and on."

"Miss Bates is lonely," said Miss Taylor. "And she's unsure of herself. She's nervous."

"I don't see what there is to be nervous about," said Emma. "Highbury is about as safe as anywhere in England, I would have thought."

"It's not that sort of nervousness, Emma. It's social nervousness. She feels that she has to talk all the time because she doesn't know quite where she stands."

Emma looked disbelieving. "Surely not."

"Yes, Emma. Remember that she's pretty hard up. Many of the people round here are actually quite well off. You yourself are, as you no doubt know."

Emma made an impatient gesture with her hands. "That's got nothing to do with it. Money means nothing."

Miss Taylor made an effort to control herself. "To you, maybe—because you've got it. If you haven't, it means rather a lot." She paused. She did not like to lecture Emma—especially now that she was no longer her governess, but she could not let this particular piece of arrogance go unchallenged. "Money confers power on people. It is there in the relationship between those who have it and those who don't. It is absolutely central to human relations and the way we judge one another, even if we like to think that it isn't. It is utterly pervasive. Utterly."

Emma did not like the reference to judgement. "I don't judge people on the basis of money," she said. "And none of my friends do."

Miss Taylor hesitated, unsure as to whether there was anything she could say to assail the confidence of youth. To be so certain—and so wrong. "Your friends," she began. "Are you sure that money doesn't come into it?"

"Into what? Our friendship?"

"Yes."

Emma sounded even more certain now. "Of course it doesn't. I've never chosen my friends on the grounds of what money they've got—or haven't got. Never."

Miss Taylor spoke quietly: "Maybe not consciously."

"Excuse me?"

"I mean that I'm sure you didn't sit down and say to yourself: I'm going to be friendly with this person because he—or she—has money. No, you wouldn't have done that, I'm sure. But think of your friends . . . What are they doing? Your Bath friends—or your friends from Gresham's, the ones you're still in touch with; Betty Slazenger, for instance."

Emma did not hesitate. "She's in New Zealand. I heard from her the other day. South Island."

"Oh yes? And it's winter there now, isn't it?"

"Yes. She's skiing. She . . ." Emma stopped herself.

"Skiing in New Zealand?"

"Yes. Betty's always been a good skier. And Rosie too. They learned when they were very small. The Slazengers had a house near Zermatt. It gives you a head start."

Miss Taylor nodded. "Yes, it must do. But let me ask you this: Of your immediate group at Bath, how many of them had the advantage of a gap year?"

Emma thought for a moment. "Just about all of them, I think. More or less. But so what? What's that got to do with what we were talking about?"

"I would have thought it was obvious," said Miss Taylor evenly.

"Well, I don't think it is."

Miss Taylor did not want to engage further. "Let's not argue," she said. "All I'm saying is that Miss Bates is not well off and must feel a little bit insecure."

"Which is no excuse for being a bore," said Emma quickly. "But don't worry, I'd never say anything to her face. Please credit me with some tact."

"Then there's this Harriet Smith," said Miss Taylor. "Should I pass the invitation on to her? She lives over at that English Language school—the one at the old airfield."

"Mrs. Goddard's place?"

"Yes. 'Mrs. Goddard's School of English,' I think it's called."

Emma looked puzzled. "Is she a teacher? I gather that any-body can get one of those TEFL qualifications and then set them-selves up as a teacher of English to innocent foreigners. Some of those diplomas take a week to get, you know—a full week."

Miss Taylor explained that Harriet Smith was not an employee—even if she helped Mrs. Goddard from time to time—but was staying at the school as a guest. Emma found this strange: How long could one stay as a guest with somebody else? Was the limit not meant to be three days or so?

"I believe that Mrs. Goddard has been providing her with a home for some time," she said. "I think that somebody pays for it."

"Somebody pays? Her parents?"

Miss Taylor did not know.

"Very strange," said Emma. "I look forward to meeting this Harriet Smith."

7

James Weston toyed with the idea of turning down the invitation to dinner at Hartfield. It was for a Friday evening, and Friday was the night on which he regularly went to a nearby gym for a session with his personal trainer, Ken. Ken was highly sought after as a personal trainer and had only taken James on as a favour for Mr. Perry, who had helped him set up his practice by lending him the money for the hefty insurance premium he was obliged to pay. ("You'd be surprised at what people can do to themselves on the rowing machines," Ken had said one day, shaking his head in disbelief.) So when Mr. Perry put in a good word for James he could hardly refuse to fit him in.

Ken, it transpired, was happy to reschedule their appointment.

"Don't let things slip, but," he said. He had a disconcerting habit of adding *but* to the end of each sentence; a linguistic quirk that betrayed his Northern Irish origins.

"I'll go on Saturday," promised James. "I'll make up for it."

"Good," said Ken. "You can lose twelve per cent of your fitness in twenty-four hours, but."

James was in his mid-fifties, but still very fit, having been a distinguished rugby player in his earlier years, coming close one season to being selected to play for England against Wales. That selection did not materialise, and an injury to his knee brought his sporting career to an end, but he had maintained at least some of his training programme and had continued to go to the gym several times a week. His blood pressure was accordingly low—something that Mr. Woodhouse had been very interested to hear about, and that he took pleasure in discussing with his friend whenever he saw him. Whereas most of us might make a general enquiry about the health of a friend when we met, Mr. Woodhouse liked to hear precise details, rather to James's embarrassment.

"You're extremely fortunate," Mr. Woodhouse said when he came across his friend in the village on the day before the dinner party. "What's your resting heart rate at the moment?"

James Weston shrugged modestly. "It's not too bad, I suppose."

"No, come on. What is it?"

James realised that an answer was expected. "Forty-eight, as it happens," he said. "The gym, you see—"

"Forty-eight!" exclaimed Mr. Woodhouse. "You know what mine is? Seventy-eight. Yes, I'm afraid that's the case. Seventy-eight to your forty-eight." He paused, looking at James with undisguised admiration. "And your blood pressure?"

James sighed. "It's OK."

Mr. Woodhouse was not to be fobbed off. "Go on. Let me hear the worst."

"One hundred and ten over sixty-five," muttered James.

Mr. Woodhouse was tight-lipped. Then he said, "I was one

hundred and thirty-five over ninety this morning. I took it twice. Same result each time."

James was tactful. "Sometimes you need to recalibrate the sphygmomanometer," he said. "They can give very inaccurate readings if you don't calibrate them correctly."

"But I have recalibrated it," said Mr. Woodhouse. "Twice. I'm afraid it's accurate."

"Oh well," said James, "you could perhaps do a bit more exercise—that helps to lower blood pressure. How about coming to the gym some day?"

Mr. Woodhouse did not respond.

"You might find it enjoyable," went on James.

Mr. Woodhouse looked away. "I have so much to do," he said. "I don't know where the time goes, but I doubt if I could find time to go to the gym."

"Then nobody's forcing you," said James.

Although they did not have much in common when it came to resting heart rate and blood pressure, Mr. Woodhouse and James had something very much in common in that both had suffered the loss of their wives. In James's case, his wife had died of a malignant tumour that had been diagnosed far too late for anything to be done about it. They had one child—a boy called Frank—who had been slightly over two when she died. James had taken his wife's death very badly, and had struggled to look after Frank, who had a milk and egg allergy—later grown out of—and who had been obliged in his early years to eat a closely supervised diet. A relative who lived in Yorkshire came forward and offered to take Frank off his hands. In his grief and his helplessness, James accepted the offer, and so Frank went off to stay with Mr. and Mrs. Churchill, where he quickly settled in. James visited him from time to time, and on each of these occasions the Churchills were worried that he would reclaim his son. At the end of each visit, though, seeing Frank so happily settled, James forbore to take him home. Eventually it was agreed that Frank would stay with the Churchills and that they would give him their name. "He can always revert to being Frank Weston," they assured his father. "Let him choose what he wants to be later on. And names are not so very important, are they?"

When Frank was eight, the Churchills left Yorkshire for Australia. The reason for their emigration was that Mr. Churchill's great-uncle had left him a wine estate in Margaret River, a choice wine-growing area in Western Australia. The estate was one of the earliest and best-established estates in the area, a much better proposition than the smaller, bijou wineries that were set up after the region became fashionable. This inheritance, fortunate as it might have appeared to those who were unaware of the Churchills' circumstances, led to days of agonising indecision and heart-searching. The prospect of going to Western Australia, to live in one of the most attractive parts of the state, on an established and prize-winning wine estate, was almost irresistible to the oenophile Mr. Churchill. He had sampled his great-uncle's wine, several cases of which had been dispatched to him with each harvest, and the thought of taking charge of an estate that produced such a fine product was immensely attractive. He knew that there was a good wine-maker on the estate, and a manager who could run the place perfectly competently, but he feared that having a distant owner would inevitably lead to problems. If he lived there, he could take personal charge of the business, and could bring his own agricultural skills to bear on the enterprise. And at the time that the news came through of his inheritance, the skies over the Churchill farm near Ripon were particularly low and grey. Western Australia, which Mr. Churchill had visited shortly after he had graduated from Cirencester, had wide, empty skies, filled with light and, as he remembered it, birdsong. The contrast was just too tempting; he had to go; he just had to.

But if they went, what would become of Frank, to whom he and his wife had become as attached as if he were their own son? While James might have been happy enough to allow Frank to stay with them in Yorkshire, would he agree to their removing him from the country altogether and taking him to Western Australia, which was about as far away from anywhere as one could get—far away, even, from Melbourne and Sydney, let alone England?

For days the Churchills debated with themselves as to what they should do. Eventually they plucked up the courage to approach James, who listened gravely to their description of the estate and their enumeration of the attractions of Western Australia. Mr. Churchill came to an end and glanced at his wife. Their fate, they knew, was in James's hands. If he said no, and refused to allow Frank to go with them, they would probably stay in Ripon.

"But of course you must go," said James. "Imagine how young Frank will love it. What a wonderful start for any boy."

They could hardly believe his generosity. "It's an awful long way away," said Mr. Churchill. "I can't imagine that we shall be back in England every year."

"No, I doubt if you would," said James. "But then I might come out to see Frank one of these days—who knows? He'll have the time of his life out there. The Australians are such a positive and cheerful people. He'll become an Australian, no doubt, which is a fate that I would gladly wish on anyone."

"So we should go?"

"Of course you should. Of course."

They left a few months later. Frank was brought to James to say goodbye, and they spent a long time talking about Western Australia and what the boy might expect there. Then, when it was time to go, James embraced his son briefly and stiffly. He was in tears, and did not wish the boy to see him cry. So he turned away, and the boy looked at him reproachfully, thinking that he was being rebuffed.

"Your daddy is very sad," whispered Mr. Churchill. "Australia is a long way away."

Although relatively few people in Highbury had actually seen the young Frank Churchill, this did not mean that people in the village and its surroundings did not know all about him. James Weston had spent his youth in Highbury, and his later prowess on the rugby field had been a source of local pride. Nobody from the area had achieved prominence in anything very much—if one discounted Mr. Woodhouse, of course, and his obscure invention—so to have somebody almost picked for the English rugby side was something of a distinction. James was popular, too, for his genial, friendly nature, and for the fact that he never appeared to make any uncharitable remarks. In the country, where memories of ancient insult can be long, this was something sufficiently unusual to be a matter of remark. "Dislikes nobody, he does," said one local, adding helpfully, "Nor he don't." No disentanglement of double negatives was required to understand this sentiment: James's amiable smile and courteous nod of the head to those he met in the street was enough to make that meaning quite clear.

People were aware at the time of the handing over of the young Frank to the Churchills, but nobody disapproved, or, if they did, nobody voiced any criticism of the sorrowing widower. It was a tragedy, people felt, that the young and popular Mrs. Weston should die so suddenly, and how could her husband—how could any man—cope with a two-year-old, particularly a two-year-old who was sickly with some food issue? It made complete sense, everyone agreed, for the late wife's sister-in-law to step in and take over, particularly since the Churchills were known to be so wealthy. In the country one of the most important measures of worth is simple acreage, uncomplicated by any other issue, and even if their land was in distant Yorkshire, they were said to possess over seven hundred acres of good arable fields and two thousand of grazing. For a young boy to be taken in by such a family was, in country eyes, good fortune on a major scale, and for a father to allow such a thing was not an indication of lack of care for a child but indeed the complete opposite.

It was not that James Weston was penniless, but at that time there was not a great deal of spare cash. His own father had been an army officer who had purchased one of the village houses when he left his regiment, the Royal Signals, extended it by the addition of a large conservatory, and had then led a reasonably comfortable life on a combination of his army pension and a small income from the sale of a family catering concern in Norwich. James had been something of an afterthought in that marriage—there were three much older brothers—and he had lost both parents by the time he was nineteen. His older brothers were by that time working in London, and doing rather well in a distribution business they had set up together. They put James through the remainder of his university course in business studies, and made him their junior partner when he was ready to join them a few years later. They were enthusiastic in support of his rugby career, giving him plenty of time off for training and touring and always attending any game in which he played. They were generous, too, in making over to him the house in Highbury—he was the only one keen to keep links with the village; when he went there for weekends, as he often did, none of them ever joined him. After his marriage, James took up permanent residence in the Highbury house, commuting to London during the week for work—a lengthy journey that he was prepared to undertake in order to allow his wife and, in due course, young son to live a more comfortable country existence.

The death of his wife ended this rural idyll, and although he kept the house in the village after Frank had gone to the Churchills, he now moved to London, to a small flat in Maida Vale. In his misery, he threw himself into his work, and into the task of coaching a boys' rugby team in Wimbledon. He emerged from his grief, of course, but loss had left its mark and it was more than five years before he felt capable of entering into a new relationship. This was with a woman who worked for a medium-sized London legal firm. She was an expert in bankruptcy law and had just become a partner. They began to live together in her flat, and were happy enough for ten years before she suddenly disclosed to him that she wanted to live by herself again. He suspected initially that there was somebody else involved—a fact that she vigorously denied, and truthfully, as it turned out; she had simply fallen out of love with him.

James reverted to his bachelor existence. He was now a senior figure in rugby-training circles, and this took up much of his spare time. He was generous, too, with his donations to a training programme he had set up to foster interest in the sport among young offenders. As one of his brothers later remarked, "OK, some of them played a bit too rough, but he saved goodness knows how many boys from prison. Ten? Twenty? Who knows? Better to assault somebody on the rugby field than on the street. Far better."

At the age of forty-seven, James was able to achieve an ambition that he had nursed for over ten years. Randalls, a small estate—not much more than two hundred acres—had come on the market after its owner, a successful commodities trader, had lost interest in it. The trader had bought it to impress his friends, but had discovered that he had the wrong sort of friends for this purpose. To begin with, they had been happy to leave London for the weekends and enjoy his hospitality, but he found that after one visit they did not accept further invitations. "Very quiet," one of them had said. "And very flat." The remark about flatness was passed without irony, and without any nod in the direction of Noël Coward; it summed up, though, the view in those particular circles that there was not much to be seen in that part of the country—the flatness of the topography saw to that—and certainly not much to do.

Randalls came on to the market at exactly the right time for James. The distribution firm that he owned with his brothers was facing take-over by a rival, and they had received a remarkably large offer for a controlling share in the company. They hesitated, but only for a short time: the offer allowed them all to remain active in the firm for five years, although none of them would need to do so. With his share of the sale, James could purchase Randalls, spend as much as he needed to improve the house and outbuildings, and have enough to live on very comfortably for the rest of his life.

The purchase made, he withdrew from the firm altogether and returned to Highbury. He was not one to retire early, and Randalls kept him busy. The previous owner had neglected the land, and it was not in good condition. James went on a fencing course and began to tackle the task of replacing the fences. Once the paddocks were secure, he purchased a flock of Suffolk sheep and a small number of cattle. He used help from the village, taking on a man called Sid, who was in due course also to work for Mr. Woodhouse, dividing his time between the two places. They got on well together and gradually began to get Randalls back into shape. "You can't ignore the land," said Sid, reflecting on the commodity trader's bad husbandry. "You ignore the land and you know what happens? The land ignores you. That's what it does, I tell you."

"You know something?" said Sid to his wife. "You know that James Weston has a son? Did you ever hear that?"

"I heard something," she replied. "They say that when his wife died he went to pieces. Couldn't do anything, and couldn't look after the baby. Who can blame him? Poor man."

"Well, that baby was a boy," said Sid. "He went off up Yorkshire way somewhere and then off to Australia. He came back when he was sixteen—visited his father, but went back to Australia."

"Where did you hear all that, Sid? Gossip down at the pub?"

Sid shook his head. "He told me himself. We were sitting in the Land Rover—finished some fencing and having a spot of lunch. He had a couple of Melton Mowbray pies—delicious they were—and he started talking about this son of his, Frank. He said that he's twenty-four now and that he thought he might be coming over to see him again. Then he went all quiet for a while. He sat there. So I just ate my Melton Mowbray pie and let him get on with his thinking."

"Guilt, maybe."

"Odd, that's exactly what he said. He said to me, 'Sid, I feel bad that I let that boy go.' I said to him, 'But, Mr. Weston, you couldn't have brought him up, you being by yourself. Far better for a boy to have a stepmother.' He listened to me all right, and I think he was pleased that I said that, but then he said, 'I feel that I let him down. When I saw him after he went up to York-shire he seemed so settled and content that I didn't have the heart to take him away from them. But I think maybe I should have.'"

Sid's words to James were comforting; the reassurance of those around us that we have done the right thing almost always helps, although it may not, as in this case, remove the under-lying anxiety that we have acted selfishly or foolishly, or even perversely. It was not the first time that James had discussed his feelings for having abandoned—the word that kept cropping up in his mind—his infant son. Shortly after the Churchills had left for Australia, his brother Edward had come across him at his desk in their London office, sitting staring into the distance as if he were a man in a trance. Edward had assumed that it was daydreaming, and had smiled at the thought that his younger brother was mentally re-enacting some triumph on the rugby field. But when he looked more closely, he noticed the tears in James's eyes. Pride, he thought, or perhaps regret at a missed try—so much could be invested in that heroic sprint towards the touchline, and yet it could all go wrong as a last-ditch tackle brought one to the ground in an undignified heap of limbs and torsos.

He had approached him, and that was when he realised that the expression on his brother's face was one of sorrow; that the tears were ones of pain rather than of pride. In the ensuing conversation there came to the surface emotions that had been concealed for too long. Edward was understanding, and at the end had suggested his brother see somebody who had helped him with a flying phobia that had made business trips a nightmare.

"She's a psychotherapist," he said. "Not a psychiatrist. I'm not saying you need a shrink. She sits and listens and then she explains it all." He paused. "I'll take you. It's sometimes hard to go on your own. I'll do it."

Edward had accompanied his brother to make the introduction. Then he had left him, and James found himself seated on the other side of the psychotherapist's desk, embarrassed at where he was, unable to bring himself to speak.

Gently she coaxed it out of him. "I stopped myself thinking about it," he said. "Every time it came into my mind, I said, *It didn't happen.* But it would always come back to me, this thought: *I gave away my son. I gave him away.*"

"And your dreams?"

He had not mentioned those—not to Edward, nor to her.

"Yes, I dreamed about playing with him. I dreamed that he was there in the flat. I dreamed that I was taking him to school."

"Of course you would."

She told him something that she knew every patient liked to hear—that he was not alone, that there were others. "I have somebody who comes to see me because she gave her baby away in adoption," she said. "Now she wants her back, but, as you know, you can't do that. And there are others. I've had people coming in here—not just women, men too—who have felt guilty about abortions, about the fact that they disposed of something they now feel was the beginnings of a baby. Not an easy subject, and not one we like to talk about. But some of these people feel regret, and it can haunt them. What you're experiencing is not all that different from what they feel."

James listened, but did not say anything.

"Every case is different, though," she continued. "Some people act selfishly. They give a child up for adoption because they can't be bothered with it. By no means everyone is like that, but some are. You didn't do that, did you? From what you tell me, you gave Frank up because you couldn't cope. You were bereaved—it was entirely understandable. And then, later on, when you could have taken him back, you realised that he had a much better life with your wife's relatives. That wasn't a selfish decision—it was quite the opposite, in fact."

"I don't think so."

"Well, I do—and I think most people would look at it that way. Most of us are quite selfish when it comes to our children, you know. We want things from them: love, the satisfaction of seeing them do well, and so on. Plenty of parents don't think just of their child's best interest. Oh, they may pay lip service to it, but they really think of themselves, of what they get from parenting."

She saw him several times, and it helped. The dreams of Frank seemed to stop, or changed in such a way that he no longer remembered them. He found himself thinking of the boy less frequently, and, when he did come to mind, his thoughts of him were free of remorse. He wrote to the Churchills and expressed his pleasure that Frank was so happy in Australia. He wrote in such a way that he made them think that their move to the wine estate had been entirely motivated by concern for Frank's future. He said that he hoped that Frank might be able to come and see him for a brief holiday sometime; he made sure to stress that it would be brief, as he did not want the Churchills to read into his invitation any suggestion that this would be the beginning of an effort to get Frank back.

The Churchills returned to England on visits three times during Frank's childhood—when he was ten, when he was twelve, and then shortly after his sixteenth birthday. On each occasion they offered James as much time with the boy as he wished, and the offer was readily accepted. The first visit was not a particularly long one, but the second was for an entire month, and James took Frank for a full two weeks. They went to Ireland together, and camped for several days on the Dingle Peninsula, enduring rain and flooded fields. Frank was appreciative of everything that his father did, and thanked him profusely, with a formality that James found strangely old-fashioned. The manners came from the school he attended—he had spent his first year at a weekly boarding school in Perth, where such things were still stressed and over-familiarity with adults was as yet unknown.

The trip to Ireland gave him an opportunity to talk to his son about what had happened. They lay in the darkness, listening to the sound of the rain on the roof of their tent; somewhere, in the distance, were waves crashing against rocks.

"You may wonder why you went to live your uncle and aunt," he said. "You must have thought it a bit strange."

"No," said the boy. "I didn't think about it because I don't really remember anything."

"It was because your mother died, you see."

"I know," said the boy. "That's why."

The conversation faltered at that point, and did not resume. What is the expression? James silently asked himself. What is the expression that pop psychologists use? Or problem-page people? It came to him. *Unfinished business.* Exactly.

By the time that Frank visited at sixteen, it was too late to talk. The cautious, rather reserved little boy had become something quite different: a gregarious, confident teenager, endowed with blossoming good looks and conscious of his power to charm. A young Adonis, he turned the heads of almost all those who even had so much as a glimpse of him. His wide smile exposed a line of white that contrasted strongly with the olive of his sun tan; a head of blond curls, like that of a Renaissance angel, topped shoulders that were broad for a boy and that gave him an air of strength and firmness. The Churchills paraded him with pride; James stared at him with unconcealed wonder, verging on dis-belief. Was this what Australia did?

"Frank wants to be a geologist," Mr. Churchill said to James. "Is that OK with you?"

"Of course," said James. They consulted him from time to time on matters pertaining to Frank's education, but he had never sought to interfere.

"There are plenty of opportunities for geologists in Western Australia," continued Mr. Churchill. "And he could help to run the vineyard too. He's good at that now. He helped a lot with the last harvest."

James nodded. Frank's life lay elsewhere—in the things that sixteen-year-old Australian boys liked to do; in a world of surfboards and freedom. There was no future for him in England, even now that he had Randalls. What were a few acres in Norfolk, bound by hedgerows and lanes, to the trackless ranges of Western Australia; what were his copses to their jarrah forests; Norfolk's chilly beaches to their sun-drenched coasts? The psychotherapist had suggested all those years ago that he should do two things: one was to enjoy Frank's good fortune—thereby validating his own, earlier choice—and the other was to envisage a sense of a future for himself. He would do both.

He followed her advice. He found Randalls and began to work on rescuing it from near-ruin. And once he had made progress with that, he started to consider his situation. He had a house; he had a farm; he had a comfortable income. What was lacking? A wife, perhaps? A lover? He had seen the bankruptcy lawyer at a party recently. She had been with her new partner, a man with horn-rimmed spectacles and a rather prominent nose. He had watched her from across the room before she noticed that he was there. He felt nothing; there was no pang, not the slightest one, and that confirmed his feeling that he was ready to find somebody who would not think him unexciting, as she clearly had.

They had talked, struggling to make themselves heard in the crowded room.

"Are you all right?" she asked.

"Yes. Absolutely. And you?"

She did not hesitate. "Yes. I'm busy."

"All that bankruptcy?"

"Yes. It never ends." She looked at him enquiringly. "And are you . . ."

He knew what the unfinished question was. "I'm by myself," he said. "But I'm seeing someone."

It was a lie, and he never normally lied. He did not know why he should wish to mislead her; it was something to do with pride, he thought. He did not want her pity.

"I hope she's right for you," she said.

He hesitated. "I think she is."

His hesitation was not caused by doubt, but by the sudden realisation that he knew exactly who it was who was just right for him; it had suddenly occurred to him. Of course she was. Of course.

8

There's nobody of your own age," said Mr. Woodhouse. "And yet you've put all this effort into this. It really is impressive."

Emma had certainly worked hard, but there was somebody of her own age, as she reminded him. "Harriet Smith is coming. Remember? She's my age."

"Of course. I'd forgotten about her."

"And then there's George Knightley," said Emma.

Mr. Woodhouse nodded. "Of course, but then he's my friend, isn't he? I don't really think of him as your friend too . . . and yet, I suppose he could be." He directed an enquiring glance towards his daughter. "You do like him, don't you? I've never asked you."

Emma shrugged. "Yes, I like him. He's just . . . well, he's just Mr. Knightley, isn't he?"

"But you don't call him that any more, do you? You used to, but not now."

"I call him George. He's not all that older than me, I suppose."

Mr. Woodhouse agreed. "No. A dozen years isn't all that

much of an age gap, although I suppose it can be when you're very young."

"Well, he's much younger than you, isn't he?" Emma pointed out. "What's the age gap between you and him? Twenty years?"

"If I'm fifty-one this year," said Mr. Woodhouse, "and he's thirty-four—seventeen years. Mind you, I never think of George's age. He's one of these people who doesn't really have an age. Do you know what I mean?"

Emma did. "There are some people with whom it doesn't really seem to matter," she said. "You talk to them without thinking about age."

"So when you were born," said Mr. Woodhouse, "George was eleven or twelve." He paused, and looked at his daughter with affected curiosity. "You *are* twenty-two, aren't you?"

"If you don't know that, Pops," said Emma, "then we shall have to have you tested to see if you've lost the plot. You do know who the Prime Minister of this country is, I hope. Do you? Isn't that the test the doctors use?"

Mr. Woodhouse pretended to search his memory. "I'm not one hundred per cent sure," he said. "But I can tell you it's not Tony Blair."

Emma laughed. "So you see there are two people who are more or less my contemporaries, and then . . ."

"Poor Miss Bates. Poor James Weston. Poor Philip Elton." He looked at Emma. "Have you decided on the *placements?* It's always so difficult."

"I shall put myself at one head of the table," said Emma. "As hostess, if you don't object."

He inclined his head. "It's your house."

"And next to me, on my right, I shall place . . . now let me think. I shall not have Philip Elton: I couldn't bear that. I'm prepared to do my duty for England and so on, but to sit next to him, frankly, is too much. So I shall have James Weston, who's quite good-looking, for fifty-something, and at least is not dead boring. Then on his right, which will be your left, I suppose, we shall have Miss Taylor. I'd rather like James to talk to Miss Taylor, I think."

Mr. Woodhouse raised an eyebrow. "Why? Do you think they have much to say to each other?"

"I do. They're both intelligent people. She can talk about anything, and so she should find some subject that they have in common. We can leave that up to them, I think. One doesn't want to have too much of an agenda, don't you think?"

"I have none," said Mr. Woodhouse.

"And then on your right, we shall have to put Miss Bates. I'm sorry about that, but I don't see where else we can put her, unless you want to sit next to Philip Elton, which I would wish on you less than I would wish Miss Bates."

"I'm perfectly happy to sit next to her," said Mr. Woodhouse. "She has some interesting anecdotes: it's just a question of separating the wheat from the chaff. And as for Philip, there's nothing much wrong with him."

"No, you're right," said Emma. "There's nothing wrong with Philip Elton—except for his personality, his attitudes, his conversation, and his views on all possible subjects."

Mr. Woodhouse sighed. "You can be very uncharitable, Emma."

"I know," she said. "I feel so bad about it. I shall try to do better." She smiled at her father. "What did St. Augustine say? Make me good and chaste, but just not yet?"

He ignored this. He did not see what St. Augustine had to do with it. "Miss Bates will sit next to Philip?" he asked.

"Yes. And that will leave Harriet Smith, this *new* person, sitting next to me. I shall be able to find out all about her. The whole story. It will be very interesting. And she can also talk to George—I'll put him between them."

There was a large drawing room at Hartfield in which the guests that evening were offered glasses of wine and canapés before dinner. Emma had prepared the canapés herself, with Mrs. Firhill offering them round. The evening was a warm one, and the late May sun was still shining, penetrating the French doors that opened on to the lawn outside, filling that side of the room with a warm glow. As Emma sipped on her glass of English wine, she glanced in the direction of Harriet Smith, who was engaged in conversation with Miss Bates, with whom she had arrived, and with Philip Elton. Harriet had been a pleasant surprise; Emma had expected somebody rather mousy, even dowdy—an expectation that had something to do with the name, Harriet Smith, which she found curiously old-fashioned. And yet Harriet could not have been more different, at least in respect of her looks, which were anything but dowdy. She was about the same height as Emma—which was on the tallish side—and had very similar colouring, which was sandy-coloured hair and a pale, almost translucent skin. But whereas Emma's eyes were hazel, Harriet Smith's were blue, of an intensity so striking that they seemed to overshadow every other aspect of her appearance. She had, Emma decided, a very particular beauty about her, a quality that required more than the possession of conventionally attractive features. Good looks could be a cliché, which meant that those who satisfied the normal criteria of beauty could fail its more more subtle tests. Thus it was that those with very regular features could just miss being beautiful because they lacked some tiny human imperfection, some irregularity that imparted to their appearance the poignancy, the reminder of ordinary humanity, on which real beauty depended. It was quite possible to be too perfect, and end up being plastic, as Hollywood stars so often were, with their well–placed curves or sculpted chins. The heart would not stop at such features, whereas it might well do so when a snub nose, or one not quite dead–centre, or ears that were just slightly too large, were combined with eyes that seem to reflect and enhance the light, or with lips that formed a tantalising bow, or with perfectly unblemished skin. That was beauty, thought Emma, of the sort possessed by that boy in Bath who had too many freckles, but whose eyes were wide and had a constant look of surprise in them.

Emma was conscious that Harriet Smith was having an unexpected effect on her. She had been curious about their new guest, but had not imagined that her curiosity could give rise to this sudden, quite intense interest. This quickening was not entirely novel; she had felt it before, and it was familiar. But what surprised her was that she had always had this feeling for men, not for women. For a moment she allowed herself the thought, guilty and unwelcome, that her interest in Harriet was of the same nature, but it was not, she said to herself; of course it was not. She had never felt that about women, and would not now. She had mistaken her feelings, she decided; this was simply excitement at meeting somebody new, somebody who might enliven her uneventful life at Hartfield; it was nothing more than that.

Emma was not interested in men in quite the same way in which some of her contemporaries at university had been. There had been boyfriends in Bath, but nothing very serious, and she had not been particularly taken with the experience. "Over-rated," she had remarked to a friend. "OK, I suppose, but not something one would go out of one's way for." The friend had looked at her in astonishment, and had said, "What planet are you on, Emma?" To which Emma had replied, "Same as you, but perhaps at a higher level."

She was staring at Harriet, and made an effort to stop herself. Harriet had now turned away from Philip and was looking in Emma's direction. Emma made a beckoning motion, and Harriet, muttering something to Miss Bates and Philip, detached herself and came over to join her.

"It's so kind of you to invite me," said Harriet. "I've seen your house from a distance and wondered about it. I saw you, too."

Emma's eyes widened. "And wondered about me?"

"Not really," said Harriet. "Well, I suppose I wondered a bit. What you were like, and so on. I'd heard people say . . ." She stopped herself.

"Go on," said Emma. "You've heard people say what?"

Harriet giggled nervously. "That you're very bright. That you're witty."

Emma reached out and touched Harriet gently on the fore-arm. "Idle gossip, Harriet. You know how people make up these things."

"But I'm sure it's true," said Harriet. "I also heard that you have a degree in art."

"Design," corrected Emma.

"I'd never get anywhere near a university," said Harriet. "I've got one A level, and it's a C in drama."

"Winston Churchill had none," said Emma. "Not even one in drama."

"Really? I thought to be Prime Minister you had to be really clever."

Emma gazed at Harriet with growing affection. She found naïvety attractive, and here was somebody who said things like *I thought to be Prime Minister you had to be really clever.* "What are you doing at Mrs. Goddard's?" she asked. "Are you teaching English to foreign students?"

Harriet shook her head. "I'm not qualified to do that," she said. "No, I'm a sort of extra in the role-playing they do. They have to do it as part of their course. There are little plays, like *Going to the Bank*, where I pretend to be the teller. Or *Making an Enquiry at the Station*, where I have to pretend to be the person at the ticket counter."

"It must be interesting," said Emma.

"No, it isn't," said Harriet. "I don't hate it, but it's boring. Can you imagine sitting there while a seventeen-year-old boy asks you for a ticket to Newcastle? Can you?"

"No," said Emma. "I can't."

There was something that puzzled Emma: Why did Harriet do this if she disliked it so much? "Do you have to?" she asked.

"I do it to help Mrs. Goddard," said Harriet. "She's been kind to me, and I need to have somewhere to live before I go on my gap year."

"Ah," said Emma. It made sense to her now.

"I want to go travelling next year," said Harriet. "I want to go to Thailand and Indonesia. But I haven't got any money, and at least I can stay at Mrs. Goddard's for nothing. I manage to save all the money I get. I'll have enough for a gap year in about ten months' time."

"She pays you?" asked Emma.

"A little. But I get a small amount from . . . from somewhere else. I save all of that."

Emma wanted to ask what this source of money was, but her father had now cleared his throat and pointed to the dining-room door. "Emma," he said. "I think it's time."

"So kind of you," said Miss Bates. "So few people hold din-ner parties these days. I think that social habits are changing, you know. People used to have the time, but now we're all so busy that there just isn't time to do it. Except this evening, of course."

"The credit is entirely Emma's," said Mr. Woodhouse. "She is the one who had the idea."

"Well, Emma," said Miss Bates, "I'm sure I speak for the entire gathering in saying that we're most grateful that you arranged this. And on such a lovely evening, too, with that sun still shining out there, warming us even at this hour when—"

"Yes," said Emma. "Thank you."

They went into the dining room, where they found their names written out carefully on pieces of card at their places. "Such a nice touch," said Miss Bates. "It's so helpful to know where to sit."

Emma caught Harriet's eye, and smiled.

"I'm glad I'm sitting next to you," said Harriet. "Thank you."

Emma was not sure what to make of this. Was Harriet expressing relief at not being next to Miss Bates, or was there something else behind the remark?

"That's fine," said Emma. "It's not a big table." She turned to James Weston on her right and complimented him on the pattern of his waistcoat.

"It matches one of the sofas at Randalls," he said.

"What clever camouflage," said Emma. "You could pass unnoticed in your own home!"

He laughed, and then turned to Miss Taylor. Emma tried to hear what he said to her, but Miss Bates was in the midst of making some remark in a moderately loud voice and she did not catch James's remark. But she did hear what Miss Taylor said in reply, which was: "It would be very nice to meet Frank one day."

She assumed that they were talking about Frank Churchill. Like Miss Taylor, she had never met Frank, but had heard all about him and had seen his picture in a silver frame at Randalls. She was struck—as everybody else had been—by how gorgeous he was, and intrigued by his story; there was something undeniably romantic about being given away and then taken off to Western Australia. Had James raised the possibility of a visit from Frank? She decided to ask.

"No," replied James. "There is no immediate plan for Frank to come, but I believe that he *might*. Just *might*. That's all."

Mrs. Firhill brought in the first course: Parma ham laid out on a plate with asparagus spears and quails' eggs.

"I love quails," said Harriet, surveying her plate. "They're the most adorable little birds. They look as if they're made out of china and somebody's painted them. And their eggs are so sweet. *Cutissimo.*"

Emma wondered whether she should tell Harriet about Italian plurals, but decided against it; the Italian plural—and gender—was a lost cause in England, where people ordered *cappuccinos* without shame and shouted *Bravo!* rather than *Brava!* when applauding a soprano. She looked again at Harriet— a quick look of appraisal. No, she would not raise the issue.

"Yes," she said, reverting to the safer territory occupied by quails. "Quails are very cute. They really are."

Harriet nodded. "So cute. Very tiny."

Emma thought that this conversation would be a difficult one to conduct with anybody other than Harriet, with anybody . . . less beautiful. Somehow, beauty made a difference; a trite remark uttered by a beautiful person is not quite as trite as the same thing said by one less blessed.

"I'd love to keep quails," said Emma. "Perhaps I could talk to Sid about it. He helps us on the farm. He probably knows a bit about quails."

Harriet brightened. "Oh, that would be such fun. Could I come round and see your quails?"

"Yes," said Emma. "But perhaps wait until we get them."

"Oh, I would," said Harriet.

Emma, feeling that she had exhausted the possibilities of quails, said, "Do you mind if I ask you about something you said before we came in to dinner?"

"Of course not."

"You said you got a small amount of money from somewhere else. You said you were saving it towards your gap year."

Harriet speared a slice of quail's egg on her fork and dipped it into the small pile of Maldon salt at the edge of the plate. "Yes. It's not very much, though."

"Is it an allowance?" asked Emma.

"Sort of."

Emma waited for her to continue, but Harriet appeared to have said as much as she intended to say on the topic.

"From your parents?" asked Emma.

Harriet put down her fork. The question seemed to have disturbed her, and Emma regretted asking it. "No, sorry," she said. "It's none of my business. I shouldn't have asked you."

Harriet shook her head. "I don't mind," she said. "I trust you. I don't mind your asking. I don't have any parents, or not parents in the accepted sense of the word. I do have a father, though. The money comes from him."

"So it is an allowance," said Emma.

"You could say that. But actually, I don't know who he is."

Emma watched her intently. "Oh, I see."

"It's not what you think," said Harriet. "It's different."

She seemed agitated, and Emma felt she should change the subject. She leaned to her side in order to be able to whisper to Harriet. "Who do you think would make a very obvious couple here?" she said.

Harriet looked about her.

"Miss Taylor and . . . your father?"

Emma drew in her breath. "Naughty! No. Miss Taylor and . . ."

"The vicar chap on my left? What's his name? Philip . . ." whispered Harriet.

"Elton. No, not him," said Emma.

"You and George Knightley?" asked Harriet, giggling.

Emma looked down the table to where George was sitting. He was half-turned away from her and so she saw only his profile. It was a ridiculous suggestion: George Knightley was . . . well, he was just George Knightley.

"He's very good-looking," Harriet continued. "I'd love to put him on my mantelpiece."

Emma's eyes widened. "What?"

"I'm only joking. I don't think he'd fit on a mantelpiece. It would be rather hard to sit on a mantelpiece without falling off."

Emma gave her a scornful look. "You really aren't very perceptive," she said. "George was the last person I was thinking about."

Harriet accepted the criticism passively. "No, I suppose I'm not all that perceptive. You are, though. I bet you are."

Emma whispered even more quietly now. "Miss Taylor and James Weston," she said. "He's not all that much older than she is and I think—and this is just my view, of course—that he's actually quite sexy. Still."

"But is that what she wants?" asked Harriet.

"Of course," said Emma. "Sometimes people don't know what they want." She paused, placing a finger to her lip in a gesture of silence and complicity. "And so we have to show them."

"I'm not sure that I know what I want," muttered Harriet.

"Then allow me to show you," said Emma.

9

Miss Taylor broke the news to Mr. Woodhouse and Emma at breakfast, two weeks after the dinner party. They were all in the morning room at Hartfield— a room that, particularly during the summer, caught the early sun. As a general rule breakfast was taken in silence, a practice that Mr. Woodhouse liked, as it gave him the opportunity to read the newspaper undisturbed. He had once breakfasted in the Savile Club in London, where a sign on the members' table, placed there only in the morning, advised *Conversation Not Preferred*. This had appealed to him, and occasionally, when his reading of the paper was interrupted by some observation from Emma or Miss Taylor, he would mutter "Savile Club" before he answered.

On this occasion, though, the importance of the announcement was sufficient to suspend any rule, and to discourage conversation after such a bombshell would have been impossible, even at the Savile Club itself.

"There is something I need to tell you," began Miss Taylor.

Mr. Woodhouse, concealed, moved his newspaper slightly

so that he could see past it to the governess. Emma, who had been reading a magazine, looked up.

"Something really rather significant," Miss Taylor continued. "At least to me."

Emma exchanged a glance with her father, who now lowered his paper somewhat reluctantly, with the air of one who is being disturbed in the execution of some important task. His eye had been caught by a report in the paper of a move to use viruses, rather than antibiotics, against bacteria. It was something that he had long been advocating, and he was pleased to see that his views were being mirrored in public-health circles.

"You may have noticed that James Weston and I have been seeing a bit of each other over the last few weeks," said Miss Taylor.

Mr. Woodhouse frowned. He had not noticed this, and he tried to remember whether there had been any particular increase in his neighbour's visits. James came to the house from time to time—sometimes on social visits, which were always appreciated, and sometimes on business connected with the farm. It made sense for them to share, and when some unusual piece of equipment was required, if one had it the other was always welcome to make use of it. What had Sid taken over to Randalls recently? A rotavator, he thought; those always came in useful when the kitchen garden was being prepared for the summer, and Randalls had rather a large kitchen garden, he seemed to remember. But had Miss Taylor been involved in any of that? She was usually indifferent to what was happening agriculturally, and he could not imagine her becoming involved with James in that respect.

Miss Taylor was now looking at Emma, as if for support. Emma smiled encouragingly; she, at least, had understood what was coming. And it was her doing, she thought. *I did this.*

"So," went on Miss Taylor, "we have decided that we should become engaged." She paused, allowing her announcement a brief moment to sink in. "He has asked me to marry him, and I have agreed."

There was complete silence. In Emma's case, this was from sheer astonishment at the fact that this had come about so quickly; in Mr. Woodhouse's case, it was from disbelief. This could not be happening. Miss Taylor was *his* secretary. She had lived at Hartfield for years and years; it was as if she had always been there, always. And then he thought: *What will happen to me?*

Having decided that the news had been given enough time to sink in, Miss Taylor went on to elaborate. "We see no reason to delay matters unduly. We haven't quite decided on a date yet, but it will be sometime this summer. We don't want anything big—just a small wedding, a few friends. We won't even be going away on honeymoon, or at least not just yet. We may go off somewhere warm in November, or even December. We haven't decided."

Mr. Woodhouse thought: *December? But what about Christmas?* Was she seriously contemplating spending Christmas without them, when every year—every year without fail—she had been in charge of the turkey and that ridiculous Scottish pudding she liked—figgy pudding, or whatever it was? Was she now proposing to forget about all that, just like that, and go off with James to some tawdry warm spot that would be full of all sorts of people exposing themselves to entirely unnecessary and harmful solar damage, which they would surely regret later on, even if their vitamin D levels were boosted . . . ?

Miss Taylor took a deep breath. This, for her, was the difficult part. "In view of this," she said, "we have decided to live together. I shall be moving to Randalls next week."

At his end of the table, Mr. Woodhouse dropped his newspaper. At her end, Emma beamed with pleasure. *Sex.* Miss Taylor and James Weston. Delicious thought: the absurd is always so tasty.

Mr. Woodhouse opened his mouth to speak. At first he stuttered, and neither Emma nor Miss Taylor could work out what he was saying, but then he cleared his throat and began again.

"This is all very sudden," he said.

Miss Taylor seemed to relax, now that her announcement had been made. "Yes," she said. "It does seem sudden. But then, if one comes to think of it, any announcement of that sort is bound to seem sudden. It involves, you see, a transition. At one moment one is not engaged, and then the next moment one is. That, I think, is largely inevitable, given the nature of engagement."

Mr. Woodhouse shook his head. "Well, I must admit that I don't really know what to say."

Emma now joined in. "You could start with 'congratulations,'" she said. "Congratulations, Miss Taylor."

Miss Taylor nodded. "Thank you. I'm very happy with the way things have turned out."

"He's such a nice man," said Emma. "I've always thought that you and he would make a really good couple." She hesitated, smiling coyly at Miss Taylor. "In fact, I seem to recall that I even suggested this to you."

Miss Taylor did not react to this revelation, but Mr. Wood-house did. "You?" he said. "You said . . ."

"All I said was that I thought James and Miss Taylor would make a good couple. That's all. I wasn't exactly Nostradamus, predicting things and so on."

"What's Nostradamus got to do with this?" snapped Mr. Woodhouse. And when Emma declined to elaborate on the connection, he picked up his paper and folded it. This was to absorb the emotion that he felt. He had to do something; he could not sit there and see their world collapse without at least doing something with his hands.

"Well, Pops," said Emma. "You are going to congratulate Miss Taylor, I hope."

Miss Taylor came to his rescue. "Your father, quite under-standably, has been surprised by my news." She gave him a sympathetic look. "And of course I can understand that."

Mr. Woodhouse pouted. "Of course I want to congratulate you," he said. "I'm very happy for you."

This was said with great misery.

Miss Taylor turned to Emma. "There you are," she said. "Your father has said congratulations."

"From his heart," muttered Emma, unheard by the others.

Mr. Woodhouse now seemed to recover some of his com-posure. "You say that you'll be moving to *Randalls?*" His emphasis on the word *Randalls* seemed to carry with it the inference that no sensible person could contemplate such a move.

"That is James's house," said Miss Taylor. "It will become, I have reason to believe, our *matrimonial home*." Her stress-ing of the words *matrimonial home* was similarly weighty.

Nobody could criticise anybody, surely, for moving to a matrimonial home.

Mr. Woodhouse digested this information. "But Randalls," he said, after a while, "is in a parlous state. It has been for years." He paused, looking down at his folded newspaper with renewed misery. "In fact, I'm surprised that the house itself is still standing."

This brought a spirited response from Miss Taylor. "Oh, no," she exclaimed. "James has done a great deal to it recently. The roof has been substantially repaired. He's had a lot of work done on that this spring."

"But what about the walls?" retorted Mr. Woodhouse. "What use is a roof if your walls are unreliable? If your walls go, your roof goes. That's just my opinion, but I believe that many will share it."

"Oh come on, Pops," said Emma. "James's walls are pretty solid. They've been standing for the last two hundred years or so."

"Precisely," said Miss Taylor, glad of this support from Emma.

"Miss Taylor would not become engaged to a man with questionable walls," said Emma brightly. "That would be a very foolish thing to do, wouldn't it, Miss Taylor?"

Miss Taylor was not sure how to take this. "I don't think I'd judge anybody by his walls," she said.

"Well, there's a dangerous view of things," said Mr. Woodhouse.

"I honestly don't think we should be talking about walls anyway," said Miss Taylor. "Walls are irrelevant."

"Of course, there are Chinese walls," interjected Emma.

Mr. Woodhouse looked at his daughter with irritation. He did not see what bearing China had on this.

He addressed himself to Miss Taylor. "You can hardly say that walls are irrelevant," he protested. "But be that as it may, what about bedrooms? How many bedrooms has Randalls got? Three? Four?"

Miss Taylor was on firmer ground here. "Eight," she said. "It is hardly a suburban bungalow."

Mr. Woodhouse shrugged. "You'll be moving from eleven bedrooms to eight. That's three fewer."

"But one only needs one," said Miss Taylor.

Mr. Woodhouse seized on this. "But what if somebody comes to stay? What then?"

"Well, we'll actually have seven left over," said Miss Taylor calmly. "We could no doubt fit a visitor in."

Emma now decided to change the subject. "If you're going to be doing any redecorating," she said. "I wonder whether I could help."

"Of course," said Miss Taylor. "I'd come straight to you. And yes, we shall be doing some redecorating, I imagine."

"James's house is very masculine," said Emma.

"Well, he is a man," said Miss Taylor. "I suppose we shouldn't be surprised if men live in masculine houses." She paused. "But there is always room for improvement."

Mr. Woodhouse was not interested in this talk of decoration. "I do hope you will come and see us," he said. "Emma and I shall be sitting here worrying about you, I imagine."

"But Randalls is only a mile away," said Miss Taylor. "I shall be able to look out of my window and see you. If I use binoculars I shall probably be able to make out exactly what you're doing. I might even be able to lip-read, which will mean that you will have to be careful not to talk about me." Even as she said this, she realised that binoculars would not be necessary; Mr. Woodhouse always did the same thing, and Emma did very little. But she could hardly give voice to this conclusion.

Mr. Woodhouse suddenly rose to his feet. "If you'll excuse me," he said. "I've had enough breakfast. I have rather a lot to do."

He had nothing to do; Emma knew that, and so did Miss Taylor, but they sensed that his world had been thrown into disarray by that morning's announcement, and he needed time.

"Of course," said Miss Taylor. "You should get on with it."

With Mr. Woodhouse out of the room, Emma felt that she could talk freely. "I'm really thrilled," she said. "I had more or less given up on the idea that you would get married."

"So had I," said Miss Taylor. "I'm very lucky."

"Is he well off?" asked Emma. "I've never really thought about him in those terms, but I suppose that Randalls is worth quite a bit, even if it has only eight bedrooms."

"I imagine he has enough," said Miss Taylor. "I've never discussed it with him."

"Well, he can't live on air," said Emma. "He had a business in London, didn't he?"

"With his brothers. He sold it, I believe."

"Well, he probably invested the proceeds and lives off those. You won't have to worry."

Miss Taylor nodded. "It's one of the nice things about getting married at this stage of life. It solves a number of problems."

Emma nodded. "I won't need to, of course."

"Need to what?"

"I won't need to get married for financial reasons. I shall have enough not to worry."

Miss Taylor smiled. "But you may want to get married for other reasons."

Emma shook her head. "I doubt it. Why should I? I have everything I need."

Except love, thought Miss Taylor, although she loved Emma, and Mr. Woodhouse loved her too; but that was not the same thing. That was a different sort of love—a comfortable, unthreatening love of long standing; a form of love that was far removed from passionate, romantic love. And that made her think: *Do I know what romantic love is? Is that what I feel? Yes*, she thought. *Yes. I feel that when I see James, when I think of him. I do. I feel exactly that.*

She looked at Emma with fondness. "I think you'll find somebody who'll stir you."

Emma made a face. "That is not a particularly appealing metaphor, if I may say so. I have no desire to be . . . stirred."

"Perhaps it's an unfortunate word," conceded Miss Taylor. "I think that it is men who are stirred—women perhaps not."

"Men are aroused, rather than stirred," remarked Emma. The remark was made carelessly; Emma did not always think. She blushed.

Miss Taylor laughed. "Let's move on," she said. "There is a limited amount that one can say about men, I've always felt. More to the point: I have plans for the kitchen at Randalls. And for the bathrooms, too. Would you like to hear about them?"

At first, Emma found herself unable to decide whether Miss Taylor's announcement of her imminent departure fell into the category of bad news or simply that of dramatic news. There was, she felt, a crucial difference: bad news usually had no redeeming features, whereas dramatic news often did. Eventually she decided that this was clearly dramatic rather than bad news because of the clear joy and excitement that the prospect of marriage had brought to Miss Taylor and also, she assumed, to James. And it was, after all, what she had herself contrived at; she was sure that she had planted the idea in Miss Taylor's mind and that without that intervention on her part it would never have occurred to the governess to signal to James—as she surely must have done—that she was receptive to his overtures. So this really was a triumph on her part—an achievement that might cost her companionship but could still bring considerable satisfaction. Even when Miss Taylor had gone to live at Randalls, Emma was confident that her old governess and friend would naturally turn to her for support and advice in the running of her new home. Already, in their discussion of bathrooms, Emma had succeeded in interesting her in wet rooms, of which she previously had been largely ignorant, Edinburgh not being a place noted for that sort of thing.

"You tile everything," she explained. "From floor to ceiling. Or rather you do it in stone, or one of these new stone-effect surfaces. Limestone looks very nice. Then you have the shower in one corner and nothing between it and the rest of the room. No glass partition—nothing."

"Limestone?" asked Miss Taylor. "Remember 'In Praise of Limestone'? And that line about why we love it—precisely because it dissolves in water?"

"These days—" Emma began.

Miss Taylor interrupted her. "I should hate to have a new

bathroom that was visibly dissolving before my eyes. It would be disconcerting, to say the least."

"Limestone bathrooms don't dissolve," said Emma patiently. "It would take hundreds of years. That poem was about lime-stone *landscapes.*" She cast a firm glance in Miss Taylor's direction: there were occasions on which the governess could deliberately obfuscate.

"Conventional bathrooms are boring," she said. "One bath. One loo. One basin. That's very . . . how shall I put it? One-dimensional."

"I should hate to be one-dimensional," said Miss Taylor. "But, on a serious note, I do like the idea of these wet rooms."

"Wet rooms *are* serious," said Emma. "They give you a sense of freedom. You move from zone to zone within the room in a very fluid way."

Miss Taylor had nodded. This, obviously, was what one learned in Bath—where they should know about such things, of course, with their long experience of spas. And Bath was evidently the place where one learned to talk about something as simple as showers and basins in a way that implied great sensitivity—great multi-dimensionality. *I shall miss Emma,* she thought. *I shall miss this young person whom I have had such a hand in creating.* And with that, she felt a pang of remorse. It is never easy to let go of another life.

A few days later, Emma came into her room, after knocking on the door, as she had always done, and after Miss Taylor had called out *Entrez!* as she had done from that very first day in the Woodhouse household nearly twenty years ago. She called out *Entrez!* because that was what a governess should do—long generations of her profession had called out *Entrez!*

Emma had found Miss Taylor with her suitcases laid out on the floor, the doors of her wardrobe wide open.

"You're packing?"

Miss Taylor nodded. "Yes. James is bringing the Land Rover over tomorrow."

She's going away in a Land Rover, thought Emma. She stared at the suitcases; two were empty, ready for filling, while one was already packed with what Miss Taylor had always called her *underthings.* She imagined the underthings being loaded into a vehicle that was normally used to convey dogs and fence posts and the like. Her gaze moved to the open wardrobe. There were only eight or nine dresses there, she noticed. Did Miss Taylor have so few dresses?

"Will three suitcases be enough?" she asked. "I could lend you mine. I brought four back from Bath."

Miss Taylor shook her head. "Thanks, but I think three will be adequate. I've always travelled with only three suitcases. One for . . ."

"Underthings," supplied Emma.

"Yes, one for underthings. One for dresses. And then one for shoes, belts, and so on. I have a few papers as well, and those can go in with the shoes."

Emma wondered what the papers were, and Miss Taylor, it seemed, knew what she was thinking. Seventeen years could do that; could bring about unspoken understandings between two minds. Words were not always necessary.

"One doesn't need all that many documents in this life," said Miss Taylor, moving over to the wardrobe to take out the first of the dresses. It was cotton lawn with a curious paisley pattern;

very old-fashioned, thought Emma—it would not look out of place in a clothing museum.

"I saw something just like that dress in the Fashion and Textile Museum in London," Emma said. She spoke without thinking. Miss Taylor's hand froze, just as she reached for the dress.

Emma noticed, and became flustered. "They had modern things too," she said hastily. "High fashion. Everything. It's quite a place."

Miss Taylor resumed her task. Slipping the dress off its hanger, she held the fabric briefly to her cheek, to feel it, as if to embrace it.

"You said you don't need many papers," Emma blurted out, eager to move on from museums. "I suppose we don't, do we? A birth certificate? A passport—if we want to go somewhere." She paused. "My father hasn't got an up-to-date passport, you know."

Miss Taylor moved across the room and laid the dress carefully in the suitcase. "No? I suppose he hasn't gone anywhere for a long time."

"Not even to London," said Emma. "Or Norwich, for that matter."

"Some people don't like to travel," she said. "And one can understand. Travel can be very vexing these days. All those people." *Us*, she thought; *we are those people.*

"He doesn't go anywhere because he's anxious," said Emma.

"Yes, he's anxious. But that, you know, is because he loves you so much. He's worried about you. He's worried about me. He's worried about the house. He won't let go of things. He wants everything to remain the same."

"I know," said Emma. "Your leaving us—even to get married—is quite hard for him to accept."

"I can understand that," said Miss Taylor. "But I'm not exactly going far. I expect we'll see each other every day. I can come round every morning. It'll take me no more than twenty minutes to walk here, after all."

Emma conceded that this would be possible. But it would not be the same, she pointed out. It would not be the same going off to sleep at night knowing that Miss Taylor would be taking to her bed in an entirely different house. "I'm going to miss you so much," she said. "I just am."

They stood and looked at each other across the half-empty suitcases.

"And I'm going to miss you too," said Miss Taylor. "I'm going to miss you, even if I see you every day. Does that sound odd to you?"

"No," said Emma. "It doesn't sound odd, because I think that's exactly what I'm going to feel."

Miss Taylor moved forward; she hesitated, as she seemed to consider taking another step, but did not. Each was still separated from the other by several feet. A suitcase of underthings lay between them.

"Darling Emma," said Miss Taylor. "Will you do one thing for me? Just one thing?"

Emma nodded. "Of course. Anything."

"Will you make an effort?"

Emma frowned. There were times when Miss Taylor sounded like a Scottish school teacher—which she was, when one came to think of it—an old-fashioned Scottish school teacher in a high-ceilinged Edinburgh classroom, some Jean Brodie–like figure encouraging her pupils to work hard. But what did she mean by *make an effort?*

"Yes. I'll make an effort."

"Good," said Miss Taylor. "You'll find that effort will be repaid. Always—or almost always."

10

It took a few days for Emma to become accustomed to the absence of Miss Taylor. Breakfast, although it had always been a quiet meal, seemed now to be even more silent yet, punctuated only by increasingly audible sighs from Mr. Woodhouse from behind his newspaper. These sighs might have been taken as a commentary on the state of the world—his newspaper revealed news that became worse and worse with each succeeding page—but they were not that at all: they were really expressions of regret over Miss Taylor's departure.

"Poor Miss Taylor," he said. "I shall never be able to understand it. She was perfectly comfortable here." He fixed Emma with a gaze that was at the same time both concerned and injured. "Do you think we should have offered her a better room? Do you think that might have made a difference?"

"No," said Emma. "It was not a question of her room and how she felt about it. It had absolutely nothing to do with that. She met James. She fell in love."

This elicited an even deeper sigh from her father. "I see no reason for her to have fallen in love; for the life of me, I just don't. Why fall in love with poor Weston, of all people?"

Emma shrugged. "People fall in love with all sorts, Pops. It may seem odd to us, but presumably there are those who think James is attractive. I, for one, think he's passable—just."

Mr. Woodhouse shook his head. "Impossible," he said. "Poor Weston may have a very low resting heart rate, but can you imagine anybody finding his face appealing—with that nose of his? And his eyebrows? No, I can't understand how anybody could like such a face. Imagine waking up every morning to see that face on the pillow beside one. Imagine it! What an awful shock it would be."

"Miss Taylor might like it," said Emma. "In fact, I suspect that she would have settled with having *any* face on the pillow next to her."

Mr. Woodhouse raised his paper and resumed his reading. It was too painful a subject to be discussed any further—at least for him. Miss Taylor was now lost, even if she had telephoned to say that she and James would come for tea at four o'clock that afternoon. It simply would not be the same. He wondered what they would talk about. They would have to talk about something, because when people visited you had to say something to them, and they had to say something back to you. It was different when they lived with you; then you could either spend time in silence, not having anything fresh to say, or you could say whatever came into your mind, not expecting any response.

He tried to recall what he had talked to Miss Taylor about, and found it difficult. Of course they had conversed, and done so frequently, but it had never been necessary for him to remember anything of what she actually said, and she, no doubt, had felt the same about his conversation. And yet it had all been so satisfactory—so secure—and now the whole thing was ruined by her going off to Randalls like a headstrong schoolgirl. What could have possessed her? Was it something to do with sex? It had never occurred to him that Miss Taylor might have needs of that nature—why should she? He had always felt that there was a vague primness about Miss Taylor—that was something to do with coming from Edinburgh, of course, but it went further than that. Miss Taylor was asexual—she was pure—and the thought of her harbouring a passion for James Weston of all people was almost inconceivable. Weston! It would be like sleeping with a farmyard animal—all sweat and grunts and . . . he shuddered. It was uncomfortable even to think of it.

Emma, of course, had other things to think about. She had been surprised at the pleasure that she had derived from bringing Miss Taylor and James together. There was something creative about making a successful introduction—something almost god-like. As a teenager there had been a brief period— no more than six months or so—when she had come under the spell of a visiting chaplain at school. This young man was only there to stand in for the regular chaplain, who was on sabbatical, but in the short time he was at the school, he had enthused a number of the pupils, largely owing to his looks, which would not have been out of place in a catalogue of male models—the sort who wear golf jackets or casual sweaters with such ease and conviction, gazing off in their photographs towards a horizon considerably more exciting than the horizons of most of us. The dreamy interest that Emma, and a score of other girls, had shown in his religious-education class had not lasted beyond his departure, but had meant that for the first time in the history of the school theological discussion among at least some of the pupils had overtaken any debate about some of the more usual subjects of teenage interest (music, the opposite sex, the incorrigibility of parents, clothes, and so on).

Emma remembered in particular a class discussion with this chaplain about the creation of the world and the granting to humanity of free choice.

"I can't quite see why God would have made the world in the first place," she said. "And in particular I can't see why he should have made it imperfect. Wouldn't it have been better to avoid all this suffering by just not making it? I mean, why would he?"

The chaplain had smiled. "A very good question, Emma."

And then there had been silence while the pupils awaited the answer.

"We shouldn't imagine that the divine mind works in the same way as ours does," said the chaplain at last. "But even if we do that for a moment, surely it's possible to imagine the pleasure that comes from setting something off on its course and then watching to see what happens. I'd like that, I think. I'd rather like to get a few lives going and then see how they cope with the challenges."

That had made an impression on her, and it came back to her now as she thought about Miss Taylor and James. The chaplain had been right, she thought, even if she was not sure that his basic premise—the existence of God—could be defended. There was, she decided, a very particular pleasure in bringing two people together and seeing what would happen; in a way, it was rather as God might feel—if he felt anything. Of course it was quite possible that the results of one's intervention might not be what one hoped they would be; there would be introductions, no doubt, that had dreadful consequences—Anne

Boleyn would certainly have been introduced to that rotund psychopath Henry VIII, and the outcome of that was undeniably unpleasant. But the risk, she thought, was worth taking, and James, benign and relaxed as he was, would hardly treat Miss Taylor as Henry had treated Anne.

It occurred to her that she might do it again, and she thought of Harriet Smith. There she was, this rather naïve but very beautiful young woman, wasting her time teaching English to puzzled students at what was, after all, a disused airfield. What a waste that was, when Harriet could be livening up her life— or having it livened up for her—with a love affair. She imagined that there were plenty of young men at Mrs. Goddard's who would leap at the chance of a relationship with an attractive girl of the English-rose type such as Harriet was. But the problem with that would be that their command of English would not be quite up to it: there would be something vaguely comic about these young men saying things like, "Please can you tell me the way to the railway station and, by the way, I love the colour of your eyes." No, it would not come out like that at all, but would probably be: "Excuse me please, the colour of your eyes is very blue, is it not, and what is the way to the railway station?"

She smiled at the thought, and decided that Harriet should not be wasted on a student, but should be brought to the attention of somebody of greater possibilities—somebody who could sort out the financial problems that she had alluded to and, at the stroke of a pen over a chequebook, make possible the gap year for which she was trying to save. You had to be realistic about these things, thought Emma; a hard-up boyfriend living in a garret was material for a romantic opera, but was not necessarily what you were looking for if you had no money your-self. There was no reason why solvent boyfriends could not be good-looking—and entertaining too. If she could only intro-duce Harriet to somebody like that—somebody who would take her away from Mrs. Goddard's school and whisk her off some-where exotic . . . or at least take her out to dinner in London now and then, and to parties where people had fun and did not talk about the way to the railway station and such matters . . . The trouble, though, was that Harriet did not appear to know anybody, and that meant that she would need assistance in finding the right candidate for this affair she was planning—or rather that Emma was planning on her behalf. Emma thought for a moment: Whom did she know who had the money to give Harriet a good time?

The issue of Harriet Smith's emotional future arose rather sooner than Emma had planned. It was a week or so after the departure of Miss Taylor that Emma drove into the village in the Mini Cooper her father had given her for her twenty-first birthday—given, but then immediately regretted. Cars were dangerous, and he was entirely conversant with the information that the Consumer Association published on the survivability of accidents in various types of vehicle. It was not that a Mini Cooper, even one painted, as Emma's was, in the colour known as British Racing Green, was more dangerous than other makes of car, it was just that *every* car had a mortality risk associated with it, and Mini Coopers were no exception. The only entirely safe car, Mr. Woodhouse felt, was one kept resolutely in the garage. However, Emma had pressed him for a car, and he'd realised that if he did not provide her with one, then she could end up buying one for which the safety ratings were lower than anything he might produce.

Emma liked to drive into the village from time to time. There was not much for her to do there other than to buy the newspaper and occasional groceries, but it was an outing and it took her out of the house. After dropping in at the post office that doubled up as a newsagent, she would walk along the short village High Street to the newly opened coffee house at the crossroads. A coffee house was something entirely new for Highbury, which was more tea-room territory than anything else, but it was proving popular with the locals, particularly with those who felt that the village pub had become unbearable since it had declared itself a "gastro-pub" and put up its charges by almost forty per cent. Not that the coffee house was cheap, but its brews were good, and there was always a selection of shortbread, muffins, and scones that could be eaten while reading one of the magazines the owners thoughtfully provided for their customers. Emma liked a table by the window and would sit there for half an hour or so, checking her emails and watching the progression of people down the High Street. She knew virtually everybody, of course, and they recognised her, sometimes waving cheerfully when they saw her looking out of the window.

On that particular morning she was not aware of Harriet Smith coming into the coffee house, as she was engrossed in reading a long and rather emotional email from one of her Bath friends. This friend, who had been going out with the same young man for three years, had recently split up with him and was bemoaning the fact that now that he was gone she would have to go to all the trouble of finding a replacement. "I know that you don't care one way or another about having a man on hand," she wrote. "Frankly I need to have one about the place. I just do. But finding one is such a bore, Emma, and I wish I could just close my eyes and, bang, there'd be a man."

Emma's reply was succinct. "Get someone to set you up," she said. "Either that, or Internet dating, but with that I suppose you run the risk of getting some dreadful geek. Try being a nun. (Only joking.)" She did not believe in emoticons, but this was an occasion when she thought she might just add one. While she was trying to work out how to do a wink, she heard a voice behind her and looked up sharply.

"If you're busy, I won't disturb you," said Harriet.

Emma pressed the send button without bothering about the emoticon. "I'm not busy," she said. "Just reading an email from a friend."

"I love getting emails," said Harriet. "But I don't get all that many. I wondered whether my spam filter was stopping them all, but it wasn't. I don't even seem to get much spam."

Emma was on the point of saying that she had heard that there were such people, but stopped herself. "I'll send you an email," she said.

"Oh, that would be so nice," said Harriet as she sat down opposite Emma. "And I'll reply to you."

"That would be really kind," said Emma. She was staring at Harriet. Surely somebody who looked as beautiful as that, she thought, would be constantly pestered by men. Did Harriet have to fend them off? Was there something about her—some vaguely fragile quality—that made men fear that if they got too close to her, if they actually touched her, she would break?

There were some people who gave one that impression; they were not made for the rough and tumble of ordinary life.

The cappuccino Harriet had ordered was now brought to the table. "You're so kind," she said to the owner of the coffee bar. "And your coffee's so lovely. I could drink cup after cup, but it would just make me all jumbled up! And heaven knows what I'd do if I were jumbled up."

Emma looked at her with interest. "You could do something really dramatic," she said.

"Oh," said Harriet, looking momentarily concerned. "Do you really think so?"

Emma laughed. "Not really. I don't see you doing anything to be ashamed of. Not really."

"Well, that's a great relief," said Harriet. "I can drink my coffee now without worrying about dashing off and doing something I might regret."

Emma's eye ran down the clothes that Harriet was wearing. They were nothing special, she decided; in fact, they looked rather cheap. And when it came to her shoes, these were a pair of trainers that had once presumably been red but were now a washed-out colour somewhere between khaki and pink. Somebody like Harriet, with her china-doll build, should not be in trainers, thought Emma. She should be wearing dainty soft leather shoes like ballet pumps, perhaps with a delicate bow on each toe. Shoes like that were expensive, of course, and if you didn't have the money, or were saving it for your gap year, then they would be beyond your reach. But trainers! It would be interesting to see what a small amount of money spent on Harriet could achieve, thought Emma. It would be a transformation.

Harriet raised her cup to her mouth and took a small, cautious sip—as if the ingestion of any more copious quantity of coffee might have an immediate jumbling effect. She lowered the cup and dabbed daintily at her mouth with a paper napkin. Her lips, Emma saw, were perfect: a Cupid's bow of a mouth.

"There's something I wanted to tell you," Harriet began. "I hope you don't mind. It's a bit of a secret actually, but I felt that I could share it with you."

"Oh?" said Emma.

"There's a boy who lives on the edge of the village," said Harriet. "He's the same age as me—twenty."

"Oh yes?"

"Robert Martin? Do you know him? I expect you know everybody."

Emma frowned. Robert Martin?

"His parents have that little hotel. The Oak Tree Inn."

It dawned on Emma whom Harriet was talking about. The Martin family had owned the hotel for over ten years, and yes, she knew Robert Martin very slightly—enough to exchange a few words if they met in the street, but not much more than that. "Actually," said Emma, "it's more of a bed-and-breakfast place. It's not a real hotel."

Harriet looked crestfallen. "It's quite nice inside," she said. "They've got a bar and a television lounge."

Emma smiled. A television lounge! Could Harriet really be impressed by the thought of a television lounge, which would almost certainly have patterned carpets and smell vaguely of fried food and furniture polish? Surely not.

"What about him?" Emma asked. "What about this Robert Martin? Does he help with the B&B? Perhaps he makes the breakfasts. Fries the sausages and two rashers of bacon. Makes the cold toast." She wrinkled her nose, but the gesture was wasted on Harriet, who beamed through the uncomplimentary description of the breakfast.

"Oh no," said Harriet. "His mother makes the breakfasts. Robert helps to take them through to the guests."

"So he's a waiter," said Emma.

"No," said Harriet. "He just helps his parents—that's all."

Emma waited for Harriet to say something more; she did not like where this was leading.

"He's asked me out," said Harriet. "For dinner at the Chinese restaurant. The one on the Holt road. You must know it."

"I don't really go for Chinese restaurants," said Emma. "But some people do, I suppose."

"Twenty per cent of the world's population do," said Harriet, and then added the explanation, "That's how many people are Chinese—one in five."

Emma shrugged. "That's fine," she said, adding, "for them." She paused. "And are you going to go to this Chinese restaurant with him?"

Harriet nodded. "I think so. I haven't replied to him yet, but I think I will. I love the way they cook duck, you know. I love duck anyway, but the Chinese make it taste really delicious with that special sauce of theirs."

"Monosodium glutamate," said Emma.

"They don't always use that stuff," said Harriet, now slightly on the defensive.

"But do you like him?" asked Emma. "It's all very well liking the way the Chinese cook duck, but do you like this Robert Martin?"

"He's rather sweet," said Harriet. "He's got these big eyes, you see, and when he smiles there's a dimple right there on his chin. It's really sweet."

Emma frowned. She had thought Harriet was weak—just the sort of person to have her head turned by the first young man to show an interest in her—but she had not imagined that she would be quite this weak. To be struck by a dimple; could she really see no further than that? It occurred to her that she could not allow Harriet to be that easily conquered, and that she would have to act to prevent this. It was not selfishness or jealousy—nothing like that—it was a simple desire to get the best for her new friend. And Robert Martin, surely, was not the best she could do, whatever dimples he may have on his chin.

"Oh, Harriet," said Emma, "you know you really mustn't fall for such things. Dimples? What are dimples but indentations? Are you sure you're prepared to judge somebody on their indentations?"

Harriet looked confused. "He's nice," she said. "Really sweet. I met him in the pub when I went with some students from the English course. He was kind to them: they asked him the way to the railway station and he was very—"

"Oh, Harriet," repeated Emma, her voice rising with exasperation, "don't be so gauche. Of course he's going to be nice to your students—with you standing there. What do you expect? What he really wanted to say to them was 'Get lost!'"

Harriet looked uncomprehending. "But why would he say that?"

"Because that's what people say if a bunch of ridiculous English Language students come up to them and ask them the way to the railway station."

Harriet shook her head. "I wouldn't."

"But of course *you* wouldn't, but then that's what you're paid for. You're *meant* to tell people the way to the railway station."

Harriet's tone was meek. "They're only practising."

"Of course they're only practising," snapped Emma. "But the point is this: he was being nice to them in order to impress you. He'll be interested in only one thing."

"Which is?"

Emma's exasperation now showed. She had hoped that she would be able to water down Harriet's attention to Robert Martin without having to be too specific. But Harriet, it seemed, was not susceptible to subtlety. "Oh, really!" she said, her voice rising in irritation. "Do I have to spell it out?"

"Maybe you do."

"All right. S . . . E . . . X. There. Clear enough?"

Harriet looked down at her faded pink trainers. Emma's eyes followed her gaze. She noticed, now, that the thick white laces were frayed, and that one of them was about to give way.

"Not all boys are like that. I don't think that Robert is."

Emma gave a dismissive laugh. "*All* males are like that, Harriet, and I'm surprised you haven't discovered that simple fact of existence. They're *all* like that. Unless they're not interested in *us*, in which case they're like that to *them*."

She was sure of her ground here. There was absolutely no doubt about how men thought and about the designs they had on young women, particularly young women with Harriet's looks and innocence. All she was doing, she told herself, was protecting a naïve young woman from a young man who would use her and then, without any shadow of a doubt, toss her aside. That's what men did; it was just what they did.

She wondered whether she sounded prudish, or, worse still, whether she *was* prudish. If Robert Martin wanted to have a relationship with Harriet, and if Harriet liked the idea, then what was wrong with that? People slept together, and was there any reason why Harriet shouldn't sleep with this boy? What would she—Emma—feel if he were to come along and proposition her rather than Harriet? Would she respond? She shivered, and thought: *Why do I shiver when I think of sex?* Did everybody else shiver, or was it just her?

Harriet was quiet. "I don't know . . ." She looked up at Emma, who realised, at that precise moment, that Harriet was clay in her hands.

"I don't think you should go out with Robert Martin," she said firmly. "You're wasting yourself. It's going to go nowhere, you know. It's *not* the way to the railway station, so to speak."

"He's—"

Emma interrupted her. "He's nothing, Harriet. He works in a B&B that masquerades as a hotel. You could aim much, much higher than that, you know. You owe it to yourself."

"To myself?"

"Yes. It's a question of what you could make of yourself. You told me that you don't have parents." She hesitated, but decided to continue. "Or you said that you don't really know your father. That's a big disadvantage in life—not coming from somewhere."

"You're very lucky," said Harriet. "You've got your dad and that house and your Mini Cooper."

Emma acknowledged her good fortune with a tilt of her head. "You could have all that. You could do something with your life—if you don't go and jump into bed with the first *random* who comes along and asks you."

"I wasn't going to leap into bed with him," protested Harriet. "I was going to go to a Chinese restaurant. There's a difference, you know."

"So the second date would be a Chinese restaurant too?" challenged Emma. "And then the third as well? Think of your monosodium glutamate levels, Harriet Smith!" She laughed. "No, he's got his head screwed on the right way, that Robert Martin. He knows how to get what he wants."

Harriet fell silent. Emma watched her carefully as she lifted her coffee cup and took another sip. She did not think that she had overstepped the mark, but she was not quite sure. She had been a bit extreme, she decided, but it was so clearly in Harriet's best interests that a few possibly rather extreme things be said; of course it was.

She need not have worried. Harriet put down her coffee, dabbed at her lips again, and looked earnestly at Emma. "You're really kind," she said. "I've got nobody to tell me these things, I suppose. I just wouldn't realise."

Emma stretched out a comforting hand. "I just didn't want to see some very ordinary boy getting his grubby hands on you," she said. "Not when you could do so much better."

"But what should I do?" asked Harriet. "I told him that I could probably go with him on the date. I said I just had to check."

"Then there's no problem," said Emma. "Do you have his number?"

Harriet nodded. "It's in my phone," she said.

"Then text him," said Emma firmly. "Say *I'm sorry but I can't come out. Got to work. Sorry.*" She paused. Harriet had taken out her phone and was searching for Robert Martin's number. "And then you could add something like *See you sometime.* That's clear enough."

"But maybe I shouldn't see him . . . You said . . ."

Emma would have sighed had she not reminded herself that she did not want to turn into her father, with his frequent, eloquent sighs. "Saying to somebody that you'll see them is utterly meaningless," she said. "*See you* means, in fact, goodbye. *Sometime* means never. But if you want to be absolutely unambiguous, you could add the word *not.* That, though, would be cruel, and I wouldn't do it."

She watched as Harriet sent the text. She had not imagined it would be so easy, and for a moment she felt a pang of guilt. That surprised her because guilt should not come into it: this was helping somebody who very obviously needed her help; it was not idle interference. She looked out of the window. There were people in the street, and one of them, getting out of a rather more expensive car than one would expect a clergyman to drive, was Philip Elton.

She watched as the young vicar locked the car door behind him and made his way into the newsagent's. He was wearing jeans, and they were well cut, and his shoulders, from behind at least, were quite broad for a clergyman's shoulders. She wondered what age Philip Elton was. Vicars were usually ancient and wore baggy cardigans with buttons up the front. This one was very different. Late twenties? Twenty-eight maybe? Not much more. And he owned a large office block in Ipswich, they said, and somebody had said that there was a block of flats in

Norwich too. Not a large block of flats, but if one thought of the rent for just a single flat these days and then multiplied it by the number of flats in the block—say ten, because most blocks of flats had at least ten flats in them—then that gave you at least seven thousand pounds a month, once one had allowed for maintenance costs and so on. If the flats were better, of course, or if there were more of them, then that figure would be even greater and would allow Philip Elton to have an even more expensive car, and a great deal more besides.

She looked at Harriet. It was very unfair that there were so many people who were able to take gap years that they often did not really appreciate, and yet here was this vulnerable, rather sweet girl who was having to scrimp and save to have any prospect of affording even a modest gap year which would probably end up being somewhere cheap and utterly obscure, such as Malta, perhaps, where she would teach English to people who wished to be able to get to the railway station, or working in a chalet in a French mountain resort, trapped in the kitchen, washing up and making soup while well-heeled skiers enjoyed themselves in the snow outside, shooting down the black runs, drinking mulled wine and eating cheese fondues at high-altitude restaurants.

She turned to look at Harriet once more. Of course, Philip Elton was the obvious candidate: single, well off, good-looking . . . The fact that he was a bore was neither here nor there—Emma did not think one actually had to *listen* to a man, and Harriet's conversation was pretty frothy anyway. They might just hit it off, both talking but neither paying any attention to what the other was saying. The difference of a few years or so between Harriet and Philip was hardly significant, and anyway he would not be a permanent fixture. Harriet could continue to work at the school for a few more months and then he could relieve himself of his parish duties—he was after all, non-stipendiary and therefore could not be told what to do by his bishop—and then they could go off on the gap year together, staying in comfortable hotels and allowing Harriet to spend the whole year on a succession of beaches if she so desired. What was wrong with that? And then she could come back and she would have a bit more sophistication and worldly wisdom to her and she could apply to a university and get rid of Philip. She might even get a place, possibly at Oxford, where the C in drama might be perfectly adequate provided that Harriet could describe herself as sufficiently disadvantaged—and she did come from a disused airfield, after all; surely that would count for a lot. Or she could get a job in London and be launched. There would be numerous eligible young men after her by that stage and she would be able to pick and choose. There would be no more trainers; those would have long since been replaced by expensive designer shoes—in several colours. There would be no more cheap-looking clothes. There would be no more naïve remarks. Harriet would be transformed. Who said, ". . . changed, changed utterly"? Some poet they had studied at Gresham's. Yeats or Keats: their names were so close that nobody could be blamed for mixing them up.

11

On that Saturday, a few days after Emma's meeting with Harriet Smith in the Highbury coffee shop, George Knightley called at Hartfield, as he did once or twice a week. These meetings tended to be spontaneous, with George dropping in without prior notice; he knew that Mr. Woodhouse never went anywhere, and that he would therefore always find him in. Both of them enjoyed these visits; in spite of the age gap between them, they found they were able to converse with all the ease and intimacy of coevals. This was because both Mr. Woodhouse and George had that relatively rare talent of dealing with other people equally, without regard to age. For his part, Mr. Woodhouse could talk to a seven-year-old with the same seriousness and respect as he could talk to a seventy-year-old; it simply made no difference to him, and he always felt slightly taken aback when a young person addressed him with deference or held back in a conversation.

"I don't see why age should make the slightest difference between people," he once said to Miss Taylor. "I suppose that people who've been around a bit longer know a bit more . . ."

"Not all of them," interjected Miss Taylor. "There are some

people who start off knowing very little about the world and end up years later knowing even less. Never underestimate the capacity of the human mind for ignorance."

Mr. Woodhouse found this very amusing. "Yes, perhaps you're right. And, in addition to having a great capacity for ignorance, some people seem to enjoy concealing what they know. They act as if they are less intelligent and less well informed than they really are."

"Precisely," agreed Miss Taylor. "That particularly applies to politicians. Those people do not wish to appear elitist and seem to believe that to be well-informed and to speak correctly—that is, to use subjects, objects, and verbs in their sentences, indeed to use sentences at all—is a sign of elitism and therefore to be avoided at all costs."

"Not me," said Mr. Woodhouse.

Miss Taylor smiled. "I shall assume that the verb in that sentence you've just uttered is implied, and that the phrase that you had in mind was *That doesn't include* . . . which would, of course, justify the use of the accusative *me,* rather than the nominative *I.* I assume that."

"Splendid stuff," said Mr. Woodhouse.

Mr. Woodhouse never had that sort of conversation with George Knightley, who was not really interested in the grammatical points from which Miss Taylor derived such enjoyment. He and George talked about just about everything else, though; George's background was agricultural—he had a degree in land management from Exeter University—but he was interested in scientific matters too, and much appreciated the copies of *Scientific American* that Mr. Woodhouse passed on to him after he had finished with them himself. They also talked about art, farming, national politics, and local affairs, although Mr. Wood-house knew relatively little about the last of these, as he never went out.

Although George Knightley bore some resemblance to his brother, John, the London photographer, the two men were in many respects very different. George was courteous and considered; he was tactful in his dealings with people, and he occupied his position as a substantial landowner with an unas-suming modesty and a strong sense of social responsibility. He encouraged people to picnic and ride on his land, and had gone so far as to create a cycle track through his woods to allow local children to race their bicycles through the mud and over small, artificial hillocks specially created for them. The children loved this, as did the horse-riders who galloped across his fields or the kite-fliers who launched their kites from the parkland sur-rounding George's house, Donwell Abbey.

Anglers were not forgotten. A good trout river ran through the land and fishing permits were granted on this to locals on the payment of two pounds—one pound in the case of boys and the retired. This liberality was appreciated even by the neighbourhood poachers, Ted and Morris Worsfold, who went so far as to report three outsiders who fished without first obtaining a permit. "There's no excuse for poaching on *that* river," said Morris. "No excuse at all."

His generosity went even further. Donwell Abbey, a sub-stantial Strawberry Gothic building, was an ideal setting for a wedding. There was a large hall in which the ceremony could be conducted, and the walled garden to the west of the house was perfect for receptions if the weather allowed. A money-conscious owner would have recognised this potential and made the house available for rent for such purposes, but not George Knightley. Rather than charge for the use of the house, he made it available for free as long as the bride or groom lived in Highbury or in one of the five villages within the immediate vicinity. This meant that a young couple without much money could have a wedding that would normally have cost thousands of pounds, allowing them to keep such funds as they had for the deposit on a mortgage or the purchase of furniture for their new home.

Such generosity may be unappreciated, as people often resent those who help them. This was not so here: everybody in Highbury liked George and passed on news of how he had helped this young couple or that; everybody knew that if a local cause needed help, then he was the first port of call, even if he was not always in a position to give a major donation.

The fact that he was a bachelor was regarded by many local women as a tragedy. "How can such a nice man still be single?" people asked. "Why?"

There was a simple answer to this, although not many in the locality knew it. George might at this stage have been by himself, but this was not always so: for four years he had been closely involved with a woman a few years older than he was, Caroline Throke, a potter who lived in King's Lynn. Caroline was an attractive redhead whom George had met when he was at university in Exeter, and with whom he had fallen in love. This had been reciprocated, and they had enjoyed four years together, although living separately. George spent weekends with her in King's Lynn, and she came, although less frequently, to spend time with him in Donwell Abbey. They regularly went off on holiday to France or Italy, and they had also spent two months travelling in India and Sri Lanka. They were ideally suited, their friends said, and nobody ever imagined that Caroline would suddenly fall for the young installer who came to fit the solar panels on her roof.

This solar-panel installer was called Ronnie, and he was good at his job. He had two main interests in life: solar energy and football. He was a supporter of Norwich United football team and prided himself on attending every game Norwich played, whether at home or away. He had a yellow scarf and a yellow sweater that he wore in honour of his team, which was known for its yellow colours. He also had a canary called Robert that he had bought in honour of the football team, which was fondly known as the Canaries. Ronnie still lived with his parents, and Robert filled their house with song from morning until evening, at which point a towel was draped over his cage to keep him quiet.

Caroline had made Ronnie a cup of tea when he first came to install the panels, and she had clumsily spilled some of this tea on his forearm. He had winced from the scalding, but had quickly recovered his composure and told her that it had not hurt at all and that he was always spilling tea over himself any-way. This reaction struck her as charming, and she had watched him thoughtfully as he climbed up his ladder and began to put the panel fixings on her tiled roof. By the time he came down from the roof two hours later, she realised that she was destined to become Ronnie's lover. She knew nothing about him, but was drawn towards him by a curious force that made her feel like a swimmer in a powerful current. She could not struggle against it; she simply had to remain afloat while the current took her away. It was entirely physical.

Ronnie felt this too. He had lived with his parents long enough and wanted to have his own place. Here was an apparently unencumbered woman who was also attractive and friendly. He had noticed her watching him, and had correctly interpreted her gaze. He understood such looks, as he was undeniably attractive himself, and knew what it meant when people said something to you and then let their eyes linger on yours before they slipped down, as if drawn by some internal bodily gravity, to the chest. He knew what that meant.

Caroline was dismayed to discover that she felt so little for George as to be able to abandon him for a solar-panel installer whom she had just met. She did not deceive him, though, and she told him immediately.

"I'm very sorry, George," she said. "I never thought this would happen, but it has. I've fallen for somebody else. I didn't set out to; he came to me. It just happened, and rather than hurt you in any way by prolonging things, I've decided that we should each go our separate ways. I'm so sorry, George, because you're the kindest, nicest man in Norfolk and I would never, *never*, do anything to cause you pain."

Except leave me for a solar-panel installer, thought George, but he did not say it, of course. Others were more direct. "She obviously wants a bit of rough," said one friend, adding, "Stupid girl." Another simply said, "D. H. Lawrence," and sighed.

George was resilient, and hid his sense of betrayal, but he had become wary, as people who are hurt by others may do. To some of his friends he now seemed to be slightly distant, to have become more of an observer than a participant; it was as if he was standing on the sidelines, watching, while others got on with the business of life—and of love. In many circumstances, when others might have commented on something, or joined in the cut and thrust of an argument or debate, George would hold back; he would smile in a slightly wry way and keep his views to himself. "Come on, George," they encouraged. "Tell us what you think. You must think *something*." He would not rise to the bait. "Of course I think something," he might say. "Who doesn't think something?"

The truth of that observation was undeniable. We all think something, all the time—the human brain being so constructed—even if it is not necessarily of great consequence. This does not deter many of us, though, from sharing those thoughts—even those of decidedly little consequence.

There was one exception to this reticence, and that was in George's relations with Mr. Woodhouse, Miss Taylor, and with Emma herself. When he came to Hartfield, he appeared ready to relax and open up. Not only did he have wide-ranging con-versations with Mr. Woodhouse, but he also spoke freely to Miss Taylor and Emma, with whom he had developed a more relaxed relationship in recent years. Certainly, the distance that had existed between them during her childhood had faded, and they had become used to having fairly lengthy—and frank—chats during his Hartfield visits. So the exchange that took place between them on that Saturday, after George had said goodbye to Mr. Woodhouse in his library and was making his way to the front door, was not atypical, even if the intensity with which views were expressed was rather unusual.

It started innocuously. Emma had been playing the piano. When, on leaving the music room, she bumped into George coming down the corridor, neither was surprised; she knew that he had been drinking tea and chatting with her father in the library, and he had heard her practising the piano when he arrived in the house.

"I see that Emma's playing Erik Satie," he said to Mr. Woodhouse. "That's one of the *Gymnopédies*, isn't it?"

"I believe it is," said Mr. Woodhouse. "I don't care for it very much. In fact, it gives me the creeps. It's the sort of thing a spider would play if spiders played the piano."

This amused George. "I suppose the intervals are a bit . . . how would one put it? Elongated? Yes. It's meant to stretch the hands. And it's languid—it's certainly languid. It makes me think of Paris on a wet afternoon in a quiet time of the year. Drops of raining falling on the Seine. Cobbled stones. The streets quite empty, and faintly, drifting down from one of those mansard windows, the sound of somebody playing Satie."

Mr. Woodhouse's eyes widened. "Spiders?" he repeated, a note of concern on his voice. "I suppose that a piano is an ideal place for a spider to make a nest. All those nooks and crannies between the keys: a spider could well find it a very attractive place to be."

George made a dismissive gesture. "Oh, surely not. What if the spider went for a walk about the sounding board and somebody started to play? He could be hit by the hammers coming down on the strings, couldn't he? No, a piano would be a lethal place for a spider—let me assure you of that." He was aware of his friend's tendency to anxiety, and sought to change the subject by asking about the long-range weather forecast that he knew Mr. Woodhouse followed with some interest.

"Not good," said Mr. Woodhouse. "There are signs that a storm is building up out in the Atlantic and will be heading our way. There are bound to be people washed off beaches down in

Cornwall. Why do they go there? Don't they know it's dangerous to stand within reach of waves when the sea is so rough?
Why won't people stay inside, George? Can you explain that to
me? Why do they have to go and court danger?"

The conversation had improved, of course, as it usually did
after any initial issues had been disposed of, and after half an
hour of talk about government policy on agricultural subsidies—
a matter that had some effect on the finances of both friends—
George said goodbye, insisting on showing himself out.

"I know the way," he said. "And there's nothing much that
can happen to me in the corridor."

For a second or two a shadow passed over Mr. Woodhouse's
face. But he said nothing, and George closed the library door
behind him and began to make his way down the corridor. It was
then that he heard the piano stop, Satie having been replaced
by Beethoven's "Für Elise," not particularly well played. He
hesitated, and then Emma appeared.

"George," Emma exclaimed. "I have had an audience, it seems.
And I thought that this was a purely private performance."

George laughed. "I like your Satie. Your dad doesn't, but
I do."

"He has very conventional tastes, I'm afraid. Poor old Pops.
He doesn't really like anything twentieth century. It's the same
with opera. He goes for Mozart and so on. Not that he ever gets
to see an opera these days."

"Maybe we could take him to one," said George. "We could
go to Covent Garden. Perhaps even Glyndebourne, if we were
feeling adventurous."

"It's impossible to get tickets for Glyndebourne," said Emma.
"You have to put yourself down years in advance. Do you know

there are children of five on the waiting lists? Parents put them down for seats for when they're eighteen. Can you believe it?"

"No," said George. "I can't."

"I can't imagine thinking that far in advance," said Emma. "It's like planting an oak tree. You know that you're not going to be around to enjoy it, but you still do it."

"And just as well that people take that view," said George. "Otherwise we wouldn't have . . ." He waved a hand in the direction of Ely. "Otherwise we wouldn't have cathedrals."

"Yes," agreed Emma. "Perhaps you're right. But I still find it hard to worry about things that are going to happen after I'm gone. Global warming, for instance."

"That's happening right now," said George. "That's not the future—that's the present."

"Oh well," said Emma. "Did Pops offer you any cake? Mrs. Firhill's been baking and we have cake coming out of our ears."

"He did, thanks very much. I had two slices."

They walked together towards the front door. In the hall, standing beneath the large Venetian canal scene—"our non-Canaletto" as Mr. Woodhouse called it—George remarked that he had seen Harriet Smith in the village with a group of English Language students from Mrs. Goddard's.

"She'll have been showing them the way to the railway station," said Emma.

George frowned. "Railway station?"

"A metaphor," said Emma lightly. "There are real railway stations, of which we have none in the village, and metaphorical railway stations, of which we have as many as anybody else—perhaps more."

George smiled. "Emma, you're very opaque sometimes."

"At least I'm not transparent," said Emma. "I should hate to be seen through." She paused. "So you saw Harriet Smith?"

"Yes. And then, when I went into that new coffee place, she was there—by herself now."

"I see."

"I had coffee with her. We had an interesting chat."

"Oh yes?"

"Yes. She has an interesting story, that girl."

Emma was intrigued. She had been hoping to get Harriet's story out of her, but no opportunity to do that had presented itself so far. Could George tell her?

"I didn't hear it from her," he said. "I heard it from Mrs. Goddard. She and I are on the Lifeboats Committee—we raise money for them, you know. Anyway, she told me a bit about her."

"Is she a sort of orphan?" asked Emma. "Or not quite an orphan, but heading towards being an orphan?"

George smiled. "You could put it that way. Mind you, you could say that about everybody, couldn't you? All of us are either orphans already or destined to become orphans."

"But what about Harriet?" pressed Emma.

"It's a very strange story. Her mother, apparently, had a dance studio in Chichester: the sort of place where little girls go to ballet lessons, with floors covered in French chalk—that sort of thing. Anyway, she was unmarried and there was no prospect of anybody turning up. But she wanted a child—pretty desperately, apparently. That's understandable, of course. And so she looked for a man who would oblige."

Emma smiled. "There are such men," she said, adding, "So I'm told."

"Not in the usual way," George went on. "This was a case of home–based artificial insemination."

Emma drew in her breath: Harriet had been an AID child. She knew, of course, that such people existed, but she had never met one.

George continued with his story. "This fellow, apparently, did the decent thing, and the result was Harriet. But there was a firm agreement in place, as I believe there often is in these cases, that his identity would be kept secret. And you can understand that."

"Of course," said Emma.

"Because if you didn't have that, then you wouldn't get donors to donate, would you? A man could find himself faced with quite a few children if he'd been helpful more than once."

"I can see that," said Emma. "But then what happened next?"

"Just a couple of years ago, when Harriet was eighteen, her mother died and she found herself . . ."

". . . alone in the world," supplied Emma.

George ignored the provocation. He had been about to say exactly that, and he saw nothing wrong with the expression. "Yes," he said, and thought: *And you could find yourself alone in the world too, Emma.* "The dance studio was sold and raised a bit of money, but that wasn't really enough to keep Harriet. Mrs. Goddard came to the rescue. She and Harriet's mother had been penfriends when they were children, and had kept up with each other. She effectively took Harriet in."

"Poor Harriet," she said.

"Well, at least she had somewhere to live," said George. "And then came the big surprise. Harriet was contacted by a lawyer in London, who said he was acting on behalf of a client who did not want his identity revealed. He was, the lawyer explained, the man who had helped Harriet's mother to become pregnant. He was the father."

Emma listened, enrapt, as George continued.

"All that the lawyer would reveal was that this man was a teacher. He did not have a great deal of money but he wanted to make a contribution to his daughter's expenses until she was in a full-time job. He said that he would pay a small sum into her bank account each month. He wished he could give more, but he couldn't."

Emma let out her breath. "Astonishing," she said.

George agreed. "So there are at least some decent people left," he said.

"Does she know?" Emma asked. "Does she know that the person sending her money is her father?"

"Yes."

"But does she know that he's only her father in a biological sense?"

He shrugged. "What does it matter? The biology's much the same whether it's a natural or assisted conception."

"So she doesn't know how she was conceived?"

"Apparently not. She thinks that her mother had an affair with the man who was her father."

"I'm glad," said Emma. "It must be difficult to accept something like that about yourself."

He did not agree. "I don't see it that way," he said. "I really don't see that it matters a damn how one comes into existence."

George now made for the door. "You won't tell her, will you?"

Emma promised him that she would not say a word to Harriet.

"Good," he said. "She's a nice girl and I wouldn't like to think of her being distressed. I suspect her life is hard enough as it is. Mind you . . ."

Emma waited.

"Mind you, she's having a bit of romance, at least. There's that boy from the little hotel outside the village."

"B&B," said Emma quickly. "Actually, it's a B&B."

"Well, it's him, anyway: Robert Martin. His father happens to rent one of my fields. They have a couple of Jacob's sheep they keep there. He said to me—the father, that is—that his son was cock-a-hoop because he was going to have dinner with Harriet in a Chinese restaurant. Apparently the father had never seen his boy so happy."

A trace of a smile appeared on Emma's face. "No, he's not," she said.

"Not what?"

"If he thinks he's having dinner with Harriet Smith, he's got another thing coming," she said. "She's going to cry off."

George seemed to be intent on examining the non-Canaletto. "Oh yes?" he muttered. "She's told you that, I suppose."

"She has," said Emma. "She's already texted him to let him know. No Chinese restaurant. No date. That's it."

George turned round gradually. "I see," he said. "And you had nothing to do with that, Emma?"

Emma's eyes were wide with innocence. "Me? I'm not the one he invited."

"That's not the question I asked. I asked you whether you had anything to do with Harriet's refusal of his invitation?" He was staring directly at her now, and she flinched. "Did you?"

Her reaction had given him his answer. "Emma, you disappoint me," he said.

Now injured innocence returned. "I really don't know what you're talking about, Knightley."

"I wish you wouldn't call me Knightley," he snapped.

"But that's who you are," she replied. And then smiled sweetly. "It's fond, I promise you. It's not formal."

He looked at his watch. "I have to go, I'm afraid. Somebody's coming to see me at Donwell."

"I wouldn't want to keep you," said Emma.

He showed no signs of leaving. "All I'd be interested to know is this: What have you got against Robert Martin?"

Had Emma not answered, George's departure might have been less acrimonious. But she did answer.

"He's not up to her," she said. "That's all."

It took a few moments for this to sink in. Then he said, "I simply don't believe what I'm hearing. Not up to her? Not up to Harriet Smith?"

She was too far committed, and decided to stand her ground. "No, he isn't. He's a sort of waiter in a B&B. You may think that's fine, but I don't. If she went off with him—and just think of it for a moment—if she went off with Robert Martin, what would she become? I'll tell you. She'd be working in the parental B&B with him, that's what."

George drew in his breath. "He hasn't asked her to marry him, for God's sake. He's asked her to a meal in a Chinese restaurant. And, anyway, what exactly is wrong with working in a B&B?"

Emma laughed. This was a mistake.

"Oh, you think that's funny," said George, his voice rising. "What do you *do*, Emma Woodhouse? What useful contribution do *you* make to society?"

He regretted it the moment he said it. He was surprised, too, at the pain this exchange caused him. He was prepared to have an argument when the occasion called for one, but he did not want to argue with Emma, because . . . He was not sure why. Because he was fond of her? How fond? he asked himself.

"And you?" she retorted. "What do *you* do?"

There was something in her tone that made him want to fight back. "I run a farm—quite a successful one, in fact. It provides three people with a job." Now there were short, angry phrases. "I am responsible for that. I also run the house, which provides two jobs and a lot of work for local tradesmen." He knew he sounded pompous, but he could not help himself.

"I run *this* house," retorted Emma.

"And Robert Martin, whom I happen to know, is a perfectly decent young man. That girl is nothing out of the ordinary, Emma. She's not exactly Einstein."

Emma hesitated, uncertain as to whether or not to mention Harriet's C in drama. She decided against it. "Einstein!" she retorted. "And him?"

"What makes her so special? Go on, tell me; I'm waiting. What makes her better than him?"

"She's gorgeous," said Emma. "That's point one. And sweet. That's point two. And she could do far better than this boring young man from a two-star B&B. Point three." She paused. "Yes, two-star. I looked it up."

George moved towards the door. He looked agitated, and

his face was flushed red. "Has it occurred to you that you're a snob?"

The insult did not seem to disturb Emma unduly, but it had a surprising effect on him. The effect was erotic, and it was all he could do to prevent himself gasping.

Emma was smiling, as if she were enjoying the affray. "Because I want something better for my friend? That makes me a snob, does it?"

He opened the door, struggling to cope with his conflicting—and disturbing—feelings. His Land Rover was outside. Emma noticed that there was mud splashed across the front of the vehicle. "You should wash your car," she said.

He shot her an injured glance, and walked out of the door. Halfway to the vehicle, he turned and called out to her. "I'm sorry. I shouldn't have lost my temper. I'm very sorry."

Emma came out of the house towards him. "And I'm sorry too. I don't want to fight with you. I really don't."

He swallowed hard. "I think sometimes you're a bit harsh on people—that's all."

"I was just trying to protect Harriet."

He stared at her. "Were you?" He answered his own question immediately. "All right, you were. I just think you're wrong about Robert Martin. Let's leave it at that."

Her relief was evident. "Yes, let's leave it at that." She smiled at him. "You know, I could wash your poor Land Rover for you. Sid has got one of those high-pressure thingies. I rather like using it. The water goes round and round in a circle, shoots out. I could get the mud off."

"Mud sticks," said Mr. Knightley.

She did not hear him. "What?"

"I said: mud sticks."

He got into the Land Rover, waved—unenthusiastically, thought Emma—and drove off. She had not felt it during their sparring, but now she felt the rawness that followed from the argument. Disagreements, even with people she knew, made her feel like that—shocked, perhaps, at the animus that can lie behind mere words. She was surprised, though, by the intensity of her dismay over the fact that George had expressed disappointment in her. Why should she care what he thought? Why should she bother if she had somehow fallen short of whatever standards he had mentally created for her? It was as if she had been *moved* in some way by the encounter, and that made her feel uneasy in a way that she neither expected nor fully understood. It was unease, yes, but it was something else, she thought—and she was not quite sure what that something else was.

Turning round, she went back into the hall. Her father was there, standing under the non-Canaletto, but looking at his daughter rather than at the painting.

"You look like a Doge, Pops," said Emma.

Mr. Woodhouse frowned. Doge? "Did you and George have some sort of disagreement?"

"A very small one," said Emma. "About nothing."

"I heard raised voices, you see. I wondered if it was Sid shouting at somebody. You know how he shouts at people sometimes."

"We weren't shouting," Emma reassured him. "We were having a heated discussion."

"About what?"

Emma shrugged. "A Chinese restaurant. Nothing important."

Mr. Woodhouse was gazing at her affectionately. "You're a very odd girl, Emma. But you're my little darling, aren't you? You're your daddy's darling, and I'm really proud of you."

"Unlike your other daughter?" teased Emma. "Unlike my *fecund* sister?"

"I'm proud of her too." The look of satisfaction faded. "Although she lives in London."

"You never know, Pops. People who live in London often come to their senses and move out. Isabella could do the same."

Mr. Woodhouse shook his head. "She won't. And all my little grandchildren will talk like cockneys. All drop their *h*'s and swallow the ends of words." He shook his head again. "So much for education."

"That's nothing to do with education, Pops. It's the culture. That's what happens. Isabella herself is losing her *h*'s. When she comes here for the weekend, I find them all over the place once she leaves. Loads of them. Dropped with utter abandon."

"You're teasing me," said Mr. Woodhouse. "These things are serious."

"You're right, Pops. Now, how about a little walk round a few of our acres? You need to take more exercise, you know. You have to keep your brain in good shape."

He crossed the hall and took her arm. "You're right. A little walk would do us both good. Although . . ." He stepped aside to allow her through the door first.

"Although what?"

"Although when it comes to the brain," he said, "we would probably be spending our time better if we sat down to a plate of smoked salmon."

"Oh come on, Pops, I thought that was an old wives' tale: fish being good for the brain and all that. It's the sort of thing you hear Mrs. Firhill saying."

Mr. Woodhouse wagged a finger at her. "She may be right, you know. Omega-three oils. Has it ever occurred to you that Mrs. Firhill might be right?"

"No," said Emma. "It hasn't." But then she thought: *Listen to me!*

She turned to face her father. He was looking at her with amusement in his eyes, but with a trace of sorrow, too, perhaps.

"No, maybe she is right."

"Mrs. Firhill?"

"Yes, maybe she is right . . . about fish . . ." She hesitated, before adding, "And other things too."

He reached out and took her hand, silently.

12

Emma had given some thought to how she might invite Philip Elton and Harriet Smith to tea at the same time without making the invitation look suspicious. She wondered whether she could persuade Harriet to join her on a small, impromptu committee to raise money for a suitable charity, and then ask Philip to address them on the relative merits of the various local charities. As a vicar, he could be expected to know all about charities, even if, as Emma suspected, he was not excessively charitable himself. That would bring the two of them together without raising Philip's suspicions; if Harriet herself suspected anything, that would not matter—her compliance, Emma thought, could be assumed: Harriet was not one, she thought, to make any sort of fuss.

Of course she had already lost one valuable opportunity for this particular piece of matchmaking. This had come at her dinner party, at which they had both been guests, but at that stage her plans for Harriet had been inchoate and the seating plan had not brought them directly together. She tried to remember whether the two of them had exchanged any words at all that evening, but she could not recall seeing them talking to each other. He must have seen her, though; no man could sit near Harriet Smith at a dinner table and fail to notice that he was in the presence of exceptional physical beauty. And if he had noticed her in that way—which he must have done—then she would not have much work to do. All that would be required of her was the facilitating of a meeting; nature, passion—call it what you will—could be expected to do the rest.

Emma decided not to bother with a pretext; she would simply invite both of them to tea, though not at exactly the same time— Harriet would be invited slightly early, so that certain ideas might be placed in her head, and then twenty minutes or so later Philip Elton would arrive. If either felt manipulated, then so be it; resentment would in due course be replaced by gratitude as each of them realised what the occasion had led to. In Philip's case this would be an introduction to a young woman far more attractive than he could normally have expected to encounter; Philip, for all his interest in Byzantine history and his good looks, was not exciting company, and his boring conversation and irritating views would limit his social opportunities. So he would be grateful, thought Emma. And then, as far as Harriet was concerned, the financial problems that so constrained her would be convincingly solved: Thailand, India, and indeed all those places in which well-funded gap years might be spent, would suddenly be open to her, along, of course, with rather better clothes—and shoes, it must be said—than she had up to now been able to afford. Many women made such a bargain and endured the consequences stoically and with good humour, putting up with tedious and opinionated men in exchange for material comfort. Emma would never do that herself, of course;

but she had no need to—she was well off; so well off, in fact, as not to require a man at all.

"Oh, I'd love to come to tea with you, Emma," enthused Harriet over the telephone. "It's just what I need. We've just said goodbye at Mrs. Goddard's to a whole lot of students and I'm feeling a bit flat."

"Off to the railway station?" said Emma. "Well, at least they'll know how to ask the way."

"Ha!" said Harriet, and then, after a short pause, added, "I hope they do. I'm a bit worried about some of them. One of them couldn't get the hang of the future tense and spoke entirely in the past. I'm really worried about him."

"It could be difficult," agreed Emma. "He probably won't get very far."

"Yes. I never really found out much about him. We had lots of conversations, but I'm not quite sure whether he was talking about things that he had done a long time ago or whether they were things that he wanted to do."

"Oh well," said Emma. "Would you like me to fetch you?"

"In your Mini Cooper?"

"Yes. I can bring that."

Harriet was excited. "Oh, that would be so nice, Emma. I've never been in a Mini Cooper."

"Well, now's your chance," said Emma, rolling her eyes at her friend's naïve enthusiasm; she was just like a ten-year-old schoolboy eager for a ride in a fast car. "I'll come over to Mrs. Goddard's at three."

"You know where it is, don't you?" said Harriet. "At that disused airfield. There's a sign that says *Hangars* and then there's one that says *Mrs. Goddard's Academy of English.* You follow that road. I live with Mrs. Goddard in the building that's labelled *Principal's House.* It used to be the officers' mess in the days when the RAF were here."

Emma looked thoughtful as she put down the phone. If she had any lingering doubts about her intervention, these were now dispelled by the thought of Harriet's current circumstances. To be living on a disused airfield—what a fate for anybody, even if it would be precisely the sort of domestic circumstances to secure a place at an ancient university. And the company . . . Presumably when the students went away, as they had just done, Harriet was left alone with Mrs. Goddard, with whom she would have to make conversation in the evening over dinner. There was no Mr. Goddard, as far as Emma knew, and she imagined the two of them sitting at the table, facing each other, searching for subjects to talk about while swallows and house martins, tiny Spitfires perhaps, dipped and swooped in the dusk about the eaves of the old officers' mess and the crumbling control tower.

The reality, it turned out, was somewhat different. When Emma arrived at the Mrs. Goddard's house, she found that the officers' mess had been painted a cheerful shade of pink, and the garden, which the officers themselves surely must have ignored, had been planted with flowering shrubs. Mrs. Goddard, who greeted Emma at the front door, was not the forbidding schoolmistress-type that Emma had imagined, but was a comfortable-looking woman—a bit overweight perhaps—dressed in what seemed to be a kimono, with her hair, which was auburn and frizzy, barely constrained by a striking head-

band. This headband, perhaps the brightest item of her clothing, featured Native American motifs and had the word *How!*
emblazoned on it.

"So," said Mrs. Goddard, as she beckoned for Emma to come
inside. "So, you're Henry's daughter."

Emma was momentarily taken aback. "Yes . . ."

"I haven't seen your dad for years," said Mrs. Goddard. "He's
gone all quiet, hasn't he?"

Emma was not sure how to respond. "He doesn't get out
much," she mumbled.

"Such a nice man," said Mrs. Goddard, shaking her head.
"Such a pity. Anyway, come in. Harriet's almost ready. She saw
your car coming up the drive and went off to get her things from
her room. Want something to drink?"

"I'm driving," said Emma.

"Oh no, not something strong. I meant elderflower. I make a
really good elderflower cordial, although I say so myself."

Emma accepted, and was left alone in what appeared to be
Mrs. Goddard's sitting room. It was comfortably furnished,
with Eastern printed throws draped over the chairs, piles of
books and magazines on the floor beside these chairs, and with
large, brightly coloured abstract paintings on the walls. It was
not what Emma had expected; and nor was Mrs. Goddard herself, who now reappeared with two glasses of cordial on a small
brass tray.

"It's delicious," said Emma as she sampled the cordial.

Mrs. Goddard smiled. "I do blackcurrant as well, but we've
run out. I make that in the autumn and hope that it lasts me until
the following year, but it often doesn't. Our students love it."

"You must miss them when they go," said Emma. "Harriet said she did."

This pleased Mrs. Goddard. "I hope they miss us too. Some of them say that they do. We get postcards from all over, and they're usually very careful with their grammar. You'd expect that, wouldn't you?"

Emma glanced about the room. "Do you teach them here?"

"Oh no," said Mrs. Goddard. "We've got a classroom block, which is near the students' accommodation. There's a language lab there, and a couple of tutorial rooms. Then we have a place for the teachers. We usually have three of them—straight out of university, in most cases. They do their Teaching English as a Foreign Language qualification and then come to us for a few months before they go off to teach English abroad. I regard them as the equivalent of the missionaries we used to send off to all sorts of places to stop the locals dancing. We don't stop anybody dancing any more, of course. A sign of great progress, don't you think?"

Emma smiled. She liked Mrs. Goddard.

"Now, of course, there are countries sending missionaries back to us," Mrs. Goddard continued. "We get people coming over from other parts of the world to reconvert the locals here. Some chance! Still, they try, I suppose, and they're usually very polite about it. They don't try to stop dancing and things like that. At least, not to begin with. They don't go up to people and say, 'Stop dancing or you'll go to Hell,' which is what I fear some of our missionaries used to say to those unfortunate South Sea Islanders. Can't you just see it? The South Sea Islanders would have been having a good dance and then along comes a missionary and says, 'Oh, stop dancing, you sinful people!' And the poor South Sea Islanders freeze in mid-step, one foot above the ground, and look at each other in dismay, and the music stops."

Mrs. Goddard took a sip of her cordial. "Of course, they believed that dancing led to other things, and it was the other things that really worried them. Dancing in itself might have been all right as far as the more liberal missionaries were concerned—as long as you didn't dance too close, but when dancing really got going, then, well, you know the consequences of that."

She looked at Emma. "We get the occasional American missionary coming to the door. They're usually very polite young men from Utah and they wear peculiar underpants. Did you know that, Emma? Those very courteous and well-behaved young men wear unusual underpants called temple garments. I've never seen them, of course, because those young men are quite unlike our own youths who wear their underpants half outside their trousers. You'll have noticed that—who could miss it?—those young men with their underpants showing. They aren't even builders. Builders are *entitled* to wear visible underpants; it goes with the job. Perhaps that's the great service the American missionaries could do us. Rather than converting us to anything, they could get our young men to tuck their underpants back inside, where they should be. That would be a great achievement, and we'd all be so grateful to them for doing it."

Harriet came into the room. She smiled at Emma. "I'm so glad you two have met," she said.

"So am I," said Mrs. Goddard. And then, to Emma, "You must come and have supper with us some day. I'll make a special cake."

Emma noticed that this invitation caused Harriet to give Mrs. Goddard what appeared to be a warning look.

"Emma is very busy," said Harriet. "She has a lot to do, Mrs. God."

"Oh well, some day," said Mrs. Goddard. "Now you two should go off and enjoy yourselves."

In the car on the way out of the disused airfield, Emma remarked to Harriet that she very much liked Mrs. Goddard. "She's not at all as I imagined her," she said. "To be called Mrs. Goddard and to have an English Language school conjures up a very different image." She paused. "And I heard you call her Mrs. God."

"That's short for Goddard," said Harriet.

"I see." Emma bit her lip. "It's just that it sounds a bit odd. I read somewhere or other about a man who heard a massive peel of thunder above him and said—he was a bit camp—'Oh, there goes Miss God up to her tricks again!' And just as he said it, there was a massive bolt of lightning and he was struck down dead."

"What a terrible thing," said Harriet. "But I'm not being in any way disrespectful. I'd never laugh at God."

"No," said Emma. "Why risk it?"

"She's very kind," said Harriet. "She was my mother's best friend. She's the only friend of my parents I know."

"That's sad," said Emma.

"Yes, maybe. But she makes up for it."

"And Mr. Goddard?" asked Emma.

"I never met him," replied Harriet. "I wish I had. All she ever said to me about him was 'I gave my husband his freedom.' That's what she said."

Emma was intrigued. "I wonder what that means."

"I asked," said Harriet. "And all she replied was 'Existential freedom.' I didn't understand, I'm afraid."

Emma referred to the invitation to supper. "You seemed worried about that. Do you mind my asking why?"

Harriet hesitated before answering. "It's the cake," she said eventually. "I don't think she should go round offering her cake to people. I've told her that before."

They had reached the end of the airfield road and Emma turned the Mini Cooper on to the main road back to Highbury. "What's wrong with her cake?"

Harriet looked out of the window. "She puts something in it," she muttered.

"Oh," said Emma.

When visitors came to Hartfield, Mr. Woodhouse would usually entertain them in his library—a large, untidy room on the north side of the house—while Emma would see her guests either in the kitchen or in the small sitting room she had taken over when she had left university. This room had been her mother's, and had been kept almost as a shrine to the late Mrs. Woodhouse, as people do when they cannot find the heart to change a room that had been used by somebody who has grown up and gone away, or died. Emma and Isabella had understood this, and as children had rarely entered the room that to them was one of the few reminders that they had of their mother. Now, however, Emma had begun to use it, and had slowly begun to stamp her own personality on the room. The shelves were beginning to fill with her books; the small writing desk by the window had started to be covered with her laptop and papers—such as they were. A sketchbook lay opened on the sofa table.

"I didn't know you drew," exclaimed Harriet. "May I take a look?"

Emma put down the teapot and made a careless gesture of dismissal. "I'm hopeless," she said. "I wish I could draw better."

Harriet repeated her question. "May I look?"

"Of course. But, as I say, I'm useless."

Harriet turned the pages of the sketchbook with almost reverential care. "They're very good," she said. "You're not useless at all. They're fantastic."

Emma came to Harriet's side and looked over her shoulder. "I went to drawing classes in Bath," she said. "For about two years. They encouraged us if we were doing the design course. I suppose you need to be able to sketch out your design ideas and it helps if you can draw."

"Which you obviously can," said Harriet, gazing in admiration at a watercolour still life in which ink had been used for emphasis. "I like that combination of watercolour and ink. It's very delicate."

"Yes," said Emma. "Ink by itself is really hard. You can't shade with it. But it goes well with watercolours."

Harriet turned a page. "Who's he?" she asked, pointing to a pencil sketch of a young man seated in a kitchen.

"That's Mark," said Emma. "He was my friend's boyfriend."

"He looks nice," said Harriet. "He's got big eyes. I like people with big eyes."

Emma smiled. "What big eyes you've got, Grandma."

"What?"

"I was just thinking about Little Red Riding Hood," said

Emma. "You know how the wolf's dressed in Grandma's clothes and Little Red Riding Hood sees his great sharp teeth . . . All the better to *eat* you with, my dear!"

Harriet gave a shiver. "Don't!" she said. "I get scared really easily, Emma."

"All right," said Emma. "No nursery rhymes. Most of them are pretty scary, aren't they? They're all about cruelty. Miss Taylor used to read to us from a book called *Struwwelpeter*. Did you ever come across it?"

Harriet put down the sketchbook and took her cup of tea from Emma. "No, I don't think so."

"If you think that Little Red Riding Hood was scary, you should look at *Struwwelpeter*. There's the story of a little boy who sucked his thumb and had it chopped off by the Suck-a-Thumb Man. He had a large pair of tailor's scissors and he cut off children's thumbs. The picture showed the blood."

Harriet shuddered. "I'm glad I never read that."

"In fact," Emma continued, keeping her gaze on Harriet, "I read somewhere that the story of the Suck-a-Thumb Man is really all about castration. Little boys understand that, even though it's never spelled out to them; little girls don't. They think it's about thumbs."

Harriet shuddered again. "Oh," she said.

They sat down with their tea. Emma looked at Harriet across the rim of her cup. *Botticelli*, she thought. *She's exactly like one of those women in his* Spring *painting. Or is she Venus herself, floating on her shell?* She would draw Harriet. She had to.

Harriet had said something that Emma did not catch because she was thinking about Botticelli. "What?"

"I was wondering about when you were going to start your practice? Remember? You told me that you were going to do design or decoration, or whatever you call it."

"In the autumn," said Emma. "I'm working on a website. I'm going to get those sample books—fabrics and wallpapers and so on. There's quite a lot to do."

"You're so brave," said Harriet. "Starting your own business is really brave."

Emma shrugged. "There's not much risk for me," she said. "I'm lucky. I've got somewhere to live and Pops pays the bills."

"That's really lucky," said Harriet.

Emma was studying her friend. Had it occurred to her, she wondered, that she might find herself in a similar position?

"It's quite hard for us these days," she said. "We have to—"

Harriet interrupted her. "We?"

"Us girls. Women. We have to work. Guys have always had to do that, I suppose, but now it applies to us too. Unless one's, well, unless one's lucky."

"You mean unless you get married?"

Emma shook her head. "Oh, it's not that simple. Most women have to run the house, look after the kids, *and* work."

"I know," said Harriet. "It's really unfair."

Emma laughed. "Fairness doesn't come into it, Harriet. The world has never been fair. It wasn't fair when women couldn't work, back in the old days. Then you had to get married or you were done for. You ended up being a domestic worker of some sort—a kitchen maid or something like that. If you came from a middle-class background you could be a governess or a lady's companion perhaps. It was harsh." She thought of Miss Taylor. She had never asked her why she had become a governess; it had always struck her as simply being Miss Taylor's destiny, in the way in which so many people just seem destined to do what they do or to be what they are. She was destined to be Emma; her father was destined to be Pops—poor, worrying, generous Pops; Sid was destined to be Sid, with his rotavator and his trailer that he used to cart firewood and manure about the place.

"Well, it's better now," said Harriet. "We have choices."

Emma looked doubtful. "Have we? Such as?"

"We can do the jobs we want to do. We can qualify to do various things. We can have a career."

Emma conceded grudgingly. "Maybe," she said. "That may be true—to an extent. But there's one choice you've left out."

Harriet waited for her.

"You've left out the possibility of leaving it all up to men."

"What do you mean by that?"

Emma looked out of the window. The thought had occurred to her that she should not interfere, but it was only a passing notion, and was discarded. "I mean that one can let men pay the bills." She paused. Harriet was listening. "You can still find men who are prepared to look after women. There are still a few women who don't have to work."

"They stay at home? Men do the work?"

Emma shrugged. "That's a simple way of putting it. You could say that it's an exchange. Men might have the money. Women exchange their . . . their friendship for practical support. They look after the men emotionally. They cook for them and so on. In return, men worry about the bills. Don't you think that sounds like a fair exchange?"

Harriet did not require much time to think. "I do," she said.

"It's not as if you're committed to the man forever," said Emma. "Men can be a temporary fix." She smiled, and noticed that Harriet smiled too. "They don't mind, of course. Everybody knows where they stand."

She was suddenly aware that she had lost Harriet's attention. The other young woman was looking out of the window.

Emma followed her gaze. A woman in blue dungarees was digging in a flowerbed. "That's Mrs. Sid," said Emma. "She's the one who does the garden for us. She's really good with flowers—she knows all the botanical names. I can't remember them. They go in one ear and out the other."

"She looks strong," said Harriet.

"She is. She's very nice too. She's married to Sid. He's a sweetie; he works on the farm."

Harriet watched as the gardener tossed weeds into a trug. "What's her name?" she asked.

Emma frowned. "I'm not sure. I suppose she's got one. We just call her Mrs. Sid because she's married to Sid. She doesn't mind. We've always called her that." She paused. "Mrs. Firhill's called Betty. I know that. Betty Firhill—not that I'd ever dream of such familiarity. She'd faint if I called her Betty—and so would I. Both of us would be out stone cold."

Harriet had noticed something else. "There's somebody coming up the drive. There's a car."

Emma affected surprise. "Is there? Oh, that's Philip Elton's car. It's a BMW Something-something. I don't know exactly what, but it's very expensive."

Harriet smiled. "But I thought he was the vicar."

"Only part-time. And he's a sort of voluntary vicar. They call them non-stipendiary or something like that. It means that he doesn't get paid."

"But he's young. So how can he afford a BMW Something-something if they don't pay him?"

Emma explained about the office block in Ipswich and the flats in Norwich. Then she added, "He's quite well off." And then, "He's not too bad, actually. If you don't mind him going on about Byzantium, he can be quite nice."

She realised that Harriet did not know where Byzantium was. And then she realised that, witty and well informed though she was, she was a bit hazy on the subject herself. Justinian, Constantinople, and . . . and . . .

The truth of the matter was that Philip Elton, although relatively well off, was not nearly as wealthy as people generally believed. He did indeed own an office block in Ipswich, and he owned it outright, just as he owned the portfolio of flats in Norwich. These properties brought him rents, but they were nowhere near as large as those imagined by Emma, and were offset by expenses that sometimes made him wonder whether he would not be better off disposing of the properties altogether.

The problem with the office block was that throughout the first thirty years of the building's existence, very little maintenance had been done on it. Had the block been well built in the first place, that lack of maintenance might not have been too serious, but the original design and construction had been typical of the shoddy standards of the time, with the result that the external concrete panels of the building had been penetrated by water, rendering the cladding unsound. Here and there sections of this cladding had already fallen off, disclosing patches of damp and unsightly wall. This gave the building a neglected look that discouraged tenants; who would want business customers to see them in such shabby premises? As rents plummeted, it became increasingly uneconomic to spend money on repairs, and rents declined even further—a vicious cycle into which rental properties can so very easily fall. Tenants seemed to be unwilling to sign leases for longer than six months, hoping that as their business fortunes improved they would be able to move to more impressive and salubrious offices. No number of assurances by Philip seemed to convince his tenants that remedial work would be done, even when these assertions came in clerical garb. "Sorry, vicar," one of the tenants replied, "I wouldn't accuse you of actually lying—you being a man of the cloth and all that—but I just don't believe you."

The problem with the flats in Norfolk was not dissimilar. Although these were in a respectable enough part of the city, they too had been built at a time when the authorities were keen to encourage new construction and were ready to turn a blind eye to the activities of builders who promised to complete projects quickly. The Norfolk flats looked all right from the outside, but were very badly insulated. As a result, their tenants had to spend considerable sums to heat rooms whose warmth immediately escaped through ill-fitting windows and thin walls.

Philip had commissioned a report on the problem from a firm of surveyors, and this made sombre reading. The cost of insulating each flat to contemporary standards was estimated to be at least fifteen thousand pounds, and although there would be some assistance from the local council, most of the money would have to come from the owner's pocket. Once again, the deficiency in the properties depressed rents.

The office block and the flats were not the only assets that Philip possessed, but they made up a large portion of his wealth. Unless he could find about five hundred thousands pounds for the necessary repairs, his property would simply diminish in value until eventually it became worthless. That concentrated his mind. The easiest way of getting money, he decided, was to marry it. That had been done by one of his university friends, who had married the daughter of a transport magnate and now lived in Monaco. Philip heard from him from time to time and was regaled with stories of his sybaritic existence. "Getting married," he wrote, "was the most intelligent move I ever made. I am now blissfully happy, and, incidentally, rich. I thoroughly recommend it. Both states are highly desirable."

Philip did not think there would be any difficulty in finding a suitable candidate. He had a very clear idea of his own good looks—he had always been aware that women found him attractive, and he had simply accepted it as his due. He was not particularly interested in the opposite sex, although he was far from being a misogynist. People in general did not interest him a great deal, except for himself, perhaps, a subject of considerable fascination to Philip.

He did not think that his life would have to change very much were he to get married. He could continue to do exactly what he was currently doing—working on his thesis on Byzantine History—while his wife, whoever she turned out to be, could run the home, cook, and generally look after him. All that was required of her was that she bring with her a suitable dowry—not that anybody called it that any more—and, if at all possible, a good-sized house.

Such as Hartfield.

Now, having had the front door opened for him by Mrs. Firhill, he stood in the hall and looked about him with new eyes. He had been privately dismissive of the paintings on previous visits, but having made a decision as to his future, the contents of the house seemed to be of considerably greater interest. Philip was, in fact, rather well informed about art; he was a regular visitor to the Wallace Collection and the Royal Academy in London, and occasionally paged through the catalogues of the auction houses when an interesting sale was in the offing. He owned few pictures of note himself, other than a small preliminary sketch of Tobias and the Angel by Stanley Spencer and an indifferent Romney portrait of a young boy reading a book; now, looking about him in the hall, he saw that he had perhaps been wrong to dismiss the Woodhouse paintings as being little more than what one would expect in a unexceptional English country house. He knew that the non-Canaletto was merely by a "follower of" an obscure Venetian painter who himself was never more than "circle of" anyone better, so that it was worth, at the most, twelve thousand pounds, but he had no idea that the rather reticent watercolour on the opposite wall was a Nash and that next to it was what appeared to all intents and purposes to be a Ravilious.

"Nice pictures," said Mrs. Firhill. "They attract the dust no end, though."

"Hah!" said Philip. "Dust is no respecter of art, is it, Mrs. Firhill? No, I don't think it is."

Mrs. Firhill shot him a sideways glance. She had always disliked him, and she would never go to his services on Sundays. Never. He was far too young and far too opinionated for her. And if she died, she hoped that this would happen while she was somewhere else so that Philip would not have the privilege of burying her.

"You'll find Mr. Woodhouse in his library," she said curtly, giving a toss of the head in the direction of the library corridor. "That's where he always is."

"Actually," said Philip, "I've come to see Miss Woodhouse. She's invited me for tea."

Mrs. Firhill pointed down the other corridor. "She's down there in her sitting room."

"I know the way," said Philip, looking down the broad corridor that led to Emma's room. *Once I'm established here,* he thought, *that old bat will go.* "Thank you so much. And I hope we'll see you in church one day."

"Maybe," said Mrs. Firhill in the tone of one who rather doubted it.

"Oh well," he said. "I would never force anybody to listen to any of *my* sermons."

"Not in a free country," Mrs. Firhill mumbled.

He kept his tone light. "Well, yes, I suppose it is a free country. Not that our dear government isn't seeking to limit such freedoms as we currently enjoy."

"There are too many freedoms," said Mrs. Firhill. "Some people think they can do exactly as they please."

Philip wagged his finger at her in mock disapproval. "Tut, tut! Mrs. Firhill! Charity. Charity." And he thought: *Old bag.*

He began to make his way down the corridor, but stopped after a few paces. The corridor was not particularly light, and this, he thought, was why he must have missed it. How otherwise could he have walked past a Stubbs?

He peered at the painting. The subject matter was right: a racehorse beginning its exercise on the downs; trees in full leaf; a sky of stacked cumulus cloud. And there, helpfully placed beneath the painting, the attribution etched into a small brass plate: *Stubbs, Morning Gallop.*

Philip drew in his breath. A Stubbs of this size could be worth at least two million, possibly much more. One had sold at auction recently for over twelve million pounds; he had seen a picture of the painting in the newspapers and read about the attempts to keep it in the country. The Australians had wanted that one, and presumably would jump at this painting too. For a brief moment he allowed himself to imagine his interview: "I'm keen to keep this in the country, I really am, and I'll do whatever I can to ensure this result." He would be credited with saving the picture by allowing the National Gallery to purchase it at reduced price. "What's the difference of a million or two when the nation's artistic patrimony is at stake?" And they would say: "It's difficult to find the words to express our gratitude—it really is."

"It's nothing," he would say. "Nothing at all. Such a small gesture."

"But so well targeted."

"Oh well, one does what one can." Of course one only does that sort thing *after* one has improved the insulation of one's rental properties. "I can't have people being cold, you know."

Philip's train of thought was interrupted by the sound of high-pitched laughter from behind the closed door of Emma's sitting room. He stepped forward and knocked.

"Philip!" exclaimed Emma. "You're just in time. I was eyeing the last scone and struggling with temptation."

He was gracious. "Such temptations should never be resisted," he said, smiling first at Emma and then at Harriet. "And if one falls, then there is no need for regret."

"Such an unusual thing for a clergyman to say," said Emma. "But then you're non-stipendiary."

Philip gave a short laugh. "That makes no difference. Holy orders are holy orders."

Emma gestured for him to sit down next to Harriet on the sofa. As he did so, he noticed the sketchbook.

"I'd forgotten that you enjoyed drawing," he said. "I'd give anything to be able to draw and paint. But some of us, alas, lack talent."

"I'm not much good," said Emma. "But I enjoy it. The important thing is—"

"She's really good," interjected Harriet.

"I'm sure she is," agreed Philip.

"I'm thinking of doing more portraits," said Emma. "If I could only find a suitable subject." She glanced at Harriet, who looked down at the floor.

Nobody spoke.

"Harriet," said Emma brightly. "I could do your portrait. How about it?"

Harriet opened her mouth to say something—to demur, but it was Philip who spoke. "That would be a most wonderful thing," he said. "A portrait of Harriet Smith by Emma Wood-house! What a picture that would be! I'd love to see it."

"I don't know," said Harriet. "I'm not all that good at sitting still."

"Nonsense," said Emma. "And the artist doesn't expect the subject to sit completely still. A portrait is not a still life."

"Exactly," said Philip. "A portrait should never be . . . be . . ." He struggled to find the right word.

"Static," said Emma.

Philip flashed another smile at her. *There is something on one of his front teeth*, Emma thought. *A piece of spinach? Spinach often gets stuck on one's teeth.* She gave an involuntary shudder.

"If you really wanted to," said Harriet. "I could sit if you really wanted to."

"Then that's arranged," said Emma. "And you, Philip, will be the first person to see the sketch. I'll even lend it to you, if you like."

"It will be an honour," said Philip.

"Of course it will be difficult to capture Harriet's looks," said Emma. "It's never easy to capture beauty."

Harriet squirmed with embarrassment. "Oh really!"

"No," said Philip. "Emma's right. It will be *very* difficult to capture Harriet's quite exceptional looks on paper. No pencil, no pastel, no paint would ever be up to the job."

The broad smile that he now directed at Harriet was intercepted by Emma. It was clear to her now that he was smitten—just as she had thought he would be.

"I'll do my best," Emma said modestly.

"Which is all that any of us can do," said Philip. "In your case, though, your best will undoubtedly be quite exceptional. Royal Academy standard, I'd say."

After her guests had left, Emma picked up her sketchbook and paged through it thoughtfully. Harriet had agreed to do a sitting the following day, but she had yet to decide what the backdrop would be.

"I don't want it to be too formal," Harriet had said.

Emma agreed. "No, of course not. Something natural."

"Oh, natural . . . yes."

Emma smiled; to be making a risqué suggestion without even realising one was doing so! *Au naturel.* It was Harriet her-self who had made the suggestion, and there might well be a case for a nude study. What could be more natural than that? But she was not quite sure how to propose it, and she was not sure whether her friend would agree.

"But you suggested it yourself," she would claim.

And Harriet would look at her with that slightly confused look that was at once so irritating and so utterly appealing.

13

It was about this time that Jane Fairfax came to stay with her aunt, the unfortunate Miss Bates, and her grandmother, the even more unfortunate Mrs. Bates. The two Bateses lived in the centre of the village, in circumstances that were cramped both physically and financially. It was widely believed that both of them had suffered a serious financial loss at more or less the same time—a loss that obliged them to exchange a comfortable existence for an uncertain life of near-indigence. The financial loss was said to have come about when they had both been persuaded by a helpful relative to become Lloyd's Names—private backers of insurance syndicates who, in return for standing behind the contracts, took a share of the often very considerable profits. They did this and prospered considerably in the first year of the investment, only to be rudely reminded the following year of the unlimited personal liability that the system entailed should claims paid out exceed premiums paid in. Re-insurance could take the sting out of most losses, but occasionally events just became too much, and the Names had to make good the deficit. People said that the loss of a ship off the Horn of Africa, closely followed by the grounding of a tanker on a reef off Kochi, consumed most of Mrs. Bates's capital. A series of destructive storms in Taiwan and Japan did the same for her daughter's.

The response of Mrs. Bates to this change in her fortunes was to more or less lose the power of speech. From being an enthusiastic conversationalist, she withdrew into a world of brooding silence, rarely opening her mouth other than to make occasional requests of her daughter. Miss Bates may have been upset by what had happened, but did not appear as traumatised as her mother. She had always been optimistic and cheerful, and continued to be so, very rarely, if ever, referring to their reduced circumstances, and bearing the indignities of genteel poverty—turned blouse collars, for instance—with remarkable fortitude.

Jane Fairfax's own circumstances were similarly straitened. She was an orphan, and her misfortune was therefore twice that of Emma or Frank Churchill, both of whom had lost only one parent. She had, however, been supported by a generous and understanding family, the Campbells, who had made it their business to ensure that she was given a good general education and, most importantly, piano lessons. That, however, was all that they could provide, and Jane was every bit as hard up as Harriet Smith—more so, perhaps, as, unlike Harriet, she had not been working. Teaching English as a foreign language was her destiny too, it seemed, and she would be looking for a suitable job doing that at the end of the summer.

Emma had not met Jane Fairfax before, but had heard a great deal about her from Jane's aunt. Miss Bates would talk on any topic with an equal degree of pleasure, but when it came to the subject of Jane her enthusiasm seemed to know no bounds.

There were no limits, it appeared, to Jane's talents, and her musical ability, in particular, had always been prodigious. "I'm not saying she's Mozart," Miss Bates gushed. "I'm not saying that at all."

But you are, thought Emma. *That's just what you're saying.*

"Put it this way," Miss Bates continued. "She has just the sort of ear that Mozart had. And it's the ear, you know, that counts." Miss Bates said this to Emma without any intention of implying that Emma could never approach Jane's level of accomplishment, but that was the way that Emma, and those who overheard the comment, understood her remark.

"And do you know something?" Miss Bates continued. "She's the most amazing cook! Yes, our Jane. As you know, Mother and I are simple eaters and pick at our food."

Except when you come to dinner with us, thought Emma. *Then you make up for it.*

"She's one of those *artistic* cooks," continued Miss Bates. "She transforms a plate—positively transforms it. And it's not just the look of the food that's so wonderful—those dribbles of sauce and so on—it's the flavours too. My dear, the flavours! Do you like truffle oil? I certainly do, although Mother's a bit suspicious of it—she says that it smells a bit like the socks that she wore at school. I know what she means, although we had nylon, which isn't terribly comfortable but doesn't smell quite as bad, although I think it's something to do with the sort of skin you have. But Jane works wonders with it. She takes the tiniest slice of truffle—a fragment, really—and uses it to infuse olive oil with the most delicate perfume. I can't imagine where she got this from because I gather that Mrs. Campbell keeps a very simple kitchen, just as Mother and I do."

"Perhaps she went on a course," offered Emma. "Or maybe she spends a lot of time watching those cookery programmes on television. Some people watch an awful lot of those, I think."

If there was any criticism here of those who watched too much cookery television—which there was—it was lost on Miss Bates. "Oh, I think she's *been* on one of those," she said. "There was some sort of competition, and Jane won, not surprisingly, I suppose. Mother and I watched her on television. 'There's Jane,' I shouted out, because Jane was far too modest to warn us she would be on. 'There's Jane, Mother!' And Mother, who's a bit short-sighted at the best of times, tried terribly hard to see Jane, but I think was confused by all those lights on the set—studio lights are so bright. It must be as hot as the Sahara in there, with all those bulbs. Poor Mother thought that one of the cooking pots was Jane, and although one may laugh about it now, I suppose it was a mistake that was made easily enough, with all that glare and the shape of the human head—not Jane's in particular, but of all heads—being not all that dissimilar to a cooking pot."

There had been many such conversations, and on several occasions Emma had had to bite her tongue to avoid giving voice to her thoughts about the remarkable Jane Fairfax. If she was so talented, she asked herself, then what was she doing spending three months of summer cooped up with aged relatives in a two-bedroom cottage in Highbury? Why was she not in London, or even New York, impressing people there with her musical and culinary skills? And if she was as brilliant academically as Miss Bates claimed—"Jane has not thought it necessary to do any A levels," her aunt had boasted. "She is well

beyond them, you know"—then why were universities not falling over themselves to offer her a place, fully funded of course?
No, thought Emma, *this Jane Fairfax is impossible—she simply*
cannot be.

It was not until Jane had been in Highbury for several days
that Emma decided that the time was right to pay Miss Bates a
visit. It was not the aunt she wished to see, of course, but the
niece, the news of whose arrival had quickly spread through
the surrounding area.

It was Miss Taylor who told Emma of Jane's arrival. "I met
her," she said as she stopped to speak to Emma in the High
Street. "It was a brief meeting, but . . ."

Emma was impatient for news. "Tell all," she urged.
"Everything."

Miss Taylor watched her. She knew Emma. "She's fairly
attractive," she said. "Dark hair. High cheekbones. A bit exotic—
in a refined sort of way."

"Oh," said Emma. Her curiosity was now more aroused than
ever. This Jane Fairfax, with her high cheekbones, might liven
Highbury up a bit.

"But she has a rather—how shall I put it?—a rather yearning
look to her."

Emma's eyes widened. "I wonder what she's yearning after.
Or who." She remembered that she was in the presence of her
governess, for whom grammar mattered. "Or even whom. Or
do you think one can just yearn in general, without any particular object for your yearning?"

Miss Taylor smiled at the thought. "Possibly. Perhaps she's
had some disappointment—or more than one."

"Perhaps," said Emma. "It must be fairly disappointing being Miss Bates's niece, poor girl. One might feel that one could have been allocated a more exciting aunt in life."

"I'm sure that she's very fond of her aunt—and her grandmother."

"Possibly."

"Not possibly," said Miss Taylor firmly. "Highly likely." She paused. "It's useful to remember that it's only a matter of chance that we are who we are, you know. You could be Jane Fairfax, for instance. You're not, as it happens, but that's only a matter of the purest chance. We do not choose the bed we are born in."

Emma said nothing. Now Miss Taylor seemed to relent, and softened. "There's something else," she said.

With the argument about genetic chance out of the way, an almost conspiratorial tone—the sort of tone that accompanies the revealing of sensitive or surprising information—crept into the conversation.

"Yesterday," began Miss Taylor. "Yesterday afternoon, to be precise, a van drew up outside Miss Bates's cottage."

"Her things?" suggested Emma. "Jane's impedimenta?"

They both smiled. *Impedimenta* was a word that Miss Taylor had taught Emma and Isabella when they were very small. *The playroom is littered with your impedimenta. Please tidy it.* They had loved the sound of it, and had named a kitten "Impedimenta."

"No," said Miss Taylor. "Not her impedimenta. I imagine that she has not brought a great amount of impedimenta with her—there wouldn't be room in the cottage. No, it was a piano."

Emma's eyes widened. "They've got hold of a piano just because she's coming to stay?"

Miss Taylor shook her head. "No. That's what I thought to begin with. But then I happened to meet Miss Bates in the greengrocer's the following day and I asked her about it. She said that it was a gift that somebody had sent to Jane. That was all. I asked her who had sent it, but she just ignored my question—you know how she can be when she's prattling away about something. She went straight off the subject and started talking about growing kiwi fruit in Cornwall or some other such nonsense."

"What sort of piano was it?" asked Emma.

"A Yamaha," answered Miss Taylor. "I saw it because I was walking past just as the men were unloading it. Two young men covered in tattoos. They brought it out on a sort of trolley thing—pianos can be terribly heavy, even for those with tattoos. It was a spanking new Yamaha."

"A Yamaha," muttered Emma. "Upright?"

"They'd never get a grand in that place," said Miss Taylor. "Not even a baby grand."

"It doesn't really matter," said Emma. "A new Yamaha will sound really good. They do. It's a bright sound, quite different from my old Collard and Collard."

"There is nothing wrong with English pianos," said Miss Taylor. "They are reticent for a reason—just like the English themselves. But the crucial question we might ask ourselves is this: Who would have bought Jane Fairfax a piano?"

It was the crucial question, and it hung in the air for almost a minute, as crucial questions can do, defeating both Miss Taylor and Emma. Of all the things that one might buy for another, a piano was perhaps the least obvious.

Miss Taylor finally had a suggestion; at least one possibility could be eliminated. "Those people who've been looking after her? What's their name again? The Campbells? Are they the sort to buy pianos? As gifts? No, I suspect that they're the sort of people who have never bought anybody a piano."

Emma agreed; the Campbells sounded very *solid* to her. "Maybe she has a man. A sugar daddy—the kind of man who goes around buying young women pianos." She paused. "One reads about such things. And isn't there a song? 'Have a piano, m'dear, m'dear . . .'"

"Pianos, Madeira . . . it all comes down to the same thing, doesn't it?" said Miss Taylor. "But I don't think we should pre-sume anything about sugar daddies."

"Why not?" asked Emma. "If it's a reasonable presumption, then why shouldn't we presume it?"

"Because it's uncharitable," said Miss Taylor.

"Does charity require one to close one's eyes to the obvi-ous?" challenged Emma.

"Maybe," said Miss Taylor.

Miss Bates greeted Emma warmly. "I must say," she enthused, "it's so nice to see you again, Emma. I love it when you pop in like this, even if, as happens to be the case, I haven't a crumb to offer you. I baked some scones yesterday and there were at least seven in the tin but now . . . It's Mother, I'm afraid; when she sees a cheese scone, something comes over her and she doesn't seem to be able to control herself. She becomes like a woman possessed; like a wild beast, I might go so far as to say. So there are no scones, I'm afraid. Not one."

"Please, Miss Bates," said Emma. "I haven't come for scones. I've come to see you. Scones were the last things on my mind."

Miss Bates looked pleased. "Well, that's nice to hear. And I must say, I always love having a chat, and today, well, today, I have a special surprise for you."

From within the house, from beyond the door that led from the small hallway into the cottage's sitting room, Emma heard the sound of a piano. She knew what to say. "The radio's on," she said. "Classic FM?"

Miss Bates gave a shriek of laughter. "Classic FM! Oh, Jane will be very tickled by that when I tell her. Mind you, it's not surprising that you should mistake her playing for the radio." She paused to take breath before continuing. "No, my niece, Jane—I believe I've told you about her."

"Many times," said Emma.

"Well, Jane is here with us now for a whole three months. Three months! Mother and I are deliriously happy at the thought of all that time with her. We have such plans for the things we'll do together. We might even go to London for the day—well, Mother obviously can't go to London, but Jane and I could. We thought that we might give Mother one of her sleeping pills in the morning rather than the evening so she will sleep all the time while we're away and won't be anxious. Perhaps two pills would be better, just to make sure."

Emma wanted to laugh at the thought of Miss Bates drugging her mother, but controlled herself. "I didn't realise you had a piano, Miss Bates," she said. "And it sounds lovely."

"It's Jane's piano," said Miss Bates. "Neither Mother nor I play."

"So she brought it with her?"

Miss Bates hesitated. "Not exactly. The piano arrived a day or two after she did. She's been playing a great deal since then—not that she has to practise very much, of course. I must say that I—"

Emma cut her off. "So she bought the piano recently?"

Miss Bates blinked. "It's a Yamaha. Do you know that sort? I thought that Yamahas were motorbikes, but apparently they're pianos as well. They're very ingenious people, the Japanese. It's remarkable how they manage to make pianos and motorbikes in the same factory, isn't it? I do hope they don't get them mixed up from time to time—it would only be human, after all, to put some of the wrong parts in the wrong place. Good heavens, I've done it myself in the kitchen often enough. Do you know *The Mikado*, Miss Woodhouse? I love Gilbert and Sullivan and *The Mikado* is one of my absolute favourites. I was in a school production of it, you know—I was Yum-Yum, who, as you'll know, was engaged to Ko-Ko. It's such a colourful operetta, I think, and I also believe it teaches us so much about Japan. Perhaps Jane will play us some *Mikado* on her Yamaha, which will be very appropriate, don't you think?"

"Where did she get it?" asked Emma quickly. "Where?"

Miss Bates closed her eyes again. It was as if she had not heard the question. "I think we should go through to see Jane now," she said. "Don't you?"

Emma, realising she would never get Miss Bates to address the issue, said that she was very much looking forward to meeting Jane. Miss Bates smiled conspiratorially, and moved towards the sitting-room door. Knocking gently, but not waiting for a reply, she pushed it open.

Emma saw Jane seated at the piano, an album of music before her on the stand. As the door opened, Jane stopped playing mid-phrase and turned round on the stool.

"Look who's come to see you," said Miss Bates triumphantly. "Emma Woodhouse herself!"

Emma moved forward to greet Jane. "I didn't want to stop you playing the piano," she said. "You're very good." Then she added, "I'm Emma."

Jane blushed. "Oh no, I'm not all that good. I'm hopeless."

"No," exclaimed Miss Bates. "You are *not* hopeless, Jane. You are very, very good. Emma here thought that it was Classic FM playing. She really did; didn't you, Emma? Your very words: Classic FM."

Emma could not miss Jane's embarrassment. "I'm sure you're good enough for that," she said.

Jane now stood up and Emma, in a single, lingering glance, took in the new arrival. She was about her own height, but with a more boyish figure. She was wearing a pair of blue denim jeans and a creased white linen top of the sort sold in ethnic clothing stores. There were heavy silver bangles on her right wrist—Indian, thought Emma. And as far as her manner was concerned, there was a reserve about her, she felt; a slightly distant air. Was that the yearning that Miss Taylor had mentioned?

Miss Bates suggested tea. "Mother has eaten all the scones," she said to Jane. "We're going to have to start hiding them."

"My grandmother loves cheese scones," Jane explained to Emma. "Sorry about that."

"I don't mind," said Emma, and then, casually, "I love your

new piano. I'm a little bit envious. In fact I'm green with envy. Deep green."

Jane put a finger on one of the keys. "It has a lovely tone."

"We've got an ancient Collard and Collard," said Emma. "It stays in tune for ages, but it's a lot quieter than your Yamaha."

"I'm sure it's very nice," said Jane.

Emma stepped forward to touch the wood of the casing. "I don't know how they get this deep shine on these things. It's lovely."

"Yes," said Jane.

"Where did you buy it?" Emma asked. "Do you mind my asking?"

She noticed that Jane exchanged a glance with her aunt before she answered. "It was a present," she said.

"A present! That's wonderful. I wish somebody would give *me* a present of a piano."

Jane smiled. "Perhaps they will."

"I doubt it," said Emma. Then, after a few moments' hesitation, she continued, "A pretty generous friend."

Jane reached forward to close the lid on the keyboard. "Yes, it was very generous."

Emma laughed. "Where does one find a friend like that, I wonder?"

Jane said nothing.

Emma laughed again. "Maybe you could introduce us. My piano is so old."

Jane hesitated. She had been looking away from Emma, but now she met her gaze. "It's actually very strange," she said quietly. "I don't know who gave it to me. It was . . . how would you describe it? An anonymous gift, I suppose." She paused. "Look, I'll go and make the tea."

"I'll do that, dear," offered Miss Bates.

"No, let me," Jane insisted.

Emma could tell that Jane wished to avoid any further discussion of the piano, and wondered whether she had been too insistent. But it was perfectly reasonable, she thought, to be interested in the source of another's good fortune. That was not nosiness—it was sympathy, and that was a very different thing, and nothing to reproach oneself over.

Emma sat and listened to Miss Bates while Jane was out of the room, although she did not bother to follow closely the twists and turns of what was said. When Jane came back into the room, Miss Bates was talking about cochineal beetles, although Emma had no idea how that subject had arisen.

"The interesting thing, Emma," said Miss Bates, "is that it was the Aztecs who developed cochineal cultivation. They were the ones who raised beetles on cactuses. That's how the Spaniards got hold of the cochineal for their lovely red dyes. Red dye, you see, was frightfully expensive, which is why red was associated with power. Cardinals wore it. Kings and princes. Charles V of Spain loved it—absolutely loved it—although he had that ridiculous Hapsburg jaw. Apparently he had great difficulty keeping his mouth shut because his jaw was so heavy, poor man."

"Some people do find that difficult," muttered Emma.

"What? Having a heavy jaw? Oh yes, these hereditary things can be so difficult. Or they can be good, if it's a good trait being passed on—like memory. Mountbatten had an amazing memory apparently, and I think Her Majesty herself is pretty good at remembering things. She has all those prime ministers to remember—all those different countries—and she remembers them all apparently. Can you believe it? She talks to all those people and never loses her temper with them, when most of us would be tempted to say, 'Oh, do shut up.' I'd never be a good politician, you know, because sooner or later I'd say, 'Oh, do shut up,' and it would be all over the press and I'd have to make a public apology. I feel so sorry for politicians, having to control themselves and never being allowed to tell people to shut up, whatever the provocation. They have to say things like: 'Thank you for sharing that with me,' when all along they want to say, 'Oh, do shut up.' Why, Jane, here you are; that was quick."

Jane poured the tea.

"You must come and see me at Hartfield," said Emma as she took a sip. There was a small chip on the rim of her cup, she noticed, and a crack in the saucer had been glued in an amateurish way. This was all a result of being a Lloyd's Name; perhaps there were former Lloyd's Names up and down the country drinking tea out of chipped cups, struggling to glue broken saucers, all reduced by the insurance market to such straits.

"I'd love to come," said Jane. "I've heard a great deal about it."

"Do you play tennis?" asked Emma. "We've got a tennis court. It's a bit in need of TLC, I'm afraid, but you can still play on it."

Jane was polite, but not enthusiastic. "Thank you," she said.

"And I was thinking of having a dinner party," Emma went on. "I like cooking."

"That would be very nice," said Jane.

Emma glanced at Miss Bates, who for once seemed to have nothing to say. From a clock on the mantelpiece there came a slow ticking sound.

Emma made an attempt to restart the conversation. "I love clocks that sound like clocks," she remarked. "Tick-tock. That's what clocks should say, don't you think? You can *believe* a clock that goes tick-tock."

It was a desperate remark, and would normally have drawn comment from Miss Bates, in whose mind it would certainly have triggered some clock association. But this time, she simply nodded her agreement.

The silence stretched out. Then Jane said, "My aunt says you went to uni in Bath."

Emma was relieved. She was intrigued by Jane and wanted to talk to her, but there was something about her that made it difficult. Was it aloofness? Superiority? Now, at least there was something to talk about. "Yes," she said. "I studied design."

Jane nodded. "That's what I heard. It sounds . . . sounds interesting."

"Oh, it was," said Emma. "We did all sorts of things. Architectural history, for instance."

"Fascinating."

"It was."

Emma waited. Then she said, "Do you know Bath?"

"I went there once," she said. "I was in a choir. We sang early music. Byrd, Tallis, that sort of thing. We gave a concert in Bath once. Then we went on to Wells and sang in the cathedral there."

"I love Wells. I love . . . I love the . . ." She tried to think what it was about Wells that she loved, but it was difficult to be specific. She loved it, she thought, because it was English.

Jane was less enthusiastic. "Yes, there is something special about it, I suppose."

Miss Bates put down her cup and saucer. "More tea, Miss Woodhouse?"

Emma had drunk only half her cup. She thought that the milk was slightly off, and she was not sure that she could face the rest. It occurred to her that perhaps Miss Bates might not have a fridge, or that it had broken down and they did not have the money to repair it. She declined the offer of more tea.

"This choir?" she said.

"It was nothing special. There were one or two people in it who had really good voices, but I wasn't one of them, I'm afraid."

Miss Bates now found her voice. "But you were, Jane, you were. Mr. Whitehead always said that you had a lovely voice. He always said that, and he should know."

"He was being kind," said Jane. "I really wasn't all that good."

"Was it a church choir?" asked Emma.

Jane shook her head, but did not expand, at least at first. Then, after a minute or so, she said, "It was when I was at university."

Emma had assumed that Jane had not been to university; Miss Bates had said that she had not bothered with examinations because she was above them, and one did not get to university without at least some qualifications.

"I didn't realise . . ." she began, and then tailed off.

Jane looked at her politely. "Realise what?"

"I thought that you didn't go to university."

"But I did," said Jane. "Not that it's all that important. I know lots of people who never went to university and who have done just fine afterwards."

"Me, for instance," said Miss Bates.

"Yes, of course," said Jane.

Emma looked at Miss Bates. She had not done just fine. She had done nothing, as far she could work out, and then she had made matters worse by losing all her money on the insurance market. How could she possibly think that she had done well? She shifted her gaze to Jane. "Where were you?" asked Emma. She imagined that the answer would be some safe, provincial place: Nottingham, perhaps, or even Durham, at a pinch.

"Not far from here," said Jane.

Jane seemed unwilling to expand, and again Emma found that the other young woman's reticence only served to enflame her curiosity. Proximity suggested that it was the University of East Anglia in Norwich, or possibly the University of Essex at Colchester, which was a little further away.

"Norwich?" she asked. "I knew quite a few people who went there."

"No," said Jane. "Not Norwich."

When Emma realised that Jane was not going to offer any further information, she decided to be direct. There was no reason for Jane to be so coy, she thought; it was frustrating for others—surely she understood that.

"Where then?" she said.

"Cambridge," said Jane.

Emma had not expected this, and it took her a moment or two to absorb the information. She frowned. You had to have A levels to get into Cambridge—and impressive ones at that; yet Jane, according to Miss Bates, had been above all that.

"I was under the impression you needed As to get into Cambridge," she said.

Jane looked down at the floor. "Yes, you generally do."

Miss Bates was smiling benignly. Emma now turned to her. "I thought you said that Jane didn't take any A levels."

Miss Bates did not stop smiling. "Did I really? Oh, I do get things wrong. I'm sure that Jane got whatever it was she needed for a place at Cambridge—although heaven knows what that is. I thought they took you if you were good at rowing or something like that, but that might just apply to the young men. I suppose they have to make sure that you've got plenty of brains as well. It's all very well knowing *how* to row, but you must have some idea *where* to row to. It would be no good at all having a whole lot of nice young men rowing around in circles, would it?"

Emma turned back to Jane. "What did you study?" she asked.

"Music," she said. "Mostly the history of music, but quite a bit of theory too."

"Bach, and people like that," interjected Miss Bates. "Jane knows an awful lot about Bach. All I know is that there were several Bachs. There was only one Mozart, of course, but there were any number of Bachs. I'm not sure which one was which; they all sound much the same to me."

Emma ignored all this. "Which college were you at?" she asked.

"St. John's."

Emma swallowed. The University of Bath was below Cambridge in the pecking order of universities, and this disclosure that Jane had been at St. John's, studying Bach and singing in a choir, made her feel that her own experience of the department of design at the University of Bath was distinctly inferior. She was not accustomed to intellectual inferiority, and she felt it keenly. Of course it occurred to her that Jane might not have got to Cambridge solely on the basis of examination results; she was an orphan, and that would count for a lot in the admission process. Cambridge colleges liked orphans, she imagined: there were plenty of meritorious people who had the misfortune to have two parents, but lacking the cachet of being an orphan they could hardly expect to find a place at Cambridge. Perhaps, she thought, there were people who disposed of their parents purely in order to obtain a place at a prestigious university; that was going a bit far, she told herself, and Jane, so thoroughly wholesome-looking in her white linen blouse, would hardly have gone to those lengths to become an orphan and thereby get into St. John's. No, Jane would certainly not have a past like that, although . . . She hesitated. Somebody had given her a piano—an expensive one at that—and that could only mean that she had a secret; people who received pianos as gifts almost always had something to hide. Somewhere there was a secret, and she decided at that moment that she would find it out. It might take some time, but Jane Fairfax was there for three months and that, surely, was quite enough time to discover the truth, whatever that should turn out to be.

14

Over the days that followed, Emma thought a great deal about Jane Fairfax. She was impatient to see her again, which rather surprised her, as she had been irritated by Jane's guarded manner and barely concealed disinclination to open up to her. Every time she had asked her something—and she did not think that her questions about the piano had been too probing—she had been greeted with an evasive or enigmatic reply. The conversation about Cambridge had been typical of that: she had had to prise out of Jane the fact that she had been at St. John's. She wondered why this should be so; was it modesty on Jane's part? It might have been that she did not wish to draw attention to the fact that she had been at Cambridge, believing—although there was no justification for such a belief—that anybody who had been at Bath would feel envious of those who had gone to Cambridge. If that were so, then her reticence could be construed as consideration, and she deserved credit for it. It was equally possible, though, that Jane had simply not wanted to engage in conversation with somebody whom she considered to be beneath her. That was clearly a less charitable explanation, but could very well be true: some people simply could not be bothered to engage with people with whom they felt they had nothing in common. Perhaps Jane thought that of her; had written her off as a typical county girl who was going to end up decorating people's drawing rooms with chintz until she married some rather dim young man, a land agent or surveyor perhaps, and who would then have three children and a couple of Labradors. The mere thought of this possibility angered her. How dare she; how dare she imagine that she, somebody who came from . . . from nothing could condescend to her, to Emma Woodhouse of Hartfield. *It takes my breath away*, she thought, *just to think she considers me to be of no consequence.*

Yet any affront she suffered was more than outweighed by the interest that she felt in Jane. She found herself thinking of the other young woman's piano-playing, and of how confident it had been. She found herself thinking again of the white linen blouse and wondering whether she might not buy one herself. Perhaps she could also look for some of the Indian bangles that had looked so good on Jane's wrist. She conjured up a mental picture of Jane's boyish figure and wondered whether she had to follow a diet in order to get that effect or whether it came naturally. Some people could get away with eating anything because their systems burned up the calories before they could get stored as fat. Was Jane like that, she wondered—did she have an efficient metabolism? She could always ask her, of course, and see what her reaction was. "Do you have an efficient metabolism, Jane?" She smiled at the thought. There would be an evasive answer to that, she imagined.

There were other people to think about, though, and these gradually began to replace thoughts of Jane Fairfax. The first of these was Harriet, whom Emma had rather neglected after Jane's arrival; and the second was Frank Churchill. It was the first who told Emma of the imminent arrival of the second.

Emma had not invited Harriet to Hartfield that day, and was mildly surprised when she spotted her friend talking to Sid near the entrance to the vegetable garden. Seeing her from the staircase window, Emma quickly slipped out of her inside shoes and put on a pair of green waterproof boots.

Harriet saw her as she approached from the side of the house. "I just popped in," she said. "Mrs. God was going into London, and I decided to take the opportunity of coming with her. She left her car at the railway station."

"She must know the way there by now," said Emma.

Harriet looked puzzled. "Excuse me?"

"Nothing," said Emma. "What I meant to say is that I'm really pleased to see you."

"Oh, thank you," said Harriet. "I normally don't like dropping in on people without any warning. I'm always worried that they might be in the loo, or something like that."

Emma laughed at the odd, almost juvenile remark. "I don't think that people are too embarrassed about that," she said.

Sid was standing by. He was grinning. "I used to work for a fellow—he was a pukka earl and all—and he used to telephone people from the loo. They had no idea that he was there, of course, and they had a perfectly normal conversation."

"I don't see why one wouldn't," said Emma. "Didn't kings conduct their court business from the bath?"

"Yes," said Sid. "So I believe. There was a programme on the box about it some time ago. They showed how one of those kings, see, would run everything from his bedroom."

They went inside. "I'm glad that you came," said Emma. "I wanted to find out when you might be free to come to lunch. I thought I'd invite Philip Elton as well. Just the three of us." She glanced at Harriet.

"Oh, but he's already invited me," said Harriet. "Or rather, us. He's invited both of us to have lunch with him at the pub. He asked me to find out when would suit you."

Emma was momentarily nonplussed. She could understand Philip's inviting Harriet to the pub, but why would he invite her as well? Her puzzlement, though, was brief. She only had to think about it for a few moments before an obvious answer suggested itself: Philip, for all his good looks and eloquence, may have felt anxious about asking somebody out on what was obviously a date; men like that often suffered from a lack of confidence. Asking both of them was a way of paving the way for the next invitation, which she imagined would be extended only to Harriet.

"That's really good news, Harriet," said Emma. "I could tell he liked you, you know. It was perfectly obvious—right from the beginning." She grinned at her friend. "Men are so trans-parent. You can read them like a book."

"He's very kind," said Harriet.

Emma would not have chosen that description for Philip, but she was content to let it pass. She thought that he was probably somewhat selfish, but that this defect could be ignored as long as he treated Harriet considerately, which he probably would. What man would not be delighted to have the attention of such an astonishingly beautiful young woman, and what man, in his delight, would not be careful to indulge her financially? This was never going to be a permanent arrangement, and the whole point of it was that Harriet should get her gap year, with a little bit of spoiling thrown in. He was certainly kind enough to provide that, she thought, even if ultimately he was not a person she would saddle anybody with on a permanent basis.

"How about next Tuesday?" asked Emma.

Harriet was free, and she thought it would suit Philip too. "He said that he had nothing on all next week," she said.

Emma made a mental note. Philip had told her father on more than one occasion that he was overworked; the truth, it seemed, was rather different. She had noticed that people often claimed to be busier than they really were; there had been a lecturer at Bath, the aptly named Dr. Snail, who had very little, if not nothing, to do and yet who always claimed to be overworked. It was guilt, she thought, that made them protest their busyness.

Emma led Harriet into the kitchen, where she made tea for them. "Are you an Earl Grey person?" she asked, opening the cupboard in which the tea caddies were kept; with her delicate features, Harriet could well have been a drinker of Earl Grey tea.

"Not really," said Harriet. "I'm not all that keen on Early Grey. I know that sounds frightfully unsophisticated, but I just go for . . ."

"Builders' tea," prompted Emma. Early Grey, she thought: Was the curious name a mistake or another example of Harriet's childishness? Early Grey . . . Mrs. God . . . *Wetness*, thought Emma. *Poor Harriet is simply wet. Dripping.*

"Yes. But why do they call it builders' tea? Do builders really drink it?"

Emma shrugged. "I suspect they do. I don't know many builders, but when we had one here repairing the conservatory he drank lots of Indian tea. He liked it dark and with three spoons of sugar."

Harriet made a face. "Three!"

"It must have tasted disgusting," said Emma. "But he liked it. He was a rather nice man. He had an Alsatian dog that stayed in his van all day, except when he took him out for a walk at lunchtime. He was careful to keep him on a lead because he said his dog was dangerous. He said it was wanted by the police for biting somebody."

They took their tea through to Emma's sitting room.

"You haven't forgotten, have you?" said Emma as they sat together on the sofa near the window.

"What?" asked Harriet. "Forgotten what?"

"That shows you have forgotten," Emma chided her. "Your portrait."

She noticed that Harriet blushed.

"I hadn't. I was going to ask you . . ."

"When I was going to do it?"

"Yes."

"Well," said Emma. "We could start right now. Or not right at this very moment—after we've finished our tea."

Harriet did not object.

"It needn't be a long sitting," Emma continued. "Half an hour maybe—this time. Something like that."

"I don't mind," said Harriet. "I've got nothing to do all day. The students are having a holiday. We call it a study day. Study days happen when Mrs. God wants to go to London."

Emma smiled. People suited themselves; more and more that was the lesson she was learning. "Do you have any preferences?" she asked.

"For?"

"For how you'd like to sit?"

Harriet thought for a moment. "I don't want it to be too formal," she said.

"No," said Emma. "A formal portrait usually says very little about the sitter. The more informal the better, I think." She paused. "You said the other day *au naturel*."

"Did I?"

Emma struggled to keep a straight face. She nodded.

"Well, maybe I did."

"That means starkers," said Emma.

Harriet appeared not to understand. She must know the word, thought Emma; perhaps she was just pretending.

"Starkers," repeated Emma. "Nothing on. A nude study."

Harriet's mouth opened in surprise. "But I didn't . . ."

Emma cut her short. "I've been to life-drawing classes," she said. "I've worked with models. It's nothing unusual."

Harriet looked about her. "In here?"

"Yes. This is as good a place as any. Unless you wanted to do it in the bathroom. Do you know those pictures Bonnard did of his lover in the bath?"

Harriet put down her teacup. "I've never done anything like this before," she said.

"Most people haven't," said Emma. "It's nothing unusual. What normally happened with the models at my life classes was that they wore a dressing gown to begin with. Then they took it off for the actual pose."

Harriet looked about her again. "Were they just women?" she asked. "Or were they men too?"

"Both," said Emma.

Harriet looked thoughtful. "Oh," she said.

Emma grinned. "It was all very straightforward," she said. "Nobody batted an eyelid."

"I wouldn't know where to look," said Harriet, and giggled.

"You look at what you're doing. You just get on with the drawing."

"You're more experienced than I am," said Harriet.

Emma was not sure how to take this. Was there a barb to it? She gave Harriet a searching look, but decided that, as usual, there was neither irony nor sarcasm in what she said. It was rather like talking to a child, Emma decided.

Emma returned to the models. "We never knew which model we would be drawing. It could be a man or a woman. They just turned up. They were very ordinary."

Harriet frowned. "In what way?"

"What they looked like. They were all ages. Some of them were fat and some were thin. There was one male model who was a body-builder and had all sorts of muscles one wouldn't have known existed, and then there was one who was really weedy. I remember his knees. They were really bony. I think he didn't get enough to eat."

"Have you got a dressing gown?" asked Harriet nervously.

"I'll fetch you one," said Emma, getting up to leave the room. As she went into her room to fetch her Japanese bathrobe, she stopped and thought about the enormity of what she was about to do. There was nothing inherently wrong about doing a nude study—artists did such things all the time, and she was, in a sense, an artist. No, more than that: she had every right to consider herself an artist; she had studied life drawing and she was a graduate of an arts-based programme; she was *not* just some untutored amateur. But even if all of that was true—which it was—she was still asking somebody she knew socially to take her clothes off; moreover she was asking this of somebody over whom she seemed to have a measure of influence. There was no reason why Harriet should feel either beholden to her or in her power, but it was obvious that she looked up to Emma. And here she was using that influence to persuade her to sit for a nude portrait. She saw herself in the mirror. *Emma Wood-house: Is this sexual?* The question, brutal in its directness, seemed to come from nowhere. She had posed it, of course, but she had done so without intending it.

No, it's not, she said to herself. I am not interested in girls. I'm just not. *Nonsense, of course you are. Everybody is interested in beauty—and Harriet is beautiful.* These conflicting answers came from somewhere within her, from some hidden centre of self-knowledge.

She reached out to take the Japanese bathrobe from its peg. It was too late to change her mind, and she did not want to do so anyway.

Back in her sitting room, she handed Harriet the robe. "I'll leave you to it," she said. "I'll come back in a few minutes."

"You don't have to go," said Harriet. "I don't mind."

She did not watch Harriet undress, though. She stood by the window and looked out, only turning round when Harriet told her that she was ready.

"That Japanese motif suits you," Emma said. "Mind you, you could wear anything, I think. You're very lucky." She pointed to a small sofa on the other side of the room. "You could sit there. Just sit normally."

"Without the gown?"

Emma hesitated. It was not too late to go back. But then she said, "Yes."

Emma opened her sketchbook. *Yes,* she thought. *Harriet Smith is entirely beautiful.* She had taken a stick of pastel in her hand, but she noticed that she was holding it so tightly that she caused it to fragment. "That's fine," she said. "Yes, that's fine. Just like that."

"I don't know what to think," said Harriet.

Emma took command of herself once more. "Actually," she said, "I don't think models think very much."

Mrs. Firhill said to her husband that night, "I certainly wasn't imagining it, Bert. You know me: Do I imagine things? I wasn't imagining it because I had no reason to imagine it in the first place, if you see what I mean."

Bert Firhill was not sure that he did. "You say that you saw them . . ." He lowered his voice. "Larking about unclothed."

"No. Just one of them. That Harriet Smith girl. I didn't see Emma—I was in the corridor, you see, and you get a view into the room through a side window; it's difficult to explain. I couldn't see it all."

"So they were up to something."

She shrugged. "There was nudity—that's all I'm saying. And call me old-fashioned if you will, but I don't expect to see nudity at eleven-thirty in the morning, do you?"

Bert did not. "Are you going to tell Mr. Woodhouse?"

His wife did not hesitate. "No. It's nobody's business but theirs."

"You're right."

"Anything goes these days, as you know. But it still makes

one think, doesn't it? That girl is a troublemaker. I've always said that. Bert, haven't I? She's trouble."

Bert nodded. He agreed that Emma was trouble, but he rather liked the idea of young women larking about, as he put it, in a state of undress. It enlivened things, he thought. But of course he could not say that; there were many things that Bert Firhill thought but could not say, and this was one of them.

15

Miss Taylor had been at Randalls for a short time when the news came through that Mr. Frank Churchill was definitely coming to spend a few weeks—possibly more—with his father, James Weston. This information was disclosed one Friday morning by an excited James, who had just received an email from his son himself. The message said:

Hey, Dad, definitely coming this time. You know how difficult it is with . . . well, it's just difficult. However, the Cs have said that London is on and so there's no stopping me now. They are going to be staying in some club in London and then renting a house in Cheltenham for a couple of months—there are Churchill cousins down there, and one of them isn't too well. I'll come straight to you at Highbury. Put the beer on ice!

Love, Frank (Churchill but really Weston!)

Miss Taylor readily shared in her fiancé's pleasure; she knew how much he had been longing to see his son again, and she had felt vaguely aggrieved that Frank had already called off promised visits more than once. She had imagined at first that this displayed thoughtlessness on the young man's part, and had been prepared to feel cross with him over what she saw as cavalier cancellations. When she found out the full facts, though, she changed her mind, and realised that if there was to be any blame for these aborted visits, then it rested fairly at the door of Mrs. Churchill.

Mrs. Churchill was not popular in Highbury, even if there were few people who had actually met her; those who had, spoke of her high-handed manner; those who had not, talked of how other people spoke of her haughtiness and sheer bossiness. There was nobody who was prepared to say a good word about her.

Miss Taylor, who was aware of Mrs. Churchill's reputation, thought this unfair. Although not one to overlook the failings of others—she was no Pollyanna—she nonetheless felt that Mrs. Churchill must have at least some good points, even if these generally went unremarked. After all, she and her husband had provided a home for Frank, and even if self-interest was involved in that, taking on the child of another was surely an act of extreme generosity. And if she had proved to be a possessive stepmother, then that was more likely to be caused by insecurity than by selfishness. Miss Taylor's Scottish upbringing had taught her that blame requires free will and the making of choices; we answer for what we choose to do, a simple enough concept to grasp. Weaknesses of character or personality issues—such as insecurity—are hardly a matter of choice. So if Mrs. Churchill's undue possessiveness had its source in insecurity, and if this insecurity were not something Mrs. Churchill had chosen for herself, then her possessiveness was not a failing for which she could be blamed. That was what Miss Taylor thought. Everybody else, however, thought differently.

Frank Churchill arrived shortly before noon on the day on which his flight from Perth touched down at Heathrow. Leaving the Churchills to make their own way into London, Frank picked up the German sports car that he had reserved—at considerable expense—and left for Highbury.

Mrs. Churchill had expressed misgivings. "I don't know why you need a car like that, Frank," she said. "You can't drive fast on these English roads, you know."

"You can't drive fast anywhere," said Frank. "Oz is just as bad. All those traffic cops."

"Speed is not essential," said Mrs. Churchill. "Anyway, when are we going to see you? When will you be coming into London?"

Frank was non-committal. "I'm not sure," he said. "It's difficult to find parking in London, I think. You just go ahead and make your plans yourselves, Ma. Don't worry about me."

"It's not a question of worrying about you," said Mrs. Churchill. "It's just that . . . well, we thought it would be nice if we could do a few things together."

Mr. Churchill had intervened. "Let Frank do his own thing, Enid," he said. "He's a big boy now."

Mrs. Churchill shot her husband a glance. This would be discussed later on. "Will you phone?" she said to Frank. "I'll keep my phone switched on."

Frank nodded. He looked at his watch. "You mustn't miss your train," he said. "The Heathrow Express doesn't sound like a train that hangs about."

They parted, and Frank, relieved to be the master of his own destiny, even if only for a short time, loaded his luggage on to the minuscule back seat of the high-performance sports car. Then he set off for Highbury, where his father, anxiously looking at the clock, willing its hands round the dial, awaited him.

When it took place, their reunion, although emotional, was a matter of few words.

"I'm so glad you've come," said James, struggling to control the tears he knew were just beneath the surface.

"And I'm so glad I'm here," said Frank. "You know that I wanted to come long ago? You know I wanted to come before this?"

James nodded, but did not say anything. He knew whose fault it was that Frank's previous plans to visit England had been suddenly dropped. Frank had not spelled it out, but it was obvious to everybody that the sudden bouts of illness Mrs. Churchill had experienced just before Frank's departure were as dubious as they were convenient. Only George Knightley had suggested that it might be Frank himself who simply could not be bothered to come.

"I fail to see why somebody of twenty-whatever-he-is should be incapable of telling her that it's his life," he said to Mr. Woodhouse. "No, her illness might just be an excuse he's come up with for his selfishness."

"But why?" asked Mr. Woodhouse. "Why would Frank Churchill not want to see his father?"

"He's probably too busy socially," said George. "Better things to do. That's the usual reason why people don't make time for their parents."

"Perhaps we'll never know," said Mr. Woodhouse. "But we

should, perhaps, bear the background in mind. Perhaps young Frank Churchill is punishing his father. After all, he did hand him over to the Churchills. Maybe Frank resents that."

"But he's had a much better life in Australia," said George. "I gather that place of theirs is one of the best wine estates in Western Australia. He'd have nothing like that in this country."

Mr. Woodhouse considered this. He was not always one to understand matters from the point of view of the other, but on this occasion he did. "But people may not judge things purely on the basis of material advantage," he said. "It's rather like this foreign-adoption issue they've been talking about in *The Economist*."

George did not read *The Economist*. This sometimes put him at a disadvantage when talking with Mr. Woodhouse, who read it religiously, and who liked nothing more than to air some item of recondite knowledge gleaned from its columns. "I may have seen something about it in *The Times*," he said.

Mr. Woodhouse did not believe this. Nobody seemed to read *The Economist*—except him—and it did not become people to claim to have read things in other papers or magazines when it was clearly the sort of thing that one would only read about in *The Economist*. "What all that's about is this," he explained. "There are some countries that are saying they won't allow foreigners to adopt their babies any more. Russia's starting to make those noises, apparently. And some other places too. They say the child is deprived of its cultural birth-right if it's taken to another country—even if conditions are much better there."

"So they would prefer a child to be an orphan at home rather than have parents abroad?"

Mr. Woodhouse made a gesture that indicated his tolerance of Russian stubbornness. "That's what it looks like."

George looked thoughtful. He was thinking of what it would be like to be an orphan. It would be lonely, he imagined—unless one had brothers and sisters one knew about, which might not be the case. He at least had his brother, John, even if their relationship had never been particularly close. John occasionally telephoned him from London, but would never have bothered to come back to Highbury had it not been for Isabella, who liked the children to see Mr. Woodhouse. He could envisage losing contact with John eventually, or seeing him only once or twice a year, unless he made an effort to keep in touch.

He felt lonely. John would never be a soulmate, and he could not think of any of his friends who were obvious candidates for that role. There were one or two men he had got to know at the pub, but they had young families and demanding careers and had little time for the sort of conversation that he wanted to have. He could talk to Mr. Woodhouse, of course, and they did in fact spend hours in wide-ranging discussions of all sorts of topics, but these discussions would often go off at a tangent, with Mr. Woodhouse bringing up some issue of viruses or food safety, or some obscure point about scientific method. Then there was Emma . . .

In recent months he had found himself looking forward more and more to their chats. He had been surprised to find how much he wanted to share his thoughts with her; if he heard a piece of music that appealed to him or read something that made him think, he would say to himself, *What would Emma make of that?* And then, if he drew it to her attention, he found that she always raised some interesting perspective on the matter and would make some amusing comment. She made him want to laugh, with her dry humour and her mischievous remarks. Sometimes too mischievous, of course; if only she could learn to be more charitable and to let people get on with their lives without giving the impression that she would like to interfere.

He was unsure why she did that. He had thought about it a great deal, and was coming round to the view that she did it because she had nothing better to do. If she had a proper job, then her energy could be channelled into that and she would not feel the need to interfere. He thought of Harriet Smith. He had seen them together, and it was clear to him that she was fascinated by Harriet. Why? Because Harriet was the next best thing to having a doll, whose life could be organised, who could be dressed up and made to do things to enliven an otherwise uneventful life?

There was so much to think about once one started to think about Emma, but now, he thought, was not the time. Mr. Woodhouse had started talking about Russian adoption, and so he should respond.

"One can understand this Russian reluctance to allow foreign adoption—to an extent. If you think it's a good thing to be Russian, that is."

Mr. Woodhouse frowned. "And is it?"

George had views. "It depends, I suppose, on what sort of life you have. If your life is intolerable, then you no doubt think that it would be better to be something else. And it may also depend on how you feel about your fellow citizens. If they're behaving badly, then you probably wish that you were something else—perhaps to avoid guilt by association."

Mr. Woodhouse reverted to the subject of Frank Churchill. "I suspect that he's rather pleased that he's Australian rather than British. You carry less history when you're Australian."

George shook his head in an animated fashion. "Everyone has some history to bear, and to feel sorry about. Mind you, the Australians do seem to have apologised to some of their people for treating them badly." He paused. "Perhaps we should do a bit more of that ourselves."

George looked anxious. "Apologise for what?" he asked.

Mr. Knightley sighed. "Take your pick. Slavery, perhaps. We might start there."

"But that was a long time ago."

"Not all that long, actually. And the social consequences of it are still being felt in the West Indies. Ask them—they'll tell you that. We created a society in which family life was pretty much impossible. The society at the receiving end of that was irretrievably wounded while we grew rich on the proceeds. Sugar fortunes came from all that, remember."

"But that's ages ago. It's got nothing to do with us."

"We've still got the capital that we built up through slavery. It's still there."

They lapsed into silence, as if both were cowed by the sheer weight of post-imperial guilt. For a brief moment, Mr. Woodhouse closed his eyes and saw, rather vividly, an image of distant plantations, of Spanish ships sunk, of a viceroy riding an elephant in a durbar, of a lifeless tiger being carried upside down on a litter of bamboo poles. And he thought: *If we can't find it within ourselves to apologise to the descendants of our victims, then our hands will remain forever dirty.* He looked at his own hands, and there came into his mind the troubling question: What does historical guilt look like on the skin?

No such reflections accompanied the discussion of Frank Churchill that took place between Emma and Harriet Smith. This conversation occurred after Harriet Smith came for the second, and final, sitting for her sketched portrait. Emma had undergone a change of heart since the first sitting, and had decided to draw Harriet wearing the Japanese dressing gown rather than in the nude. Harriet seemed relieved about this; how could the portrait have been shown to anybody, she pointed out, if it portrayed her naked? "It would have to be kept secret—locked up like one of those stolen paintings that unscrupulous collectors stash away. And that would be such a pity, Emma, when it's bound to be so good."

Emma agreed. "Philip Elton wanted to see it," she pointed out. "And perhaps it would have been a bit embarrassing for both of you."

"Oh, I couldn't have borne that," said Harriet. "I would not wish Philip to see me in the nude." She blushed. "I mean, to see a picture of me in the nude."

Emma smiled. "No. So why don't I do you in the Japanese dressing gown? You looked so good in it."

Now, with Harriet adopting once more her position on the sofa, Emma began to add the dressing gown by the simple expedient of sketching over the original with more pastel. It was not too taxing, and rather reminded her of how, as a very young girl, she had dressed her cut-out dolls with paper cut-out clothes. And Harriet, after all, had precisely the pertness, the neatness, that those dolls possessed.

"You won't believe what I saw," remarked Harriet as she settled into her pose.

"Try me," said Emma.

The pastel moved across the page; light, shade, smudging.

"I was in Highbury with Mrs. God, I mean Goddard—"

"No, Mrs. God," Emma interjected. "It seems to suit her."

"We were going to buy gin," Harriet continued. "Mrs. God loves her gin."

"I'm beginning to like her more than ever," said Emma. "And?"

"And we saw a really smart car drive down the High Street. It was a silver sports car of some sort—it was German."

"And?"

"It stopped outside Miss Bates's cottage."

Emma paid more attention now. "Really? Why would any-body in a silver German car want to stop there?" She paused. "Unless by accident, of course. I suppose one might very easily *break down* in front of Miss Bates's cottage. Not that German cars break down."

"This guy got out," said Harriet. "A young guy."

"How young?"

"Our age," said Harriet. "Maybe a year or two older." She lowered her voice. "He was to die for."

Emma put down her pastel and stared at Harriet. *To die for* . . . Nobody said *to die for* any more. "Good-looking?" she said.

"To die for," replied Harriet.

"And then what happened?"

Harriet paused before delivering the next instalment of her story. "He rang the bell, and then went inside. We went off to do our shopping and we weren't back for at least half an hour. The car was still there. I'd thought that maybe he'd stopped to ask directions, but it must have been a social visit. Anyway, there we were, and he came out and I said to Mrs. God, 'You see that guy? Could we just watch where he goes?' And Mrs. God said to me, 'You mean, follow him?' She liked the idea. She watches those police series on television, you see, and she rather liked the thought of following a German sports car in her Fiat 500. So we did."

Emma put down her pastel; really, this was too ridiculous for words. "So you gave chase?"

Harriet nodded. "He drove off to Randalls. You know that house just off the Holt road? Quite close to you. It belongs to James Weston."

"Of course I do," said Emma, with some irritation. Did Harriet really imagine that she might not know her own neighbours?

"Well, when we saw that, Mrs. God said, 'Of course, of course! It's Frank Churchill.'"

"Frank Churchill," muttered Emma. "So he's arrived at last."

"Do you know him?" asked Harriet.

Emma thought very quickly. The interest that Harriet was taking in Frank Churchill unsettled her. Emma had not yet had the chance to look at Frank Churchill on this visit, and she did not like the idea of Harriet suddenly falling for him. That was *not* in the script.

"I've met him on previous visits," she said. "He's James Weston's son, you see. He was sent off to Australia when his mother died—some relatives called Churchill took him. They've got pots of money."

Harriet listened intently. "He looks so cute," she said. "He's got this really nice face, you see—very regular features—and his shoulders . . ."

"Too bad," muttered Emma.

Harriet looked puzzled. "No, there was nothing wrong with his shoulders—in fact—"

She did not finish. "Harriet," said Emma, "sorry to have to tell you this, but I don't think Frank Churchill's going to be interested."

Harriet stared at her. "You mean . . ."

Emma waited for her to finish her sentence, but she did not. She inclined her head slightly; that was all—just a slight lowering of the head. She was not going to tell any lies; Frank Churchill may or may not be interested in Harriet—who could tell? All she was doing was expressing her own opinion as to whether or not he would notice her. There was nothing wrong with that. She would not tell Harriet that he was gay, but if that was the way she chose to interpret what she had said, then was she under any obligation to correct her? She could not be a nursemaid to Harriet, responsible for protecting her from every misunderstanding.

And yet conscience pricked her. "All I meant," she said, "was that I thought he might not be interested. That's all."

Harriet groaned. "It's so unfair."

"What's unfair?"

"These nice men—all these really nice men are . . . aren't interested."

"I'm sure he's perfectly happy with himself," said Emma.

For the rest of the sitting, she sketched in silence. An hour later, the portrait was finished, and she stood back to admire it. It was good, she thought; not just adequate, but good.

She showed it to Harriet, who said that she was pleased. "I love a pastel drawing," she said. "And this one makes me look so . . ."

"So intriguing," suggested Emma.

"Yes, maybe. Goodness, I'm not that clever and yet here I look as if I'm thinking very hard!"

Emma started to remove the portrait from the sketchbook so that she could frame it. She was glad that it was finished, as she was beginning to feel bored with Harriet's company. There were so many more interesting things to think about, she felt; poor Harriet was so superficial. Her destiny was to be handed over to Philip as soon as possible and to go off on a well-funded gap year. That was what was contemplated for her. And as for her own life, Emma thought that there were numerous possibilities. There was Mr. Frank Churchill to start with: something might well come of him. And there would be no difficulty in seeing him, as she and her father could easily invite James and Miss Taylor over for dinner and then add, "And do bring anybody staying with you." She was not sure about inviting Harriet, as the last thing she would want would be for Frank Churchill's head to be turned by Harriet's looks. That would not do at all. But she could hardly not invite her, she decided, as she was bound to hear of the dinner party and wonder why she had not been included. She had so much in this life, and Harriet had so little; it would be a kindness on her part to include her. So Harriet would get an invitation, but would not be seated anywhere near Frank Churchill.

Later, after Harriet had left, Emma sat in her study and thought. Why, she wondered, had Frank gone to see Miss Bates? It seemed so odd; unless, of course, he was paying a dutiful call on an old friend of his father. That was entirely possible: Miss Bates and James had known each other for years, and Frank might just have been calling in to find out how Miss Bates was, not having seen her for so long. That was the most likely explanation; she was sure of it, and saw no reason to think about it any more. *Cadit quaestio,* one might say.

16

The guest list for the dinner party ran to more names than Emma had originally envisaged, including Mrs. Goddard, who had not been on Emma's initial list, but who had been invited by Mr. Woodhouse. "I've added somebody to our dinner party," he announced. "Floss Goddard. I bumped into her in the village and asked her. I hadn't seen her for a long time."

"The English as a foreign language woman?" asked Emma.

"That's her."

Emma bit her lip. "I wish you hadn't. This dinner party is getting larger and larger by the minute. Have you invited anybody else?"

"Miss Bates," he said.

"That'll be fun." The sarcasm behind the remark was not concealed.

"She's a nice woman, Emma. And her niece too."

Emma sighed, although she was secretly pleased that Jane Fairfax would be there. Jane would be no threat to Frank Churchill's attention, as long as they could make sure that she did not play the piano; some men admired talent, although most of them, she thought, were far too unsubtle to do that. She would make sure that Jane was seated near her, as there was still a lot she wanted to find out about her.

Mr. Woodhouse, though, should not be let off that easily. "You may as well invite the whole village." She paused. "How do you know Mrs. Goddard, anyway?"

"We go back a bit," said Mr. Woodhouse. "When she bought the old airfield I was on the Parish Council and she submitted her plans to us. I got to know her then. That was about fifteen years ago."

"Well, I suppose you've gone and done it. We can't uninvite people, Pops. Mrs. Firhill is going to have to make double quantities of everything, since we're feeding the entire community, more or less."

"Oh, and I invited Philip Elton," said Mr. Woodhouse. "I forgot about him."

Emma did not mind about that. She had been at the vicarage the previous day—Philip had been out at the time—and she had posted her sketch of Harriet through the letter box as he had said that he knew a good framer and could get it framed at an attractive price. She wanted to hear his views of the sketch, and this would provide an opportunity to do so, even if it meant putting up with his company for the evening.

"And George Knightley?" asked Emma.

"Of course."

Mr. Woodhouse now became silent. He frowned, and then looked out of the window, as if whatever was worrying him was outside.

"Something wrong?" asked Emma.

He hesitated briefly before replying. "All these guests," he said. "I enjoy these occasions, as you well know, Emma. But a thought has suddenly occurred. Do you think that all these people have . . ." He broke off, looking slightly embarrassed.

"What? Have what?"

"Have all their immunisations up to date? Do you think we could ask them?"

Emma looked at him with frank disbelief. "Oh really, Daddy!" The *Pops* disappeared at moments of stress and her earlier, more authentic way of addressing her father returned. "Really!"

"You may laugh," he said, "but it's a thought. You know that you can catch whooping cough as an adult. It's very unpleasant. It lasts for months."

Emma knew that nothing she could say would reassure him, but she tried. "You can use sanitizer after you've shaken hands with them," she said. "Discreetly, of course."

"Perhaps," said Mr. Woodhouse. He was not entirely convinced, though, as he had read the small print on the labels of those sanitizers. "Kills 99.9% of known germs," they claimed. And what about the remaining 0.1 per cent, he asked himself. What about them? Ninety-nine point nine per cent of household germs were probably quite harmless anyway; 0.1 per cent, however, were not. And then there were the unknown germs; nothing was said of them, and, as everybody knew, what manufacturers and advertisers did *not* say was often much more important than what they did say.

On the day of the dinner party, Emma was ready well in advance. She herself had not helped with any of the preparations, having left these to Mrs. Firhill, who had in due course invoked the help of both her husband and Mrs. Sid. To Bert Firhill was delegated the task of laying the table and polishing the glasses before setting them alongside each place. Mr. Woodhouse was fussy about clean glass; "There is nothing—nothing—worse than a glass that has fingerprints or smudges on it," he said, which was not true, of course, even as an account of his own views, as there were many things that he thought considerably worse than the minor health hazard posed by dirty glass. But wine hygiene had become a concern of his since he had read in *The Economist* of a restaurant in which the dregs of wine left over in customers' glasses was decanted into empty bottles and then recorked for subsequent service. He had been haunted by this information, and had resolved never to drink wine in a restaurant again; which made little difference to his life, as he never went out for dinner anyway—other than to Randalls, and occasionally to Donwell Abbey. He was sure that James Weston would never stoop to such practices, although there remained a niggling doubt in his mind that Miss Taylor, being Scottish, might object to any wastage and, were the idea to be planted in her mind, might do just that. He knew that she was canny, and remembered her telling, with some pride in her voice, of an elderly uncle of hers, an Aberdonian and therefore particularly imbued with habits of Scottish frugality, who had used a bicycle-tube repair outfit to patch up his hot-water bottle after eighteen years of use. Coming from such a background, Miss Taylor might just be tempted to drain used wine glasses and recycle the wine; he would have to watch very carefully, he decided, to see whether the tops of the wine bottles were properly sealed when they were opened. But what if the bottles were broached in the kitchen prior to being brought into the dining room? This unresolved question had worried him and would continue to do so. Perhaps it would be best to have it out with James and ask him outright whether his bottles had had old wine poured into them. But could one ever ask such a question? Would offence be taken, even by an old friend? These questions added to his discomfort.

Bert was used to Mr. Woodhouse's oddities, and did not object to the request that he wear white butler's gloves while polishing the wine glasses.

"Good idea, Mr. Woodhouse," he suggested. "You never know where hands have been. Or you do, perhaps."

Mr. Woodhouse frowned. What could this remark possibly mean?

"Only joking," said Bert cheerfully. "My hands are pure as the driven snow. Carbolic soap—my old dad used it to get the grime off when he finished a day's work, and I've done the same, man and boy."

This reassured Mr. Woodhouse. "That's very good, Mr. Firhill. But please use a fresh cloth. There are plenty of those blue things in the pantry, near the rubbish sacks."

Bert set to work. As he was polishing, Mrs. Sid came in with a stack of plates. "You'll observe that herself is not helping much," she said. "It's her own party and yet who's not in evidence to lend a hand? The hostess, that's who."

"She's a spoiled little baggage," muttered Bert. "Too much money. Too much time on her hands. And attitude too."

Mrs. Sid agreed. "Sid's too soft on her. He says that she's not too bad compared with some he's come across in his time."

"Oh yes?" said Bert, picking up a heavy Stuart crystal glass on which he had located an errant fingerprint. "Well, Sid hasn't seen what I seen. Naked cavorting with . . ." He stopped himself, but it was too late. He had not actually seen it—not with his own eyes—but his wife had seen it, and he felt that this was as good as his having seen it himself. For the most part, they saw the same things anyway; so what difference did it make?

"What?" asked Mrs. Sid, her voice lowered to conspiratorial levels.

"Nothing," said Bert.

"Come on, Bert. You may not have meant to say anything, but you can't put a burp back in the stomach, as they say. Naked what? Cavorting?"

Bert had not intended to speak about what his wife had seen, but now had no alternative. He told Mrs. Sid about having seen Harriet Smith with no clothes on, although this time he said nothing about not having seen Emma. Quite reasonably, Mrs. Sid concluded that Emma had been naked too. She let out a long low whistle.

"Shameless!" she whispered. "No clothes!"

"I'm not saying nothing," said Bert. "But we can draw our own conclusions."

Mrs. Sid shook her head. "I don't see how Sid will be able to shrug that one off," she said. "That'll change his tune."

In the kitchen, Mrs. Firhill laboured over the soup, and then laboured over the main course, the pudding, and the cheese course. Emma appeared a quarter of an hour before the guests were due to arrive, and sampled the soup.

"That's really good soup, Mrs. Firhill," she said brightly. "They'll love that. And what about the venison? Don't make it too dry. I can't stand venison when it's dry."

"It's coming on nicely," said Mrs. Firhill, tight-lipped.

From the corner of the kitchen, Mr. Firhill, peeling off his butler's gloves, looked sideways at Emma. His glance was intercepted by Mrs. Sid, who was cutting slices of stale bread into small squares for croutons. She narrowed her eyes to express shared affront. She was not to know, of course, what Bert was thinking, which is just as well.

Philip Elton was the first to arrive.

"Oh good," said Mr. Woodhouse as he looked out of the drawing-room window. "Here's Philip."

Emma raised an eyebrow. "I always thought that one should be at least ten minutes late."

"But he is," said Mr. Woodhouse. "We said seven-thirty, and it's now seven-forty. Somebody has to arrive first."

"Fifteen minutes is better," said Emma. "Inflation, you know."

Mr. Woodhouse shook a finger in mock reproach. "Philip is a man of the cloth, Emma. He may be hungry, for all we know."

Emma was having none of this. "Pah!" she said. "He owns an office block in Ipswich and all those flats in Norwich. *And* he drives a BMW Something-something. You don't drive a BMW Something-something if you're on the bread line."

Mr. Woodhouse had heard of the structural problems in the office block. "I hear that he has dampness—"

"Yes, he's extremely wet," interjected Emma.

"In his cladding. That is, in the cladding of that office block. The rain gets in behind the façade, you see, and then it doesn't dry off because it's behind those prefabricated panels. It's a serious problem."

"He could sell it," said Emma. "It could be advertised as a building with running water."

Mr. Woodhouse smiled. "You don't like Philip, my dear—I think I can tell that. Try not to show it, will you?"

Bert Firhill had been deputed to open the front door to the guests and to bring them into the drawing room. He had put on the butler's gloves for the task—he was rather proud of them, even if they did not go with the blazer and tie that he was wearing. Now he brought Philip in and announced him formally. "The vicar."

Philip stepped forward. He looked at Emma as he did so, and so did Bert.

"It's very good to see you, Philip," said Mr. Woodhouse. "This is just a fairly spontaneous little party, but we thought it would be nice to have people over for another dinner. People should try to get back into the habit of giving dinner parties."

"They should indeed," said Philip. "It's a very civilised practice that seems to be dying out these days. I'm very much in favour of dinner parties."

"Yet you don't give them yourself," observed Emma. She said this without apparent malice, in an observational tone of voice. And then she added, "As far as I know."

Mr. Woodhouse gave her a warning look. This was not a good start. "Philip is very busy, Emma," he said. "He has his parish work and his . . ." He waved a hand in the air. "His . . ."

"Ph.D.," said Philip, smiling at Emma. "But you're right, Emma. I should hold a dinner party, and I shall do so soon. And I hope—I fervently hope—that you will head the list of invitees. You and your father, of course."

Mr. Woodhouse looked slightly flustered. "I don't go out very much," he said. "So don't worry about me."

"Then please come by yourself," said Philip to Emma.

"Thank you," she said. She had just noticed that Bert Firhill was staring at her. Why? "I think that's the bell," she said.

"I don't think so," replied Bert. "I didn't hear it."

"Well, if it didn't ring, then I am sure that it will do so shortly." She paused. "Would you mind?"

Bert left the room and Emma poured Philip a drink. He had asked for a gin and tonic, and she made sure that it was a good triple measure. She handed this to him, and then made a whisky and soda for her father.

"It was very good of you to put that sketch through my door the other day," said Philip, as he took a sip of his drink. "I'm sorry that I wasn't in when you called. Parish business, you know."

Emma waited for him to say something further, but he was intent on a second sip of his gin and tonic. "I hope you liked it," she said. "It was just a little sketch—nothing major."

Philip lowered his glass. "But it was wonderful," he said. "It really was. You captured Harriet's look just perfectly, if I may give you my opinion. That slightly upturned nose of hers . . ."

"Retroussé," said Emma.

"Yes, that retroussé nose. And her hands—they were very delicately painted."

"They're delicate hands," said Emma. "Hands are often difficult to do."

"I'm sure they are. But you did them beautifully."

"You're very kind."

Philip raised his glass to his lips. Emma noticed that the level was going down rather quickly. At least one gin had been consumed by now; two remained. It would be amusing, she thought, to see him inebriated. He might say something highly entertaining; one never knew. But it would certainly put him in the right frame of mind to make an advance to Harriet; inhibitions never helped romance to flourish.

"Have you taken the picture to the framers yet?" she asked.

Philip shook his head. "Not yet, no. No. We may have to reconsider that."

"Reconsider framing it?" asked Emma. "Why?"

He shifted from foot to foot. *He's embarrassed,* thought Emma. Had he perhaps made a rash promise of being able to get good framers to do the job and then found that he could not? Was that the problem?

"I'm not sure if it's quite right," said Philip, looking nervously at Mr. Woodhouse, who was following this conversation although not joining in.

Emma was about to ask why he felt this, but was interrupted by the arrival of the next party of guests. This was James Weston, Miss Taylor, and Frank Churchill. She stepped forward to greet Frank.

"I last saw you when we were about twelve," said Frank. "I don't remember it very well, but I think you ignored me entirely."

Emma laughed. "Children are so rude to one another, aren't they?"

"Too true," said Frank. "But we're not twelve any more."

"I promise I won't be rude to you," said Emma.

"Good. I couldn't bear it if you were. We Australians are very sensitive, you know."

Everybody laughed. It was such a witty thing to say.

"You and Frank must have a lot of catching up to do," Mr. Woodhouse remarked to James Weston.

"Yes," said James, looking proudly at his son. "We do. But we've got Frank for months now, we hope, and so there'll be plenty of time."

"It's been a very happy few days for all of us," said Miss Taylor.

Emma was taking the opportunity to study Frank. Harriet had said *to die for,* and she was right. She studied his face. It was the regularity of the features that struck her, and again Harriet, for all her naïvety, had been right about that. The classical ideal of beauty required that nose and eyes should bear a certain proportional relationship to the brow, and whatever that proportion was—and perhaps it was that magical Greek figure, *phi*—then Frank Churchill had it. She looked at his hair: light brown turned golden at the top by exposure to the sun. He was male perfection incarnate: it was as simple as that. And he had a brain, people said. That made a difference. A dumb Adonis would have been tedious; one who thought and could speak in sentences—with subjects *and* verbs—was infinitely more attractive.

The pre-dinner drinks dispensed, and consumed, Emma led the guests into the dining room.

"Quite the little hostess," whispered Miss Taylor to James.

"Thanks to you," he replied under his voice. "Your graduate."

"The clay shaped itself," said Miss Taylor. "I couldn't have changed Emma had I wanted to. And I fear for her, I'm sorry to say."

James glanced at Emma, who was taking her seat at the head of the table. "You think she'll come a cropper?"

"I don't know. Maybe yes, maybe no. But there's a danger that she'll overstep the mark with somebody."

James nodded. As an old friend of the family he did not want Emma to be hurt; at the same time, though, he felt that a short, sharp shock might be the only way in which she would be brought down a peg or two. That was it, he thought; she needed taking down a peg or two.

With everybody seated, Emma looked down the table at her guests. She had placed Philip next to Harriet Smith, and she noticed, with some satisfaction, that he was already engaging her in what appeared to be animated conversation. The triple gin had done its work, she thought; now all that was needed was a response from Harriet, and the whole scheme would fall into place. *How satisfying,* she thought; *and I have created this. It is all my idea.*

Her gaze moved on to Miss Taylor and James. Although they were not seated together, she had seen the look of affection that passed between them as they took their places at the table; such affection as might be felt between a couple who had been together for years, rather than a few weeks; a look of friendship, a look of pleasure, of satisfaction, perhaps, at having found each other. *But it was I who found you for each other,* she told herself. *I am responsible for your happiness.*

Then there was Miss Bates. Emma felt a sudden tug of conscience and told herself that she must make more of an effort with Miss Bates; she must give her a bit more of her time. It would be easy enough; all she had to do was to call on her now and then—Miss Bates was always in—and give her a present of those violet creams that she liked so much but obviously could no longer afford. Miss Bates, she assumed, divided her life between the violet-cream days—before she was an unsuccessful Lloyd's Name—and the days in which violet creams were

just a distant memory. Lloyd's Names had suffered in many different ways—being deprived of violet creams was just one way
in which financial disaster brought hardship. Poor Miss Bates—
and there she was sitting next to James, who was being so kind
to her, as he was to everybody, whatever his or her failings.

But there was no time to take in the rest of the table, as Emma
had Frank Churchill on her right, and he had to be talked to.

"Place of honour," said Frank. "On the hostess's right."

"Yes," said Emma. "I've split up the Randalls party. I assumed
that you wouldn't want to be beside your father and . . ." She
almost said "stepmother," but remembered that this would be
premature. ". . . Miss Taylor," she finished.

"I'm easy," said Frank.

She looked at him, noticing his skin, tanned by the sun. She
noticed, too, his watch, a Patek Philippe. It was understated
and would have been missed by most people. Emma knew just
what it was.

"This must be the first time you've met her," she said.

"Yes."

He was smiling at her in a way that suggested she would
get no further information from him. She had the impression,
too, that he was thinking about something. It was as if he was
weighing her up in some way; and it was disconcerting.

"She'll be great for your dad," she said. "He was so lonely."

Frank frowned. "Was he?"

"Oh, yes."

"That's too bad."

Mrs. Firhill was serving the soup, and was now hovering
behind Frank with a tureen. He half turned, and smiled as she
ladled the consommé into his plate. Emma thought: *He's pay-*

ing attention to her. Why? She waited until he turned back. "What are you going to do after you leave Randalls?" she asked. "Are you going to travel?"

He shrugged. "I'm not sure. Maybe. I've got a friend who's in France at the moment. We had a vague arrangement to go to Thailand for a few months. I could do that on the way back to Perth."

Emma dipped her spoon into her consommé. There was a friend. She felt a certain irritation at the thought that Frank Churchill already had a friend; the first seeds of envy. "She's French?"

"He. No, Australian."

The word *he* dropped into the conversation like a small stone into a pond. Her first thought was: *I was right, again! Inadvertently, but still right. He isn't interested!* And then she remembered what Harriet had said, which was, "What a pity."

Frank wiped his lips with his table napkin. "We've known each other a long time," he said.

She had been distracted by her thoughts. "Who?"

"Geoff, my friend in France—we were at school together."

She wanted to find out more, but was trying to work out how to ascertain the nature of the relationship. Perhaps she had jumped to conclusions; in fact, she was now sure that she had. Old school friends could go to Thailand together without there being anything more to it.

"You're lucky still to be in touch with friends from school," she said. "I hardly ever see mine. Except for one or two I occasionally hear from."

He looked at her intently. "It's different with me and Geoff."

She did not know what to make of this. "Oh . . ."

"Yes."

The situation was now unambiguously clear. "I'm fine with that," said Emma.

Frank lowered his voice. "One thing, though—I like to flirt."

Emma was unprepared for this. "Flirt?"

"Yes. It's cover. I'm fed up with people suggesting that I have to get a girlfriend and get married. I get it all the time. You've got no idea."

"Can't you come out? Doesn't that take the heat off you?"

Frank shook his head. "No, I can't. It's fine for most people, but I can't because I have the Churchills to think of. They wouldn't understand—they just wouldn't. My aunt is ill, too, and it's simpler for her not to know. Later, when she's gone, I'll think again. And I'm not sure if I want to hurt my real father's feelings. He feels guilty, you know."

"Are you sure?"

"Yes, dead sure. And I think that if I came out, then he'd feel even guiltier. No need for him to do that, of course, as the way I feel is nothing to do with my father having handed me over to my aunt and uncle. Nothing at all. But he'd think: *Oh my God, it's my fault for being an absentee father, et cetera, et cetera.* Believe me, it's simpler—at least for now."

"If you say so."

"I do." He paused. He was looking directly into her eyes. "Would you mind if I flirted with you? Just a bit?"

Emma's first reaction was to say no. She saw no reason why she should be drawn into Frank's problems, especially since she thought they were largely of his own creation. She was not convinced that James would take the disclosure badly—he was a tolerant man, with modern attitudes. Why not just tell him?

Why try to conceal something that most people now thought of as perfectly natural—as just one of the possibilities of being human?

But then she looked at Frank, who was smiling back at her in a way that immediately weakened her resolve. Why not? It tickled her that she should be the object of the attentions of such a breathtakingly good-looking young man. She could even imagine that when he flirted he meant it, while at the same time she could have the reassurance of knowing that he did not, for Emma was wary of involvement with men.

"All right."

His smile widened. And it was at that point that Frank leaned over to her—just as Mrs. Firhill was beginning to clear the soup plates on the opposite side of the table—and whispered into her ear: "Sex!"

It was perfect. Emma was genuinely taken by surprise, and reacted as anybody into whose ear the word *sex* had been whispered might be expected to react. She gave a start, and then, reverting to her agreed role, pouted. Leaning forward herself, she whispered into his ear, "Consommé!"

That made him laugh, or begin to laugh and then apparently struggle to suppress it.

Everybody saw what was going on—or at least everybody on the opposite side of the table saw it. James's eyebrows shot up, and then shot down again. Miss Taylor's brow furrowed, and then became smooth once more. Jane Fairfax's mouth opened very slightly, and then shut. Mrs. Firhill raised her eyes to the ceiling and then lowered them again.

The dinner party continued. The hubbub of conversation increased during the second course, and by the third—

a chocolate mousse of which Mrs. Firhill was particularly proud—the level of sound was almost deafening. Shortly after eleven, though, Mr. Woodhouse began to yawn, and several of the guests, noticing this, started to suggest that they leave. This was the signal for all to rise to their feet and begin to drift out into the hall. Emma had intended that they should finish in the drawing room, where coffee, decaffeinated and otherwise, was waiting, but the host's obvious tiredness had put paid to that.

She met Harriet in the small morning room where the women had placed their coats. They were alone, and she took the opportunity to find out how her friend had got on with Philip. "Things seemed to be going well at your end of the table," said Emma.

"Really well," said Harriet. "We talked and talked all evening. He barely said anything to the person on his right. He's got such a lovely voice, Emma. He really has. I could listen to him for hours."

I couldn't, thought Emma. But she said, "Yes, you're right. It's lovely." She looked at Harriet encouragingly. "And?"

Harriet smiled coyly. "I think he likes me."

"Good."

"I think he's going to ask me out."

"Also good."

Harriet picked up her coat and they went out into the hall. There were few guests left now: Mrs. Goddard, Harriet, and Philip. Mrs. Goddard embraced Mr. Woodhouse, planting a kiss left and right, preventing him from recoiling by embracing him firmly. "Dear Woody," she said. "It's been such a treat. And promise me you'll remember."

Mr. Woodhouse looked anxiously at Emma. "Yes, of course. Of course."

"Now, Harriet, dear," said Mrs. Goddard, releasing Mr. Woodhouse and turning to Harriet. "That's us offski."

Emma smiled. *Offski.*

"And you, dear Emma," continued Mrs. Goddard. "You must come and hang out with us. Promise me you will. Go on, promise."

Emma smiled again. "Any time," she said.

"Any time *soon*," enthused Mrs. Goddard. "Now come on, Harriet, time to split."

Now it was just Philip, Mr. Woodhouse, and Emma.

"I must go too," said Philip. He had been watching Mrs. Goddard with a certain morbid fascination, and Emma even thought that she detected a suppressed shudder. Well, that was not surprising; cold fish meets warm, effusive fish, she thought; and for all the *offski* and *splitting*, she instinctively liked Mrs. Goddard, or Mrs. God as she now thought of her. What if God, if he (she) was actually like her: rather casual, with a fondness for cannabis (which he, after all, would have created in the first place) and a benign, rather folksy manner? What if God actually hated Gregorian chants and the Anglican liturgy, strongly disliked the smell of incense the Catholics kept wafting in his direction, and had a strong sympathy for ageing hippies who taught English as a foreign language? What if God actually knew the way to the railway station but understood that others needed to be told as well?

Mr. Woodhouse yawned. "Oh goodness, I am sorry. You see Philip out, Emma," he said. "I'm afraid I must get to bed before I collapse. Such social excitement!"

He shook Philip's hand quickly and disappeared down the corridor.

"He gets so tired," said Emma. "He's always up early—that's the problem. He's up at five most days."

"Emma," said Philip. "Can we talk?"

Emma affected surprise. "Of course. But about what? We've all just covered every subject under the sun in the dining room. Politics?"

Philip swayed slightly on his feet. "Could we go outside? It's a lovely night."

Emma looked out into the garden. "It could rain."

"It won't rain. It's perfect. Couldn't we go and sit on the lawn for a few minutes?"

She looked at her watch. "It's so late . . ."

He took her arm, gently, and moved towards the front door. She did not resist; he probably had something to say about Harriet, and she would, of course, encourage him. *I can tolerate this* creepy *man for the sake of Harriet*, she told herself.

There was an almost full moon outside, painting the garden an ethereal silver. "Look at the moon," she said. "So bright. So lunar!" She had to say something.

They were standing on the lawn now. "I don't want to sit on the grass," she said. "It gets so damp at night." She thought of his office building in Ipswich, and its chronic damp.

"Emma," he said. "I need to tell you something."

It occurred to her that he wanted to discuss the portrait. That was it.

"What did you think of my portrait of Harriet?" she asked. "You can be absolutely frank, you know." Frankness, of course, was the last thing she wanted; praise was the first.

He seemed to regard her question as a distraction. "Oh that. Well . . ."

She waited. "Yes?"

"You did it in pastel."

"Yes, it's a pastel drawing. I thought that would work rather well for Harriet. Her colouring, you see, rather lends itself to pastel, don't you agree?" And then she added, "There's nothing wrong with pastels, you know. Vuillard used them a lot. They look like oils until you get up close, and then you realise they're not."

He sighed. "You didn't fix it."

What was he talking about? She always fixed her pastels. "I did. I sprayed it with fixative. I always do."

He shook his head. He was standing with the moon behind him and she could not see his expression. "You fixed the first drawing—the one underneath. You forgot to fix what you did on top of it. So when I smudged it—inadvertently—I saw what was underneath."

Emma caught her breath.

Philip seemed to be waiting for her to say something, but at first she did not. Finally she said, "Major embarrassment."

"I should think so."

Emma decided to brazen it out. "I'm very sorry. I'm sorry that you've seen Harriet in the nude, but . . ." She hesitated. "Don't let it put you off her. Please. Nothing need be said. You should just go ahead anyway."

"Go ahead with what?"

"With Harriet. With seeing her."

This remark was greeted with complete silence. Then Philip

emitted what sounded like a groan. "You don't think that I'm interested in *her*, do you?"

"Yes."

"But, Emma, no, no, no. You've got it completely wrong. It's *you* I like. I like you a lot. In fact, I think I'm in love with you."

She stood quite still. She heard him breathing. She felt his hand upon her arm.

"Say something, Emma. Please say something."

She struggled to speak. The awfulness of the situation seemed to have constricted her throat. It was hard enough to breathe, let alone to speak. Eventually she said, "I don't really think so."

He let out another groan. "Please review the situation. Please reconsider."

She felt her confidence grow; he sounded like a business letter. "No. You should stick to Harriet."

"Her!"

"And what's wrong with her? She's a very attractive young woman."

"She's an airhead."

This was too much for Emma. He was right, but she would not have him say it. "Since when did vicars call other people airheads? You should be ashamed of yourself, Philip."

This silenced him. She waited a few moments, and then announced that she had to get back into the house. "And you," she said, "should not be driving. You had three gins before din-ner and then . . ." She stopped herself, but he had heard what she had said.

"You deliberately gave me three gins?"

"You didn't have to drink them." She knew this was a weak response.

He snorted. "I'm quite sober, thank you. Talking to you is enough to sober anybody up."

She watched him as he strode away. When he reached the BMW Something-something he was briefly illuminated by the automatic switching on of the interior light. She saw him lower himself into the driving seat and slam the door. Then the engine roared into life and the car spun round in a tight circle, the beams of its headlights sweeping across the lawn and catching Emma for a second or two before they moved away.

Emma went back into the house, her mind a confusion of conflicting thoughts. But one thought seemed to rise above the others: *I created this mess. I did it.*

17

E mma decided to visit Harriet the following day. She had toyed with the idea of leaving matters exactly where they stood, but it seemed to her it would be better to put Harriet off Philip before she learned of his lack of interest in her. This would be easily achieved, she felt: Harriet had shown herself to be remarkably malleable, and a few words of advice, judiciously chosen, would undoubtedly be enough to bring the whole thing to an end.

She had not yet decided exactly what she would have to say to Harriet. It had occurred to her that she might tell her that Philip was already involved with somebody else—possibly even that he was already married—but that, she realised, would simply be untrue, and she did not tell lies. Far better, then, to tell the truth about Philip—that he was a flawed character, which was true and could be put to Harriet in perfectly good faith. There might be an issue as to why Emma had changed her view so quickly, but this could be explained as a falling of scales from the eyes, as sometimes happened, even to the best judges of character.

She had phoned Harriet to let her know she was coming.

Harriet explained that she was teaching earlier in the morning, but would be free from eleven-thirty. "Will you be driving over in your Mini Cooper?"

Emma bit her tongue. Oh, silly, silly girl! "Yes," she said with as much patience as she could muster.

"I'd love to go for another spin in it sometime. I'd love that."

"I'm sure we can do that, if not today, then some other day."

"Thank you."

By the time Emma parked the Mini Cooper outside Mrs. Goddard's house, she knew exactly what she was going to say, and how she would say it. She waited in the car until she saw Harriet returning from the teaching block, then she got out and approached her friend.

"You said you wanted to go for a spin in the Mini Cooper," said Emma. "How about now?"

Harriet was enthusiastic. "Ooh, I'd love that. I'll just get my hat."

Emma, wondering why Harriet would need a hat to go for a drive in the Mini Cooper, returned to the car and cleared the various newspapers and unopened letters cluttering the passenger seat. Then Harriet returned, sporting a wide-brimmed straw hat around the crown of which a garland of spring flowers, fashioned out of coloured fabric, had been carefully wound. The flowers were of different sorts: freesias, daisies, tiny rosebuds.

Emma had decided that she would deliver her news while driving the car. Harriet would be in her territory then, and would not wish to argue with the driver. She would also have to listen just as long as Emma wished to continue, since the drive and the advice could well end up being coterminous.

By the time they set off, Emma had already introduced the subject.

"I'm so glad that everybody enjoyed themselves so much last night," she said. "Or just about everybody did."

"Oh, I think it was everybody without exception," said Harriet pertly. "I didn't see anybody looking downcast."

"Not from where you were sitting," said Emma.

Harriet, who had been gazing out of the passenger window, turned to face Emma. "But I really don't think anybody was unhappy. I really don't. The party only broke up because your poor father was so tired. That's all it was. Otherwise, I think it could have gone on for ages."

"I'm not sure that would have been a good thing," said Emma. "Then the guests with a drink problem would have had the chance to drink even more."

It took Harriet some time to respond to this. Emma could see she was thinking, torn, no doubt, between curiosity and discretion. Curiosity won out. "With a drink problem? Surely none of your guests . . ."

"Oh, yes," said Emma. "You'd be surprised."

Harriet looked away again. "Mrs. God likes a drink, but I don't think she has an actual problem, you know. And she has lots of other really good qualities. She's generous: she's been very kind to me, and to loads of other people too. She bought a ticket to Portugal for one of the students who needed to get home because his mother was ill. She didn't ask him to pay her back."

"I wasn't thinking of Mrs. God," said Emma.

"Oh." Harriet paused. And then, she said, "Who, then?"

"I'm not sure if I should tell you. It's not that I don't trust you to keep it to yourself—I do, it's just that . . . Oh, all right. Have another guess."

"Miss Bates?"

"Miss Bates!"

"Well, she sometimes looks a bit red."

"That, Harriet, is what she would call rouge—in other words blusher. Somebody like Miss Bates would use a lot of it. Rouge and cologne. No, not Miss Bates."

They turned a corner, rather too fast, and the Mini Cooper listed to the side. "Oops!" said Harriet.

"It's Philip Elton, I'm sorry to say."

They had come to a stop sign, where the lane on which they had been driving joined a larger, busier road. Emma drew in to a rough, informal parking place that had been used as a temporary campsite. There were several old refrigerators and piles of rubbish.

"Look at all that rubbish," remarked Emma. "This is not to criticise travellers, it's just to say: look at all that rubbish."

Harriet sounded distressed. "Philip?" she said.

Emma switched off the engine of the Mini Cooper. "I know it sounds extraordinary. After all, he is a vicar, and an expert in Byzantine history. Neither of these things is particularly associated with drink—I know that. But then all sorts of people drink too much—you'd be surprised."

"But he didn't have all that much," objected Harriet. "Three glasses of wine, maybe four. That was all."

Emma sighed. "But what did he have before we even got into the dining room, Harriet? I'll tell you: three gins. Three *large* gins. I saw him. I'm not making this up—in fact, I promise you: three large gins. Straight down."

Harriet appeared to be digesting this information. Emma pressed on with her attack. "Now you see, Harriet, if you start off with three large gins in your bloodstream and then you have four generous glasses of wine, what then? You're drunk. You're certainly not fit to drive, which I may say, he did."

"I suppose . . ."

"Yes, you are, Harriet. You're drunk. And then to drive a car in that state is criminal. You could cause awful damage to somebody else. Everybody knows that—except, it seems, Philip. Or perhaps he does know it and simply doesn't care." She watched the effect of her words. They were hitting home now. "People who know that they could be harming somebody else and just don't care—you know what they are, Harriet? They're psychopaths." She paused, amazed by her own effrontery.

"Surely not . . ."

It was too late to retract. "No, surely yes. Psychopaths are people who have a personality disorder, Harriet, and they don't care what the impact of their acts will be. They're prepared to hurt other people in whatever way takes their fancy. They're prepared to kill people at the drop of a hat. Many of the top Nazis were psychopaths, Harriet. Goering, Goebbels. You know, it's a funny thing, and probably no connection with anything—probably just a complete coincidence—but I've always thought that Philip looks extraordinarily like Joseph Goebbels. Odd, that."

She could hardly believe she had said this. It was that ridiculous. It was outrageous—but it was so easy to say; so easy, the words just tumbled out.

Harriet had taken off her straw hat and was twisting it in her discomfort. One of the flowers, a tiny linen daisy, came off and tumbled to the floor of the Mini Cooper.

"And there's something else, Harriet. I didn't want to tell you, but I feel that as your friend—your particular friend—I can't let you remain in ignorance. And so I've decided to tell you. Are you prepared for this?"

Harriet nodded her head. She looked miserable.

"In his inebriated state, just before he left—drove off while unfit to drive—Philip manhandled me into the garden. He took my arm and hauled me off."

Harriet gasped. "No!"

Emma closed her eyes briefly, as if trying to obliterate a painful memory. "Then he tried to get me down to the ground. I said, 'No, no, you mustn't,' or words to that effect, and I was able to fend him off. But he actually made a pass at me, Harriet. Although you and I know that he's keen on you, he was still prepared to tell me that he entertained a passion for *me*, Harriet—for *me*, your friend! He's . . . he's indiscriminate."

Harriet gasped. "He didn't hurt you, I hope."

"Just a slight bruise on my arm," said Emma. "Nothing much."

"What happened then?"

"After I had refused him, he went off in a real rage. He said something about talking to me being enough to sober anybody up—a really nasty remark—and then he got into that BMW Something-something of his and went off in a shower of stones. I saw the marks on the driveway the next morning and went over them with one of Mrs. Sid's rakes so that my father wouldn't see them and say, 'What's all this?' and I would have to answer—because I do tell the truth, Harriet—'That was where the vicar made his escape after propositioning me.' Sorry to be so brutally frank, Harriet, but there are occasions when one has to tell the truth."

Harriet reached across to Emma and held her arm tenderly. "Poor, poor you. Well, at least you're safe and sound. It could have been far, far worse."

"It certainly helps to have the support of a good friend," said Emma. "Thank you, Harriet."

"And to think he might have seen my portrait," said Harriet.

"Oh well," said Emma quickly. "Let's just put the whole thing out of our minds. You know, Harriet, there's a lot to be said for denial." She paused, and laid her own hand upon her friend's hand. "So why don't you put on your lovely straw hat again and we can continue our little journey without a thought of anything—or anyone—unpleasant, such as Philip Elton?"

Harriet replaced the hat.

"You look so lovely in that," said Emma. "The shape is just right. It really suits you."

"Mrs. God gave it to me," said Harriet.

Emma smiled. "A divine gift. How fortunate you are, Harriet, to have Mrs. God on your side."

Harriet had reached a decision. "Philip Elton," she said, "is history."

"Byzantine history," agreed Emma.

They both laughed.

They drove off. As she steered the Mini Cooper along a lane bordered on each side with hawthorn hedges, Emma told herself that she had not told a single lie. Not one. Philip really had drunk three gins; the fact that she had given them to him did not detract from the truth of that. Then, it was incontestably the case that he had driven on top of all that alcohol. And he had tried to get her to sit on the grass and declared his passion for her. Everything she had said was completely true.

But then again, it was not, and she suddenly knew it. She thought of what she had said, and she felt an abrupt sense of shame, the feeling that one has when one realises that one has committed a social solecism or caused grave offence. *I said some terrible things,* she told herself. *No, I didn't—what I said was true.* But the rationalisation, the attempt to put the best possible light on what she had said did not work. Her shame increased. *Psychopath*—she had called him a psychopath and Harriet, naïve, gullible Harriet, had believed her. She had plied him with drink and then described him as a drunkard. She had been responsible for his intoxicated driving. Her fault. *Her fault.* But then she only wanted to protect Harriet, and that made it legitimate, didn't it? There was a big difference between twisting the truth a bit to harm somebody and doing the same thing to protect somebody. Everybody knew that, didn't they? She decided that they did, and she felt slightly better.

The assessment of summer that year varied widely. It was a "passable summer," said Mrs. Sid. Her runner beans were doing very well, and her salad vegetable bed was ripening nicely, but she was not at all pleased with her Victoria plums (measly) and her apples (very few, very few). From the perspective of Mr. Woodhouse, the summer was a good one, and rather better than the previous year. He judged the seasons by the incidence, throughout the world, of major weather disasters. He was a close observer of hurricanes in the Caribbean, following the daily bulletins of the American hurricane-tracking service. Any sign of unusual activity—an unexpected typhoon, a delay in the arrival of rains, an unusual pattern of heat-encouraged bush fires in Australia, was taken as further evidence of global warming, a subject in which he had a strong interest. That summer there had been little: the earth's weather seemed to be unusually stable, with comfortable high-pressure zones settling over the Atlantic and over Europe, bringing sunshine and soft breezes to Norfolk, and in particular to Highbury and Hartfield. Such cloud as there was seemed benign and friendly: little patches of cotton-wool cumulus drifting lazily across a blue sky; the occasional wisp of high stratus, but no ominous mares' tails; nothing that would disturb the rambler or the swimmer.

For Philip Elton the good weather was neither here nor there. He found no cause for satisfaction in days of comfortable sunshine, which in no way mirrored his angry and embarrassed mood. The main cause of his embarrassment was the aftermath of Emma's dinner party. It was not the fact that he had made a fool of himself on the lawn, resulting in his firm rebuff—that was a painful enough experience, but it faded into insignificance beside what subsequently happened. That was the real disaster of the evening.

After he had shot down the Hartfield drive in the BMW Something-something, Philip had made his way home at considerable speed. The speed limit for most of the journey was either forty miles an hour, where the road was narrow and winding, or occasionally sixty, where it became more substantial. Philip exceeded the limit on both sections, but it was not this that was to prove his undoing. That came when, travelling at a rather low speed in order to negotiate a tricky bend in a lane, he misjudged the curve of the road and ended up in a ditch. No damage was done to the car, and he himself suffered no injury. Had he been given the opportunity to reverse back on to the road, he could have extricated himself from the ditch and resumed his journey, with nobody having been any the wiser. He did not get that opportunity, though, for the first car on the scene—just a minute or two after he had toppled into the ditch—was a car from the police station at Holt, driven by Sergeant Tom Mayfield, returning from a call to investigate a burglary attempt in a nearby village. In the passenger seat of the police car was Constable Martin Horsley, who was not only tired but was suffering from toothache caused by an area of sensitivity in one of his teeth.

"Hello," said Sergeant Mayfield as they rounded the corner. "What have we here?"

"A Beemer Something-something," replied Constable Horsley. "And I don't think it's going anywhere. My God, my tooth!"

"Get yourself to the dentist first thing tomorrow," snapped Sergeant Mayfield. "And I don't want to hear any more of your precious tooth. I'm pulling over. That fellow's lights are still on."

The two policemen got out of their car and approached the stricken vehicle. As they did so, Philip, who had seen them coming, opened his door and took a deep breath.

"Thank goodness you've turned up," he said. "I seem to have slipped into this ditch. It's a tricky corner."

Constable Horsley shone his torch into Philip's face. "Oh, it's you, vicar," he said. He recognised him as Philip had presided over the funeral of his late uncle. Sergeant Mayfield also knew who he was as they had both spoken at a social-responsibility day at a nearby school.

"This is a bit of sorry to-do," said the sergeant. "You been out and about, vicar?"

Relieved to be recognised, Philip was effusive in his explanation. "At a dinner party, as it happens. At Hartfield—you know the place—Mr. Woodhouse's house. A jolly good dinner. His cook is Mrs. Firhill and her chocolate mousse . . ." He stopped. Sergeant Mayfield had taken the torch from Constable Horsley and had played the beam over Philip, from head to toe, as if looking for something.

"Did you have a drink at all, vicar?" he asked.

Philip stared at the policeman. "A drink?"

"Yes. Alcohol, you know. Wine, for instance. I'm sure Mr. Woodhouse has a good cellar at that big place of his."

Philip swallowed. "A sip or two. With the meal, of course."

Sergeant Mayfield glanced at Constable Horsley. "Of course," he said. He then cleared his throat. "I'm sorry, vicar, but there's a requirement that we breathalyse drivers involved in incidents. It's the law, you see."

"But this isn't an incident," said Philip, his voice wavering. "I haven't hit anything. I just sort of . . . slipped off the road. It wasn't my fault."

Constable Horsley had retrieved the breathalyser kit from the police car and was preparing it for use. "If you just breathe into this little tube, vicar. It's completely painless."

With fumbling hands, Philip complied. Then he stood by awkwardly while the two policemen considered the result.

"Oh dear, oh dear," said Sergeant Mayfield. "I'm afraid you're well over the limit, vicar."

"I find that hard to believe," said Philip. "I really do."

There was now a note of firmness in Sergeant Mayfield's voice. "Be that as it may, sir, you must accompany us to the station for another test."

Philip made a strange, moaning sound.

"Are you all right, sir?" asked Constable Horsley.

"My car," complained Philip. "I can't leave my car in the ditch."

"You can't drive, vicar," said Sergeant Mayfield. "You're in no fit state. We'll sort the car out later."

In silence and in misery, Philip accompanied the two policemen to the police car. He sat morosely in the back seat with Constable Horsley, his hands clasped firmly together, his eyes downcast. "What will happen to me," he asked, "if I'm convicted?"

"You lose your licence," said the constable. "No driving for a year, I'm afraid."

"Most unfortunate," added Sergeant Mayfield from the front seat. "You being a vicar and all. Most unfortunate all round."

And it was most unfortunate. Two weeks later, having pled guilty and therefore been fast-tracked through the criminal-justice system, Philip appeared before the local magistrates' court and was duly fined and banned from driving for a year. The case was fully reported in the local press under the headline: "Boozy Rev Revs Up and Ends in Ditch." Humiliated and ashamed, Philip decided to take three weeks' leave pending his bishop's decision on his future. He had a cousin in London who offered to lend him his flat in Notting Hill while he was in the British Virgin Islands. Philip accepted the offer with relief, and sneaked off to the blissful anonymity of London—by public transport. Slowly he began to recover from the embarrassment and self-reproach that the whole incident had caused him, and found himself drawn into a social life organised by friendly neighbours in Kensington Park Road. It was through them that he met, during his second week in London, a woman who was introduced to him as a popular contestant in a television talent show, *Look at Me!* She was a dancer and Edith Piaf impersonator, although she was blonde and buxom, and not at all like the French chanteuse. She knew the limits of her talent: these were severe, as she could not really sing, least of all in French, which she sang with the American accent that bad British singers for some reason feel they must adopt. She also misunderstood the words, thinking that "Non, je ne regrette rien" was a song about sending one's apologies for being unable to accept an invitation; she understood very well, though, that her C-list celebrity status was best exploited by finding a man who was capable of supporting her in the style to which she aspired. In conversation Philip had happened to mention the office block in Ipswich as well as the flats in Norwich. She had been listening. He had said nothing about dampness or insulation problems. She was immediately interested.

18

For Emma, the fine summer weather meant the opportunity for a picnic. She had raised this possibility with Mr. Woodhouse, who had listened attentively to her suggestion before he asked, in a deliberate and considered way, "Why?"

Emma's reply was equally considered. "Because a picnic is what one has in fine weather. Ask anybody, 'What do you do on a fine day?' and they will reply, 'Why, we picnic, of course.' That's why I suggested it."

The sarcasm with which Emma had clothed her response was lost on Mr. Woodhouse. "But why, Emma? Why? It's not enough, my dear, to say that's what people do. People do all sorts of things. The real question is why do it? You can eat the same food—in fact, rather better food—in your own dining room. You don't get ants in your own dining room. You aren't subject to the vagaries of the weather."

"The weather is absolutely settled," interrupted Emma. "Look at the sky."

"The sky tells us very little, Emma. The isobaric charts reveal the real truth. And I can tell you that they show things brewing up over Iceland. They'll be having no picnics over in Iceland, I can assure you."

Emma sighed. There was no point in arguing with her father, who would always produce some good reason not to do anything. The only way to proceed was to proceed.

"Well, it's a great pity," she said, "but I've already invited people. We're committed."

It was not a lie in the true sense of the word. Emma had invited Harriet—that was true—but she had not invited anybody else. The issue then was whether having invited one person justified the claim to have invited "people." Emma considered this, but only briefly, and only after she had made the statement. She decided that the grammatical distinction between the singular and the plural was now so weak—*they* being used as a third-person singular pronoun, for instance—that it was quite acceptable to refer to a person as *people*. That disposed of that; what she had said was true.

Mr. Woodhouse looked peeved, but only momentarily. His anxieties could shift very quickly, and what had been an overwhelming problem could within minutes, indeed within seconds, become no more than the background to a greater, more pressing issue.

"But what will we do about the sandwiches?" he asked. "They become limp and soggy so quickly. Have you thought about that yet, Emma? Have you discussed it with Mrs. Firhill?"

"We don't have to eat sandwiches, Pops," said Emma. "There are plenty of other things to eat on a picnic. There are those rather nice pork pies—Melton Mowbray pies. People love those on a picnic."

This had the desired effect, firmly shifting the conversation to dietary matters and away from picnic issues.

Mr. Woodhouse shook his head. "Those pies," he said gravely, "are full of salt. And pork."

"Well, they are pork pies . . ."

"I know that you like bacon, Emma, but I wish you would eat less of it. I was reading the other day that each slice of bacon you eat takes several minutes off your life."

"And years off a pig's life," interjected Emma.

Mr. Woodhouse frowned. "I don't see what pigs' lives have got to do with it."

Emma did not answer for a while. Then she said, "I shall make all the plans. You just attend—that's all you have to do. You come along and be your usual, cheerful self. That's what people will want."

"Who's coming?"

Emma composed a quick mental list. "The usual suspects," she said. "The Weston–Taylors, Frank Churchill, *la veuve* Bates, Miss Bates (yawn), Jane Fairfax (iceberg), George Knightley, Mr. Perry (crank)—if you'd like him to come . . ."

"Yes, we must invite him," said Mr. Woodhouse. "He's very good on wild plants. He knows all their healing properties and he can identify any mushrooms we find."

"That will be very useful," said Emma. "And then there's Harriet Smith and Mrs. Goddard."

She watched her father's reaction. "Mrs. Goddard?" he said. "Do you think she'll come?"

"I think she enjoyed that dinner party, and I like her." She paused. "You like her too, don't you?"

He looked away. "Yes, I like her. She's . . . she's unusual, isn't she? We don't get many people like that around here."

Emma waited for more, but he fell silent. "Did you know her quite well?" she asked.

"Reasonably well."

The subject of Mrs. Goddard, she judged, was now closed.

Mr. Woodhouse suddenly thought of somebody else. "What about Philip Elton?" he asked.

"I don't think so. And anyway, I think he's away."

Mr. Woodhouse shook his head. "He was. He's back now. And I would like to have him there, Emma—I'd like that very much."

Emma was thinking of the complications of having Philip: she did not want Harriet to be reminded of her attempt at matchmaking, and she did not want to run the risk that the true nature of affairs be revealed. She also felt something to which she was unaccustomed and that was largely unexpected: a niggling sense of guilt. She had given him those large gins, and he had subsequently lost his licence and been publicly humiliated. Did he blame her for that?

Mr. Woodhouse now explained why he was so keen for Philip to be invited. "I feel sorry for that poor man," he said. "He may not be to everyone's taste—I'll admit that I find him a bit on the pompous side—but his heart's surely in the right place. When Sid had his prostate operation, he went to see him in the hospital and offered to pick him up when they discharged him. Sid said that the other patients in his ward didn't receive any visits from their vicars. They were obviously quite indifferent to their poor parishioners' prostates."

"That's his job," said Emma.

"Yes, it may be, but remember that he doesn't get paid for it. He does it out of the goodness of his heart."

Emma said nothing.

"And then we have to remember that on the evening in question—the evening when he went into the ditch—he had been at our house, Emma. He had been under *our* roof. I really don't know how it happened, and yet poor Philip was quite a bit over the limit when they tested him. How can that be, I wonder?"

Emma looked out of the window.

"Did you notice what he had beforehand?" asked Mr. Wood-house. "You gave him a drink when we were in the drawing room. What did he have?"

"He had gin," muttered Emma.

"Just one?"

"One glass," said Emma. "I gave it to him. He didn't get a refill."

Mr. Woodhouse shook his head. "Most puzzling," he said. "But, be that as it may, there is a more important consideration here. The fact of the matter is that Philip has been publicly humiliated. He has been shamed. He owned up—he pled guilty, you know—and he was then punished. We must assume that he is contrite, and in those circumstances it is for us to show that he is not going to be ostracised."

Emma listened. "Maybe I . . ." she began, but did not finish.

"When somebody does wrong, Emma, we must remember that that person is still a human being like the rest of us. We must not rush to throw the first stone. We must remind our-selves that all of us do wrong from time to time, unless we're saints, which we aren't."

"And neither were half the saints themselves," interjected Emma.

"Possibly. But we mustn't join the mob of witch-hunters who love to expose and shame people. We mustn't do that. We must show that Philip has paid for what he did and is not going to be spurned. We need to take the lead here."

He seemed to be waiting for a response. "All right," said Emma.

"And I believe that he has a girlfriend in tow," said Mr. Woodhouse. "Somebody he met in London. I'm sure she's very nice. She should be invited too."

That was welcome news. That Philip had a new girlfriend meant he would not embarrass Emma with any further declarations. So Emma said, "Good. It's really nice to hear that he's found somebody—at last."

It was Mr. Woodhouse's picnic now. "And I think we should get in touch with Isabella and get her and John and all those children of hers along. It will be good for them to get out of London and get some country air. All those people in London breathing the air in and out; just think of it, Emma. Just think of all that breathing going on in London—it's a wonder there's any air left for the rest of us."

Nobody turned down the invitation. Some of those invited offered to help: Harriet said that she was happy to do anything that Emma felt needed to be done, and Mrs. Goddard said that she would bring two, possibly three, cakes that she would bake specially for the occasion. This offer was made by Mrs. Goddard directly to Mr. Woodhouse, whom she telephoned after she had received the invitation, rather than through Harriet, who would have discouraged it. And it was accepted by Mr. Woodhouse, rather than by Emma, who would have heeded Harriet's warning and declined it.

Miss Bates was particularly excited. "My goodness me," she enthused, "a picnic! You know, I was just thinking the other day: When did I last go on a picnic? And do you know, I couldn't remember, although it came back to me a little bit later when I was listening to Jane playing an arrangement of Verdi. And I remembered that it was many years ago in Tuscany, when I went there with a friend who was recovering from an operation on her arm, I think it was—or it might have been her hand. I think she had carpal-tunnel syndrome, and she had to have surgery more than once; once on the left hand and then again on the right hand, or perhaps it was twice on the left hand: you know, I really can't for the life of me remember which it was. She obviously couldn't carry the picnic basket and so I did that, and carried the rug too, and then I slipped—we were on a path that led down into a rather pleasant little gorge— and I tumbled over and over and ended up in an olive grove. I was quite unhurt, but my friend was distraught. I remember that quite well now."

Even Mrs. Bates, who had been included in the invitation, appeared to be excited about it: sufficiently so for her to say, "Picnic."

"There!" said Miss Bates. "Mother's thinking about picnics. That's far better than sitting there brooding about Lloyd's."

This was a mistake. At the mention of Lloyd's, Mrs. Bates's brow furrowed and she retreated once again into silence.

Isabella and John Knightley also responded warmly to the invitation, and arrived from London in their Volvo estate,

accompanied by their four children, on the day before the picnic was due to take place. They were given the guest wing at
Hartfield, where there were corridors down which the children could run without unduly disturbing Mr. Woodhouse in
his study or Mrs. Firhill in her kitchen. The children had been
told of the picnic, and had talked of little else since they left
London. Would there be cake? Would there be somewhere to
swim? What were the chances of meeting a bull while crossing
a field, and would Daddy be prepared to draw the bull away
with his coat while they climbed over a stile to safety?

"Whatever you do," Isabella warned them, "do not mention
bulls to your grandfather. Just don't."

She was right about that. Although Mr. Woodhouse had now
become actively involved in the planning of the picnic and was
keen for it to take place, his concern had grown over the risks
that he felt were an inevitable concomitant of the entire adven-
ture. Foremost among these was the possibility of rain.

"If it rains," he said, "and I'm afraid we must accept this as a
near certainty, then we shall have to have cover for everybody."

"We could always just go back to the cars and come home,"
suggested Emma. "That's the obvious thing to do."

He shook his head. "And what about that journey from the
picnic site to the cars? What about that, Emma? That could
take a good fifteen minutes; I've measured it on the Ordnance
Survey map. And during those fifteen minutes we could all get
soaked to the skin."

"That won't be the end of the world," said Emma. "It's only
rain, after all."

"Oh, Emma," he said, "you're thinking of yourself. You

and Isabella and Harriet and that Frank Churchill will all be fine because you're young and healthy. But what about poor Mrs. Bates? She's in no position to survive a soaking and would be a candidate for pneumonia. And if she went down with pneumonia, we could well lose her, and what a tragedy that would be."

"Mrs. Bates has to die sometime," said Emma. "I don't want anybody to become ill, but surely some things are inevitable."

"You heartless girl!" chided Mr. Woodhouse.

She tried to defend herself. "But I'm not being heartless. I'm merely saying that we can't all live forever, and I, for one, don't want to. Who wants to end up in a hospital bed, unable to do anything for yourself, and stuck full of tubes? What for? For more days and months of lying in bed, feeling miserable. Far better, surely, to go on a picnic and—"

"Enough!" shouted Mr. Woodhouse.

"I'm only trying to—"

"No, I shall not hear any more of your cruel views. Enough! Your problem, Emma, is that you can't see it from the point of view of those who are old and frightened and unable to speak because of what happened at Lloyd's."

They left it at that, and Mr. Woodhouse in due course placed a large order for plastic ponchos—one for each guest—that could easily be carried and unfolded in the event of rain. It was, he thought, his gesture against the whole pro-euthanasia movement that talked so glibly of choice without realising the fire with which one played when tinkering with fragile taboos against killing others. Yes, he thought, Mrs. Bates's life did not seem to amount to much, but to her it was all she had.

· · ·

The spot they had chosen for the picnic was no more than three miles from Hartfield, on land owned by George Knightley. Donwell Abbey had once been one of the largest estates in that part of England but had been considerably reduced by the enthusiasm of George's great-grandfather for risky investments. Yet even after the sale of several parcels of land in the 1920s and again in the 1950s, the home farm remained, and this was by far the largest holding in the area. It was at one end of this, where a gentle meadow was bounded by slightly rising ground, that the picnic was to take place. This rising ground was wooded, largely with oak, and this would provide a place for Isabella's four children to play games of concealment and pursuit, and for such adults as wished to do so to take a break from the main picnic site.

Those who had cars offered lifts to those who had none, or whose licence had been suspended. Miss Bates and her mother travelled with George Knightley in his estate car, while Jane Fairfax, Philip, and his new girlfriend were driven by Sid in his old Land Rover. Emma had invited Harriet to accompany her in the Mini Cooper, while Mrs. Goddard, along with James Weston and Miss Taylor, joined Mr. Woodhouse in his ancient Lea-Francis, which he had taken out of its garage for the occasion. Frank Churchill, who said he was keen on getting some exercise, rode there by bicycle, and arrived several minutes before anybody else.

Sid had been put in charge of spreading the picnic rugs on the ground and unpacking the hampers. By the time that everybody was assembled, a fine lunch had been laid out—enough to feed twice the numbers present, as Mrs. Firhill always over-catered.

"We shall never get through all of this," observed Emma. "Look at all those sausages and chicken drumsticks."

"You never can tell," said Harriet. "Men eat an awful lot, you know. They have such appetites."

Emma gritted her teeth. Harriet said such stupid things: *Men eat an awful lot.* Of course they did. Men did all sorts of . . . she searched around for a suitable adjective . . . such *gross* things. She looked up at the sky. She was not sure that she could face an entire afternoon of Harriet's company, and she would have to make sure that she created a buffer zone between herself and her friend by placing Harriet firmly next to people who would keep her busy. Not Philip, of course, nor Frank Churchill. Perhaps Harriet could sit between James and Miss Taylor—a safe place to be where the conversation would move along nicely without ever leading to anything untoward.

She clapped her hands to attract everybody's attention. The buzz of conversation faded. "Everybody should sit down," she said. "Find a place and then we can start with smoked salmon. As you'll see, there is bags and bags of it, so don't hold back."

They sat down. Emma made sure that she had Frank Churchill on one side of her and Isabella on the other. If Frank chose to flirt with her again—as there was every chance he would do—then she would have the satisfaction of having her older sister witness her receiving the attentions of such a handsome young man. Isabella had always tended to condescend to her slightly, and it would do her good, thought Emma, to see that men like Frank thought her worth flirting with.

She smiled at Frank, and she was encouraged when he returned the smile. "So," he said, "what have you been up to?"

"Planning this," said Emma. "And you?"

He shrugged. "Chilling," he said. "Talking to the old man. Nothing much."

She watched him as he spoke. She noticed something that she had not seen before: a small cleft in the middle of his chin, perfectly placed. Harriet had said something about that, she remembered, but she had ignored it because it was only something that Harriet said.

They ate smoked salmon in silence, although it seemed to Emma that they were communicating fully through their eyes. She reached for a bottle of white wine that was standing, in its frozen sleeve, beside a plate of sandwiches. "Can I pour you some?"

He nodded, passing her two plastic glasses.

As she poured, she noticed that the plastic sleeve, inflated like the waistcoat of a tiny Michelin man, completely obscured all evidence of the wine's origins. "You must know a bit about wine," she said, "living on a wine estate."

"Yes, I suppose I do."

She finished pouring. "All right. Tell me what this is."

Frank held up his glass and peered at the contents. The liquid, the colour of straw, refracted the rays of the sun. He lowered the glass to his nose and sniffed at it appreciatively before taking a first sip.

"What do you want?" he asked. "Region, type of grape, or estate?"

"Could you give me all three?" asked Emma. "Or maybe just two. I'll settle for region and grape."

He tasted the wine again. "It's definitely Italian," he said. "Veneto maybe. Yes, I think I'll say Veneto and Chardonnay."

After he had delivered his verdict, he reached for the bottle, and without taking off the sleeve, he poured himself another glass.

"It's very nice," said Emma. "I like it."

"It's all right," said Frank. "I wouldn't rate it that highly. But it's all right for a picnic."

"Where did you learn all this?" asked Emma.

"At home, mostly. But I've been on courses. I blended our last vintage on the estate."

"That must be tricky," said Emma.

"You have to know what you're doing," replied Frank. "But let's take a look. Pass me the bottle and I'll take the sleeve off. All will be revealed. I think I'm right, but we'll just confirm it."

Emma reached for the bottle and passed it over to Frank, who began to slip off the sleeve. He stopped halfway and stared at Emma.

"Is this your idea of a joke?"

Emma had no idea what he was talking about.

"Come on," said Frank. "Tell me: Is this your idea?"

She was at a complete loss. "I don't know what you mean."

He gestured towards the bottle. "That's our wine. You knew it all along and you tried to show me up."

She snatched the bottle from him and slipped the sleeve off completely. *Churchill's Ground, Western Australian Riesling.* She gasped. "Is that your . . ."

"Of course it's us," snapped Frank. "And are you satisfied now? Satisfied that you've shown that I can't even identify my own wine?"

"I didn't know," hissed Emma; she did not want anybody to

hear their argument. "I didn't choose the wine. Mr. Firhill does that—or my father. I had no idea."

She felt dismayed that the picnic should have started with a row with Frank Churchill. This was not what she had intended; in fact, it was the opposite of what she had anticipated. There would be no flirting now.

Frank was not to be placated. Red with embarrassment, he looked at Emma with undisguised hostility. Then, picking up his plate, he rose to his feet and moved to a neighbouring picnic rug. Emma looked about her in horror. Isabella had been watching, and so, she thought, had George. She realised that they would not have misunderstood the situation, and that the looks of admiration or envy that she had expected were now replaced with looks of pity.

Isabella leaned over towards her. "Darling, what on earth did you say to Frankie-boy?"

Emma wanted to cry, but was determined not to. This was Frank's fault; he was the one who had been rude; he was the one who had taken offence over something that she certainly had not planned. She had had nothing to do with the choice of wine for the picnic; and if Frank could not even identify his own wine, then surely he was the one who should be smarting over his pretentious claim of expertise.

"He tried to identify this wine," she said to Isabella. "He got it wrong and then he flounced off."

Isabella commiserated. "Men are so fragile," she said. "It often comes as a surprise to us girls to discover just how sensitive they are. But they are."

"I don't care about him," snorted Emma. "He's seriously pleased with himself."

"Good-looking men often are," said Isabella. "It's because we let them be like that." She reached out and touched her sister's shoulder. "Look, don't worry about that. Don't let a little tiff spoil your picnic."

"I won't."

"Good for you. Now let's go and check up on the children. Last seen, they were heading for those woods. John was meant to be keeping an eye on them, but he often forgets."

While the two sisters made their way from the picnic site to the edge of the woods, Mr. Woodhouse, James, and Miss Taylor had been joined on their rug by Philip and his new friend, Hazel. Philip seemed to be in a light-hearted mood, and was wearing a wide-brimmed Panama hat at a jaunty angle; nobody who was unaware of his recent difficulties would have been able to guess that this was a man who had stood in court and been stripped of his driving licence. Hazel was dressed in tightly fitting jeans and a low-cut black top. With a cigarette in one hand and a glass of wine in the other, she took alternative sips and puffs; nobody who was unaware of who Philip was would have imagined that this was the girlfriend of a (non-stipendiary) vicar, let alone a Byzantine historian.

"Do you know Norfolk, Hazel?" asked Miss Taylor.

"Can't say I do," said Hazel. "Know where it is—yes, vaguely. It's here, isn't it? More than that, no chance. Hardly get out of London most of the time, though now that . . ." She glanced at Philip, who smiled at her benignly.

"I hear you're a singer," said Miss Taylor.

"Quite well known," said Philip. "Hazel has sung on television. More than once."

Miss Taylor raised an eyebrow. "On television?"

"Yes," said Hazel. "I was on a show called *Look at Me!*"

"I'm afraid I didn't," said Miss Taylor.

"It's a well-known talent show," explained Philip. "Hazel was very successful. I'm surprised you haven't heard of her."

"It's for a slightly younger age group," said Hazel. "No offence, of course."

Miss Taylor glanced at James, who merely closed his eyes, briefly, and then reopened them. "I see," she said. "So what *do* you sing?"

Hazel shrugged. "How long's a piece of string?" she replied.

"I haven't heard that one," said Mr. Woodhouse.

Philip smiled. "She means that she sings all sorts of things. But she's best known for . . ."

Hazel took over. Blowing the smoke from her cigarette up into the air she said, "Piff."

Mr. Woodhouse, James, and Miss Taylor all looked puzzled.

"What?" asked James.

"Piff."

Philip waved his right hand airily. It was the hand in which he was holding his glass; a small amount of wine slopped out. "Edith Piaf," he explained. "You know—the little sparrow."

"Oh," said Miss Taylor. "I see what you mean."

"It's very atmospheric," said James. "When I hear Piaf I can almost smell the Gauloises. Cobbled streets. The prospect of freshly baked bread."

There was more to be said about Piaf, and Mr. Woodhouse was preparing to say it when they were interrupted by the arrival of Mrs. Goddard, who had come over from one of the other rugs bearing a large open cake tin.

"This is a nice little party," she said. "How about a bit of my special cake? I baked it just for today and it's getting very good reviews over there." She nodded in the direction of the rug she had just left, where Miss Bates could be seen holding forth while those seated around her, having finished their cake, looked up at the sky in a somewhat dreamy manner.

They each helped themselves as the cake tin was passed round. "Very good," said Mr. Woodhouse, as he bit into his slice. "You're a marvel, Goddy."

James smiled at the nickname. He had been called Westy when he was at school, but fortunately it had not stuck. He far preferred to be James Weston.

Isabella and Emma found the children just inside the wood. They had stumbled upon a fallen oak that had been hollowed at its base by rot and the action of the weather. Round this upturned oak they had created a small feast of their own, having brought cupcakes and sandwiches over from the main picnic. The adults checked that all was well and then returned to the main body of the gathering.

When they reached the picnic site, they found that people had rearranged themselves. George had now joined the group sitting on the same rug as Miss Bates, while Frank was sitting with Jane and her grandmother. Emma sat down next to George, who cleared a space for her.

"It's all going very well," he said. "I know you did a lot of work to arrange this—well done, Emma."

"The weather has held," said Emma. "That was my greatest fear—that it would rain."

"Well, it hasn't rained," said George. "And look how happy everybody seems."

Miss Bates had been speaking about music. "I'm not sure," she continued, "what instrument I'd like to play if I played in an orchestra. I think something . . ."

"Something loud," said Emma. "I think you'd be very good, Miss Bates."

"Oh, that's kind of you, Emma. I'm not so sure about that, though. I used to be able to read music quite well, but then I let it slip. I learned rather a lot of music theory—indeed I did Grade Six in music theory many years ago. I never played in an orchestra, even at school, although I once bumped into Benjamin Britten in Aldeburgh. It was when I was very young, just a girl, really, and I was staying with a cousin and we were in the butcher's shop when Mr. Britten came in and asked for a pound of sausages. The butcher gave them to him—just like that—and didn't make any remark about music or anything of that sort. He just said, 'Here you are, Mr. Britten.' And Mr. Britten said, 'Thanks, Tom,' and that was it. I felt quite shaken."

It was at this point that two people on the rug seemed to doze off at much the same time. One of these was John Knightley and the other was Mr. Woodhouse, who had come over from another rug with Mrs. Goddard. John had leaned back and rested his head on the sweater that he had been wearing but had taken off as the afternoon got warmer; Mrs. Goddard was still seated, but her head dropped forward in somnolence.

"My brother appears to be asleep," said George.

"And Mrs. Goddard too," said Miss Bates. "It must be the heat."

"Or the company," muttered Emma.

Her remark was not uttered loudly, but it was heard. Miss Bates, who had been on the point of saying something, was silenced. She stared down at the rug, and brushed at crumbs, real and imaginary. She looked crestfallen. "I can perhaps get a bit carried away with a subject," she said quietly. "I know it is a fault, and I shall try to do something about it. I know that."

George placed a reassuring hand on Miss Bates's shoulder. "I don't think Emma was referring to you, Miss Bates," he said. "It is very clear to me that it was my own failings that she had in mind."

"Oh, I don't think so," said Miss Bates. "Nobody would accuse you of being boring, George. How could they? No, I think this was a gentle reminder to me not to talk too much."

George rose to his feet. "I must stretch my legs," he said. "There is always a danger of cramp." He did not look at Emma, and he seemed to give her a wide berth when he moved off the picnic rug. She looked up at him, hoping to catch his eye, but he would not make eye contact.

Emma said nothing. It had occurred to her that something very significant had happened, although she was not sure exactly what it was. She felt ashamed. At her own picnic she had been humiliated by Frank and now she had, in turn, insulted poor Miss Bates. Nothing good could come of this occasion now, she thought, nothing good at all.

She looked about her. There was no sign of Frank, or of Jane. And where were her father and Mrs. Goddard? *At this rate,* she thought, *I shall be left here by myself, surrounded by the detritus of the picnic, covered in shame.*

19

Isabella and John Knightley stayed on at Hartfield for several days after the picnic. The suggestion that they should prolong their stay came from Mr. Woodhouse, who pointed out that a few more days in the country would help the children to clear their lungs after uninterrupted months in London. "They might also rediscover the existence of the letter *h*," he muttered, a remark which, fortunately, was not picked up by John Knightley. He had always scoffed at the countyish ways of both his father-in-law and his brother, and had succeeded in assuming the linguistic cover of an accent described as Chelsea Cockney. This had been achieved with the aid of a voice coach, an expert on the mastering of the glottal stop. For hours John had been coached in the proper pronunciation of the word *butter*, managing at last to pronounce it as *bu-er*, skilfully eliding the double *t* in the middle. His children, he was pleased to note, did not require to be taught to get rid of these otiose *t*'s, and said *bu-er* naturally and unself-consciously.

While his brother and his family were staying at Hartfield, George was invited to have every meal there, with the exception of breakfast. George was particularly good with his nephews and nieces. With that innate ability that children have to detect an adult who treats them as an equal, the young Knightleys were all over their uncle, climbing up his legs, pulling his hair, ambushing him in corridors, and setting traps for him on the garden path. He took all of this in good part and gave them uninterrupted hours of his time, reading them *Winnie-the-Pooh* and *Orlando, the Marmalade Cat* without complaint.

The ease with which George fitted into the expanded household at Hartfield could not disguise the fact that between him and Emma there was, after the debacle of the picnic, an atmosphere of tension that came to a head when Emma made a remark at the lunch table in the course of a discussion of islands. This discussion was triggered by a report in that day's *Times* of the identification of a hitherto unknown lizard on a remote South Sea island. This discovery had interested the children, who speculated at length as to whether the lizard could climb trees, eat snakes, and be susceptible to domestication.

Emma had at this point said, "It must be strange living on some remote island in the Pacific—Tristan da Cunha, for example—even if you're not a lizard."

"Please pass the bu-er," said one of the children.

"Tristan da Cunha is actually in the Atlantic," George pointed out dryly. "Or it was, when I last looked at the map."

Emma shot him a glance, and avoided him for the rest of the day. Nor did they speak to each other over the dinner table, at which they had been joined—at Mr. Woodhouse's invitation—by Mr. Perry, who spoke for some time about the properties of echinacea, Philip, who had eyes only for Hazel, and by Mrs. Goddard and Harriet Smith. After dinner, though, when everybody was having coffee in the library, George drew Emma out into the corridor.

"I'm sorry, Emma," he said. "I spoke rudely at lunch, and I shouldn't have done so. I didn't mean to show you up in front of the children."

She looked away.

In spite of her hostility, he continued, "It's just that Tristan da Cunha *is* in the Atlantic."

She turned to face him. "Do you think I care about Tristan da Cunha? Do you think I care whether it's in the Pacific or the Atlantic? It makes absolutely no difference."

"But it would," protested George. "It would make a great deal of difference if you lived there."

"Oh, don't be so ridiculous!" snapped Emma. "You're such a . . . such a pedant."

George caught his breath. "Me?"

"Yes, you. You're always going on about where things are."

It was an absurd accusation; she knew it and he resented it. "You're the one who's being ridiculous," he said. "And as far as I'm aware, I don't always go on about where things are. In fact, I can't recall a single instance in which we've talked about the location of anything at all, let alone an Atlantic island. Can you?"

She looked at her watch. "It's very late. I need to go to bed."

He caught her wrist. He did it gently, but he held it when she tried to pull away. "You can't run away from things indefinitely, Emma."

"Let go of me."

He let go.

"I have to talk to you about the picnic," he said. "I know you don't want to, but we can't let the issue sit there, festering."

"I don't know what you mean," she said.

"You know very well," he returned. "You know very well that you behaved appallingly."

She stood quite still.

"Yes, you do know that, don't you?" George went on. "You know full well that you gratuitously and cruelly humiliated Miss Bates. You didn't have to do it, you know. You didn't have to insult a poor, rather vulnerable woman who's seen her whole world collapse about her ears, who's got to cope with a mother who's virtually catatonic, and who depends on benefits to get by each week. And you, with everything that you have—this house, your money, your looks, your coruscating wit—you still think that you have to put that poor woman down. Everyone knows that at times she can bore the pants off all of us, but the point is that she is our neighbour, Emma, our neighbour in more senses than one." He paused. Emma was staring at the floor. He lowered his voice. "That was badly done, Emma. That was badly done."

She did not reply. She let him finish what he had to say, and she walked off, not turning back to say good night, not wanting her tears to be seen. She had always liked George, even admired him, and now she had offended him, goaded him into this denunciation of her. She had no idea why she had mocked Miss Bates. George was quite right: it had been ungenerous and unkind. Was that the sort of person she was? She had never asked herself that question—that uniquely unsettling question—but now she did: *What sort of person am I?*

She went up to her room and flung herself down on her bed. She did not turn on the light, but lay there, fully clothed, immobile in her wretchedness. His words sank in; they sank in. It can happen; in the lives of all of us there are points, sometimes unexpected and barely salient, when somebody says something that may change us—and our lives—to an extent that is truly surprising. This was such a moment for Emma Woodhouse.

The following morning Emma drove briefly into Holt before going on to Highbury. Parking the Mini Cooper outside the Bateses' cottage, she made her way up the front path with its cracked and broken paving stones. She looked at the house with new eyes, where once she had failed to see the paint peeling off the windowsills, now she saw it; where once she could not have noticed the crumbling mortar protruding from between the bricks, now she wondered how she could possibly have missed it. She pressed the bell and then looked down at the doormat of worn brown bristle; previously she would have sneered at its message: *Welcome to Our Home.* Now she felt instead its poignancy. She was puzzled, and vaguely ashamed. She had known that Miss Bates was hard up, but had not really thought about what that meant. Something within her was telling her to look at things in a very different way.

There was a scuffling noise within, followed by the sound of a chain being taken off. And then the door opened, and Miss Bates, wearing a grey woollen skirt and a thin, faded linen blouse, stood before her. The blouse had pictures of swallows in flight, and in the background a line of hills could still be made out, but only just; the material was well worn.

Miss Bates's face lit up. "Emma! What a pleasure. Please . . . please come in."

Emma felt herself blushing; the back of her neck was warm. "I'm sorry I didn't phone to warn you about dropping in. I hope you don't mind."

"But why should I mind?" said Miss Bates. "We're always delighted to have visitors. Sometimes we just sit here, you know, and wish for visitors. And then, as often as not, a visitor arrives, as if sent by Providence, which is perhaps the case."

She ushered Emma into the cramped hall off which rose the staircase to the upper floor. Emma noticed that one of the bannisters had been broken and had been inexpertly repaired with green string. On the way in she saw on the wall a picture of a characteristic Edward Lear illustration: that lonely figure, the Yonghy-Bonghy-Bò, traced in ink by the poet, taken, she imagined, from some old book and then mounted in a somewhat battered frame. She stopped in front of the picture. "That's Lear, isn't it?"

"Yes," said Miss Bates. "Mother was always very fond of him. She doesn't read him any more. She doesn't read anything, I'm afraid."

Emma peered more closely at the drawing. Miss Taylor had read the poem to her as a child; it was one of her earliest memories of her governess. She heard her again, reciting in her clear Edinburgh tones, "On the coast of Coromandel . . ." She looked at Miss Bates. "You know the poem, do you? The Yonghy-Bonghy-Bò?"

Miss Bates reached out to touch the glass in front of the picture, with reverence, almost as a believer might touch a reliquary. "On the Coast of Coromandel," she began:

> Where the early pumpkins blow,
> In the middle of the woods,
> Lived the Yonghy-Bonghy-Bò.

Emma took up the recital.

> Two old chairs, and half a candle,
> One old jug without a handle,
> These were all his worldly goods,
> In the middle of the woods . . .

"It's very sad, isn't it?" said Miss Bates. "The Yonghy-Bonghy-Bò falls in love with Lady Jingly Jones, who can't marry him because she has pledged herself to the man who gives her Dorking hens. It's so sad. She sends him away, doesn't she?"

"Yes," said Emma.

> Down the slippery slopes of Myrtle,
> Where the early pumpkins blow,
> To the calm and silent sea
> Fled the Yonghy-Bonghy-Bò,
> There, beyond the bay of Gurtle,
> Lay a large and lively Turtle.
> "You're the Cove," he said, "for me.
> On your back beyond the sea,
> Turtle, you shall carry me!"
> Said the Yonghy-Bonghy-Bò,
> Said the Yonghy-Bonghy-Bò.

"I think I used to cry when I read that," said Miss Bates. "Lear was very funny, but also very sad. He was a very lonely man, I believe."

They both stared at the picture of the Yonghy-Bonghy-Bò, a small, spherical figure with a tiny hat perched on his outsize head. He was astride the turtle that would carry him across the sea to his exile.

"We should go and sit down," said Miss Bates. "Jane is out, I'm afraid."

"But I came to see you," said Emma.

Miss Bates seemed surprised. "To see me?"

Emma had a bag with her, a linen tote bag with a picture of Covent Garden market printed on both sides. "I have a present for you."

Miss Bates looked at the bag in astonishment. "But why, Emma? I've done nothing to deserve a present."

Emma reached into the bag and took out the four large boxes of violet creams that she'd bought earlier that morning.

"I remembered that you liked these," she said, passing the gift to Miss Bates. "You do like violet creams, don't you?"

Miss Bates made a slight, fluttering sound. "But I adore violet creams. I love violet creams more than virtually anything else. They are my favourite."

"Then these will keep you going for a bit," said Emma. "I hope you enjoy them."

Miss Bates indicated the door behind her. "We can go into the little parlour. You'll be more comfortable there."

They entered the room. It was very small, and was just capable of accommodating the two chairs and low table it contained. Emma thought of the Yonghy-Bonghy-Bò; in just such a parlour might he have spent his time on the coast of Coromandel, spurned and lonely. "Two old chairs, and half a candle . . ."

They sat down, and Emma launched into her apology. "I've come to say sorry for my stupid rudeness at the picnic," she began. "I said something very silly, and I wouldn't want you to think that I meant it."

Miss Bates looked down at her folded hands. "I did not think it was silly. It was a reminder to me not to get carried away." She paused. "You see, I have so much to say—or I think I have so much to say. It's not that I want to impress anybody, or anything like that. It's just that I find I want to share my thoughts with others. I get excited about that, and I'm afraid it shows. I have learned my lesson."

Emma wanted to protest. "No, no," she said. "I'm the one who's learned a lesson. I have."

"I don't think you had any lessons to learn," said Miss Bates. "Nobody thinks *you* speak too much."

"It's not that at all."

"Well, whatever it is, you don't have to apologise to me, Emma. I am happy enough to have your friendship—if I don't presume too much in saying that."

"No," said Emma. "You don't presume in the least, Miss Bates. I am really happy that you consider me a friend." She paused, staring hard at her hostess. "Then you accept my apology?"

Miss Bates raised her hands as if fending off something unwanted. "Of course I do. But, as I said, I don't think it needed to be made. So let's draw a line under the whole matter and begin with what? A cup of tea? I believe that we might have a bit of coffee, too, as Jane brought some with her. I could make you a cup of coffee, if you were to prefer it. And . . . and, yes, I believe we still have a couple of cheese scones, unless Mother . . ."

"A cup of tea and a cheese scone would be perfect," said Emma.

Miss Bates went out of the room and returned a few minutes later with a tea tray on which there was a plate with a single scone. She poured Emma a cup of tea and they drank it in near silence. Emma made various attempts to start a conversation, but Miss Bates seemed unwilling to say very much. She smiled a great deal, though, and nodded in agreement with what Emma said, but the usual stream-of-consciousness commentary was absent. Miss Bates, it seems, was making every effort not to do what Emma had implicitly accused her of doing: talking too much. When, after fifteen minutes, Emma stood up to go, she thought: *I have extinguished something. I have dampened another's spirits.*

As she left Miss Bates and made her way back down the garden path, Emma noticed that there was a familiar Land Rover parked immediately behind her Mini Cooper. The figure in the driving seat was equally familiar. It was George.

She stopped in her tracks. She was still smarting with shame over what he had said to her the previous evening, and had remembered every word of his criticism. She felt disinclined to face her accuser just yet, but she could hardly turn and go back into the cottage. Nor could she simply get into her car and pretend that she had not seen him.

She decided to continue towards her car and see what he did. It was possible that he was parked in the street for some reason other than to confront her—the post office was not far away—and if he was, then she could simply wave to him and drive off. But, as she approached the car, the door of the Land Rover opened and George stepped out.

"Emma," he called. "May I have a word with you?"

She nodded.

"I was in the shop in Holt," he said. "I was speaking to Mrs. Edwards, and she said that you had been in and bought up their entire supply of violet creams."

Emma shrugged. "So?"

"I know why you did that," he said. "I'm right in thinking they were for Miss Bates?"

"Maybe." She wanted to say, *What's it got to do with you?*

"Then I want you to know how much I admire that. It's a kind thing you've just done."

He looked at her expectantly, but she did not know what to say.

"I'm sorry," he said. "I've interfered, but I must say how proud I am of you."

She frowned. *How can he be proud of me?* she wondered. *What am I to him?*

He answered the question she had not openly asked. "I feel entitled to be proud of you because I count you as one of my closest friends. We go back quite a long time, Emma, and that means something to me. I don't know if you know that, but it does."

She was uncertain what to say. A few days ago she might have made some witty remark about going back with people—reactionary friendships?—but this was not the moment for that sort of clever levity. Now she felt something quite different: a fondness for her old friend, which was combined with something altogether new—a sense of George as a person with an existence that was quite independent of hers. And this made her realise that if she were to be written out of this world today, it would still go on with its essential concerns and objectives; she was nothing really. She had no job; she had nobody who depended on her; she did little to make the world easier for those she knew, other than, perhaps, to hand out boxes of violet creams.

George was going back to his Land Rover. Over his shoulder he said, "Don't fight it, Emma."

She opened the door of the Mini Cooper and had already started the engine when she thought of his words. *Don't fight it.* What precisely was *it*? Her better nature? Did she have one?

Her route home from the village took her past the turning for Randalls, and it was there, at the intersection of the two lanes, that she saw Jane Fairfax walking across a field at the edge of the road. Emma saw Jane before Jane saw her; she stopped the car and waited until Jane climbed over a rickety old stile at the field's edge. She called out, and Jane looked up in surprise.

"Are you going back to the village?" Emma shouted through her car window.

Jane looked momentarily confused. Then, smoothing her hair, which had been ruffled by the breeze, she came over to speak to Emma. "Yes, I am. I've just been . . ." She hesitated. "I've just been for a walk. Over there." She pointed vaguely behind her.

"A nice day for it," said Emma.

"It looks as if it's going to rain, though," said Jane. She spoke rather formally, as if she was keeping her distance from Emma.

Emma noticed it. "Please let me give you a lift into the village."

Jane shook her head. "You're going in the opposite direction." Then she added, almost grudgingly, "Thank you, anyway."

"But you said it's going to rain," said Emma.

"I'll be all right."

"I can't leave you to get soaked."

"I said: I'll be all right."

Emma would not give up. "Come on. I don't mind going back. I've got nothing to do. Please."

Jane sighed, and silently crossed to the other side of the car. Emma leaned over and opened the door for her. "There's not much room, I'm afraid. You can move the seat back."

Jane said nothing, but strapped herself in. Emma switched off the engine; she had pulled in off the road and she could move if anything came. "I need to say something to you," she began. "I've just been to see your aunt. I went there to apologise."

Jane looked straight ahead.

"I know what you probably feel about it," Emma continued. "It was stupid of me—and really unkind. I don't know why I said it." She paused. Perhaps Miss Bates had not told her niece about the incident; not everybody had heard what had happened. But if she had not, then why was Jane's manner so hostile? She decided that Miss Bates must have told her.

"I've obviously offended your whole family," said Emma. "I'm really sorry. I didn't mean to."

Jane suddenly spoke. "You need to watch what you say."

"I know," said Emma. "That's why I'm saying sorry."

"Anyway, it's not that. It's nothing to do with my aunt."

Emma thought quickly. "Did I say something to you? If I did, I can't remember."

"It's the way you flirt," said Jane quietly. "You flirted with Frank at that dinner. I saw you. You can't seem to leave men alone."

Emma froze. That was it. Competition: of course Jane Fairfax would have had her eyes on Frank Churchill—what young woman would not? She turned to face Jane. "Listen, Jane. I wasn't really flirting with Frank Churchill. We were just pretending—that's all."

"Oh, yes?" said Jane sarcastically. "An act."

Emma now began to feel irritated. She was being honest with Jane Fairfax and she was being mocked for it. "Yes," she said, her tone becoming sharper. "That's exactly what it was."

"I doubt it," said Jane.

Emma was not accustomed to being disbelieved. It rankled. "But it was," she protested. "It was an act on Frank's part."

"And why would Frank act?"

She hesitated. She did not want to tell Jane what Frank had said to her, but now that she was being falsely accused of flirting with him she would have no alternative. "Because he's not interested in girls. He told me. But he doesn't want people to know."

Jane Fairfax gasped. "He said that?" she stuttered. "He told you . . ." She could not complete her sentence.

"Yes," said Emma. "He wanted to confide in me."

"What exactly did he say?" asked Jane, her voice strained.

Emma shrugged. "He told me he had a boyfriend he was going to go travelling with. He didn't tell me who it was—somebody he met at school, I think. He said they went back a long way.

It's not a big thing. It's no big deal: lots of people are that way. Who cares?"

"I do," muttered Jane.

"Well, you shouldn't," said Emma. "It's an entirely private matter. Nobody's uptight about people's sexuality any more. Why should they be?"

The rain had come on. Gently, it had crept up on them, and fell now in tiny drops across the windscreen of the Mini Cooper.

"Please take me home," said Jane. "Please just take me home."

20

Harriet Smith called Emma the following morning to invite her to accompany her on a trip to Cambridge. They would not be alone, she explained, as the outing was really for the benefit of a group of Italian students from the language school.

"Mrs. God has hired a small bus," she said. "There're twenty seats and only twelve students—so there'll be bags of room for you. Mrs. God won't be coming herself. We'll be in charge."

Emma hesitated. She was not sure that she liked the idea of spending the day in Cambridge with a group of teenagers, but there was something in her mood that disposed her to accept Harriet's offer. The meeting with Jane Fairfax had not been a comfortable one, and it seemed to her that her relationship with any member of the Bates family was now unlikely ever to be satisfactory, even if she had done her best to apologise to Miss Bates for the specific offence she had given. Certainly, Jane was still behaving towards her in a distant, rather cold manner, and all attempts to get past that seemed to be doomed to failure— which made Emma all the more keen to have her approval. But if that was not to be, it was not to be, and so she decided that she would spend a bit more time with Harriet, who had never rebuffed her and who, she was sure, never would.

She left the car at the language school and joined Harriet and the students on the bus.

"They're very excited," said Harriet. "They arrived in England only a few days ago; they came straight from Stansted Airport. They can't wait to see Cambridge."

One of the students overheard this conversation from a seat immediately behind Harriet and Emma. "And the railway station," he said. "We are hoping, please, to see the railway station."

Harriet turned in her seat. "Yes," she reassured him. "We'll show you a railway station sometime."

"Contract?" pressed the student.

"Promise," sighed Harriet. "A contract is an agreement. You promise something when you say that you'll do it. You give your word."

"Promise?" asked the student.

"Yes," said Harriet. "I promise that you'll see a railway station."

Emma was intrigued. "Why are they so interested in railway stations? Is it because you talk to them about it so much?"

Harriet smiled. "Not me. Mrs. God does. It's the first thing she teaches them and they spend rather a lot of time on it. *Can you please tell me the way to the railway station?* They go on and on about it, and I suppose they become rather proud of being able to say it."

"How odd," said Emma. "I imagine they think that this is what people in Britain talk about all the time. Railway stations. The national conversation."

Harriet was intrigued. "What *do* people talk about in Britain?" she asked.

Emma thought for a moment. "The weather, mostly," she said. "That's a very important topic of conversation. Oh, and football. People talk about football, although that's mostly men."

"What do we talk about when they're talking about football?"

Emma shrugged. "We talk about them. They don't know it, but we talk about them."

Harriet gave what sounded to Emma like a tiny, half-suppressed squeal of delight. "Oh, I think that's true. I think that's exactly what we like to talk about. Girl talk. Girl talk about men. Oh, yes!"

Emma glanced at her friend and then looked away. *What am I doing, going off to Cambridge with this air* . . . She stopped herself. Something that George Knightley had said to her came back to her, something about advantages in life. She glanced at Harriet again: What was her life? Mrs. God and the English Language school? Foreign students going on about how to get to the railway station? A father somewhere whom she had never met who was no more than a biological progenitor and who would not even recognise her if he saw her? A vague hope of a gap year that would probably never materialise?

"No, you're right, Harriet," she said gently. "Men are a very interesting subject."

Harriet leaned back in her seat as the bus negotiated a bend in the road. "But you're so much more experienced than I am," she said. "I know so few men, and I'm not sure that I know all that much about the ones I do know."

"That surprises me," said Emma. "You're very beautiful, Harriet, and men like beautiful girls. They're funny that way. You'd think that you'd know tons of men."

Harriet was pleased with the compliment, but her pleasure was soon overtaken by doubt. "Yes, I do see them looking at me from time to time, but I never seem to know what to say to men."

"Don't say anything," said Emma. "What's there to say, anyway?"

"For example," said Harriet. "I was in Holt the other day and this man came up to me and said something I just couldn't understand."

"Perhaps he was asking the way to the railway station."

Harriet shook her head. "I don't think so."

"So what did you do?"

Harriet looked embarrassed. "I screamed. Not very loudly. Just a little scream."

Emma looked at her in astonishment. "So what happened?"

"He turned on his heels and ran away."

"I should think so too," said Emma. "You did the right thing, Harriet."

Harriet was not so sure. "But what if he were entirely innocent? What if he really were asking the way to the railway station? What if he were some poor Swedish tourist or whatever who had got lost and thought that he could ask me for help?"

Emma agreed that this would have been a shame. "There are some men who are quite innocent," she said with mock seriousness. "Very few, I believe, but there are some. And yes, it would be very discouraging if one were practising one's English and all that the person to whom you spoke did was to scream. That would be very discouraging indeed."

Emma could hardly believe that she was having this ridiculous conversation with Harriet, but it seemed to her that when she was in Harriet's company she somehow regressed. And yet it was not unpleasant. Harriet was completely unchallenging; she would never say anything that required too much thought; she would never say anything that would unsettle. And what harm was there in spending time with such an undemanding friend? It was not much different, surely from spending an afternoon curled up on the sofa with a magazine—an innocent pleasure, and one to which one could surely treat oneself from time to time.

The bus dropped them off as close as it could to the centre of Cambridge, which was across the Backs. On the other side of the river, outlined against a pale blue sky, rose the spires of King's College. On the Cam, slow-moving in its August somnolence, a college punt, poled by a young man in jeans and a plum-coloured blazer, moved lazily downriver, overtaken by a family of purposeful ducks.

Harriet addressed the students, who were milling about, chatting excitedly in Italian. She explained that they had three hours, and that she would expect them back promptly, as the bus would be waiting for them. Then the students dispersed, breaking up into several groups of friends, consulting the small maps of the city that Harriet had given them at the start of the journey. Emma and Harriet followed them as they crossed the bridge and headed towards King's, but soon lagged behind and lost sight of them.

"I hope they all come back," said Harriet. "I don't know what I'd say if I had to go back and tell Mrs. God we were one or two short."

"I expect she'd be pretty relaxed about it," said Emma. "That cake of hers . . ." Harriet frowned, and Emma let the subject drop. "We can go and have some tea in one of those tearooms on King's Parade."

"And do some shopping," said Harriet.

"Of course."

"Not that I can buy anything," said Harriet. "I don't have any money, I'm afraid. But I like looking. And you can have almost as much fun shopping if you don't buy anything. You can try things on."

Emma looked down at the ground. *I don't have any money.* She wondered what it would be like to be broke. Plenty of people were in that position, scraping around for money for the most basic necessities; she knew that of course—intellectually, but not in the essential, empathetic way that such knowledge calls out for. She had never experienced that in her life. Not once. While she was at university, her trustees—a firm of solicitors in Norwich—had given her an allowance of two thousand pounds a month, and that had recently gone up to three. She had no tax to pay on that; she paid no rent; she never had to buy any food or any petrol for the Mini Cooper. All she had to do was buy clothes. She had accepted that as her due; it was her money after all.

She turned to Harriet. "I could treat you to something."

Harriet's response was immediate. "Oh no. I couldn't expect you to do that. That's really kind, but I couldn't."

"Why not?"

"Because it's your money. I can't expect you to spend your money on me."

"But I want to. I want to get you a present." She paused. "And you know something, Harriet? When somebody offers you a present, you should accept."

Harriet looked uncomfortable. "You don't have to feel sorry for me, Emma. I'm all right, you know."

Harriet's insight took Emma by surprise. She was right: she had been feeling sorry for her, and of course nobody wanted pity. She would deny it . . . No, she would not. "Yes, I was feeling sorry for you. But I can see that you don't want that."

"Of course I don't. Nobody does."

"All right. I've stopped feeling sorry for you."

"Good."

"But does that mean I can't buy you a present?"

Harriet was silent. Then, when she spoke, her voice was quiet. "I said that you don't have to. But if it's going to make you happy, then you can. If you really want to, that is."

"I do," said Emma. "I want to." And as she said that, she tried to remember when she had last bought a present for anybody. There had been a present for her father for his birthday, a subscription to *Country Life*—the same thing that she had given him every year for the last four years—but apart from that, she could not remember anything. She asked herself whether she could possibly have been that mean. *Yes*, she thought, *I have.* But then she remembered the violet creams that she had given to Miss Bates, and that made her feel better; only momentarily, though, because it occurred to her that the violet creams were not a real gift but recompense—and inadequate recompense at that—for the egregious wrong she had done.

. . .

Emma was reasonably familiar with Cambridge shops and knew one where she might find just the right present for Harriet. This was a dress shop called Summer Nights that was on a small street off King's Parade, sandwiched between a jeweller's and an old-fashioned cheesemonger's. Summer Nights catered to well-heeled visitors and to the wealthier undergraduates, being one of those shops that did not deign to put prices on the items it displayed in the window. For those on a budget, that is always a very clear indication that the shop is not for them; for those in a position to buy what was on display, it was a reminder that price was not the real issue. Emma had bought dresses there on a number of occasions, and was a regular and appreciated customer.

Harriet understood this perfectly. "We can't go in there," she said to Emma. "That's going to be far too expensive."

This merely goaded Emma on. "Yes, we can. I've been in there loads of times. I know what their stuff costs."

Harriet shook her head. "We can't."

Emma took her friend by the arm and pushed her gently through the door. "Yes, we can."

The assistant had been sitting behind the counter, but rose to her feet when she saw them come in.

"Emma," she said, smiling in welcome. "It's great to see you."

Emma made the introductions. "Sally, this is my friend Harriet. Harriet, this is Sally, who sells the best clothes in Cambridge. That's official."

"I won't argue," said Sally. She glanced at what Harriet was wearing, and then, discreetly, looked back at Emma. Emma realised that she did not need to give any explanation to Sally.

324

"Have a look round," said Sally. She glanced again at Harriet before adding, "The size tens are mostly on this rack, but I've got some other things over here, and in these drawers too."

"You're a ten, aren't you?" asked Emma, adding, "Every-body is, aren't they? Even those who aren't."

"Really," said Harriet. "You really shouldn't."

"I want to," whispered Emma. "Please let me. It's just some-thing that I want to do."

"But everything will be so expensive. And, anyway, I can't decide. I never can."

Sally's head was turned away during this exchange—she was tactful—but she had heard every word. Her hand went out to the rack of dresses. "You know, I've got something special here," she said. "It's just come in. Italian cashmere."

She slipped a dress off its hanger and held it up for inspec-tion. "A cashmere jersey dress. We'd usually have this in win-ter, but it's fine as long as the weather isn't actually boiling." She paused. "And when does it boil round here?"

"Never," said Emma.

Sally held out the dress to Harriet. "It's your colouring," she said. "You can wear blue. Can't she, Emma?"

"Yes, she can. She can wear anything, I suspect, and look like a million dollars."

"I can't," protested Harriet. "This dress is lovely, but I don't think so."

Emma ignored this. "Try it on."

"Yes," urged Sally. "Just try it. No harm. And shoes? I've got the most fabulous suede ankle boots. I promise you, they're just made for that dress. They're both Italian."

"I don't need any shoes," said Harriet. "I've got shoes."

"You can never have enough shoes," said Emma firmly.

"No," said Sally. "Emma's right. You have to have lots of shoes."

Harriet was led to the fitting booth and the curtain drawn for her. Sally nodded at Emma. "She could wear anything," she whispered. "You're right."

"Find those ankle boots," said Emma.

"You've been so kind," said Harriet as they left the shop.

Emma said nothing, but acknowledged the thanks with a smile.

"Nobody has ever done anything like that for me," continued Harriet. "I don't know what to say."

"You don't need to say anything."

They were in the street outside the dress shop but Harriet suddenly turned and embraced Emma, hugging her friend to her. Emma felt the bag containing the dress and shoes press against her uncomfortably. She felt herself flush with embarrassment.

"OK," she said. "It's OK."

A couple of young men walked past them. They did not look, but one addressed the other in a voice intended to be heard. "Cool. I like that sort of thing."

The other young man laughed. Harriet let Emma go. "I'm sorry, I got carried away. I'm just so . . . well, I'm just overcome."

Emma felt slightly flustered by Harriet's effusive show of gratitude. "Let's just walk along King's Parade. There are more shops."

"You mustn't buy me anything else," said Harriet. "Ever."

Emma laughed. "I might get some shoes myself. What did Sally say back there? You can never have enough shoes."

"No, you said that."

"Did I? Well, then, it must be right."

They walked on, making their way through the afternoon crowds of visitors. Cambridge in summer was busy, even with the regular students being away; as one set of young people departed, their place was taken by another: Australians, Americans, Koreans—a hotchpotch of nationalities eager to experience the benison of the ancient academic city. On the King's Parade, several young men, wearing straw boaters, plied their touts' trade, trying to persuade people to rent a river punt. A small group of Japanese girls giggled at the importuning; elsewhere a crowd had gathered around a street performer who was extracting coloured handkerchiefs from a top hat; the locals, indifferent, walked past on their business. Emma said, "What's the point of taking handkerchiefs . . ."

She did not finish. Harriet had gripped her arm. "Over there. Isn't that him?"

Emma looked about her. "Who?"

"That guy."

"What guy?"

"Frank what's-his-name?"

Emma looked in the direction in which Harriet was pointing. The crowds had thickened, and she was not sure whom she was meant to be looking for? Frank? Frank Churchill?

"You mean Frank Churchill?"

"Yes," said Harriet. "I'm sure I saw him. With that Jane girl."

"Jane Fairfax?"

"Yes. I'm sure it was them."

Emma searched the crowd, looking for Frank's golden head of hair. He was tall; he should be visible. There was no sign of anybody who looked like him. She turned to Harriet and asked her whether she was sure.

"I think so," said Harriet. "You can't really miss him. And it was her too—she's quite distinctive-looking."

"Where were they going?" she asked.

"That way," said Harriet, pointing down the street in the direction of St. John's and Heffers Bookshop.

Emma made up her mind. "Let's find them."

"And speak to them?" asked Harriet.

"No," said Emma. "I'm just a bit curious to find out what they're doing."

"There's no reason why they shouldn't be in Cambridge," said Harriet. "They're probably shopping."

"Maybe," said Emma.

They walked on, Emma setting the pace. She was intrigued. Earlier on, she had detected Jane's interest in Frank, but had assumed that she had disabused her of any illusions as to her chances with him. Perhaps Jane had decided on a simple friendship with Frank; that was no concern of hers, except that . . . She bit her lip. She felt a tug of envy. Frank Churchill was her property, not Jane's. Jane was nothing; she was a visitor for the summer who had not even met Frank before. She—Emma—had known him for years, or rather, even if she hardly knew him, she had met him years before on one of his trips from Australia, and James was virtually family; all of which meant that she, rather than Jane, should be walking around Cambridge with him. This was not to say, of course, that she fancied him—she told herself that she did not. He was extremely good-looking and he had that smile that she had already observed, and there was that cleft in his chin . . . but this was not about any of that. She knew there was absolutely no point in falling in love with somebody who was not going to be interested; that was *not* the point: the point was that he would have far preferred to be shown round Cambridge by her rather than by that stand-offish *iceberg* Jane Fairfax.

It did not take them long to reach the entrance to St. John's. There was no sign of Frank and Jane in the street, and the crowd had by that stage thinned out. They had paused in front of Heffers, and Emma had looked in through the open front door. Again there was no sign of the couple, and Emma shook her head when Harriet suggested they might have gone downstairs, or possibly upstairs. "I don't think so," she said. "I don't see Frank in a bookshop."

"Well, then maybe I was wrong. Maybe it wasn't him."

"No," said Emma. "I don't think you were wrong."

"Well, we don't have to find them, do we? You said that you wanted to find some shoes. There was an interesting shoe shop back there."

Emma looked up at the gate of St. John's, at the elaborate stone-carved arms. Suddenly she remembered the conversation she had had with Jane when she had called to inspect the new piano. She had mentioned that she had been at Cambridge— Emma having dragged the admission out of her—and had said that her college was St. John's. Of course; of course that was it: Jane would be showing Frank Churchill her old college.

"Let's go in there," said Emma.

Harriet was uncertain. "Into that college? Are we allowed?"

"Of course we are," said Emma. "We pay for these places. It's taxpayers' money that keeps them going."

"I don't pay tax," muttered Harriet.

"I do," said Emma. "Come on."

There was something happening at the entrance to the chapel in the First Court. A crowd of people was milling about the main door of the chapel, and when this door opened, the people surged forward. Emma's eye was caught by one of these people. "Frank," she whispered.

"Where?"

"Over there. Going into the chapel."

Harriet could not see him. "Are you sure?"

"Yes, he's gone inside."

"And Jane? Did you see her?"

"I think so, but I couldn't tell."

They crossed the court. Outside the chapel, there was a small noticeboard announcing a special concert by the choristers in aid of an organisation that supported prisoners of conscience. This was the reason for the crowd, most of which had now been admitted to the chapel.

They went inside. A student was at the door, selling tickets. Emma paid for both of them and put the change into a collecting box on the table. The student thanked her. "You can sit anywhere," she said. "It'll start in about five minutes."

Some of those admitted to the chapel had not yet sat down, but were walking about looking up at the stained-glass windows. Emma wanted an unobtrusive seat and so she pointed to a pew towards the back. More people were coming in now, and the chapel was filling up.

They sat down.

"Can you see them?" whispered Harriet.

Emma scanned the rows of heads, the backs. "Yes," she whispered back. "They're there. Right towards the front."

A man emerged from the side and stood in front of a microphone near the choir stalls. He tapped the mouthpiece with a finger to attract attention.

"Ladies and gentlemen, dear friends," he began. "The choristers of the college have kindly agreed to perform this concert this afternoon because they support the work of our organisation. As you know, we are concerned with prisoners of conscience—people who are detained not because they have committed crimes as we would understand them, but because they have expressed views that challenge those in power. In most cases, this is because they have simply told the truth, or worked for the truth as they see it.

"I don't need to tell you about the suffering of these people and about what your support means to them. I'm sure that you are well aware of that. Here, in this beautiful place, this peaceful sanctuary from the wickedness of the world, it may be hard to imagine the suffering of those who are kept apart from others, locked up in conditions intended to break both body and spirit. But that is what they suffer, day after day—day after day. We can turn away from the suffering of others; we can put it out of our minds. We can say that it has nothing to do with us. But that is always wrong, ladies and gentlemen, because the suffering of others is something that does not go away if we simply turn the other way, if we ignore it. It is still there."

Emma was gazing up at one of the windows and at the effect of the light from the coloured glass. She looked across the aisle; a man had taken a woman's hand and had squeezed it in unspoken reassurance. The woman turned to him and smiled, in gratitude for the gesture; she wore glasses with thick lenses. Emma thought: *She's just had bad news.* Emma looked back up towards the window, and thought, inconsequentially, *The properties of glass.* She was still staring up at the window when the choir began to sing "Many waters cannot quench love." She closed her eyes. She had forgotten about Frank and Jane. *We can turn away from the suffering of others.*

She kept her eyes closed. The choir was silent for a moment before they began their second song. It was about a turtle dove and love: "Though I go ten thousand miles, my dear, though I go ten thousand miles." The song had the familiarity of something heard before and half remembered. She opened her eyes. Harriet was staring at her.

"Are you all right?"

"Yes, of course."

"You seem sad."

"I'm not. I'm thinking." She paused. "I want to go now. Do you mind?"

"But they've only just started."

"I know, but I want to go."

Harriet was not one to argue. They slipped out before the choir began again. Outside, the light seemed far too intense; it had been muted and diffuse in the chapel.

"That was them," said Harriet. "That was definitely them."

"Yes," said Emma. She was no longer interested in Frank and Jane. They did not matter.

"Now what?" asked Harriet.

Emma looked at her watch. "I don't feel like doing anything in particular."

"We could go back to where we were due to meet the students," suggested Harriet. "We've got over an hour. We could wait."

"Yes," said Emma. "We could sit by the river."

On the way back, Harriet said to Emma, "Are you feeling sad?"

Emma wanted to say no, but said yes instead.

"Why?" asked Harriet.

Emma shrugged. She could not describe to Harriet what she felt, for she was not at all sure why she should suddenly and unexpectedly feel saddened. It might have been mourning that lay behind it; it might have been sorrow; it might have been regret for what she had done, for what she had failed to do; for wasted time, for arrogance and unkindness; for everything.

In the bus on the way back, the students were conversing rowdily, in Italian, about their experiences in Cambridge.

"They're meant to speak English while they're here," said Harriet. "But I can't make them. Mrs. God can, though. If she hears them talking Italian she shouts 'English!' at them. It gives them a terrible fright."

Emma stared out of the window. She thought that she did not mind what the students did, or what Mrs. God thought about it, or what Harriet said. But then Harriet remarked, "I'm going to wear your dress next week."

Emma was not particularly interested. "Good."

"I've had a very nice invitation," Harriet went on. "I'm going to Donwell Abbey. I've been invited for lunch."

Emma froze. "Donwell? George Knightley's house?"

"Yes," said Harriet. "He's so nice. He invited me himself.

Mrs. God is going to take me over—she won't stay, of course—she'll come back and collect me later. I'll wear my new cashmere and the suede ankle boots." There was a pause, before she added, "The ones you so generously bought me."

Emma said nothing. Whatever feelings had come over her while contemplating the stained glass at St. John's, this could not be allowed to happen. This had nothing to do with stained glass or light, or the transporting cadences of "The Turtle Dove" as sung by a college choir; this was altogether different; this could not be ignored.

She looked at Harriet, and for a brief moment their eyes met in what Emma decided was perfect understanding.

21

Mr. Woodhouse could tell that something was wrong. "I may not be the most observant man in Norfolk," he said to Emma over breakfast, "but I cannot help but notice that something is . . . well, biting you. It's not me, I hope."

Emma tried to make light of her father's observation. "You, Pops, have never bitten anybody—as far as I am aware. Of course, one never knows—one's parents may lead secret lives and be biting people left, right, and centre, but in your case, I think not."

Mr. Woodhouse reached for the marmalade. "Your *bons mots* are very *bons*, Emma, but they conceal nothing from me. You're upset about something." A disturbing thought crossed his mind. "You aren't unwell, are you? Sometimes a raised temperature can cause mood disturbances, you know. Are you sure you're all right?"

"Of course I am. I'm fine."

"You would tell me? You would let me know if your temperature went up, or anything like that?"

She smiled benignly at her father. "Of course I would. It's

335

just that I've been thinking about my business and about how I need to make a start. I need to get more samples."

That was true—to an extent. Emma had begun to weary of her empty summer and had already placed an advertisement in *East Anglian Living* offering her services as an "interior decorator and design consultant: kitchens, bathrooms, living rooms, bedrooms." It had been a large advertisement, occupying half a page of the magazine, and she had been slightly concerned that some of its claims—such as the description of herself as an "award-winning designer"—were slightly ambitious, or even misleading, although not completely untrue, if one considered the class prize in design at the University of Bath to be an award. It was, she told herself, every bit as much an award as any other prize that people won—even better, perhaps, as it was academic and not commercial.

The advertisement, although placed, had yet to appear, and she was nervous as to what would follow. In her more pessimistic moments she imagined the conversation that might ensue if a client asked her about her experience in designing kitchens, which of course was non-existent.

"You'll have done plenty of kitchens before, of course. You'll know the issues."

"Oh, the issues. Yes, I'm aware of those."

"Any photographs of your previous work?"

"Not to hand, but let's talk about what you have in mind. I'm very keen on islands in kitchens—as long as you put them in the right place."

"Photographs?"

"Of islands? I can get some for you."

"No, of your work—your kitchens."

It made her feel uncomfortable even to think of it. Of course, she could always tell the truth and confess that there had been no previous kitchens; she could even make something of her inexperience. "My very first kitchen, you know, and I'm *bursting* with ideas." And then they would move on to the firmer ground of fabrics for the drawing room—"I suggest a subtle red—you're north-facing, you know, and you can do with a warm colour."

"You know, I think you're right about that."

"Thank you."

Yes, truth might be the answer; in which case she might be slightly dismissive of the advertisement: "Oh, that . . . the advertising people went a bit over-the-top, you know—made me sound *so* experienced, and I'm not really, but at least my charges won't break the bank."

But it was not just these concerns over her incipient career that were responsible for Emma's distracted state; there was something else worrying her that she would never confess to her father. This was her anxiety—not to say anger—over Harriet's behaviour. She and Harriet had parted coolly at the end of the bus journey back from Cambridge. On her way home in the Mini Cooper, Emma had reflected on just how treacherous Harriet's conduct had been. She—Emma—had raised Harriet from nothingness—and she *was* nothing—and introduced her to all sorts of people she would never have met on her own. She had gone to the trouble of lining up Philip Elton, even if that had not worked out; she had invited her to Hartfield; she had done a pastel portrait of her *and* had been prepared to pay for its framing; she had bought her an expensive cashmere jersey dress *and* a pair of suede ankle boots; she had helped her

337

with her wretched foreign students and their gabbling on about the way to the railway station—and all for what? For Harriet to use the entrée—and the clothes—she had provided her with to set her cap at one of her oldest friends, George Knightley, who was far too decent and vulnerable to be able to defend himself against this sort of ambitious manoeuvre. How dare she! How dare she sit in her . . . her *disused airfield* and plot her assault on Donwell Abbey!

She tried to imagine the consequences of a successful campaign by Harriet. George was not all that old, and a difference of fourteen years or thereabouts in their ages was nothing. Harriet could well persuade him to marry her, and if that happened, she would be Mrs. George Knightley of Donwell Abbey—the largest and most important house for miles around. Indeed, Donwell Abbey could hold its own with any large house in the county, including Sandringham. Of course Harriet would want that; of course she would. Emma thought grimly of the details. There would be a newspaper announcement of the engagement, and that would make people sit up and take notice. "The engagement is announced between Mr. George Knightley of Donwell Abbey, elder son of the late Mr. and Mrs. Basil Knightley, and Miss Harriet Smith, of a disused airfield, daughter of the late Miss Smith and an unknown, but much-loved, donor." Hah! People would have a good laugh at that, but then they would think: *That goes to show how far one can get if one's ambitious enough.* But then she thought: *That's not why I'm upset. I don't care about property and money because I have plenty of both. What I care about is him. Just him.*

· · ·

It was not the advertisement, though, that brought Emma's first commission, but something far closer to home. In fact, the commission came from virtually next door—from Miss Taylor and James. Ever since Miss Taylor had moved in with James, she had been planning to do something about Randalls and the general state of shabbiness into which it had fallen under James's ownership. The barns and outbuildings were all kept in a very good state, of course, as James was a conscientious farmer, but when it came to the house he showed the indifference that men living on their own often have to their surroundings. The house had not been painted for almost fifteen years, no chairs had been re-covered in that time, nor carpets cleaned or repaired, and the plumbing arrangements in the cold and uncomfortable bathrooms would hardly have been out of place in a museum.

"We need to get somebody in," said Miss Taylor. "We can't do it by ourselves."

James did not see why not. "I don't think you need an interior decorator," he said. "Just get a painter to come round and freshen things up, and a plumber of course. These plumber chaps are jolly good at ripping old stuff out. A couple of days' work at the most."

"It's not that simple," said Miss Taylor. "We have to replace all the curtains. We have to get new flooring for the bathrooms as well as new baths and whatnot. The kitchen has to be tackled from scratch."

James sighed, but he would deny Miss Taylor nothing. "Oh well, you're the one with the good taste."

"You have it too," she said. "It requires very good taste indeed to live in a state of disrepair."

He laughed. "Genteel decline?"

"Perhaps."

He was concerned about cost; the farm and the outbuildings were expensive—everything was expensive. "I suppose you'll want some fancy *Classic Interiors* type to come prancing down here and charging the earth."

"No," said Miss Taylor. "I've had an idea. Emma. This is exactly what she wants to do. And she's got a very good eye—she always has had."

James looked thoughtful. "And she won't charge the earth?"

"I'm sure her charges will be very modest—and we'll be keeping it in the family, so to speak."

"In that case . . ."

"Good. I'll give her a ring."

Emma took no persuasion. She would do the job for nothing, she insisted, firmly refusing the offer of a fee. "After all," she said, "I'm not a *real* interior decorator—just yet." She had by now received consignments of samples from wallpaper and fabric companies, and these were loaded into the back of the Mini Cooper, along with paint charts, tiling booklets, and all the other accoutrements that served as the tools of her new trade. She was excited by the prospect of redecorating Randalls—a house that she had long admired but which she felt had been badly neglected. Her excitement was tempered, though, by the unavoidable prospect of seeing Frank, who was still staying at Randalls and whom she had last seen at that disastrous picnic. He had not apologised to her for stalking off in a huff when he failed to identify his own wine, and for her part she had felt that she had nothing to say sorry for: the incident had in no sense been her fault. But whatever view one took of that debacle, the fact remained that she and Frank were currently not on speaking terms and that any meeting at Randalls would probably be a fraught one.

Miss Taylor came out to meet her when she parked the car at the head of the Randalls drive. "We're going to do great things, Emma, you and I," she said. "This poor old house is going to be utterly transformed."

"V. exciting," said Emma, reverting to a favourite abbreviation of *very* she had used in her childhood.

Miss Taylor lowered her tone conspiratorially. "But be careful not to frighten the male department," she said. "Everything needs to go—top to bottom—but you know how men are: they like to hang on to things."

Emma nodded. "I shall be v. tactful."

"I'm sure you will be," said Miss Taylor, although in reality she was not at all sure.

They walked towards the house, the gravel of the driveway crunching underfoot in a satisfactory way. "I see ochre tones," said Emma. "I get a very strong feeling of ochre."

"Interesting," said Miss Taylor.

"Except for the bathrooms," Emma continued. "I see white, and pale blue. Eggshell, perhaps."

Miss Taylor nodded. "One would not want ochre in a bathroom, I think."

They entered the house.

"All of this will have to go," said Miss Taylor, gesturing towards the hunting prints that lined the walls of the hall. "And all that stuff too." This was the ungainly coat rack, the umbrella stand, the protruding hall table with its heavy Victorian legs, and an uncomfortable-looking oak hall chair on which a pile of old newspapers rested.

Emma cast an eye about her. "I see one of those nice Farrow and Ball greens," she said. "Once we've thrown everything out, of course."

"V. good," said Miss Taylor.

They went into the kitchen where Miss Taylor prepared Emma a cup of tea. There was discussion of the kitchen cupboards, which they both decided would have to go, and of the kitchen floor, which it was agreed would have to be taken up and replaced. Tea was poured, and it was just after this that the telephone rang. Miss Taylor took the call, and Emma indicated by pointing out of the door that she would take her tea into the conservatory adjoining the kitchen.

"Go ahead," said Miss Taylor, cupping her hand over the telephone mouthpiece. "I'll only be five minutes or so."

Emma walked through into the conservatory and examined the vines that had been trained up one side of the structure. The furniture, she noted, was shabby and would need to be replaced. And then she stopped. She had not seen him when she entered, but Frank Churchill was sitting in a chair at the far end. He had been reading a book, which fell to the ground when Emma came in.

For a long-drawn-out minute neither said anything. Then both spoke at once.

"Oh," said Emma, and then, "Oh," again.

"Um," said Frank. "So . . ."

They paused. Then Emma said, "I suppose you do live here."

The remark seemed to surprise both of them.

"I mean, here you are," said Emma.

Frank shrugged. "I'm staying here."

"Of course you are," said Emma.

The silence resumed, to be broken eventually by Frank, who said, "I think I should say sorry."

Emma listened impassively as Frank continued. "I heard from my father that he had taken bottles of our wine to the picnic. I know now that you didn't intend to show me up."

"I didn't," said Emma, quick to assume the role of the wronged party. "That's what I told you."

"Yes, I know," said Frank. "But . . . well, I suppose I'm still a bit cross with you."

"But I didn't know it was your wine."

"No, not about that—about something else."

Emma was cautious. "What exactly?"

Frank had risen from his chair and had turned to look out of the conservatory window. His back was towards Emma.

He turned round again. "You shouldn't have spoken to Jane."

Emma's mouth dropped.

"Yes," said Frank. "You shouldn't. I told you what I told you in confidence. I didn't expect you to go broadcasting it round half of England."

Emma reddened. The back of her neck felt warm.

Frank continued with his accusation. "You told her that I wasn't interested in women."

She decided to defend herself. "That's what you told me."

"Well, it's not true," said Frank. "As it happens."

Emma's voice rose. "Then why did you tell me what you told me?"

Frank hesitated, and Emma noticed a certain sheepishness come over him. "I wanted to flirt with you without any . . . without any misunderstandings."

It took her a moment or two to be offended. "Oh, I see. You wanted to use me?"

Frank nodded. "I'm sorry."

"But why?"

"Because I wanted Jane to see me getting on well with another girl." He paused. "I can see that you don't believe me."

"No."

"Well, it's true. I wanted to make Jane jealous because . . . well, you see, she and I have known each other for a couple of years—"

She interrupted him. "How . . . ?"

"We met in Australia. She came with a friend on a working visa. They worked in a hotel in Fremantle. I met her there. We kept in touch when she came back to England. Anyway, we were pretty close, but she'd decided to give the relationship a rest."

"And you wanted to give her a shock?"

"Yes. I wanted to show her that she wasn't the only fish on the beach."

"Pebble," corrected Emma. "Fish in the sea. Pebble on the beach."

"Whatever."

"And did it work? This . . . strategy of yours?"

He nodded. "It did. We're back together. But not without a big row over what you told her."

Emma now understood, but she was uncertain what to say. Perhaps he was right in saying that she had betrayed a confidence, but then she reminded herself he had misled her, he had used her. Both of them, it seemed, had something to feel sorry about.

"Yes," Frank continued. "You can just imagine. She accused me of deceiving her. She said that I should have told her right at the beginning. She asked me why I'd bothered with her if I wasn't really interested. She started to cry."

Emma winced.

"But eventually I got through to her and explained. It took ages. Three days. But we sorted it out."

"I'm very sorry," said Emma. "I didn't know that it would get out of hand."

"There's more," said Frank.

Emma bit her lip. Her world suddenly seemed like a jersey from which a loose strand of wool had been pulled, resulting in the rapid unravelling of the whole. "Yes?"

"She knows my friend Geoff—the one I told you I was going to be travelling with."

Emma waited.

"And she told him that I had said I was gay and that she believed I fancied him."

"Oh."

Frank spoke with heavy irony. "Yes. And that can really help a friendship, you know."

Emma made a gesture of helplessness. "I don't think you can blame me for that."

"What's the point of blaming anybody? The whole thing's a mess."

Emma asked about Jane. "I suppose she hates me."

"Yes," said Frank. "Sorry about that."

Emma said nothing. *She hates me.* It had never occurred to her that she might be disliked.

Frank sighed. "You may as well know: Jane and I are engaged."

She tried to look pleased. "That's really good news." It sounded flat. She repeated herself; it was still flat.

Miss Taylor came in. Emma noticed that she gave Frank an enquiring glance, and she interpreted this to mean that Miss Taylor knew and that she wanted to find out if Frank had told her about his engagement.

She was right. "I've told Emma," said Frank.

Emma looked at Miss Taylor. She felt the tears welling up in her eyes. Jane hated her: that had been spelled out to her. Frank took the view that she had grossly complicated his life through her indiscretion. Harriet regarded her as a rival, and Philip no doubt blamed her for his downfall and disgrace. Nobody, it seemed, liked her—apart from her father, and possibly George, and even then he had been cross about her rudeness to Miss Bates, even if he later gave her credit for trying to make amends.

All of these people, she thought, *could so easily see me as an enemy.* And she remembered something she had read in the newspaper that morning—an obituary for a Polish baker who had established a chain of cake shops and become a philanthropist. "He had no enemies," said the obituarist. The line, written often enough to become an obituary cliché, had stuck in her mind, and came back to her now. *It could not be said of me,* she thought, *I have enemies to spare—all of my own making.*

·   ·   ·

Miss Taylor realised that Emma was too distracted to continue with the task of advising on the redecoration of Randalls. Frank Churchill did not linger long in the conservatory after Miss Taylor came in, but mumbled an excuse about having to go to the gym and left.

"What gym?" Emma asked Miss Taylor after Frank had gone.

"He doesn't use a gym," said Miss Taylor. "It's an entirely metaphysical gym, as many gyms are. A lot of people who talk about going to the gym actually have no idea where the gym is. It's aspirational—what our dear, misguided Roman Catholic cousins would call an *intention*."

"So he just wanted to get away?"

Miss Taylor put an arm around her. "I believe he's cross with you over some misunderstanding. Don't pay too much attention to it."

"Everybody's cross with me," said Emma. "Or so it seems."

"I don't think so. I'm not. I'd never be."

Emma felt the warm reassurance of her former governess's presence. Nothing had changed, and she was eight once more, listening to Miss Taylor explaining the world, telling her not to be afraid. "I'm going to try to improve," she muttered. "I really am, this time."

"It's not called improvement," said Miss Taylor. "It's called growing up. All of us do it—well, most of us, perhaps not absolutely all. There are some who never do. You can spot them if you survey the landscape."

For a moment Emma pictured Miss Taylor gazing out over the countryside, searching, hawk-like, for immature personalities. But now Miss Taylor was looking at her with concern. "My little Emma," she said fondly. "Don't be disheartened.

Life isn't an easy business for any of us, you know. We feel our way through it, and we make a lot of mistakes on the way. And when I use the word *mistake*, I don't use it in the way in which politicians use it. They call their misdeeds—plain, old-fashioned misdeeds—mistakes. They aren't. There's a big difference between a mistake, which is all about harm that you didn't intend, and a misdeed, which is harm that you *did* intend. A big difference."

Emma listened.

"Your mistake," continued Miss Taylor, "has been to inter-fere in the lives of others. It's a common mistake—possibly the commonest mistake in the book—because it's one that so many parents make. They try to make something of their child that the child doesn't want to be. They try to hold on. They mean well, of course, but it's a mistake. You've just made that mistake in another way, I suspect. I've watched you with Harriet Smith, you know."

"Harriet latched on to me."

"Of course she did—because you let her. She's much weaker than you. You should have thought of that . . . Sorry, I don't mean to upbraid you—I really don't—but that's what hap-pened, isn't it?"

Emma made a tiny, resigned sound, an acknowledgment of the truth of what had been said.

"Yes?" prompted Miss Taylor.

"Yes." Emma was not going to argue. Miss Taylor had always been right. As Mr. Woodhouse had once observed to Emma: "When Miss Taylor pronounces on something we must remem-ber that it is really Edinburgh speaking, and speaking with all the authority of the Scottish Enlightenment, of Hume, of Adam

Smith. We cannot argue with Edinburgh." But now she raised the fear that had been nagging away at her since that ill-fated trip to Cambridge. "Harriet says that George has invited her over to Donwell for lunch. Just her. Not me. Just her."

Miss Taylor digested this information. "I see. Donwell. For lunch?"

"For lunch. By herself. And she's going to wear a cashmere jersey dress that *I* bought her in Cambridge. And suede ankle boots." *Oh, the injustice of it,* she thought, *the sheer, crying injustice!*

Miss Taylor had dropped the arm that she had placed round Emma's shoulder; the physical closeness was gone, but now there was something more powerful than that: a complicity, in a sense, an acute understanding.

"You've always liked George, haven't you?" said Miss Taylor. Her voice was measured, as would be the voice of a diagnostician.

"Yes, I have."

Miss Taylor took a step away and looked up at the vine, as if seeking inspiration from the plant. The grapes were far from ripe, but were there already, in luscious little clusters.

"Wasn't Harriet friendly with that young man from that hotel?" asked Miss Taylor.

"It's just a B&B," said Emma.

Miss Taylor looked at her sharply. "They think it's a hotel," she said. "That's what they want it to be. Maybe that means something to *them*."

Emma was chastened. "I'm sorry. Yes, that hotel. He's called Robert Martin."

"And what happened?" asked Miss Taylor.

Emma did not answer. Miss Taylor repeated her question. "What happened, Emma?"

Emma took a deep breath. "I ruined it for her," she said. "I put her off him." She stared at Miss Taylor defiantly, as if to challenge her to react to what she had said.

But Miss Taylor did not scold her; she simply shook her head. "I suspect you know what to do," she said.

Emma waited.

"I'm not going to spell it out," said Miss Taylor. "I'm no longer your governess. You're going to have to make your own decision here and act accordingly."

"Please . . ."

"No. Definitely not. And I don't think we should try to make any decorating decisions today."

Emma went back to the Mini Cooper and drove down the drive. Miss Taylor watched her from the drawing-room window, with James Weston at her side.

"Will you play the piano for me?" he asked.

"Of course," she said. "What would you like?"

" 'Take a pair of sparkling eyes,' " he said.

The Oak Tree Inn served lunch in the bar. The day's specials, chalked up on a small blackboard in the shape of a fish, were potted shrimps, steak and kidney pie, and sticky toffee pudding. There were several customers already eating when Emma arrived, although it was barely midday. She did not feel particularly hungry, as she had eaten a late breakfast, but she nonetheless took a seat at one of the small bar tables and began to study the menu. The choice was a large one for a small hotel, but it was only the steak and kidney pie and the sticky toffee pudding that appealed to her.

The bar was unattended when she arrived, but within a couple of minutes a door slammed somewhere and a young man appeared. Emma recognised Robert Martin, who spotted her, smiled, and came over to her table. He was wearing a white apron of the sort sometimes worn by French waiters, and he had a small notebook in his hand.

"Emma?"

She returned his smile.

"I thought it was you," he said. "It's just I didn't expect to see you here."

"I've been meaning to come for some time. I felt hungry and thought: Why not?"

He opened the notebook. "I haven't seen you for ages."

"No. I saw you the other day in the village, but you didn't see me. Obviously."

"No. Have you finished at Bath?"

"Yes. That's it. The world of work beckons now. And you?"

"I did a hospitality course in Norwich." He made a gesture to encompass the bar and the hotel. "It's for this place."

She nodded. She had been studying him discreetly. He was rather good-looking, she thought; he used to be a bit too thin, she thought, but now he had grown into himself—that was Miss Taylor's expression: *You'll grow into yourself.* She and Isabella had not really known what it meant, but had taken comfort in it as an assurance that somehow everything would be all right. *And have I grown into myself now?* she asked herself. *Have I?*

"I'd better get on," said Robert, nodding in the direction of the kitchen. "We're short-handed. We've got one Polish girl at the moment and that's it."

"They work so hard," said Emma, and thought, *Unlike me.*

Robert agreed. "She's fantastic."

Emma placed her order, which appeared on her table quickly. At the end of the meal, as Robert took away her plate, she said what she had come to say. "Do you get any time off? This afternoon?"

The question took him by surprise. "Yes. A bit. I have to be back to help with dinner, though."

"Of course."

"Why?"

She tried to seem casual. "Because I wondered if you'd like to drop by my place. Tea, maybe."

He looked at his watch. "I could come at four, or maybe a bit earlier."

"Do you play tennis?"

"I used to—a bit."

"Bring trainers."

She rose from her chair and gave him her credit card for the bill. He seemed puzzled by her invitation, but was polite. A certain distance, though, crept into his tone, as may happen when one accepts an invitation that one is not sure about, that is suspected of concealing an agenda.

Emma left. Now she telephoned Harriet and issued her invitation. Again she was careful to sound casual. "If you're doing nothing, come round to my place. I'll maybe ask one or two other people. Tea—something like that. Maybe a game of tennis—bring some trainers. We've got racquets."

"I didn't know you had a tennis court."

"We do. It's at the back of the house, near one of the barns. I hardly ever use it. I'm a hopeless player."

Harriet said that she would come by bicycle. One of the students had lent her an electric bicycle and she would ride over on that.

"It's such fun to use," Harriet said. "I'll give you a go, Emma, if you'd like. You can have a go and I'll watch."

It was such a childish invitation, thought Emma, but then she said, "Thanks, Harriet, I'd love to. You could show me how."

"Oh, it's easy. It's just like riding a bicycle."

"It is a bicycle."

"Oh, silly me, of course it is."

Mr. Woodhouse said, "I'm going out. What are you doing?"

"I've invited a couple of people round. We might play tennis later on."

They looked at each other with interest; he because he wondered who her guests would be, and she because he very rarely went out.

"Who?" he asked.

"Harriet."

"And who else?"

"Robert Martin—you know, his parents run the Oak Tree Inn. They . . ."

"I know exactly who they are," said Mr. Woodhouse. "They had the health inspectors in there last year. They looked very closely at the kitchen."

"I'm sure it's pretty clean. It seems well run."

"Oh, I'm not suggesting that it's not well run, but why, one wonders, would the health inspectors be there? Somebody must have called them."

She did not think that this necessarily followed. "They can do random checks. If I were a health inspector, I'd descend without notice."

"In my view," said Mr. Woodhouse, "somebody must have experienced a stomach problem and reported it. Diarrhoea. I read that book about what goes on in restaurants and hotel kitchens. Yes, I read all about it. It would make your hair stand on end. Apparently twenty per cent of people who eat in restaurants get diarrhoea as a result. Twenty per cent, Emma!" He paused to allow the statistic to sink in. "Now that's an average across the country—just imagine, just imagine what the figure for London must be like. Much, much higher. Probably something of the order of fifty or sixty per cent, I should imagine." He shook his head at the thought. "One eats at one's peril in London."

Emma tried not to smile; she knew that if she smiled, her father would say: "Diarrhoea is nothing to smile about."

"But Isabella lives in London," she said. "She doesn't spend all her time in the loo. We would have heard about it if she did. And John and the children—they don't look as if they have diarrhoea."

"Diarrhoea is nothing to smile about, Emma," he said. "It can kill, you know. Look what it did in India during those great cholera epidemics in the nineteenth century. That's when Dr. Collis Brown invented that chlorodyne of his. He knew how to deal with diarrhoea."

Emma looked at her watch. "But what about you, where are you going?"

He waved a hand in the direction of Holt. "For a drive. I might call in somewhere for tea. Who knows?"

She looked at him sideways. "Be careful. Remember what happened to Philip. Avoid ditches."

This brought a sympathetic reaction. "Poor Philip. I gather that he really misses being behind the wheel of his BMW Something–something. Sid said that he saw him being driven around in the village by that new friend of his, Hazel. Apparently she reversed all the way down the High Street for some reason, with Philip directing her from the back seat."

"The important thing is that they should be happy," said Emma.

"That's very kind of you. Is this a new Emma?"

The remark, not intended critically, went home, and stung. A new Emma, not unkind like the old Emma . . .

Harriet arrived first, as Emma had planned, riding the electric bicycle up to the front door and coming to a halt with a flourish.

"I hardly had to pedal," she said. "You just sit there and this little electric thingy does all the work."

They went inside. "I put the net up on the court," said Emma. "And I found you a racquet and one for Robert."

They had been walking down the corridor towards Emma's sitting room. Harriet stopped. "Robert?" she said.

Emma looked innocent. "Robert Martin. You know him, of course."

Harriet was flustered. "Yes, yes . . . Robert."

Emma shrugged. "I'm not sure if he plays much tennis—I don't think he does, but I asked him anyway." She paused. Harriet had coloured. She was blushing. "Have you seen him recently?"

Harriet did not answer, but suddenly continued on her way down the corridor. Emma followed.

"I have to speak to you," Harriet said when they reached the sitting room. "I have a confession to make, Emma. You're the closest friend I have at the moment and I've been deceiving you. I feel awful, but I have to tell you."

Emma gestured for her to sit down, and then joined her friend on the sofa. "So?"

"I hate to deceive people," said Harriet.

"Nobody likes doing that."

"You see, you've been so kind to me, Emma."

Emma wanted to tell her to get on with it, but did not.

Harriet sounded as if she was close to tears. "And then I go and reward you by going against your advice."

"What advice?"

"The advice you gave me about Robert. I've been seeing Robert all along."

Emma's immediate reaction was one of relief. The whole point of the game of tennis had been to bring them together because she thought that they were right for each other. "Great," she said. "That's really great."

Harriet's demeanour registered her surprise. "You think it's a good idea?"

Emma reached out to touch Harriet on the forearm. "Of course I do. He's really nice. I think that he and you are ideally suited. It's perfect."

Harriet uttered a cry of joy. "That's such good news! Such good news!"

"I'm glad you're pleased."

"Robert and I are going to go off on a gap year together—in a year's time. We're going to go to New Jersey for a couple of months and then on to Canada. Robert's uncle has a motel in New Jersey—we might be able to stay with him for a while and help him. Then we're going to go to Banff, where Robert has cousins. They stayed with Robert's parents and they're keen to reciprocate. It's good if you can pay people back for things, isn't it, Emma?"

"Oh yes," said Emma. "It's good to pay back."

Harriet's smile faded. "There's another thing."

Emma looked at her. "Yes?"

"George Knightley."

Emma stiffened. Had Harriet been seeing George behind her back too? That would be another matter altogether, and the sweetness and light of the moment might prove short-lived.

"I've been talking to him," said Harriet. "And we were going to meet in a couple of days' time."

"I know that," said Emma quietly, and thought: *You were going to meet him wearing the cashmere jersey dress that I bought you—and the suede ankle boots too.*

"George likes you," said Harriet. "And I've been encouraging him."

"Excuse me," said Emma. "I'm not quite with you."

"I said to him that he should let you know how he feels. I was going to arrange to have you both round for dinner at Mrs. God's."

Emma stared at her. "*You* were matchmaking?"

Harriet giggled. "Yes, I suppose you could call it that."

Emma drew in her breath. "You thought that I needed your help?"

"I wouldn't say you needed it, but I thought it might be useful." Harriet paused, studying Emma's reaction to her words. "It's the same with Mrs. God and your father. I did my best to bring them together. He's there right now."

"He's with her? With Mrs. God?"

Harriet nodded. "They're like a couple of love-birds." She reached out to Emma. "You're not cross with me, are you, Emma? Please say that you're not cross with me."

Emma Woodhouse, pretty, clever, and rich, was cross with her friend Harriet Smith, but reminded herself that Harriet had very little in this life, even if she had the faithful affection of Robert Martin, a good friend in Mrs. God, and all the attention that exceptional looks can bring. That was something, but it was so much less that she, Emma, had and therefore it was grounds for the dulling of anger. So Emma forgave Harriet, and reminded herself that she had done worse herself, not least to Harriet. It had been an important summer for Emma, as it had been the summer during which moral insight came to her—something that may happen to all of us, if it happens at all, at very different stages of our lives. This had happened because she had been able to make that sudden imaginative leap that lies at the heart of our moral lives: the ability to see, even for a brief moment, the world as it is seen by the other person. It is this understanding that lies behind all kindness to others, all attempts to ameliorate the situation of those who suffer, all those acts of charity by which we make our lives something more than the pursuit of the goals of the unruly ego.

George came to see Emma. They walked in the garden and he said to her, "I've never been very good at expressing my feelings; other people are so much better at that. But I want you to know that I've been in love with you, Emma, for a long time. I just have. Not a day, not a single day has gone past but that I've thought about you."

His words swam about her, and she stood quite still, as if stopped by an invisible wall. It took her a while to respond, but then she said, "I'm glad you've told me, because I've always been fond of you."

"Just fond?"

She smiled. "Seriously fond."

He looked away, and she noticed. She reached out to him and began to say something, but it made no sense. He said to her, "I was hoping you'd say something else."

Not more than a second or two passed. It was like leaping off a building. "But I want to say it," she whispered. "I'm in love with you too. Yes, I'm in love too."

She thought: *In love; not* by *love or* with *love, but* in *love.* It was a state of being; it was a state of immersion, like being *in* the sea. And love was as powerful as the ocean itself, as embracing, as strong as the sea is. Love. She was like a child playing with a newly learned word; there was the same sense of delight, of discovery. She was astonished by its force, and was struck by the insight that it seemed to bring with it. It was as if a great searchlight had been switched on in the darkness and was bathing all before it with its light, its warmth. Now the world made sense because she could see it. Now she knew why she should cherish what she saw about her: other people, the world itself, everything. Embarrassment had stopped her saying it, but now she saw that embarrassment for what it was, and it lay dismantled before her, the ruins of selfishness, of pride, of insensitivity.

It seemed as if he could sense what was happening within her, for he said nothing, as if awed by a moment that would only be defiled if he were to speak. But he embraced her with tenderness, and simply held her for a while before they drew apart and looked at each other as if they were two people who had just witnessed something miraculous. He then said, "I do wish you'd come to Donwell and redecorate it."

She thought for a moment that this was an odd thing to say at a time like this, but then it seemed right to her; it seemed just perfect. It was the best thing he could possibly have said. And she replied. "Yes, I will."

"And we could go to Italy too. Would you come with me to Florence?"

That was an offer of the world; to which she replied, "Of course."

Mr. Woodhouse saw a great deal more of Mrs. Goddard, and they too went abroad for a while, in their case to Vero Beach, Florida, where Mrs. Goddard had a small apartment. Philip Elton married Hazel, and Hazel sang "Non, je ne regrette rien" at the wedding. "Just as well she has no regrets," observed Emma to Mr. Woodhouse at the ceremony. He whispered, "Let us not be without charity, dear girl." And she lowered her eyes at the gentle reproach, for she had learned her lesson, even if there would be occasional, but only very occasional, relapses; for none of us is perfect, except, of course, the ones we love, the things of home, our much appreciated dogs and cats, our favourites of one sort or another.

Jane Fairfax and Frank Churchill eventually married in Western Australia. There was a house on the wine estate that had been prepared for their use. Jane gave piano lessons to the children of other farmers and in due course had twin boys. Nobody ever worked out who gave her the Yamaha piano, but there were theories. One of these, put forward by Mr. Woodhouse, was that the piano was bought by Miss Bates, who was only pretending to be poor in order to defeat her creditors at Lloyd's. According to this school of thought, she had squirrelled away most of her funds and was easily in a position to buy violet creams for herself and a piano for her niece. "That woman never fooled me," said Mrs. God, who claimed to be a good judge of character.

Emma was happy. She realised that happiness is something that springs from the generous treatment of others, and that until one makes that connection, happiness may prove elusive. In Italy with George, that thought came even more forcefully to her when, in a small art gallery in an obscure provincial town well off the beaten track, she saw a seventeenth-century picture of a young man giving his hand to a young woman. And the young woman takes it and holds it, cherishing it, as one might cherish something that is fragile and vulnerable, and very precious. The eyes of the woman are not on the young man, nor upon the hand that she holds, but fixed on the one who views the painting, and they convey, as do so many of the figures in art that would say anything to us, this message: *You do it too.*